# Shield of Blood

## The Mowbray Chronicles - Book 4

Mette Holm

ISBN-13: 978-87-971343-6-8

# DEDICATION

to my family, friends and loyal readers.

And to the little, ragged boy who stood in the corner of my mind and whispered: Write my story, it will be epic, you'll see.

Without imagination what are we?

# ACKNOWLEDGMENTS

There are more than a few people without whom my books would never exist.

My editor and excellent friend, Steve, who never lets me off the hook for something, I could do better. Without your determination the end result would be meagre, thank you.

The fabulous three, aka the lovely ladies who endure my endless ramblings about kings, usurpers, fiends and 'is it possible to die this way do you think'-questions on our bi-annual workaways. I am blessed to have you as companions on my journeys into the unknown.

My wonderfully critical proof-reader who finds the commas I miss, helps me soup-up the language and make every sentence a wonder to read. I am ever so grateful for your efforts and patience.

My extraordinary graphic designer who is brave enough to peep into my brain and extract what is always the perfect cover for my novels. Besides being incredibly patient, you are also just the perfect kind of crazy – and you did it again.

My family and friends who cheer me on, even when they have no idea what on earth I am doing. You make me keep going when things get rough.

Most of all, I thank you, my wonderful husband for letting me run wild with ideas, for supporting me at every turn and for never doubting my efforts, even if I do. I love you.

**And a big thank you to you, my dear reader, for going on this epic voyage with me. You are what makes me aspire to greatness.**

# GALLERY OF CHARACTERS

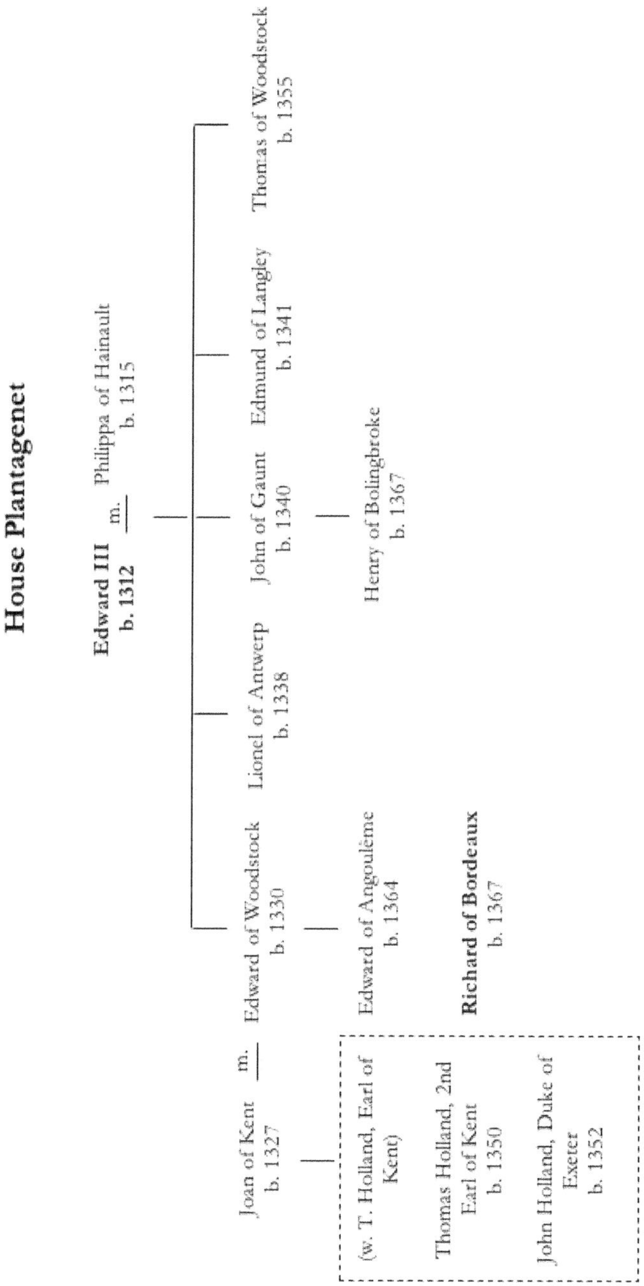

# House Mowbray

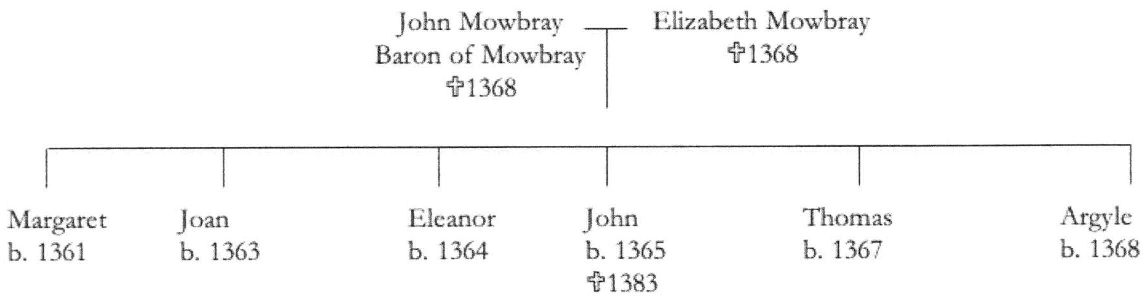

# OTHER KEY CHARACTERS

**Edmund la Fontaine** (b. 1341)

Sieur Aymard la Fontaine

Henry of Grosmont, Duke of Lancaster (b. 1310 - d. 1361)

Blanche, Baroness Wake of Liddell (b. 1305 - d. 1380)

Thomas de Beauchamp, Earl of Warwick (b. 1338)

Sir John de Montagu, Baron Montagu (b. 1350)

Sir Simon Burley (b. 1336 - d. 1388)

King John II of France

Prince Charles, the Dauphin

Prince Philip, Duke of Burgundy

King Peter of Castile

Henry of Trastamara

Princess Constance of Castile

Princess Isabella of Castile

Pascaline (d. 1370) - Lady-in-waiting to Princess Joan

Warden - Master of Arms at Beauworth

Reynold Grey - squire to la Fontaine

Alan Coxcombe – knighted by Warwick

Robert de Vere – Earl of Oxford

## 26 July 1392 – Westminster Palace

'If I had known that day what my actions would cause, then believe me, my Lord, I might have made a different decision.'

From afar came the sounds of a camp growing even as the sun set, pages and squires rushing to and from the tourney area, carpenters working into the night to erect stands and platforms for the royal household and noble families. London was teeming with visitors, some of whom had travelled the length of England to attend the tournament. Almost a hundred shields had gone up, one for each of the knights and noblemen competing in the joust and mêlée. Further afield, bowstrings sang, announcing practicing archers. Tomorrow would be a grand spectacle, and Edmund was going to be centre of attention on the jousting field.

'You were but a child,' John of Gaunt said, but the King's uncle's eyes glittered with curiosity.

'I was a cunning child.' Edmund turned from the window. 'When you grow up on the streets, honour and glory are the last things on your mind. You do not care what happens to others. You only care where your next meal will come from. Where you will sleep. If you will be safe. Such a life is hard to forget.'

For the first time that night, Gaunt put away his cup and gave Edmund his full attention, leaning in and fixing his gaze. 'I would have the truth this time, Sire, for we are short on time.'

'Let me remind you that it is you asking me for a favour, not the other way around, my Lord. And once I have told you my tale, much may be remedied. But I will not be hurried along, for I have yet to agree to your insane plan.' Though it was utter madness, Edmund could not deny that it had a certain allure; a chance to shape history.

Gaunt groaned. 'Get on with it then.'

'You are that certain, I will agree?'

'You may be many things, Sire,' Gaunt said with distaste, 'but you never turned back on a pledge. And that is what I would have at the end of whatever you mean to subject me to tonight.'

Edmund stifled a laugh and nodded. 'You will not be disappointed, my Lord.'

Impatient, Gaunt snapped his fingers for Edmund to continue, but he took his time, sorting through his thoughts. If this was to be told, it had to be told right.

One chance, Edmund reminded himself, one chance at everlasting glory. As with all the other chances Edmund had ever come across, he meant to seize this too and bend it to his will.

With a smile, Edmund gestured at Gaunt, ignoring the royal uncle's glare. 'I never saw an opportunity I did not like …'

# Part 1

# Destiny

# CHAPTER 1

## 4 May 1354 – Lillebonne

'How the Hell did you get that wrong?!'

Sieur Aymard is a short, stout man, his face is livid and his eyes black as coal. Except from the ring around them. It burns a strange amber colour.

Inside, Edmund smirks, but outside his face is arranged to look solemn and sad.

'But I … I …' The blacksmith, burly and usually quick-tongued looks about in confusion. 'But I was told … Your orders, Sieur, they were clear as day …'

'To geld my most promising stallion?!' Spit springs from Sieur Aymard's twisted mouth. 'A horse I told you not two months ago would sire a new line the like of which had never been seen before? Are you insane!'

The blacksmith wrings his big, calloused hands. 'I thought perhaps you had found something wanting …'

'Something wanting?! In the best stallion ever foaled in my stables!' The grey-haired Lord takes a step forward, it bears a warning that is almost comical, and yet the blacksmith shrinks back.

'I'm ever so sorry, M'lord, it's just that … well, I've only done what you asked.'

Sieur Aymard looks to be growing taller, broader, angrier by the second, and Edmund has to pinch his wrist behind his back not to laugh out loud.

The blacksmith who is at least two heads taller than Aymard cowers. In different circumstances, the blacksmith would be halfway through his chores by now, shoeing the horses and gelding those that were on the list. Instead, he is passing his big hammer from one hand to the other as is his habit when he deals with difficult customers, but Sieur Aymard is a different matter.

And of course, Sieur Aymard is right. The silver stallion should never have been gelded. Had it not been for Edmund. Another shiver of pure joy courses up his spine and he pinches harder to ensure his serious expression does not falter.

'Come here boy!'

Obediently, Edmund steps forward, careful not to look at the blacksmith, whose face is white underneath the dirt and grit.

'What have you to say?'

'My Lord,' Edmund says with extra care, 'I was in the stables when I heard Master Guy tell Master Thibaut which horses were up for gelding. But …'

He pauses and glances sideways at the blacksmith Thibaut, as if to apologise and then Edmund looks straight at Sieur Aymard again. 'But I did not hear mention of the silver.'

Aymard holds up his hand and stills whatever argument the blacksmith might have come up with. As it is, all Thibaut can do is glare at Edmund while his face slowly turns puce.

'Fetch Guy.' Sieur Aymard's voice barely reaches a whisper and yet Edmund sprints for the stables.

When he passes the stable master's table, Edmund is quick to replace the parchment he laboured over for hours in the schoolroom two days ago with the real order from Sieur Aymard. Edmund still remembers the tutor's admiring words when he handed it in for examination. How he had praised Edmund's craft and told him that he was a fast learner.

Wiping a smile off his face, he runs down the aisle in the centre of the stables and finds Guy, knee deep in horseshit, pinching the ear of some unfortunate stable boy who will not last the week. Edmund has long since stopped caring about the boys that come and go in the stables. Beside himself, only Guillaume has lasted more than six months, and Edmund rather suspects that is only because Guillaume is somehow related to Guy.

'Master Guy.' Edmund adds a pant to his voice, a sense of childish urgency. 'Sieur Aymard requests your presence in the yard. At once. And would you bring the list of horses for the blacksmith?'

With a final twist that makes the dirty little boy scream in agony, Guy lets go of his victim and stomps down the aisle with Edmund trailing right behind. He is careful to stay close to the stable master for he considers him an ally of sorts and Edmund has few enough of those as it is. The children in the villages spit at him when he passes through, and the children in the castle take no notice of him. Not that he needs them; children are a waste of time, but the adults too shy away from him. Except Guy. And yet Edmund could not contain himself. Had to play a little joke on him. A big joke on Thibaut, who has already thrown Edmund out of the smithy twice for looking at his girls. If only Thibaut knew what else they got up to when he was away. Anyway, the last time he had thrown Edmund out on his ear, he had decided to get even.

Too bad that Sieur Aymard's horse had to pay the price, but there it is. Edmund picks up the piece of paper from Master Guy's table: 'Best not forget this, Master.'

'Good lad,' Guy growls and stomps out into the feeble sunlight. 'My Lord, you sent for me?'

'Read the list, Guy.'

With a curious glance at Thibaut, Guy clears his throat and begins listing the horses by name. Of course, this list is one name short, but Guy, who likes his drink, will hardly remember what he told the blacksmith four hours ago.

Edmund crumbles the piece of parchment in his hand and slides it inside his sleeve, reminding himself to burn it first chance he gets.

When Guy reaches the end, the blacksmith's face has gone from white to a strange yellow colour. To Edmund it looks a little like the tallow candles that he sometimes gets for his room. Though he would rather not admit it, Sieur Aymard is kind to him. None of the other stable boys are allowed time off to study or get candles for their rooms. They sleep above the stables in what hay there is while Edmund has a room off the back over Master Guy's cottage.

'There's one missing!' It seems Thibaut has finally worked through the list of names. His voice is confused but carry warning too. 'Read it again.'

'No need,' Sieur Aymard sneers, 'there are no more names. Tell me, you scoundrel, which of my competitors put you up to this? Who is such a fiend that he would let a magnificent beast that the whole town would have benefited from be gelded?'

Thibaut looks at Sieur Aymard, and Edmund can tell that the blacksmith is about to turn from fear to anger. He is pricklish about his girls, but he is fierce about his honour. The look he shoots at Guy is enough for Edmund to resume laughing inside. What fun it would be to see the two of them meet at the tavern later tonight. For certainly this is far from over. Certainly, Thibaut will be looking for some way to redeem himself, and preferably at the expense of Sieur Aymard's drunkard of a stable master.

Little love lost there, Edmund thinks and soaks up the tense atmosphere. It lends a strange protective layer to his own skin, a suit of armour made from other people's actions.

'Well?!' Sieur Aymard curls his fist around the hilt of his sword.

Thibaut knows he is beaten, and yet in the pause before he says something, Edmund begins to wonder if perhaps the blacksmith will meet his end today, right here on the cobbled stones of Sieur Aymard's courtyard where not half an hour ago, Thibaut gelded the lord's most prized possession.

'I must've misheard,' Thibaut says in a meek tone. His words are crusted with loathing. 'Beg' pardon, M'lord.'

Sieur Aymard seems to be considering if it is worth the effort of finding a new blacksmith for the town and then he releases the grip on his sword. What irony it would be, if Thibaut is struck down by a sword forged by his own father. Edmund is a little disappointed that nothing more is done.

'You will work for free for me until the debt is paid,' Sieur Aymard says, his face slowly regaining its usual pink shade. 'Three years will suffice, I should say, and then I have been very generous. For Jouyex would have fathered hundreds of foals to be sure.'

You do not know, Edmund thinks but nods along anyway, the stallion has been on the field these past many weeks with several mares in heat and has only spared them a few attempts. But the sight of Thibaut's face by the mention of working for free for three years is worth all his painstaking hours copying Sieur Aymard's list and adding Jouyex' name at the bottom.

If nothing else, Edmund muses, I can always turn my skills with a pen into a useful trade along the way. But he rather hopes not to. He wants to fight in the war not putter around taking other people's notes. Or forging their signatures to get at their goods. Edmund knows of a few men who make their living that way, but he wants greater things for himself.

'Better go now, Thibaut.' Guy gestures for the gate. 'Before my Lord has a change of heart. He has been most generous.'

The blacksmith picks up his enormous toolbox and pushes past Guy muttering something too low for Edmund to hear. Whatever it is, it makes Guy's face sour and Edmund feels fear steal up his arms. When Guy is in a foul mood it is best to be elsewhere and stay out of sight. Most of the boys working the stables never learn that, which is why they do not last. But Guillaume and Edmund, they know when to make themselves scarce. Except there is nowhere to hide here in the middle of the open courtyard.

'Boy!'

Sieur Aymard becomes Edmund's saviour and, for a second, he is sorry that he gelded the lord's favourite stallion. It is a fleeting feeling.

'Yes, my Lord.'

'I want you to wait at tables tomorrow,' Sieur Aymard says without looking at Edmund. 'I am expecting a large retinue to make rest here, and I was hoping - until this morning - that I might sell some of Jouyex' future offspring to my visitor. Now, I must choose other horses for him to invest in.'

'Might I help you, my Lord?' Edmund hates the submissive way he has to speak to this old bag of bones, but if he is to stay warm and dry this winter, he must do what needs doing. 'I know most of the horses very well.'

Sieur Aymard exchanges a look with his stable master and Guy nods. It is a hesitant nod. But it is there. Edmund straightens his back a little more. He might only be about twelve years old, no one really knows his true age, but already he is as tall as Sieur Aymard and soon will be as tall as Guy.

'I keep forgetting you are not the little lost soul I found in the gutter, Edmund,' Sieur Aymard mumbles and puts a hand on Edmund's shoulder. It is awkward and does not linger. 'Yes. You may help me. But that does not excuse you from waiting tables tomorrow. Or scrubbing floors today.'

No doubt at the sight of Edmund's disappointed face, Sieur Aymard gives a rare and somewhat frightening smile. 'Not to worry, you will still have time for your lessons.'

Guy waits for his lord to disappear into the old, crumbling house before he clips Edmund around the head. 'You're up to no good, boy! Don't you deny it. I saw the smirk on your face before. Now, you'll tell me and I'll decide if it goes to Sieur Aymard.'

As a well-rehearsed actor, Edmund bows his head and pauses before he speaks. 'I apologise for my behaviour, Master Guy. It is only that Master Thibaut does not care for me, nor I for him, and so … well … Perhaps I did relish in his misfortune.'

'And now you'll tell me, you'll pray for him at church and ask God's forgiveness?' Guy gives Edmund another clip around the head and, this time, Edmund's teeth rattle. 'Don't take me for a fool, boy. I'm not one and you know it! I also know you've been hanging around the forge waiting for his two fair girls to prance about.'

Edmund rubs his ear. 'Yes, Master Guy, it is true, and Thibaut did not appreciate my attentions.'

'He'll be wanting men of honour and wealth to carry those two little tarts off. Not some gawking boy who's no name to him and no prospects.' Guy coughs and spits. 'Much good may it do those two doves, for they need to get away from him before they come of age.'

They will want to get away from everyone here, Edmund thinks, not least our benevolent Sieur Aymard. He might be past his prime, but he is still looking for a wife to ensure he had an heir. Edmund has escorted his fair share of lesser lords and knights presenting their daughters, sisters and a few even their mothers for the Lord's approval. None had met his requirements. But that does not mean there is any shortage of children in the household. In fact, there are far too many who bear an uncanny resemblance with the master of the house. Too bad they are all girls.

Somewhere in the back of Edmund's mind something stirs for a moment, then comes to rest again. The feeling has come and gone ever since Sieur Aymard had found him sick and starved in the gutter, quite literally. Edmund has learned early on to listen to his gut, but it has been silent on the subject and so, once more, he pushes the niggling sensation aside, bending to slip through the wide gap between the thick timbers that make up the horse pen behind the stables.

Walking across the field, Edmund's mind begins to wander.

A few months ago, Guillaume had asked Edmund how come he got to go to lessons and Guillaume did not. For once, Edmund had no ready answer and so Guillaume had asked the question that had long lingered on the fuzzy edge of Edmund's thoughts.

'Maybe it's because you're really his?'

Immediately, Edmund had shaken his head, no he did not look at all like Sieur Aymard, and all of his bastards did, so no, definitely not. Besides, his sons had died well before Edmund was born, surely that was further proof that Edmund was in no way related to the old man.

But Guillaume would not let it go. 'Haven't you ever asked? Ever wondered?'

'I have wondered, but who knows what happens inside other people's heads?' Edmund had fired back though he was fairly certain, he knew what was going on inside Guillaume's head, after all, he was a simple boy. 'Besides it makes no difference. If he wants me to have an education, I will take it and be grateful.'

'You already talk like a nobleman,' Guillaume had said and cut open another bale of hay, scattering it into the mangers as he had moved down the stable aisle.

'What?'

'It's like you're different from me – us.' Guillaume chewed his lip; he always did when he was trying to decide on something. Edmund waited. Inevitably, Guillaume would share whatever was on his mind and there was no point in rushing him. 'You're living in your own room. You've got a bed and all. Even Master Guy pays you interest he doesn't for no one else.'

'He beats me too.' Suddenly, Edmund had felt desperate to fit in somehow. It had been a raw and very uncomfortable sensation that he would as soon have been without. 'You have seen him do so.'

'A clip 'round the ear.' Guillaume had turned for the next bale, and Edmund had slid it towards him, scowling as he did. But Guillaume ignored him. 'That's no beating, it's not even punishment. Not really. You know Master Guy; you've seen him with them other boys. He doesn't hold back. Didn't with me at first either …'

'But now you do not get more than a clip either,' Edmund had argued.

Guillaume's face had turned dark. 'Every week, when the rest of you're eating in the kitchen or working in the stables, when no one's around; he whips me.' He had lifted his shirt revealing white skin streaked red, pink and some places even dark blue. 'See?'

'He has never whipped me.' Edmund's words had come out all strange and muffled, but Guillaume had only nodded and continued filling the mangers.

'I'll take it, it don't matter,' Guillaume had said, lugging the bale behind him, his hands working tirelessly. 'As long as I've got two square meals a day, I'll take anything. I can't go home to my mother, she'll not have me, and her husband, he'll do me much worse. He did ... before ... before I ran away.'

Guillaume had shown up some six months ago, carried in on the morning mist. Edmund had never thought to ask him how he came to be in Sieur Aymard's service. Edmund never asked any of the boys, but somehow Guillaume had stuck when all the others had come and gone. Now, for lack of comparison, Edmund considered him a friend of sorts, and a most useful companion. For some reason, most of the other servants seemed to like Guillaume and would tell him secrets he had never asked for, which he repeated to Edmund when they worked together in the stables.

'Sorry.' Edmund had not meant it, but he said it anyway. 'I do not even remember my mother.'

'And your father?' Guillaume's eyes had been big as goose eggs, his own troubles forgotten.

Edmund had kicked the last bale of hay and stomped off, no doubt leaving Guillaume open for the week's whipping. But Edmund did not care. Questions about his parents always made his temper flare. But for a few strange fragments that haunted his sleep, he hardly remembered his mother, and he had absolutely no recollection of his father. Not even a pale figure without a face. The thought gnawed in the pit of his stomach. Just once, he had broached the topic with Master Guy on a night when the stable master had not been too deep in his drink, but the punch he had given in reply had been enough for Edmund not to pursue the topic. It had taken him three days to stop coughing up blood. No questions were worth that price.

'Wake up boy!'

Edmund ducks just in time to avoid another ringing slap and Master Guy laughs. 'You're a quick bastard.'

'Yes, Master.' Being called a bastard is one of the things Edmund loathes above all else. 'Shall I fetch the brown mare?'

'No, we'd best be getting on with the selection of horses for Sieur's guest.'

'Do you know who it might be?'

This time, Guy is faster than Edmund, and through the ringing he can just make out the stable master's grumbling. 'None of your business!'

## 5 May 1354 – Lillebonne

'La Fontaine!'

The grandly dressed man strides across the small courtyard and clasps hands with Sieur Aymard. Edmund is holding the reins of the man's horse; they are thick, rich leather studded with silver adornments. They feel powerful, as if some of the stranger's grandeur is seeping into Edmund's skin.

'My Lord Grosmont.' Aymard straightens but still looks withered next to the spry Duke.

Almost since the very first day when Sieur Aymard had plucked Edmund from the gutter and brought him to his house, Edmund had watched the knight take one mistress after another without producing the heir he so desired. In wonder, Edmund had asked the cook why Sieur Aymard did not simply marry someone, and after a swift smack with a ladle, the cook had given Edmund a knowing look and told him to stay close to the old man that he might one day come to his senses. It was no answer and had left Edmund annoyed and in a vengeful mood. Not long after, the cook had been dismissed when Sieur Aymard was taken to bed with food poisoning. The next time Edmund had asked about the knight's urgency in fathering an heir, the stable master had shaken his head in despair and told Edmund that once Sieur Aymard had been the proud father of two strong, healthy boys and a girl so beautiful that the sun was jealous of her. So jealous in fact that, when the girl came of age, she was sullied and cast aside, and Aymard's sons died soon after from a malady no one could account for.

What of the girl, Edmund had wanted to know. Guy had given him a strange glance and then turned his back declaring that she too had died and now, the old man was left without heirs. All that springs from the birthing cots of the young women, who are marched through his sorry halls, are girls. A wealth of dark-haired girls. Some of them die before they are churched. Edmund knows that at least two of them are still alive; one works in the scullery.

Brushing his thick blond curls from his forehead, Edmund draws the horse to the stable wall. He secures the reins to the bar behind the trough and then he pauses to splash water on his face. Through the glitter of water drops in his eyelashes, the horse looks to sparkle in the sunlight.

'You like the look of him, boy?'

Edmund turns and bows low, drops prickling his eyes. 'Yes, my Lord.'

On the steps, Sieur Aymard waits and gives a small nod as if to approve of Edmund's behaviour. He knows he should be pleased, but rebellion always lurks just beneath the surface and now it rears its ugly head.

'But it is not as fine as the horses we have here.'

The Duke gives a half-smile. 'Is that so? It ought to be, for I purchased it off Aymard some years ago and paid a hefty price. Has he so refined his breeding that this is now a lame creature not worthy of your good care?'

Edmund is tongue-tied, a rare and odd occurrence. 'No, I just … It is just that …'

'Fret not,' the Duke says and lowers his voice to a whisper. 'If you say no more on the matter then neither shall I. But pray, do pick out a good horse or two for me to inspect when I am done with business. I might just see if I can strike a good deal, now that you have told me the truth of my purchase.'

Before Edmund can say anymore, the Duke turns away with a smile and nods at Sieur Aymard: 'To business, La Fontaine! I have little time to spare.'

The two men disappear into the dark hall, leaving Edmund with burning ears to tend to the horses. For some reason, he suddenly thinks about his mother, the faceless woman who left him alone many years ago. He has but vague recollections of living in a dirty hovel somewhere outside the town, of rare visits from an old man whose donkey always bit when Edmund reached out to stroke it. Any memory of his mother always leaves a strange empty feeling in his gut.

Edmund wipes the sting of angry tears from his eyes and proceeds to water and feed the horses. He takes extra care to rub down the Duke's horse, a magnificent beast with long soft fur around its hooves and a thick black mane, setting off the deep maroon hide.

By the time he is done, Edmund smells of warm horse and straw, he is hot and has blisters on his palms. But he likes to use his body, he likes to feel the burn of strain when he lugs around big bales of hay or mucks out the stables. It makes him forget; it gives him blessed sleep. It wards off her dead eyes.

Edmund ducks into the kitchen and pilfers a couple of pieces of warm bread fresh from the oven, bites down on an apple and skips to the dairy to lure some butter from Marie, who smells of cows and milk and has a cheerful smile on her face. Sometimes he sneaks into her cot late at night and she folds her arm around him and hugs him tight. She even lets him kiss her when no one is watching. But Marie is nowhere to be found. Edmund draws two thick lines of butter across the bread where it melts into a golden sheen and drizzles through the slices onto his palm.

Licking his wrist, he turns to the paddock, whistling for the horses to come before he bites into the bread.

'Where have you been?!' Sieur Aymard's angry voice tears a black hole in Edmund's simple joy. 'When you make an agreement with someone, you honour it. Have I taught you nothing, boy?!'

'I …' Edmund struggles to swallow his half-chewed bread.

'No doubt he has worked hard, La Fontaine. A little reward of some of your fine food is called for. I have just seen to my horse, and he has rarely looked as fine and well managed.' The Duke keeps his eyes on the approaching horses. 'Which ones?'

He is not asking his host Edmund realises and steals a glance at Sieur Aymard before pointing. 'The dapple-grey. A gelding. And the one to the far left.'

'Looks like my own,' the Duke says and nods. 'Which one is your favourite?'

'The black one.' Edmund tucks the rest of the bread into his mouth and snaps his buttery fingers. The black destrier snorts and trots towards his outstretched hand. Its soft muzzle nibbles at his palm and he coughs not to choke on his meal when the tickling makes him laugh.

'A fine beast.'

'The finest,' Aymard agrees and gives a brusque nod. 'But I shall keep him for breeding. There is also the cream and white.'

'It bites,' Edmund says and earns an angry look from Aymard. 'Well, it does. It might turn out good in the end, but it needs much work.'

'All yearlings?' the Duke asks no one in particular.

'Not the cream. It is – what – three years now?'

Edmund realises that Sieur Aymard is asking him a question, and a foreign feeling of pride surges through his body. 'Almost four, Sire. Not too old to be taught better manners, but it will take some time.'

'I like the silver.' The Duke points and Aymard groans. Jouyex is his pride and joy and, if not for a mishap with the blacksmith, it was destined to start a new line of destriers. Edmund has to smother the smile that threatens to break on his face. The blacksmith got what he deserved and then some.

'Gelded,' Edmund says helpfully when the Duke gives Sieur Aymard a curious glance. 'The blacksmith made a mistake.'

'Still a fine horse, my Lord,' Aymard says, his voice all business. 'Quick to respond, not yet fully grown and yielding on the field.'

'I need a horse that is not afraid of battle.' The Duke looks at the silver gelding with interest and then turns to Edmund. 'Which one might that be, master groom?'

'The chestnut, the one that looks like yours, my Lord. It shows great promise, I have seen the training, and Master Guy is content with it. It is not yet fully broken in, but another half-year should do it.'

The Duke rubs his hands and turns to Aymard. 'You heard the boy. Another half-year. Perfect timing; would you not say La Fontaine? I shall have a horse and a squire in one fell swoop.'

Edmund looks from the Duke to Sieur Aymard, whose face has an inscrutable look to it. 'You take that one and one for the boy and we have a deal.'

'Very well! I shall take the black one too. I will need documents for the deal,' the Duke says and quickly adds: 'I trust you, of course, but I may not be able to come myself and it is best, do you not think, that whoever comes for this precious cargo is endowed with documents that hold both our seals?'

'Yes, my Lord.' Sieur Aymard throws a glance at Edmund. 'Prepare the Duke's steed and make sure the men are fitted with food for themselves and the horses.'

The Duke turns to follow and gives Edmund another half-smile. 'You did well. In case no one else tells you, you did well today, and I will see you in half a year.'

What is half a year, Edmund thinks and bows low before the Duke. He only wonders what boy they were talking about to be the Duke's squire. The cream horse has come close and bites him in the elbow. Edmund glances over his shoulder to ensure no one is watching and then he flicks the soft pink muzzle, making the horse shrink back and flatten its ears. It will never stop biting; Edmund has made sure of that.

That night, Sieur Aymard sends for Edmund and he drags himself to the great hall, half asleep after another long day in the stables. He knows, he should have washed his face and changed his clothes, but he is so tired that he cannot be bothered. Besides, the knight hardly notices and so Edmund simply goes to the table and sits across from the old man, waiting for him to speak.

Marie walks by with a bowl of stew and stops long enough for Edmund to ladle two big scoops onto his platter. She drops a piece of bread next to him and bends with a smile to whisper: 'I know you were in the dairy.'

Edmund gives her his sweetest smile and watches two little roses bloom on her cheeks. He knows what those roses mean and, very soon, he will visit her cot again. Perhaps this time, she will reward him with more than a few stolen kisses. Somehow, Edmund knows he has much to learn and he intends to learn from her.

'The Duke was pleased with you,' Aymard growls between two mouthfuls and Edmund jerks his head around. 'I had all but given up hope that he would honour his promise to come, but I should have known he would not go back on a word. Nor would he dare forget a promise made to his … Never mind.'

Mopping up sauce with his bread, Edmund dares a question: 'Why did he come, my Lord?'

'For you, though I am not best pleased that he finds it in his power to delay.'

Edmund feels a chill crawl up his spine, he is to be the squire; he is the boy they were talking about at the pen. Already, his mind is imagining all sorts of new adventures for him to embark upon. If Edmund is honest, he has long been bored in Sieur Aymard's service, and so he relishes in the idea that he can leave. What is six months when you know what is to come?

In his excitement, Edmund coughs up the wine he is trying to drink and Aymard looks at him. 'You need to learn how to be a man. When the Duke's men come for you, you must be prepared to serve the Duke as a man would. You must obey his command; you must know how to behave and when to keep your mouth shut. Any display such as the one I witnessed today will cast you out and back to me. I do not intend for that to happen.'

'I can learn, my Lord.' Edmund makes the promise quickly, easily. Now, he knows why the old man has been pouring money into the hands of a tutor, why he has had Edmund on the field riding the horses, even the most expensive ones. He has known for a long time that someone would come and claim Edmund for greater things. 'Anything.'

'There is much to do. Tomorrow, when you are done in the stables, you will come here. I have to hire a tutor to teach you what you need to know. Every day until the Duke's men come, you will study and prepare, you will work in the stables, you will ride and learn to fight with lance and sword.' Sieur Aymard drinks deep and slams his cup onto the trestle table. 'It is time you grew up. The days of being a child are gone.'

They went with my mother; Edmund thinks and hides his scowl by staring at his food. 'Yes, my Lord.'

'You are lucky, the Duke took a shine to you boy, and never forget it. Do you think I have kept you here because I enjoy your company? That I poured money and time into your training because of your fair hair and easy manners?' Sieur Aymard empties his cup and rises. 'Come.'

Pushing down his prickled pride, Edmund follows Aymard into the adjoining study, closing the door on the noise of the hall. Suddenly, it feels as if he has been sold like a horse. As if he has never been more than a thing to be bartered with and handed off to the highest bidder. It does not sit well with him. It irks him as a stone in your boot on a long walk.

'You understand what has come to pass?'

'Yes, Sieur Aymard,' Edmund says and makes his voice small. This is no time for misbegotten manners; he will have plenty of opportunity to get even later. For now, it will serve him to be meek and obedient, and so he tucks away his disdain and plays the humble servant boy.

'If, at any time, the Duke deems it sensible that your charge should change, I want you to accept it. He is a wise man and a great friend to the King.' Sieur Aymard gazes out of the window at the amassing clouds. The sky is the colour of slate. 'A very great friend.'

Not for the first time, Edmund wonders how a lowly knight who resides in the middle of nowhere knows so much about the English court and if perhaps, Sieur Aymard has even met the King of England himself. It makes Edmund desperate to meet the King too, to best his master and become his superior in every way.

It dawns on Edmund that the first step on this path is to fully understand how to serve a Duke. If that means surviving another six months in Sieur Aymard's shadow what of it? It only gives him time to dream up the perfect vengeance for being sold like a horse to a stranger.

This time, a simple bellyache will not be enough; Edmund must come up with a parting gift that the old man will remember forever.

## 26 July 1392 – Westminster Palace

'By now, you must have guessed that the visitor who bought me as you would buy a piece of meat was none other than your father's most loyal friend and your father-in-law. It was not long before I was knee deep in harrying and bleeding the French countryside dry. I never thought of it as laying waste to my fellow man, for I had never truly felt like I belonged anywhere.'

'You were no doubt also knee-deep in blood?' Gaunt lifted his cup.

'Not until I met your brother, not truly.' Edmund stretched his legs. 'Lord Grosmont kept us to the task, but he was not a man who lusted for blood. Perhaps that is why he was heralded as one of the greatest Englishmen who ever walked the earth.'

'He was.' Gaunt was clearly the spectator not the orator tonight, and in that Edmund was satisfied.

'He shaped my life and gave me all the gifts I use till this day.' When Gaunt's face contracts in disgust, Edmund merely smiles. 'Come now, to be a great courtier, a great knight and a great Lord, you must possess all of God's virtues and, at the same time, be no stranger to the dark and devious ways of the Devil.'

'I would call you devilish, but not godly,' Gaunt said. 'And my late, beloved father-in-law had many virtues, but he never sunk as low as you did.'

'Because he did not begin his life as a beggar? Was not sold to a stranger in his childhood?' Edmund laughed. 'There are worse crimes, my Lord, as you must admit.'

'Just get on with it.'

Edmund nursed his wine for a moment before he drank. After wiping his mouth, he fixed Gaunt's stare. 'I met Lord Mowbray not long before I was to see true battle for the first time. Grosmont introduced us. Mowbray was my age, but to all the world, he was everything I was not. He had fame, fortune and most importantly, he had an army of his own.'

'So, you decided to take something from him?'

'No,' Edmund paused, searched for the right words. 'For the first time, I sought the friendship of another.'

Gaunt leaned forward, one hand under his chin. 'I never understood the relationship between the two of you. For you are right, he was everything you were not. If I could choose, I would have him here in this room and you dead somewhere far away.'

'Infidels would never finish me off,' Edmund said carelessly. 'And you would not want him here, not truly, for he would never agree to do what you ask of me.'

'No,' Gaunt admitted and then sighed, 'because if the two of you had changed places, we would not be in this mess in the first place. He would have governed his son better, and you would not have been here to pour mischief into anyone's cup.'

'You truly think the King would be another kind of man if only Mowbray had been here?' Edmund shook his head. 'The Baron spoiled for adventure even more than I ever did, he would not have been happy stuck here at court. Later, you will learn what happened to him when he was summoned for one of the longest sitting Parliaments. In the end, it was being chained to court that drove him away from England and to his destiny.'

Gaunt scratched his cheek, all the while maintaining eye contact. A weaker man would have yielded to the treatment, but Edmund simply looked back. In the end, Gaunt waved. 'Tell me how you met that I might think a little better of you.'

'It was the first time I ever heard your name mentioned,' Edmund said, 'and spoken so casually, I thought you were no one at all.'

# CHAPTER 2

## 25 April 1356 – Bordeaux

'Gaunt is coming with a host of fresh soldiers.' The Duke of Grosmont splashes water on his face, and Edmund is quick to replenish the basin. 'Thank you, Edmund. It is wretched warm these days and more filthy than a devil's arse!'

Edmund bites his cheek to contain laughter and waits for Grosmont to finish his wash. He wonders idly who this Gaunt might be, probably just another sergeant providing new men for the Prince's noble cause. Though after months of harrying, Edmund has done nothing very noble, but he understands that much can be hidden, if only you cry out that it is for God and glory.

'When Gaunt arrives, we must expect for the conditions here to change.' Turning from the basin, Grosmont grapples for the cloth Edmund is holding out.

'For the better, my Lord?' Edmund takes the basin. Perhaps this Gaunt person is more important than he first thought.

Grosmont grunts into his cloth. 'There are rumours that the Prince himself judges it is time to meet the French on the field. Though if their behaviour thus far is anything to go by, he will have a hard time teasing the old King out of his Parisian lair.'

The moment the water touches the ground it is sucked away, no trace of it outside the Duke's tent. If this is what a devil's arse looks like, Edmund understands why they are always depicted with scowls on their faces.

Though he is more inclined to think that it has to do with the church wanting to keep simple folk on a narrow path to salvation. Even the Virgin Mary gives but stern looks when you gaze upon her in church, not that Edmund goes very often. He ducks back into the tent.

'All of our harassing the French these past years has served but one purpose.' Grosmont speaks as if he has not even noticed, Edmund had left. 'The Prince means to do battle with King John and once and for all return France to his father's rule. Perhaps it will come to pass, after all the French King shares his name with the most unfortunate and self-servicing King we have ever had.'

He tosses aside the streaked cloth and looks at Edmund. 'King John ... if not for him we would not have to be here today. If not for him, there would be peace in the world.'

Edmund yearns for Grosmont to continue his tale, but he does not, instead he scratches his cheek. 'I need a shave. Close and clean this time, Edmund.'

'Yes, my Lord.' Edmund opens the ornamented wooden box and examines the barber's knife. Its silver handle alone is more valuable than anything Edmund has ever owned. 'It needs sharpening.'

'Well? Get on with it.'

'By a smith, my Lord.' Turning, Edmund holds up the knife's dull edge. 'Even I cannot make this sharp enough to dare touch your skin.'

Grosmont sighs and twirls his large opal ring. 'It will keep. But mind you take that to the smith today. I shall have my shave before tomorrow morning.'

'How will his Grace the Prince engage the King of France in battle?'

'How would you do it?'

Another test, Edmund thinks and pushes aside a desire to shake his head. Grosmont believes in just one way of learning, by constantly being tested, questioned and asked to reason every word you utter. It is a good way to learn, but brutal if you get it wrong.

'Rouse the French people against their sovereign. Once he sees that even his own people will not fight for him – or cannot fight for him – he will have to act. He can hide no more, he must be seen to take action.' Edmund catches a glimmer of acknowledgement in Grosmont's eyes, it soars to his heart and swells his chest. 'But what might happen if the King does enter into battle? What if he is caught?'

'We observe all the rules of chivalry.' Grosmont nods at the pile of clothes on his cot. 'No doubt, the Prince means to take him hostage and demand a ransom from France.'

'What if he is killed?'

Grosmont pauses, his fingers dance on the edge of the table. 'If he is killed in battle, the Dauphin will become King.'

'Then he must take heed and leave the Dauphin in Paris.' Edmund rummages through the pile and comes away with a clean white shirt and high collar. When Edmund turns Grosmont is looking at him, a pondering glint in his eye.

'My Lord? Something else?'

'No, no …' Grosmont motions for Edmund to approach. 'The shirt is fine. It is what you said. Why do you say so?'

Even after serving Grosmont for all of two years, Edmund still cannot tell what the Duke thinks; his mind is closed to everyone. But it does not do to leave the Duke waiting that much Edmund does know.

'Would the French King take his son to battle?'

'Our King has sent his heir.'

Edmund pulls the shirt over Grosmont's head and waits for him to arrange it. Then Edmund shakes out the collar and weaves the silk cord through the small holes. 'But the Prince …'

'Yes?' The Duke tugs at the collar where it clings to his wet skin.

'I have never seen the Dauphin, but I cannot imagine he will be a match to the Prince of whom I have heard much.' Edmund feels heat creep up his neck. 'Have you met the Dauphin, my Lord?'

'I have seen him when he was a child. The gold chain, I think.'

While he fetches the small chest, Edmund can hear the Duke shuffle his papers. 'What is he like?'

'Nothing to our Prince.' The thick gold links come to rest around Grosmont's neck. 'And you are right, if King John takes to the battlefield, he will be best served to leave his heir behind. But then, when has a King ever thought as a common man? And he has more sons.'

'When is Gaunt expected to arrive, my Lord?' Edmund enjoys speaking with Grosmont almost as an equal though he knows they are as far from equals as two men can be. When the Duke's men had come to collect him, Edmund had been furious to be handed over as a side of bacon. But once he joined the Duke's camp, he never looked back. This is the best decision old Sieur Aymard ever made, Edmund is sure of it.

Grosmont laughs. 'Best you call him Lord Gaunt, lad, for he is the Prince's brother and married to my daughter and so, also my heir. He is due within the week. Once he is here, the Prince no doubt will rely upon his brother to make the final preparations. For battle must surely be given. The men hanker for it.' Grosmont looks up as a weak wind pushes at the tent flaps. 'Would that Gaunt would come sooner. But I am certain that King John will not disappoint the Prince – again. He cannot afford to, for it is as you say, Edmund, the French grow weary of our efforts, and rumblings must surely have reached Paris by now. They demand vengeance. For which we can hardly blame them.'

'They have been hard tried, my Lord.' Edmund ties back the flaps to let in the breeze; it dances past him clad in yellow dust. 'Is Lord Gaunt as his brother?'

Amusement lingers on Grosmont's face. 'I shall let you make your own conclusion. It is best not to let others cloud your judgement, Edmund. Even me. But I can say that Lord Gaunt is of a more strategic nature than our beloved Prince. Which is, no doubt, why the King has sent him here; to ensure everything is done as it should be.'

Gaunt sounds more as a tutor than a younger brother, Edmund thinks, and brushes down Grosmont's dark cloak taking extra care to clean his coat of arms. The golden lions glisten against the red background. When first Edmund saw the lions, he had struggled not to laugh at the ridiculous blue tongues that lolled from their mouths. Now, he thinks it makes them look fierce. Perhaps it is because now, he knows the Duke and is one of his men.

'Until Gaunt arrives though, I expect to see you on the training field every day.' Grosmont snaps his fingers at one of his pages. 'Wine. Just enough to drive this incessant dust from my throat.'

'I never miss a day's training, my Lord.' He does not mean for the words to come out petulant, but they do.

'Still better with a sword than a lance?' Grosmont shakes his head when Edmund holds out a pair of thin leather gloves. 'You will have to keep at it.'

Just as Edmund has put the gloves back in the little box, the page returns with a tray of wine and a few plain cups. 'Here.'

The boy's hands tremble a little when he lifts up the tray for Edmund to take it. 'Yes, Master Edmund.'

'I remember when you were that age.' Grosmont watches the boy scurry away.

'Surely, my Lord, I was older when you met me?'

Grosmont snorts. 'Twelve or so I believe, yes? Eugene is thirteen.'

'I do not even remember being that small, my Lord.' Edmund earns a smile. 'I have quite forgotten all that went before this life. I hardly recall being a stable boy at all.'

'A blessing perhaps?'

Edmund puts the tray on the little travel table and goes about preparing the wine. Grosmont prefers it watered down. 'Perhaps.'

'But no, you were never that small. I remember looking at your Grand-Père and wondering how any child of his could produce such a specimen as you. But since he was glad to part with you, I had no cause to ask any questions. Even a blind man could tell you were built for more than what inheritance your Grand-Père might have left to bestow upon you.'

It takes an effort for Edmund to maintain his smile. Grand-Père? What is the Duke on about? What is this madness? Surely, he must have thought Edmund is someone else.

But before he can ask, Grosmont continues, 'I liked the look of you the moment I saw you. I was pleased then that I had made arrangements to include you in my retinue. You have served me well. But you must work on your skills constantly that you do not fall prey to laziness and wind up dead before your time.'

It takes a moment for Edmund to get his thoughts in line. Just long enough for Grosmont to give him a probing glance. So, Edmund smiles. 'The men take pains to see if they can best me.'

'How many does it take these days?'

'With the sword; three.' Edmund shirks at the sharp taste at the back of his mouth from the wine. 'My Lord.'

'They grow restless from staying here too long, they need sport.' Grosmont nods when Edmund holds out a cup. 'You are sport.'

'It sometimes makes me feel …' Edmund shakes his head. 'It is good training, my Lord.'

'Most assuredly, Edmund, it is. And there is no need to feel anything but power when you spar with the men; most of the camp knows that they will have to work hard to take you down.' Grosmont empties the cup with a satisfied sigh. 'Take it as a compliment. And besides, your efforts seem to have caught the eye of some of the Prince's followers.'

'My Lord?' Off the field, Edmund would rather be equal to the other men. But on the field, he means to best them all.

'Baron Mowbray to be precise. You are of an age, and he claims that he enjoys your company. In part, he is pleased with your sword-work, no doubt, but for the most part, I believe he simply wants to get in my good graces. The Baron's wife is a distant relative of mine, you see. He has praised what he has seen in the training field.' Grosmont's low backrest creaks. 'He has asked that you be transferred to his troops.'

Unexpected joy surges through Edmund, and he bows his head to Grosmont to hide a victorious smile. He has made an extra effort to impress the Baron, and he is glad it has paid off. Now, he sends a quick prayer to the God he hardly believes in that Grosmont will release him to serve the Baron.

'Well?' Grosmont's opal ring twirls. 'What say you?'

'I am in your service, my Lord. The Baron is kind to speak of me, but my allegiance lies with you.'

'Perhaps your skills are squandered on the field,' Grosmont laughs and pounds the table in amusement. 'You have the raw makings of a diplomat! I will be sent to protect Calais soon, how like you that?'

Again, Edmund feels heat creep up his neck; Grosmont enjoys to tease him. He will have to be careful if he is to succeed. 'If you command it, I shall defend Calais for you.'

'You cannot stay a squire forever,' Grosmont says and accepts another cup of wine. The dry heat leaves throats coated in sand; the Duke is wise to water his wine. 'I think perhaps it is time you won your spurs. I have wanted it for you during our many previous encounters.'

To Edmund the pause drags on forever, but he waits for Grosmont to continue without pressuring him. 'To do so, you must see true battle. You must take up arms against the enemy in the battlefield. You must be in war proper. Spurs won another way is the coward's way, and you are no coward.'

'Yes, my Lord.' Inside, Edmund is jumping around screaming at the top of his lungs; he has longed for the moment when he might go from squire to soldier, and now the Duke is implying that he might even be a knight! What a twist of fate!

'I can tell the prospect pleases you.' Grosmont empties the cup and shakes his head when Edmund moves to fill it a third time. 'You have been a great help and a good fighter throughout our chevauhcées. I have already told the Prince as much. I believe perhaps Mowbray speaks up now because he has heard what I have said and wants as many young, able men in his company as possible.'

Edmund endures one of the Duke's prolonged stares, he knows that if he looks away now, Grosmont will reconsider and he shall not have the opportunity again. It is plain on his face that he is looking for weakness or hesitation, and Edmund will not let this opportunity slip through his fingers. Grosmont seems to come to a decision.

'Tomorrow, I will summon Mowbray, and we shall hash out the details,' he says and smiles back at Edmund. 'I will not let my best squire go without making terms for Mowbray.'

'Thank you, my Lord,' Edmund manages to say with well-rehearsed dignity.

He is pleased when the Duke sends him on an errand for more wine, and as soon as he is clear from the tent, he stuffs his hand into his mouth to still the triumphant laugh that is threatening to overpower him. To take up arms with the young Lord Mowbray, to be almost certainly near the fabled Prince whom he has but seen a few times and always from far away. It is what he has dreamed of since he left Sieur Aymard's service.

All of Edmund's hopes and dreams now rest on the shoulders of one man.

## 26 April 1356 – Bordeaux

Lord Mowbray arrives resplendent in his red and white gown and cloak, his emblem laid out on his shirt chest in gemstones and pearls. To Edmund, he looks like a peacock stuck in the chicken coop, clean and sparkling amidst the dust and grime. The Baron bows to Grosmont and then takes the seat he is offered. Next to the Duke, Mowbray looks almost adolescent, though Edmund learned last night that he is a married man.

Grosmont sends his servants from the tent and asks Edmund to serve the Baron whatever he wishes. Mowbray smiles warmly at Edmund and accepts the cup of wine he holds out on a small silver tray.

'Thank you for the invitation, my Lord,' Mowbray says in a rich deep voice that seems at odds with his youthful appearance. He inclines his cup to Grosmont and drinks.

'I am most pleased you have agreed to discuss the matter further.' Mowbray winks at Edmund. 'After all, I have often had the pleasure of being beaten by your squire in the field.'

Edmund basks in the praise although he has only managed to disarm the Baron when the fight is with swords; as soon as lances are the weapons of choice, he has Edmund on the ground more times than he cares to admit. Edmund turns for the tray of olives and sour pickled lemons, the Duke's favourite light snacks.

Mowbray waves at the offered tray and continues: 'Just yesterday, I had a message from the Prince. We wait only for his brother to bring reinforcements before we march to join forces with his Grace. Surely, King John understands that he can no longer avoid giving battle. France grows restive ...'

'A good thing for us,' Grosmont says and sucks leftover juice from the pickled lemons from his fingers. 'I believe the men Gaunt brings will tip the scales further in our favour. The King is wise to send his sons to face King John and his Dauphin.'

'You believe that the jewel of the French crown will join the battle with us alongside his father?' Mowbray asks and considers the silver tray for some time before picking a few olives. Edmund hovers in the back, his eye on the prize, his head buzzing with impatience.

'How can they not? If King John sends his Dauphin, he will be a laughing stock in all of France, since they know our Prince has called out the King for a duel.' Grosmont leans forward. 'And I know for a fact that the young Dauphin is no match for our Prince.'

And you think that the French King is not wise enough to leave the Dauphin at home, Edmund thinks, for you said so yourself just yesterday. How many times must I hear the same story?

Mowbray leans back with a hearty laugh. 'I dare say no one is a match for our Prince! But I do not think King John will accept the duel. He will come in great force, as well he should, to free France from what he thinks are her enemies. But he would be a fool to fight the Prince, which you know as well as I.'

'He would be wiser to accept our King's claim to the throne. If he played his cards right, he might even have been permitted to serve until his death before the Crown reverted to English hands, where it belongs. Unfortunately, he is as poor a card player as he is wise.' Grosmont rubs his arm; underneath his splendid surcoat with the lion crest he hides an old war wound that often causes discomfort. 'And you are right, he will come in force.'

Now that Grosmont has served the bait, Mowbray is quick to take it. He glances at Edmund and nods. 'That is why, my Lord, I believe we need Master Edmund to join our campaign.'

'That is a lot of importance to put upon such young shoulders,' Grosmont says without looking at Edmund. 'He may be important to me, but to the war, all of us are but grains of sand. Alone, one man does not make a beach – not even this young man.'

'I am given to understand that you are making for Calais?' Mowbray tries a new approach.

'Yes, we are leaving as soon as Gaunt arrives. There must be a commander of Calais, especially at this crucial time, and I have been bestowed a great honour in taking up the charge.' Edmund knows that Grosmont is working hard to hide a hint of regret. 'I was hoping to leave with a full retinue … If you want Edmund to stay behind …'

'I ask once more that he joins my troops, where he will make a real difference. Many of the men may be grains of sand as you say, but here I believe we have found a sharp rock that the enemy will fall upon and hurt themselves. If you agree, I shall ensure he is a squire no more, which will serve all of us, do you not think? For I am certain that his time has come, my Lord Duke.' Mowbray shrugs. 'Do you not agree?'

'He has served me well,' Grosmont grumbles and Edmund feels his hope crumble. 'What do you propose I do without him?'

'If I had a younger brother, I should offer his services in return for this great favour,' Mowbray says, 'but alas, I do not. However, I do have a page who is ready to serve as squire, and I have been looking for a place for him.'

Grosmont holds out his cup and Edmund pours the wine, careful to look as if he has not been listening and is not angry that the Duke is delaying his decision. Yesterday, he spoke as if it was already decided and now, simply because he wants someone to wait on him hand and foot, Grosmont sounds as if he is changing his mind. If only the Baron could offer something more.

'I see.' The Duke looks at Mowbray. 'I am to be stuck with a page?'

'It would be in your power to create another great squire. None do that as well as you, everyone knows that.' Mowbray smiles and earns a nod from the Duke. Edmund pours for the Baron too, careful not to overstep their newfound intimacy and return the smile. 'You are free to refuse of course.'

'Why is it, Mowbray, that I think you have some hidden leverage?' Grosmont chuckles when Mowbray throws out his arms in mock surprise. 'Come now, what is it?'

'The Prince agrees with me that Edmund should join us,' Mowbray relinquishes; it is his turn to laugh. Edmund turns his back, his cheeks burning with pride and glee. From behind, Mowbray continues, 'I have informed the Prince of young Edmund's talents and he agrees with me that we need all the able young men, we can muster. Battle against the French will require the full force of the English army. What better way is there for you to serve the Prince than to hand over the strongest weapon in your retinue?'

'The strongest weapon in my retinue is myself – I believe – though I am no longer a young man. And his Grace has seen fit to send me far from the field of battle.' Grosmont gives a hard laugh when Mowbray bows his head at the rebuke. 'But even I cannot refuse the Prince. And I will still guard the English realm in Calais, for if luck goes against you, the French are sure to go north immediately to throw out their English overlords.'

When Edmund turns around, Grosmont is looking at him. 'You wish to go? Though no one can guarantee that it will not be going to your death?'

'Yes, my Lord,' Edmund says, careful as always to remain humble in the company of great men. 'Let me go to represent you on the field of battle. Let me have a sword to swing and a horse to ride and I shall carve a piece out of the heart of France just for you.'

Mowbray laughs and Grosmont tips his cup to Edmund. 'Yesterday, I said you had the makings of a courtier, today, I believe you might be a poet. Although I suspect you will write your poems in blood.'

'Whatever he writes them in, his pledge is an honest one,' Mowbray chips in. 'I, for one, would never turn down a man who was prepared to carve me out a piece of France. Neither should you.'

'I shall agree, Mowbray,' Grosmont says and gives the Baron a stern look, 'if you can guarantee that upon our victory against the French, the Prince will knight young Edmund here!'

Mowbray opens his mouth as if to protest, but then decides against it and nods. 'I shall speak to the Prince as soon as we meet up with him. I cannot promise more at this moment for we do not know what the future brings. But if all of us survive the battle, Edmund will be knighted.'

Grosmont scrutinizes his guest for a moment. 'It must be the Prince himself who knights Edmund. I expect that you can persuade him to allow this folly to an old soldier and comrade in arms. He can send his acceptance of my request to Calais. We both know that spurs can be won in many ways. I mean for Edmund to win his the only way I see fit for any man, on the field of battle.'

'No place would be more valiant or chivalrous.' Mowbray nods. 'I shall strive to meet your demands, my Lord. For I have no desire to die at the hand of the French and neither does the Prince. We mean to be victorious, and I would feel a lot better knowing Edmund was there with me.'

'To that I cannot object,' Grosmont says, 'Which is why I am adamant that he be knighted by the Prince himself, as a testament not only to Edmund's skill but also to my wisdom in parting with him. Otherwise, I shall take him with me to Calais.'

Edmund wants to interrupt, he can almost smell the battle, feel the spurs. What if the Duke has given Sieur Aymard, who is apparently his Grand-Père, his word that Edmund is to be kept safe? Edmund has not had a moment to ask if what Grosmont let slip yesterday is true or not. Part of him wants it to be so, but then his own flesh and blood has sold him as easily as you would sell a sack of grain. Part of him wants Grosmont to be wrong, to have spoken falsely, because deep down, having no family is what works best for Edmund. That way he is free. Or as free as any servant will ever be.

The truth is, Edmund knows not what Grosmont and Sieur Aymard discussed almost three years ago when the deal was struck. He had only seen a rare smile play in the corner of the old codger's mouth when the Duke left. But if Edmund is refused this opportunity to prove his worth, he knows he will find it hard to forgive Grosmont, whatever the cause.

'I shall speak with the Prince as soon as we meet up with him.' Mowbray gets to his feet. 'We will be pursuing the French until they are forced to turn around and give battle. But we can both agree, I think, that it will not be long before they come bearing down on us. If at all possible, you will hear of Edmund earning his spurs not long after you have the Prince's reassurance that he will knight him.'

Without another word, the Baron makes for the flaps and Edmund opens them for him. In the brief moment they pass each other, Edmund thinks he sees encouragement and even amusement in Mowbray's eyes.

'By this time tomorrow you will be in the service of that young buck,' Grosmont says when Mowbray is gone. 'Be sure he never finds fault in his decision.'

For a moment, Edmund is speechless and then he understands: 'You believe the Prince will agree, my Lord?'

'Oh yes.' Grosmont pulls a stack of papers towards him, a cracked red seal prominent on the top piece. 'I have already struck the deal with him. His promise arrived this morning along with news that the French are mustering to give battle. Have a care you survive, boy, and you will be reborn a legend; forged by war and surrounded by Princes.'

# CHAPTER 3

## 26 July 1392 – Westminster Palace

'The first time I saw the Prince, I confess I was disappointed.' Edmund got up and weaved his way to a narrow window giving on to a small enclosed courtyard; Gaunt's room was an obstacle course of fine furniture and chests of all sizes. 'After all that I had heard of him and his merits, I had expected a giant among men. But he was just another lean soldier with a hardened if handsome face. Had it not been for the crown he wore, I would not have known it was he, I was to bend my knee to, he who would soon come to favour my advice – for better and for worse. He who would put me at the centre of all things.'

Gaunt nodded but kept silent; clearly, he was interested, but he would never own it. For once, Edmund admired the seasoned courtier his calm demeanour.

'My impression improved when he picked up his sword, for though he was slight, even at fourteen I stood a full five inches taller than he, the Prince was tough and swung his blade with the force of three men.' Edmund's fingers traced the faint scar on his neck. 'But what mattered most to me was that he was not above fighting dirty. From him more than any other man, I learned how to treat a sword and more importantly, how to make the most of any weapon available. Rarely had I seen such fierceness, such ferocity as when he took the training field. How seasoned soldiers yielded, turning their bloodied faces to him, laying down their maces and hammers and declared themselves completely at his mercy.'

'My brother liked nothing better than to wield his sword. If only he had been as adept at other matters.' Gaunt's words came out listless, but his face had turned hard.

'I do not know what I did to impress him though I would wager that at least some of his interest was spurred when I delivered to him an enemy of immense value.' Edmund turned his back to Gaunt and leaned on the windowsill. 'A prisoner who earned me not only my spurs, but left me showered in gold and gifts that many other men envied me – and still envy me to this day.'

Gaunt's chair scraped across the floor, then Edmund heard his footsteps on the hard rush matting. He had gone to the empty hearth and was looking into the dark abyss.

'Your work on the field lent a debt that could never be repaid.' Gaunt sighed. 'Though I dare say my brother and father tried. You caught their eye and they never let you out of their sight for long.'

'But even before, as soon as I arrived with Lord Mowbray to join his campaign, he began to take an interest, and so too did you.'

With a soft scoff, Gaunt sat down. 'I wish, I had not.'

'We were all young then.' Edmund leaned against the cool glass. 'Young men make mistakes.'

'None as many, nor as devastating as my brother.' Once more, Gaunt turned his head to the dead fireplace. 'And we both helped him.'

## 16 August 1356 – Saintes, France

Edmund wipes his chin. The iron taste floods his mouth when he licks his lips. His hand comes away streaked in red. Inward he cusses that he forgot his gauntlets in his tent.

'Ready to forfeit, Master Edmund?'

Swinging his sword, Edmund looks up. 'Are you, your Grace?'

The force of the blow tells Edmund that the Prince is far from done. In fact, it appears he can go on forever, the grip never slipping, the advances coming fast and strong.

Kneeling beneath the series of blows, Edmund takes every strike to his shield with gritted teeth. He knows it will be wisest to yield, but something deep inside rebels at the thought of giving in simply because his aggressor is the Prince of England.

At a minute pause in the relentless battering, Edmund seizes his opportunity and rises with a roar, forcing his own advance, his sword glittering in the sunlight, letting blow upon blow fall on the Prince's shield and arm. Every contact with the armoured arm sings in Edmund's bones and yet, he persists.

Laughing, the Prince stems Edmund's attack and forces him back, swinging ever quicker. Edmund knows he is out of his depth, but the cheers ringing from all around keeps him going, lends strength to his sword. When he slides off the Prince's attack and he stumbles, Edmund cannot hide a smile.

He kicks the Prince in the knee, and he goes down with a groan. But then, quick as a snake, the Prince swings his shield, the blow paralysing Edmund's thigh. He falls before the Prince, both of them panting. The blue eyes burn into Edmund's and then the final blow is dealt. The flat of the Prince's blade makes contact with Edmund's throat and he rolls to the side, grappling at the burning pain.

'Enough!'

Edmund squints; the Prince is still kneeling next to him, leaning heavily on his blunted sword, his golden hair fringed dark from sweat.

'Enough, brother.' Is that worry in John of Gaunt's voice?

The Prince rises slowly and offers Edmund a gauntlet hand. Gaunt's eyes dart between them. 'Are you mad? We are about to meet the enemy, and you are beating the life out of your troops?!'

Edmund tumbles to his feet, the Prince's grasp firm and warm.

'Not all of them. He is but one man.' Laughter is bubbling just below the surface. 'And while Master Edmund might fight fiercely, he knows better than to wound his Prince.' He looks at Edmund and adds quietly; 'I believe.'

Edmund's throat throbs, but the pain is dull and air once more fills his lungs. He ingests fire with every whooping breath and his blood roars in his ears. How true the Prince just spoke. Edmund spits.

'Who would you have me spar with, brother? No other man is a match to me.' There is humiliation in the words and Gaunt stops, his back turned to the Prince.

'I would have you plan our attack, not play with swords.' Gaunt stalks off.

The Prince's squire pulls off the bloodied gauntlet and takes his sword and shield. With a cup in his hand the Prince snots and spits before drinking deep. 'We must defer our match for another time.'

'Yes, your Grace,' Edmund says and bows when the Prince turns to leave. Though he will never admit it, Edmund is grateful to Gaunt right at this moment. He would not have lasted much longer. He may be taller than the Prince, and broader of chest too, but the Prince is a seasoned warrior and hides his strength behind a thin veil of a lean body.

'You fought well!' Baron Mowbray slaps Edmund on the back and laughs. 'I made a tidy sum betting on you!'

'Glad to be of service, my Lord.' Edmund's arm burns from exertion, and his stomach burns from being once more a commodity. 'Next time, maybe you would bet for me too?'

'You did too well,' Mowbray says and pushes Edmund's shield into the arms of his own squire. 'No one will be stupid enough to bet against you again!'

'Pity, I could use the money.' Edmund drinks deep from his water-skin and winces when the watered-down wine bites at his split lip.

Mowbray leads the way off the field. 'You must make your fortune some other way, my friend! Taking down the Prince before we face the French might be very tempting. God knows he might be served right with a good beating. But it would be bad for morale!'

'He would have won,' Edmund says with a grudge. Although he is still training, anytime he loses is a great insult to him, one that must be repaid threefold or more.

'For now, perhaps, but I have a feeling that some day soon, you will be more than a match even for him.'

'Is that why you have avoided the field of late, my Lord?'

'Careful Master Edmund,' Mowbray says with mock severity; 'It is still in my gift to make – or break – you.'

Edmund smiles and his lip splits in protest. 'My Lord Grosmont might take offence.'

'Unfortunate for you then that Grosmont is not here while I am.'

Mowbray looks up at the gathering clouds. 'Another storm is coming, best we find shelter before …'

A big drop lands in his eye and he growls. Edmund laughs. 'I was born in a storm.'

'You stay outside then; I prefer to stay dry and warm as long as I can. We move on at daybreak,' Mowbray says and pulls his hood up. 'You are ready?'

'Yes, My Lord.' Edmund turns his face to the rain, the cold a welcome relief, soothing his bruises and cooling his temper. 'The men are prepared, the horses rested, as much as can be expected.'

'How is it that my men are fed when many others all but starve?'

'You forget I grew up in this land.' Edmund wipes his face and grimaces when his hand brushes over his throat. Tomorrow, he will sport a black bruise where the Prince's blade struck. 'But even my frugality cannot change our situation. If we do not encounter the enemy soon, we too will starve.'

You also do not know that I steal what I can from the other lords that I might stay high in your favour, Edmund adds in his thoughts. If it comes to it, he will steal the other knights' horses and put them on the char to ensure Mowbray stays in his debt.

'Rain and starvation. Is this worth fighting for?' Mowbray muses.

'It is not our decision, my Lord.'

'No, but it is my responsibility to question even the Prince's decisions if my men's lives are at stake.'

Edmund follows Mowbray into the camp, the rain pelting them. 'When we meet the French, are not all our lives at stake?'

'It is one thing to die a heroic death on the battlefield,' Mowbray says trying to shake water from his soaked cloak now that they are inside his tent and out of the rain. 'There is no honour in starvation.'

All Edmund can do is agree, but he also knows first-hand that Death takes what he wants; he does not wait for an invitation. Better to offer up someone else to soothe Death's everlasting hunger.

## 18 September 1356 – Nouaillé, France

It seems an age since Edmund has seen the face of the Baron. He has been riding behind Mowbray for weeks, while the army makes its way to the fields outside Poitiers where the French are rallying. It is becoming dull, monotonous and Edmund despises such things above all else.

Once more, Prince Edward has challenged King John to a duel and once more, King John has refused. It is said that the English envoys laughed all the way back to the Prince with the answer, but when they saw the Prince's face, their laughter died on their lips. Within burns an insatiable fury that is but further stoked by the French King's arrogance.

Tonight, Edmund stands behind the Baron, thrilled to be attending the Prince's final war council. He thinks it is in no small part due to his unfinished duel with the Prince. One he hopes to finish before long and prove to all the world that even the greatest prince that ever lived can be cut down by an orphaned peasant boy. None will snicker then.

'The three-way split is the only way to do it.' The Prince taps his finger on the map, quick as a woodpecker searching for worms. 'Surely, brother, you understand that to make the most of our men, we must capture the French and ensure they cannot escape. I want King John as my prisoner in this tent by tomorrow evening!'

'I understand, but you are stretching the lines thin. Too thin.' Unlike his brother, Gaunt displays no emotion. Edmund likes him for that, but he also knows that Gaunt is a dangerous man, a clever man who is not afraid of playing dirty if it comes to it. Edmund would recognise a fellow creature anywhere.

'Trust me, John.' The Prince slaps Gaunt on the shoulder. 'After all, I have encountered the French before.'

'But not the entire force of the French army.' Gaunt is silenced by a single glance. Something passes between the royal brothers that eludes even Edmund. 'But if you are certain …'

Since first seeing John of Gaunt, who is but a year older than Edmund, he has tried to find the resemblance between the strong, golden-haired heir to England and his younger, coarser and shorter brother. They do share some features, the handsome face – though the Prince far outshines his brother – and their build, but Gaunt is slight by comparison and he has a wily look about him that Edmund knows all too well.

'They will need to climb the hill to get to us, your Grace.' Mowbray pours over the outline of the battlefield; in the torchlight, his crimson cloak looks a tattered brown. 'Perhaps we can use the thickets on either side to our advantage?'

'Yes, you have the right of it, Mowbray.' The Prince pushes back his golden curls and taps the map again. 'Warwick, you will command the van, and Salisbury, I trust you to command our archers. I shall take charge of the main troops, to put bravery into the heart of every soldier under my command.'

Edmund notices that Gaunt is scowling, but he stays silent when his brother continues. 'The thickets will act as extra protection and you can position yourself to ensure that you can take out the enemy easily. Their bolts will be nothing to our arrows.'

'Perhaps the archers could be put to good use on the flanks too, my Prince?' William Montagu, the Earl of Salisbury, suggests. 'If we let a company or two sneak through the cover of night, we may even be able to attack from behind.'

Edmund finds Salisbury to be a peacock with a brain matching that of the same bird. If not for his title and his birth right, he would not be invited here, Edmund thinks annoyed, but there you are. The rich will forever favour their own until someone turns up that has something more to offer. He intends to be that other.

The Prince considers Salisbury's suggestion, no doubt aware that all attention is on him and relishing in it, if Edmund is not much mistaken. Finally, the Prince says, 'I need some of them to guard our provisions.'

'Of course.' Salisbury struggles to hide his frustration. 'I shall post forty men to that effect. I still think …'

'Your suggestion has given me cause for contemplation, my Lord,' the Prince interrupts. 'Perhaps it is time we broke for a meal. Let us reconvene here in a couple of hours.' When all the men bow to take their leave, the Prince adds. 'Brother, dine with me, we have much to discuss.'

To Edmund there is a dangerous undertone in the Prince's words, but Gaunt merely smiles and watches the Lords and knights file past. Once outside the tent, everyone disperses to attend their duties and give new orders. Edmund would have paid good gold to still be in the tent, for no doubt the two royal brothers will shout rather than talk.

Salisbury hurries away to set a watch for the baggage train, nodding to Mowbray as he passes. 'My Lord.'

Mowbray offers a small smile to Salisbury's back. 'His is a position I do not envy. We are outnumbered two to one, if not more, and we need every man available to fight, not stand guard. Our archers can make this battle. If there are enough of them.'

'Surely …' Edmund stops himself knowing that Mowbray will nod encouragingly and when he does, Edmund continues, 'Surely we should put all the men on the field? What good are provisions to us if we lose? But if we win, we can have not only our own provisions but also those of the French army. I do not understand why the Prince is so interested in what little we do have.'

'He may come off cavalier, but he too knows that this might not be an easy battle. He cannot afford to jeopardise what we have left.' The Baron turns towards the Mowbray camp, his banner snapping above his tent. 'And you ought to say, "When we win". The weather may yet be with us.'

'My Lord?'

'The Prince prefers to do battle in mist and rain rather than sunshine. It provides extra cover and God knows we need it.' Mowbray raises his hand to a company of passing soldiers sporting his badge on their chests and they cry out in return. 'Trust me when I tell you that I would never allow my men to walk into a trap. I swore before God that I should not lose any more than I must. If I thought the Prince in the wrong, I would not hesitate to make my case.'

'Did you notice the French soldiers earlier?' Edmund has spent an hour under cover of the thickets with the other scouts wondering what on earth the French were doing on the field. More than once, he had to clap both hands over his mouth to not laugh out loud and reveal how close the English spies were. 'They look untrained. Bewildered.'

Mowbray laughs. 'They are! Which is our good fortune! With any luck they will soon discover that they cannot beat us and surrender.'

'You are not for a long battle, my Lord?' Edmund aches to finally be in a real battle, the past years in Grosmont's service attacking villages and burning crops has only added to his desire to meet adversaries in the field who might prove worthy of his blade. Killing animals and pilfering grain is hardly what Edmund had in mind when Sieur Aymard sent him off with one of the great lords of England. After biding his time for so long, Edmund plans to make the most of this battle.

'No.' Mowbray waits for Edmund to hold the tent flap open to him. 'No, Edmund, I am not. Whenever lives may be spared, I believe we should. God will not love us any more if we send too many innocent soldiers to their graves. You mark my words.'

Sometimes, Edmund marvels at how much the Baron sounds like an old man who would rather sit before a comfortable fire than forge his destiny by blood and steel. It annoys Edmund to no end that he has wound up in the service of what he can only describe as a coward. Grosmont may be twenty years their senior, but at least he is not afraid of blades drawn. Some nights, Edmund longs to be in Grosmont's service once more, but not for long, for in truth, Edmund wants to serve no man. He is hoping that this battle might finally set him free. If not, then perhaps death is preferable to a lifetime serving someone else.

Sometimes, he imagines death as a creature that is always poised in the dark just beyond your gaze, patient in its expectation, knowing that in the end, it will prevail over man every time.

'You disagree?' Mowbray pulls off his sword belt and tosses it to his squire.

'Outside our chevauchées, I have no battle experience to speak of, my Lord,' Edmund says to soothe the proud Baron, but inward he does disagree. Let the battle be long and bloody and let me come out victorious, he thinks and says, 'I know only that I will fight until the French either surrender or perish.'

Mowbray smiles. 'So will I, Edmund, so will I. But praying to God for a swift victory is no shame. Tomorrow, you will earn your spurs no matter what happens. It depends not on the number of people you kill, but on your efforts while battle ensues.'

# CHAPTER 4

## 19 September 1356 – Poitiers, France

*We are losing.*

The thought manifests itself in Edmund's brain as he watches the enemy in its thousands descend upon the field.

*We are losing.*

It is such an alien idea that it paralyzes him. Pins him to the ground. He has no reason to be afraid, for only few months ago, Edmund fended off three full-grown men with ease, wielding his sword and mace. He has the loot to prove it. The ring threaded on a golden chain that crushes against his chest beneath the armour. The subtle leather boots. The helmet he wears. All taken from slain enemies.

*We are losing.*

But the whole host of the French army, for all that they looked out of sorts yesterday, now charge and Edmund feels a fleeting sensation of dread. All those knights, soldiers, archers and noblemen. The entire French royal family turned out to defeat one Prince. The monster that is the army of France turns its eye on him. It watches him, it weighs him. And Edmund trembles. It makes him sick.

*We are losing.*

Until this very moment, Edmund has always thought of Death as bleak, hooded and silent. But today, he has learned that when Death takes to the field, he does so clad in bright, sparkling colour, in gold, silver and purple.

He does so with a crown on his helmet and gold gauntlets on his hands, waving at the men who salute him by the thousands. With l'Oriflamme snapping red against the iron sky.

*We are losing.*

Edmund looks about. He sees his fellow soldiers come to the same horrifying realisation. He can feel their terror. He can taste defeat; bitter and foul. His hands tremble, his grip on his sword is slipping. The sword the Duke gave him. A present to ensure he won his spurs today. This very day. The day he will die. No spurs will be won. By nightfall, if not before, this magnificent sword will belong to a nameless, faceless enemy. Idly, Edmund wonders who will wear his boots tomorrow.

*We are losing.*

They say that Death is swift. But it is not. It is cruel, it is violent, it roars and bites and stabs and tears at you. It drinks your blood and feasts on your innards. Edmund understands all of this now. In one brilliant flash, he understands all. Death is not salvation; Death is slaughter.

*We are losing.*

His faceless mother beckons him; she holds out her arms and calls to him. The faint sickly scent of her decaying flesh, not entirely washed away by the passing years, lingers in his nose. She lifts her head, her dark hair still despite the wind that whips the standards and lifts Edmund's hair from the nape of his neck where the helmet does not quite reach his chainmail. Her hands reach for him. White bone. He turns away from her.

*Death has come.*

*We are losing.*

*Death is here.*

Edmund swallows back the bile of defeat. He closes his eyes against the charge of the enemy, the strength of numbers, Death in purple at the head of the French army. His heart beats quickly and hard against the breastplate, his hand searches blindly for the hilt of his sword. How can it be that he is afraid? He who has nothing to lose and everything to gain. He who should be the first to charge and prove himself to the Prince and all the lords and knights surrounding him. He is disgusted with himself.

He licks his lips; they are chapped and salty against his tongue.

'We fight together, in victory or to the death!'

Edmund stares into the face of the Prince, his eyes ablaze, fierce. He lifts his sword to the sky and Edmund follows suit.

'We are all fellow companions!' the Prince roars. 'We all drink from the same cup!'

The Prince turns and nods to the Earl of Warwick who breaks the line and starts withdrawing. Edmund can feel all the men around him take a collective breath. Is this it? Are we running from a force so large that it will devour us before we are even off the field? With a look of utter disbelief, Edmund turns to the Prince once more.

A flicker of rebellion.

That is all Edmund sees race across the Prince's face. Or is it? How can he tell? But he recognises it as an old friend, for it has often enough visited his own expression. He feels a surge of bravery rise from the pit of his empty stomach.

This is a ploy, a ruse.

The Prince has formed a plan; there is method to the madness. But Edmund feels confusion spread among his fellow comrades. The Prince must act soon, or they will turn and run.

From the field below, the French cavalry form up and gather momentum. They aim straight for the bowmen; they know to keep their horses and their heavy armour directly in front of the arrows, so that they fly in vain, hitting only plate.

Under Edmund's now watchful eye, Warwick returns to his position, but too late, the French cavalry is upon them, smashing through the hedges, scattering the archers and men-at-arms. French soldiers armed with javelins follow the cavalry, pouring up the slope, gutting their enemy where it stood.

Edmund's ears threaten to burst under the roar of the approaching army, the trumpets and horns blowing, the beat of the hooves and the din of men fighting for their lives. Below him, the field turns into a rolling ocean of colour, gold and silver, purple and red. Enemy waves wash over their lines of defence, the French cavalry leading a manmade storm

Suddenly, the French horses begin to rear, throwing their riders and trampling the men-at-arms who trail in their wake.

The archers! Edmund spins around to see that they have shifted their position and have clean lines of sight, picking horses off one by one, pelting the French in a hail of arrows. To his left, the vanguard pushes back the attack, cutting down the enemy, closing the line. Nothing can stop an English arrow once it is released, no weapon of war is mightier than the longbow. The French ought to know, they have encountered the longbowmen before, but to Edmund it seems they have learned nothing. What fortune, he thinks and raw joy runs through his body, what fortune that the French are mindless fools.

Right in front of him, the hedge crumbles. He grasps his sword with both hands and ducks the first blow, hacking his blade into the flank of the oncoming destrier. It goes down with a scream, and Edmund draws his sword from the flesh, a spray of blood warm on his chin. He steps on a dying soldier to get a better vantage point and parries a blow, twisting to bring down his sword upon a defenceless neck.

The world blurs.

Death stirs in his seat.

Time stretches and billows.

Edmund leans on his sword, too tired to wipe it clean. He forces himself to look up and sees the Prince standing in the middle of mayhem, his face turned to the skies, his knights and lords in silent prayer around him; Grailly, Chandos and Audley awaiting orders.

Wiping his forehead, Edmund's hand comes away bloody and filthy, but he cannot tell if it is his or the blood of the enemies he has slain. Dull, he watches the Prince huddle with his comrades, a foxy smile growing on Grailly's face. Audley nods. Points.

The trumpets sound.

'MOUNT UP!'

Edmund looks about. Mount up? The soldiers around him exchange confused glances. Squires hustle horses on lines forward. His own grey destrier stomps and snorts. Edmund takes the reins and is boosted into his saddle, his sword thrust into his hands. He looks at it. Black with blood.

Audley and four knights ride out in front of the line of horsemen. Edmund reins in his horse, he understands. Around him soldiers look up, their faces hard, their gaze determined.

'ARCHERS AT THE READY!'

To his right, near enough to hear their voices over the roar of battle, Warwick joins Salisbury and looks across the field where the French army is advancing at a steady pace, certain of their victory.

Warwick gives a half-smile: 'Let us slay some Frenchmen!'

Salisbury nods and slams down his visor. Perhaps his peacock brain is what will save him. He is too stupid to die, Edmund thinks and smiles inside his helmet.

At the centre of the English cavalry line, Audley spurs his horse into a trot leading the way towards the bulk of the French troops. Edmund watches the four other knights follow suit. Below, the French lines begin to break as some of the men-at-arms are slow to receive the English cavalry while others quicken their pace to take on the enemy in their stride.

The Prince holds up his sword and spurs his horse into a trot. Edmund dose the same, he is second in the line of cavalry. If you are to make your mark, be sure it is seen, Grosmont had told him, and for once Edmund heeds advice from another.

English arrows blacken the skies. The Prince's horse canters. Edmund looks down the slope, Audley is almost upon the French line. The Prince spurs his horse into a gallop.

'SAINT GEORGE!'

The war cry goes up, it soars to the heavens, and Edmund lends his voice to the choir just as Audley plunges through the French line, hacking as he goes, his four sworn knights following him into the belly of the French beast.

Edmund grasps his sword, the rider before him lowers his lance. Just before they meet the enemy, Edmund sees movement at the back of the field. Charny with l'Oriflamme! He must have the French battle standard; he must bring it to the Prince when the battle is over.

In front of him, the horseman goes down. Edmund turns to avoid impact and crashes into the French army.

Blood everywhere.

Edmund coughs and spits, his arms explode in pain every time he lifts his sword to strike at another enemy. He swings his mace; he screams the battle cry every time it comes up: 'SAINT GEROGE!' till his throat is raw.

Blood makes his grip slip, he has lost his mace, it is lodged in some Frenchman's skull, he is on foot, his horse gone, and Edmund is tired, so very tired.

'TO ME! TO ME!' A host of men rally to the Prince's side.

In the carnage, Edmund cannot make out Mowbray's banner of red and white and he is grateful; if he is forced to leave the heart of the battle to help reinforce the rear or worse yet, sent to watch the provision carts he will go mad. To ensure he does not see the Mowbray standard, Edmund scrambles to the Prince's position and hurtles towards the oncoming attack along with the men who have formed a natural circle around the Prince and his standard bearer.

'SAINT GEORGE!'

A French cavalry charge is let loose on the advancing Prince, but from their vantage point, the last of the archers are quick to change their positions and create an iron blizzard that swallows up the charge. Twenty horses fall to the ground kicking and screaming, and then Edmund and the rest are upon them, slicing, hacking and slipping in the blood-soaked, churned up dirt.

From below a horse, a hand grips Edmund's leg and sends him sprawling. He rolls away; his strength returns in the face of danger, and without seeing he thrusts a dagger into flesh. Whoever is caught under the horse screams and throws a gauntleted hand at Edmund breaking his nose and blackening his sight. He struggles to get up and kicks his enemy in the face; the impact sends flashes of searing pain through his knee. It is a good pain; it is life thrashing and holding on.

'Saint George!' the battle cry resounds further afield, and Edmund curses when his enemy, although caught under a dead horse, lashes out again. He has somehow gotten hold of a broad sword and is flailing it about.

Edmund staggers away and turns to face a blinded man, an arrow has taken one eye, the other dangles down his cheek, no doubt squeezed out when the horse fell on him. His whole skull looks wrought and squashed in and still, he fights on. Edmund sneers and severs the Frenchman's head from his body.

'To me!' Warwick is slashing at two Frenchmen who have somehow escaped the arrow rain only to face a fierce enemy. 'TO ME!'

Edmund pushes his helmet back in place and leaps forward to cut off one of the approaching men's arms. Relieved of an enemy, Warwick makes short process of the remaining Frenchman, ramming the butt of his sword into the helmet opening.

'WHERE IS THE PRINCE?'

Too weary and hoarse to answer, Edmund points to the right of the field, where the Prince is engaged in a deadly battle with a troop of French soldiers. Some look to be standing their ground, but already others are turning to run. French orders are barked from a man lodged beneath a great brown horse; its chest littered with iron tipped arrows. Next to it, a banner is trampled into the ground.

'The Duke of Bourbon!' Warwick moves, his one leg dragging behind, the thigh soaked in blood, white bone peering out from a deep gash. 'If we can …'

Edmund looks up to see one of the Prince's sworn men grab a lance and thrust it through the Duke's chest. He opens his mouth to protest, but the man has already moved on and the Prince is leading the way, his battle-worn suit of armour as black as the clouds gathering above. Skirting the brown horse, Edmund loses no time looking at the dead Duke; dead men are worthless. If he wants to win more than his spurs, he has to catch a nobleman.

The Prince keeps his pace, his eye firmly set on something further afield. Edmund looks up and, for a moment, he is blinded when the sun peers at the field through the dark clouds and bounds off something. King John's crown! Now that is a price worth losing an arm over.

'AUDLEY!' Warwick shouts, and Edmund sees Audley's horse go down only a few paces from l'Oriflamme.

All sounds return suddenly and sharply, screams from men and horses, death cries and the ring of swords, battle-axes and maces all around him. A sword flashes before his face and he parries it, grunting at the force of steel against steel. At his back, someone tries to get through the slits of his armour where the shoulder meets the back-plate, but even though the force of the blow knocks the wind from him, Edmund fights on, blocking the knight in front of him. He catches the sword with his own and twists the blade. The knight loses his grip, Edmund bends to avoid another attack from behind, picks up a battle-axe and buries it deep in the knight's groin. He falls to the ground, and Edmund yanks the axe free. The knight bleeds out next to him as Edmund turns to face his next opponent.

'SAINT GEORGE!' The force of the battle cry presses against his ears as he rages against what might be a nobleman. The surcoat is smothered in blood, but here and there, gold thread and bright yellow peeks out. He has to keep this man alive, only wound him enough to ensure he can capture him.

'Surrender!' Edmund roars, he hardly recognises his own voice. 'Surrender!'

The enemy raises his sword, and Edmund blocks the blow, but just as he is about to push back, the man falls to his knees tossing aside his blade. Edmund groans; sweat and blood mingling with a strange, warm drizzle. He looks up to see an impaled Frenchman, his blood sprouting from a wound where the lance has torn open his neck. He lets the blood sprinkle his forehead for a moment longer, relishing in the death of another enemy.

Then Edmund turns to his prisoner. 'Your name!'

'Philip.' The Frenchman pulls off his helmet, grey eyes swimming in a sea of red. He is but a boy. 'Duke of Burgundy and Prince of France.'

Edmund smiles, finally, the prize he was looking for. Finally, he has something that the Prince will want.

'Surrender! Surrender yourself – or you are a dead man!' an unknown soldier yells next to Edmund, and he turns to see King John pull off his right-hand glove and hand it over.

'I surrender myself to you.'

Warwick steps in and seizes the French King, a scuffle ensues but whoever the soldier is, he is pushed aside and the King escorted from the field by three English Lords, two of whom can hardly walk.

Edmund hisses with spite and anger, but it is too late to do anything. Once more, someone who has had life handed to him on a silver platter has bested him. If only the battle still raged then Edmund would have buried the French battle-axe deep in Warwick's back and taken King John for himself.

He turns to Prince Philip and nods. He places his glove in Edmund's hand and together, they leave the field. Perhaps a prince will be enough.

# CHAPTER 5

## 19 September 1356 – Poitiers, France

'All hail King John of France!'

Hoarse voices bark the greeting and Edmund looks up. His neck is stiff and although his nose has been put right, the snap loud enough to split his head, he can smell none of the food set out before him. He stands with the rest of the men assembled in the great silk tent to salute the captured King.

Once King John joins the Prince at the dais, the men attack the food as if they had seen none for months. Edmund chews on a piece of meat, but it tastes of little and smells of nothing. He groans at every movement; it feels as if his skin is too tight for his body.

'There's only one way out,' the soldier next to him says. 'Drink! Drink till you're senseless, or you'll not sleep a wink tonight!'

Edmund wipes his mouth and winces when he grazes his nose; little dark scabs dust his food. He gulps down tasteless liquid that burns his throat and winces again.

'First battle?' Across from Edmund, a man with the Mowbray crest on his chest nods in understanding. A patch covers his left eye, and he has a sick look about him, but he eats all the same. 'I 'member that. You'll do well to drink, lad; there'll be no rest for none of us for many weeks to come.'

A roar rolls across the hall as King John's son Philip enters the room. Edmund handed the Duke of Burgundy over to Baron Mowbray on a promise of a rich reward. Now here is his prisoner, free to join his father and the Prince on the dais. It sets Edmund's teeth on edge more than any of his wounds.

'A toast to King John, the most valiant man on the field today!' the Prince calls out, and all men assembled bang their cups against the tabletops creating a thunderstorm. 'An adversary as no other!'

Another roar answers the Prince's speech, and King John raises his cup. 'A toast to my captor! The finest Prince in Christendom!'

'Saint George!' the English soldiers chant and Edmund chimes in, because not to do so is sure to stand out. 'Saint George! Saint George and Prince Edward!'

The Prince laughs and nods to King John; they were mortal enemies on the field, but tonight all acts of chivalry must be upheld, and the King made to look almost a victor although he is defeated and has lost so many men that he has hardly an army left, never mind all the nobles who fell on English arrows and blades.

'What happens when word reaches the Dauphin that his father is a prisoner of England?' Edmund asks.

'He'll be in a rage,' the soldier with the patch predicts. He is green now, and Edmund can tell that no amount of drink will take away his pain. 'It'll be long before the ransom's set.'

The soldier next to Edmund takes over when the man with the patch falls silent. 'They'll send the French King to England, but I think Prince Philip'll be set free and sent to the Dauphin as a sign of good faith.'

The solider with the patch slumps forward, folding in on himself. Detached, Edmund wonders if he is dead. Then he pulls the soldier's bowl of food from under his limp chin and dips another piece of bread into the steaming sauce. Waste not; want not.

'It seems a folly to take so many prisoners only to set them free.' Edmund's irritation burns under his skin when he understands that all he fought for will be undone with a single word from a Prince. But he can also feel the wine working wonders on his pain, and for that he is grateful.

'It is too expensive to keep them locked up.' A hand closes on Edmund's shoulder and he looks round, his neck protesting in spite of the drink, to see Baron Mowbray. 'Come with me.'

The men at the table rise to toast their leader, and Mowbray drinks with them before turning away with his hand still on Edmund's shoulder. 'You should rest.'

'The others …' Edmund begins but a glance from Mowbray silences him. There is pain and a strange new distance in his grey eyes.

'They drink because it takes their minds off what they have done.' Mowbray raises a tired hand to the Earl of Salisbury before leaving the tent. 'But tomorrow, they will wake and still remember everything that happened, all the lives they took, all the pain they suffered and blows they dealt.'

'You sound uneasy, my Lord.' Edmund's irritation turns on his own master, what do dead men matter? Edmund has already forgotten what he did; he only remembers the Baron's promise that he will be richly rewarded. That is what war is about. 'We won the battle.'

'But we have yet to win the war,' Mowbray says. 'Tonight, you will sleep in my rooms. The Prince was kind to bestow on me good accommodation because I brought him Philip of Burgundy. But in truth, it is you who should sleep there, for it was you who captured Philip as I told his Grace.'

'Thank you.' Edmund pretends to force back a sob of gratitude. 'Anyone …'

'You won your spurs today,' Mowbray cuts him off. 'Even if I had not pledged to Grosmont that you be knighted once the battle was done, I would ask the Prince to knight you this very moment, if it was in my gift. As it is, our Prince is engaged in the tiresome affairs of courtesy and knightly display, and thus, you must wait for the sun to rise before you can feel his blade upon your shoulder.'

'I can wait.' What is one more lie now that Edmund knows what will come to pass?

Mowbray walks from the tent towards a nearby house and works his way up the stairs. From behind, Edmund can see he is limping and holding his left arm tight to his body. Perhaps his days of ordering Edmund around are numbered.

He is suddenly curious to know what happened to Mowbray, where he made his battle, who – if any – he took captive, but he cannot voice the words. They cling to his tongue and he cannot force them out. What if Mowbray did better than he did himself?

They walk down a passageway, torches sending dancing lights across the stone walls. The sound of their panting is a testament to their joint agony and exertion.

'Here we are.' Mowbray pushes the door open and enters a room bathed in a warm, inviting light. 'I asked for wine to be sent up and some stew.'

Edmund sits down on a low stool before the fire and pours two cups of wine. When he hands one to Mowbray, he finally looks up, his face white.

'I was caught in a mêlée and one of our fine archers put an arrow in my calf,' he says without prompt and lifts up his gown to reveal a bandage that reaches from his ankle to his knee.

'How bad?'

'It was burned, but I am certain it will keep me up at night for some time,' Mowbray says ruefully and looks at Edmund, the whisper of a laugh in his eyes. 'I see you ran into something?'

'Someone,' Edmund says, and forces a smile though he hates to be made mockery of. 'I have never met a fiercer enemy than he who did this, and he was caught under a horse, one eye picked out by our archers.'

Mowbray drinks deep and stares into his cup. He makes no move towards the stew. 'How do you like war now?'

'Not much,' Edmund says, though that is as far from the truth as can be, but he can tell that Mowbray does not share his excitement. The battle made him feel alive, it brought him a deep sense of having a cause, a destiny and now, finally, all of it was revealed to him. Though he had been dead on his feet by the time King John had yielded, Edmund is certain he could have gone on fighting well into the night before someone might have been lucky enough to cut him down.

'It was carnage,' the Baron mutters.

Edmund ladles two bowls of steaming stew, his hand shakes as he offers one to Mowbray.

'The Prince kept his army together; it was well performed. For our part at least.' Mowbray takes the bowl and sets it aside. 'But the French … have they learned nothing from Crécy? I thought they would know by now that cavalry charges and crossbows are no match for our archers.'

'You regret our victory, my Lord?' A mush of vegetables, fat and chunks of meat fills Edmund's mouth, but it is bland. He is happy that the French have learned nothing. It bodes well for future battles.

'One should never regret victory. I simply wonder why they have learned so little from their previous losses? Too many lives were spent today. They speak of as many as two thousand! King John has lost most of his noblemen and knights – and has himself been captured. The Prince would never have allowed such a disaster.'

Edmund is fascinated by Mowbray's account of the day; it is cool and prosaic. 'What would he have done, my Lord?'

'Fought to the death.' The Baron sighs. 'He is his father's son and would never let an enemy capture him. It is not in the nature of their family.'

'But Richard the Lionheart …' Edmund protests, he had the tale from Grosmont when he first joined his army and had thought; at last, here was a king he could understand. They say that the Prince aspires to be as his ancient ancestor. One of his few redeeming qualities, Edmund thinks.

'That is precisely why the Prince would choose death over capture.' Mowbray gives the side door a longing glance. 'I shall retire. You can sleep here, in a feather bed, as a reward for your bravery on the battlefield and for capturing King John's son. A pity it was not the Dauphin.'

A great shame, Edmund thinks and rises to bow to the Baron, for I would have liked to capture him even more than his younger brother. What would a Prince of England not do to get his hands on the heir to the French throne?

'Bid you good night, my Lord.' Edmund's words come out in punches.

'Try to get some sleep. Tomorrow is a great day for you, but before it is over, it will also feel the longest day of your life,' Mowbray says and closes the door.

Knighthood.

Spurs.

Edmund has the best night's sleep he has ever had in his life. In the early hours of the morning, he awakes when the Baron screams from behind the door. Not all men are made for war, Edmund thinks and rolls over. Certainly, he is better suited for slaughter than a delicate lord. With a smile on his face, Edmund returns to his dreamless sleep.

# CHAPTER 6

## 26 July 1392 – Westminster Palace

'I always did wonder what my brother saw in you.' John of Gaunt peered at Edmund. In the gloom of his stately rooms, Gaunt looked haunted and old, the strain of keeping close to the King, to offer council he ill liked was taking its toll.

'You mean beside the obvious?' Edmund smiled at Gaunt. 'In truth so did I.'

Rather than rage, Gaunt leaned back with a serene look upon his face. 'I did ask once. Edward looked so baffled that, afterwards, I resolved never to ask about his peculiar friendships again. I could manage them. Most of them.'

'But not all of them,' Edmund said and tried to read Gaunt's expression.

'He praised you for your valour on the battlefield. He would probably have had a minstrel prepare a song about your many attributes had you ever taken a wife,' Gaunt mused. 'But I think he liked you most because of your appearance. He saw some of himself in you. He never did in me.'

'Did it distress you, my Lord?'

A harsh laugh answered Edmund's question. 'I had better things to do. And I had my father's ear. Which was much better than anything Edward might have conceded to giving me. I was content for many years, you know, to be their go-between. Yes, my father loved my brother more.

Everyone did. He was the first-born, he was the heir, it was the natural order of things.'

'Do you still have the King's ear?'

'In so much as anyone does.' Gaunt slides off the question. 'No, I think Edward loved you best because of your innate desire to always be in the midst of the battle. You never skirted a fight; you sought it out. It was as if you did not know fear.'

'I knew fear.'

Gaunt reached for his cup. 'You never showed it.'

'At Poitiers, I nearly shat myself from fear.' Edmund acknowledged Gaunt's smirk. 'I was a boy. No matter what you teach a boy, no matter how many grown men try to beat sense into a boy's head, nothing can prepare him for true battle. I had never seen true battle before.'

'You were in Grosmont's chevauchees.'

This time, Edmund laughed. 'Stealing grain from farmers and harrying the land is no match for the full force of the French army descending upon you. You know this as well as I, my Lord.'

'I suppose.'

Edmund rose again to stretch his legs and get away from Gaunt's probing eyes. 'Perhaps your brother simply recognised in me what he could not be at all times.'

'A soldier you mean?'

'Yes. You know how he longed for battle even while in the midst of one.' Edmund turned to the window. 'As did I. Poitiers lit a fire in me that has burned bright ever since. If I could but die on a battle field, I should be content.'

'That is what I do not understand, Sir Edmund, why you – both of you – so longed for death that you would seek it out time after time.'

'For my own part, I confess that I sought battle not to die but to defeat death.' Edmund looked out into the summer night; faint speckles of light illuminated the grand courtyard beyond Gaunt's apartments. 'And I did. I conquered death more times than I care to remember. But I want battle for another reason too.'

'Glory and gold.'

'Glory and gold I have, and plenty of it, what would I do with more?' Edmund turned from the view with a half-smile. 'But bringing war to an enemy keeps me out of trouble, in as much as that is possible. You see, I cannot help myself; everywhere I look there are opportunities ripe for the plucking. Even tonight here in your presence, I see at least three or four opportunities to stir up trouble. I suspect it is in my blood.'

'We all know what is in your blood.'

'Thus, you must concur, my Lord, that mischief is a large part of me.' At Gaunt's weary nod, Edmund continues, 'and I made much mischief when I first set foot on English soil.'

## 4 May 1357 – Plymouth, England

Edmund drags himself down the swinging gangway. His legs are stiff and the wobbling planks do little to ease his awkward stride, but no one notices him. They are busy either on the docks or ships unloading baggage, horses and loot. Looking to the left, Edmund sees the Prince's enormous vessel being tied up. On the deck, the Prince's hair glistens in the sunlight and when he raises a hand in salutation the men on the docks cry out in pleasure at the sight of him. Somewhere in the back of Edmund's mind, he wants to be standing where the Prince is, but then, it seems he is as close to realising his desire as he can ever dream to be.

'Move on.' One of the other soldiers eager to get off nudges Edmund, and he stumbles forward as the gangway shifts when the current catches the ship's bow and swings it sideways. 'I'll be off this bloody ship if I've to push you over to get on dry land!'

Without grace, Edmund tumbles onto English soil for the very first time. Not quite sure what he had expected, he knows full well that this was not it. England looks so like France that, for a moment, he thinks they have turned about in the middle of the night and sailed back. He sends a scowl after the man who pushed him, would that he had more at his side than his eating knife.

'Sir Edmund!' Mowbray's rich voice reaches Edmund and he looks left. 'Welcome to England!'

'My Lord.' Edmund bows to the Baron who has sailed with the Prince, while Edmund had to cross the sea with the rest of Mowbray's men on a smaller vessel.

Mowbray scrutinises Edmund for a moment. 'How fare you now?'

'Better, my Lord, thank you.' Edmund decides to share a little secret with Mowbray, what harm can it do to better his relationship with the man who brought him to the battle field and showed him what he is meant to do for the rest of his life. 'The sea has little love for me.'

Mowbray nods and rubs his arm, a gesture that has become almost second nature to him. 'The Prince has decided that we are to go to London with him to deliver King John into the hands of the King. Walk with me.'

Edmund falls in behind Mowbray, there are so many men on the docks that, for a moment, Edmund fears that the wood will give way and the water will swallow them all up. No, he most certainly does not care for the sea, and eleven days of it is quite enough for him. It was excruciating to see the thin sliver of land on the horizon taunting his gaze and never growing in size. Yet, here he is, delayed the possibilities spring to life in his mind, he is returning to his true self, what a relief.

'I shall petition the Prince to let us move on to Nottingham once King John is safe in London,' the Baron calls over his shoulder, his voice drowning in the noise of the docks. 'Careful!'

Edmund skirts a company of soldiers marching for land, carrying crates between them. 'What is that, my Lord?'

'Loot no doubt,' Mowbray says with scarce a glance at the soldiers. 'War is a costly affair. The soldiers often come only because they might return home with gold lined pockets. As you did. Though you did not have to pack it in a crate.'

I am not home, Edmund thinks darkly, but I will make of it what I can. And if nothing else, I will meet the King and see if he is all that they say he is. Perhaps if Edmund plays his cards right, he will, in time, come to view England as his home.

Mowbray turns. 'What is it?'

'How far is London?' Edmund shakes off his gloom and looks about again. 'I thought we would sail straight to the castle doors to deliver the royal prisoner.'

'It will be some time before we are there, but never fear, the south of England is a friendly place, especially at this time of year.' The Baron watches one of his squires lumber by on a cream mare, holding the reins of his destrier. 'Careful, Simon!'

'And how far is Nottingham?'

'I forget you do not know the country,' Mowbray says. 'If the Prince releases us, we could be there within a month. And when you meet my sweet wife, Sir Edmund, you had better think her the most beautiful woman in England.'

## 12 May 1357 – The Tower of London

This makes for a pleasant change from tents, ships and tawdry inns, Edmund thinks and leans back his head and looks into the vast expanse to spy the arched wooden beams high above. The hall is packed with people, each more wonderfully dressed than the next; there are so many jewels, pearls and links of gold and silver to make his pauper heart leap with joy. The sight also makes his fingers itch, but he is not a little boy who needs to steal anymore.

Next to him, Mowbray has transformed from a worn and haggard soldier into what he truly is, a great English Lord, styled in lavish fabrics and twinkling gems. On his shoulder, a large pin piled with green stones set in gold glitters in the light of a hundred candles. Though it is warm outside, it is cool in the stone hall, all corners swallowed by perpetual darkness. Now, the Baron nods at an old man, who walks by with a girl on his arm young enough to be his great granddaughter.

When she turns to look over her shoulder, Edmund smiles at her. Though his garb is plainer than most in the hall, he is refreshed and wearing the finest clothes he has ever had. He feels as if he is wearing his entire fortune on his sleeve, but that is the way of the rich, and he must learn to behave as they do if he is to fit in. The young woman nearly stumbles when her ancient husband yanks her to a halt. Her attention leaves Edmund, but he knows she will think of him when the old man visits her bed tonight.

The doors to the inner rooms are ajar, but no one goes near them. No doubt, the Prince and Gaunt are in there right now, but Edmund must stay by Mowbray's side until such a time as the King sees fit to summon them. At least, he caught a glimpse of the King when they first arrived in London riding at the heart of the great procession that took King John to his prison. Though Edmund would happily have traded places with him, for the French King is put up in more splendour than any prisoner of war should be awarded. Then again, apparently it is costumery to treat important prisoners more as guests who cannot leave the party than common criminals. Edmund has tried and failed to understand the practice, and in the end, the Baron refused to broach the subject.

Mowbray moves and Edmund follows his gaze. 'Who is that, my Lord?'

'That, Sire,' the Baron says with a boyish grin, 'is the Queen and her youngest son, Thomas of Woodstock. They go everywhere together; it is a great jest at court that she cannot be without him. They say she pampers him, but perhaps that is simply because she knows that she can have no more children, and so the last she bore beneath her heart is all the more dear to her.'

Edmund looks at the boy who is tall and fair. For a moment, they lock eyes and something springs across the boy's face that makes Edmund's hair stand on end. It is gone before he can decide if it was even there at all.

'When will we see the King?'

'When he summons us.' Mowbray weaves his way across the hall and pauses here and there to greet some courtier or other. They all sound the same to Edmund, but he vows that before they leave, he will know all of the most important men at court. 'King John is put up now and messengers sent to the Dauphin to relay that his father is in good health. Soon, the negotiations for his release will commence. No doubt, they will go on for a long time and take up much of the King's time.'

A servant rushes by with an empty tray, and Edmund's stomach growls. He turns to Mowbray. 'He will head the negotiations himself?'

The dark-haired Baron smiles. 'He will preside over the initial negotiations here at court, but once a venue for the true negotiations is settled, I believe he will send emissaries and embassies. The hard work has no doubt already been done in taking down the King's demands, and now that the Prince has added his own set of requirements there will be much to discuss that does not require a King's attention. He has a land to govern.'

'And a war to win,' Edmund mutters to himself when Mowbray is hailed by a courtier. To the steady drone of high-pitched squalor, Edmund looks about again. It is the first time he has been this close to the King's chambers, and though he will never admit it, everything he has seen in London has taken his breath away.

First the Baron's house, which is more of a palace than a house. Then Grosmont's Savoy Palace, prominently placed at the banks of the river, glittering against the sky and in the water. They say that, in time, Gaunt will inherit the place, which Edmund thinks a great shame, for such a castle should be in the hands of someone more alive and intriguing than the Prince's dull brother. Yesterday, they went to see Westminster Palace, situated at the outskirts of the great city and near dense woods with good hunting with large lavish green fields and parks leading up to it. Nothing had Edmund more amazed at Westminster than the large array of hawks.

But all of it paled to the first sight of the Tower, white against a blue sky. Edmund had struggled to believe his own eyes when he had seen the large menagerie that the Baron had told him about. For some reason, Edmund had thought the Baron was teasing him with his ignorance, but today, when they rode in under the Lion Tower, his doubt was put to shame. The sounds of the savage beasts and the rancid smell of predators had unsettled Edmund in a way he had never imagined. More than anything, he now wants to go back and see the beasts through the thick iron bars, but he must bide his time and hope that he can manage to slip away at some point.

'... long now.' Mowbray looks at Edmund. 'Are you paying attention, Sir Edmund?'

The distinction makes Edmund smile; he is a knight, anointed by the blood of his enemies and risen up by a Prince. Bursting with pride, he puffs out his chest and pushes aside his childish fancies of visiting the lions.

'I am sorry, my Lord,' Edmund says with deference, 'I was marvelling at the hall.'

'It is quite spectacular, though for my part, I prefer Westminster to this place,' Mowbray says under his breath. 'But here, you must know, lies the true heart of power. If ever a King wants to impress his own importance upon his people, he will do it from the Tower. It is a castle now, but it was built to withstand invading armies and fierce enemies. It is said that there has been a fortress here of some kind these past two hundred years, when the Normans freed England from her enemies.'

Edmund can feel history flutter beneath the beams, he can feel power surge from the stones and into his skin and he nods. 'Surely, no enemy could gaze upon this place without feeling dejected.'

'Surely, no man alive would come here and feel he is more than what he is,' Mowbray says. 'They have put King John up in one of the finest apartments in the Tower, and yet, they say that when he was taken there, his eyes welled up for he knew now that he was well and truly beaten.'

They should have thrown him in the dungeons, Edmund thinks, but he knows that it is impossible to treat an anointed King in such a manner. Besides, he is more interested in what King Edward means to do now that the French army is in tatters and France is ripe for the taking. But when he asks, Mowbray only shakes his head.

'The negotiations must run their course.' He reads Edmund's expression as one of despair, which is not far off, and continues, 'it is better to win the war by settling the succession than to beat an enemy bloody and never get what you want. I have no doubt that our King knows what he is about and that he will do anything he can to ensure that he is made heir to the French throne once King John dies.'

'What about the Dauphin and the other French Princes?' Edmund is still angry that his captive, Prince Philip, was set free and returned to his older brother. At least, Edmund was showered in gold and glory – for a time.

Mowbray rubs his arm. 'They will object, as all heirs should. But King Edward's claim to the throne of France is stronger than theirs will ever be. In the eyes of God, King Edward and his kin must be returned what is theirs by right. They must be restored to the throne of France and so they shall be. Perhaps it will be achieved by other means than battle and bloodshed.'

'How so, my Lord?' Edmund feels his jaw tense up.

'Marriage makes for strong alliances. And our Prince is in need of a wife.' The Baron nods to a bench under a high window. 'Let us sit, this damned leg is acting up again. I swear, they may have burned the wound but they did not burn away the pain inside.'

'If marriage is all that is required,' Edmund says and takes a seat next to Mowbray, 'why has it not been settled long ago?'

'The Prince is less eager to wed than his father is that he be wed,' the Baron admits with a snort. 'Sometimes, it seems, fathers cannot have what they want, no matter how much power they wield over their children. Lord Gaunt was happy to marry the heiress to Grosmont's estate, but the Prince … he is a different matter.'

The dry air in the hall makes Edmund drowsy and his attention slips between his fingers. 'Perhaps the Prince has his sights set on someone else.'

Mowbray laughs. 'They say he is in love, but that the lady is not free to accept him. Though I imagine that it is a tale he has spun himself that he might be spared the pain of having all the princesses of Europe paraded before him.'

'Perhaps this time he cannot avoid it?'

'Perhaps,' the Baron agrees and bends to nurse his calf, which Edmund knows is still pink and sore from the wound Mowbray took in battle. 'And perhaps the King is making plans of his own. They are both wilful men, but as you may soon find out, the King has something that the Prince does not.'

Edmund gives Mowbray an inquisitive glance and he smiles. 'He can demand obedience from everyone.'

But blind obedience is dangerous, Edmund thinks, and as for the Prince, I am not sure he will do anything but what he wants for himself, no matter who tells him otherwise. Besides, how can the King make demands of the man who brought him the greatest prize of all, a royal hostage?

## 14 May 1357 – The Tower of London

It is another two days of feasting and babbling and dancing before Edmund is finally summoned to the King's presence. Mowbray has been holed up with the King and all of the council for most of the day, and Edmund has been going mad in the hall, listening to idle talk, gossip and pretending interest in the many women who prance about. But when he looks up, all of his pent-up irritation evaporates.

A man covered in gold stands before the gathered men, his head adorned with a glistening crown decked with rubies, pearls and blue gemstones. He looks as a god, he stands as a god, and most importantly, when he speaks, his voice is that of a god. Booming. Deep. Powerful.

Edmund is not often speechless, but even if the King had asked him to speak right at this instance, he would not have known what to say. Something deep inside tugs at him and then disappears.

Next to the King, the Prince looks slight, but he is every inch his father in all other ways. His commanding presence is overshadowed only by the man who fathered him. The Prince nods at Edmund and then turns to his father, his whispered words drown in the fragments of conversation that float about the room. The King nods and claps his hands just once.

'My Lords, I am told we are to give thanks to a young man who excelled on the field of battle.' The King shoots a piercing glance in Edmund's direction. 'He handed Prince Philip of France to my son and was rewarded with a knighthood, as is befitting. I have no doubt, we can expect great things from you in the future, Sir Edmund.'

When Edmund merely gawps, Mowbray appears by his side and nudges him. Edmund clamps his mouth shut and sweeps a bow. Next he knows, the tall figure of the King towers above him and gestures for him to stand. Up close, the King loses a little of his lustre, but none of his presence.

'Kneel.'

With a lump in his throat, Edmund kneels, keenly aware that all eyes in the room are on him. He has to perform to perfection, there must be nothing these great Lords can protest to or find wanting in him. Not for the first time these past days, Edmund grudgingly gives thanks that Sieur Aymard took care to have him trained from an early age.

The King accepts his ceremonial sword, a long shimmering blade, the hilt so heavily adorned that it is useless at anything but to make knights and lay out to be admired. Now, the cool blade rests on Edmund's right shoulder.

'Sir Edmund, do you swear fealty to the Crown of England, to his Grace King Edward, rightful heir of the kingdom of France and ruler of England and Wales?' the herald calls out in his uniquely clear voice.

Edmund bows his head and the blade shifts, carving a curve in the air just above his bare head.

'Sir Edmund, do you swear fealty to England herself, to all those who will govern her for as long as there is breath in your body? Do you swear to give your life to keep her safe?'

Once more, Edmund bows his head, and the King's jewelled hand slides into view. Taking it, he knows what comes next, and still, the blow of the King's hand is hard enough to rattle Edmund's teeth. But he does not move his head even an inch, and in the fleeting moment when he clasps eyes with the King, he sees amusement and a flicker of something else, lurking in the outskirts of the blue eyes that look back at him. Then the moment is gone and Mowbray steps up to congratulate him.

'Well done! Now, you are truly bound to England for perpetuity. Beware you do not cross her rulers and you will be fine.' As he steps aside, the

Baron whispers, 'your rewards will not be far behind. Just be patient. This is the first of many praises that will be sung about you.'

From the back of the room, Edmund watches silently as the great Lords of England discuss politics, France and, most of all, their new captive. The King looks lively and pleased, the Prince is clearly in his element, though Edmund senses a restlessness that he recognises from himself. All this chatter, and for what, when there is a war yet to be won and more battles to be had.

'Dreaming of glory, Sir Edmund?'

John of Gaunt's slick voice carves a slice out of Edmund's pride and he turns. 'My Lord, I did not see you there.'

'I saw you.' Gaunt nods towards the dais, where the Prince and his father are deep in conversation, deaf to the rumble of the room. 'They are plotting and planning no doubt. What to do with King John, how much to demand for demands must be made, we all know that. I have already put in my opinion, but I prefer to do it out of the public eye.'

I wonder why, Edmund thinks, but he controls himself and gives a stiff nod. 'No doubt there is much to be settled, my Lord. Are you to stay here in England when an embassy is sent to negotiate?'

A loud laugh makes some of the men turn, but they snap their heads away when Gaunt glares at them. 'Who is to say what my father desires from one moment to the next? If he wants for a politician to go, he will do well to send me. If he wants the French to tremble, he will do well to send my brother.' Gaunt pauses and gives a disapproving sigh. 'If he wants to make himself a laughing stock, he will send my youngest brother.'

Thomas of Woodstock has appeared in the room, his clothes so smooth on his young body you would think they were rolled right onto him. His golden curls bounce as a girl's would, and Edmund has to bite his tongue not to laugh.

'In any event, it is a long time in the future, Sire, and we must all wait while a couple of grand men play the game of crowns and inheritance.' Gaunt turns away. 'Perhaps they will settle on something entirely different, a wife and some land, perchance, or a division of power between Princes. I should put nothing past my kin, and neither should you. But fear not, you will be richly rewarded, your patron saint Mowbray has seen to that.'

Before Edmund can express his doubtful gratitude for the Baron's interest in him, Gaunt is gone and Edmund is at the mercy of some of the lesser Lords and knights of England, all of whom are interested to know who this boy of just fifteen is, now elevated to knighthood and sworn to England by the King himself. Rather than slink away, Edmund lets them have little trinkets to bring home to their gossip mills. He knows that if he is to make a name for himself, best he be in charge of what is said and when.

It is some time before Mowbray breaks up the circle of men and drags Edmund away, leaning in to whisper, 'the King is pleased, and so am I. But now, we have had our fill of court, and we are granted privilege to retreat to my home. I cannot wait to show you all the pleasures of Nottingham.'

# CHAPTER 7

## 26 July 1392 – Westminster Palace

'How long have you known?' Gaunt tapped his finger on the paper laid out in front of him. It was part of the reason they were meeting tonight and it sat as a barrier between them.

'Almost from the first moment I saw him.'

'My father.'

'And mine.' Edmund sank the wine with an effort; it had grown tepid and sour. 'It was like looking into a mirror, only one that had aged me by thirty years or more.'

'Did he ever speak to you on the matter?'

'No,' Edmund said, irritation flared at the thought. 'In the end, it was Lady Blanche who took pity on me after … after Limoges. When I returned here for good, only to find that what few men I would have called friends had perished.'

Rolling his shoulders, Gaunt leaned back and looked at Edmund with renewed interest. 'You speak of Baron Mowbray.'

'Him too.' The memory of the Baron was still a dagger in Edmund's side, unwanted but necessary to remind him never again to stray from the right path. 'He suffered more by my hand than most others, and either he did not know or he did not care, but he was – I learned much too late – a rare and true friend.' Turning away from Gaunt's intense gaze, Edmund thought, Mowbray told me I had to say that his wife was the most beautiful woman in England, and that was an easy task, for she was.

## 10 June 1357 – Framlingham Castle, Nottingham

'My Lady,' Edmund bows and brushes a kiss on the back of her creamy hand. He feels it tremble ever so slightly and smiles, holding it a moment longer before he releases it. 'I have heard so much about you and now, I see for myself that none of the praise was exaggerated.'

Baron Mowbray smiles too and tucks his blushing wife's hand into the crook of his arm. 'I told you; she is the most beautiful woman in England.'

'Every man boasts that of his wife, no matter how ugly she is,' Edmund says and lets his eyes linger on Elizabeth Mowbray's flawless face. 'That does not make it so. But I should have known that you would tell no lies to make your wife more beautiful than she is, for no such lies exist.'

'You must be wary, dear wife,' Mowbray says with a contemplative air, 'I fear that Sir Edmund is a notorious flirt.'

Her blue eyes widen and her blush deepens, painting roses on her cheeks. 'Surely not, husband, what way is that to speak of our guest.'

Baron Mowbray turns his grey eyes to Edmund and, for a moment, he would swear that a little doubt flees across the Baron's face, but it is gone in a flash and his smile returns. 'I speak as I find, wife, best get used to it, for we are to dwell here for some time, I believe.'

'It is true then? The war is over …'

'In respite I should say, my Lady, rather than over.' Edmund enjoys the way she looks at him, lips slightly parted, a little short of breath. 'There will be more battles before it is over, for the French are not likely to let go of their crown simply because we have their King.'

'What Sir Edmund says is the truth.' The Baron lets his squire unfasten the heavy travelling cloak. 'Since we were fortunate enough to capture King John, the French will be preoccupied trying to gather the ransom our King is bound to demand. And it will be hefty, of that I have little doubt.'

'For his folly on the field, he should be shut away forever,' Edmund offers, 'I have rarely seen a poorer performance than that given by the French at Poitiers. And I am used to harrying peasants and villagers.'

'On that we can agree.' Mowbray winces when he begins walking across the grand hall, the walls decorated with the Mowbray coat of arms, a fire burning in the hearth although it is the height of summer outside. Everything about Framlingham Castle suggests great wealth and surplus. 'But this time they will have learned their lesson, and they will not give battle in such a headless manner when we take the field against them again. You helped put fear into their hearts and wit into their heads.'

'I rather doubt that,' Edmund mutters and feels the blue gaze upon him.

'Sir Edmund won his spurs that day, wife,' the Baron says and pats her hand, which is once more tucked under his arm. They enter what has to be the Baron's study, the furniture large, sparse and almost entirely free of clutter. Except for a great table set against the far wall offering a view of the grounds and good light for reading. 'He captured a French prince and, now, all of us must bow before him, for that feat won him more than spurs and gold, it won him the friendship of the Prince himself.'

Edmund gleans a little discomfort in the Baron's words and inclines his head. 'He will forget me soon enough now that he is home, surrounded by friends to sing his praises and basking in his father's attention.'

'There was praise enough for both of you, or have you forgotten that, of all the new knights, you were the only one to earn a private audience with the King? Do not be humble, Sire, it does not suit you.' Mowbray squeezes his wife's hand and plants a kiss on her forehead. 'Go and see that all is prepared for our guests, wife, I have business to attend to with Sir Edmund. The two of you can speak tonight. I suspect, I will be occupied for most of the evening.'

'We are having a feast in your honour, Sire. Yours and my husband's.' She pauses at the door, which Edmund is holding for her, and looks up at him. 'I shall pray that this is the end of the war, no matter what you and my husband say, for I would have you here and not in France.'

'Pray all you like, my dear,' Mowbray says from somewhere behind Edmund, 'it will make no difference.'

'You should have more faith, husband,' Lady Mowbray says and smiles up at Edmund. 'I might just surprise you.'

Edmund allows himself a moment of pleasure from watching her walk away, her hips swinging under the layers of expensive fabric, before he closes the door. A woman such as her might make a man forget himself.

'The war will not end on a woman's prayer, or it would have ended a thousand times over,' Mowbray grumbles and shoves a pile of papers aside on his desk. 'Nothing has been done since I left! What use is a wife if she does not run the household in my absence?'

'Your house still stands, my Lord,' Edmund says and makes an apologetic gesture when the Baron scowls, 'the fields are thick with crop, the pens bursting with livestock. If this is not a house well run, I do not know what that might look like. But there are things you cannot leave in the hands of a woman. What of your steward?'

Mowbray joins Edmund at the window, giving the empty glass pitcher a fleeting glance as he passes it. 'It seems my steward is on my northern estate at the moment. But look here, no wine for me in my rooms, no fire, no beds made up for us, though she has known for a week at least that I would return.'

'Perhaps she has been too busy preparing the hall for a feast, instructing the cooks what your favourite dishes are and making sure that there is food in the larder and fish in the barrels.' When the Baron snorts, Edmund points into the courtyard. 'There.'

Lady Mowbray is rushing across the courtyard pointing left and right, calling out instructions as she goes, everyone jumping to as she passes.

'That hardly looks like a woman remiss of her duties, my Lord.'

'Perhaps.' Mowbray turns from the window and looks around the room, his face gloomy. 'But there is still much more to do than I would have liked. Never let anyone tell you that to own land and houses is a blessing. All it is, is more work.'

'I know you have a large estate, my Lord,' Edmund says with some admiration and a little jealousy, 'now that we are here, I should like to see it.'

'If there is time, you shall, but my wife's talk of the war being at an end has unsettled me, Sire.'

'Why?'

'Because one of her chief merits is that she knows what the common folk think and speak of.' The Baron seems to notice Edmund's confusion, because he sits down heavily in his great chair, the back covered with shiny, red cloth and embroidered with Mowbray's crest. He sighs, 'If all of England thinks this is the end of the war, they will be disappointed, and soon, I should imagine. For this is no more than a regrouping. Can you envision the Dauphin simply laying down his arms and swearing fealty to an enemy who slaughtered most of his noblemen and took his family hostage? Can you conceive that our King would let up on his hold on French territory, simply because a group of noblemen meet to make terms to hand back his French opponent?'

'No, my Lord.' Edmund is more preoccupied with thoughts of the Baron's young, delicious wife than a war of Kings, which right now is leagues away. He will be in the thick of battle again soon enough and wants to spend his waiting time more pleasantly than pondering what kings might or might not do.

'Good, because your spurs also earned you new responsibilities, Sire.' Mowbray once more shuffles his papers, cracks a wax seal and begins to read.

Edmund's heart sinks a little. 'What might those be?'

Looking up from his letter, the Baron rubs his forehead. 'Being the Prince's companion is a blessing and a curse, my friend. He knighted you and, now, his family owns you till you draw your last breath. Do not think they will not hold you to the words spoken as you bent your knee. Make no mistake; the Prince will be generous, not least because you put a prince in his stockade. But more than anything, he will call on you to assist him on the battlefield for that is where you will best serve his purpose.'

'If the Prince needs my sword on the field, I shall be glad to bring it.' Edmund feels unease steal through his body. He may be a knight, but he is still a serf. Nothing has changed at all.

'Most of those who are fortunate to serve the Prince do not last long,' the Baron says with a strange sadness in his voice. 'I have seen it too often.'

'I am not most men,' Edmund argues and continues in thought; and what do you know, surrounded as you are by splendour and fortune that you have inherited. If you do not want to go to war again, you can simply say no and stay where you are. You can rally your own army. You are someone, I am no one – that is what you are telling me.

'No, you are better than them. I have rarely seen a man more at ease with a sword in his hand and blood on his face. If you wonder why the Prince has named you one of his friends there is your answer. He sees something – perhaps even a lot – of himself in you.' The Baron returns to his stacks of paper. 'But be careful, for so too does his brother Lord Gaunt. And he does not like what he sees.'

Whenever Edmund begins to think the Baron walks blind through the world, he proves him wrong. Edmund dons an amused smile. 'Why not?'

'Gaunt does not like anyone who stands in his way. Be it you, his brother or an enemy, to him it is one and the same. If you want to survive in England, you need to win over Gaunt. Which is no mean feat.'

Edmund draws a hand through his hair; it is stiff from dirt and sweat. He wonders briefly if perhaps a serving girl will help him bathe, but even that prospect does not liven him up.

'Being the Prince's friend is also being Gaunt's enemy.' Mowbray sighs, his eyes on his paperwork. He reaches for an ornate silver inkwell, a large gem on the lid. 'Mark my words. Before long, both of them, if not the King too, will demand something from you that is not worth all the gold in the world. And you will have to give it to them, because without them you are nothing.'

'Is that how you see me, my Lord?' Edmund hears the anger and so does the Baron.

'I wish it were different Edmund, truly I do, for I find myself lucky to call you friend, but I would be a poor friend in return, if I did not warn you.' The Baron gives a tired smile. 'Still, we need speak of it no further, for until the ransom is set, there is nothing neither you nor I can do, and so we may as well enjoy ourselves. God knows when we are summoned once more to wage war.'

'Whenever that might be, I shall be ready,' Edmund says and pushes away the screams that haunt his rare dreams. The screams of men who fell beside him, of enemies slain and of horses caught in a rain of arrows.

'We all shall, for we have no other option.' The Baron waves Edmund away. 'Go rest, bathe, get a change of clothes. Go prove me wrong about my wife.'

'With pleasure, my Lord.'

Closing the door, Edmund pauses for a moment before he turns for the stairs. After all, the Baron has all but given him a task to perform and what a friend would he be, if he does not go about it diligently.

Edmund stops a passing scullery maid. 'Where is Lady Mowbray?'

## 10 August 1357 – Nottingham

'What happened next?'

Her blue eyes blaze in the light of a hundred candles, and Edmund gives her a half-smile which does exactly what he intends, it makes her breath catch, her plump lips part.

'We were outnumbered and battle weary. I could hardly join the battle cry when it went up, and every time our archers let loose another hail of arrows, we would have to stop and crouch under our shields not to be killed by one of our own.'

At his other arm, a woman some years older than the young, blushing Lady Mowbray, exhales and puts her hand on his upper arm, her grip tensing when he looks at her. Ripe for the plucking, Edmund thinks and gives her a smile too.

'Then what? Oh, do not keep me in suspense, Sire, for I shall call you no friend of mine or my husband if you do not tell the tale to its end right now!' Lady Mowbray's words are pushed into Edmund's ear by her soft lips, to ensure he hears her above the clamour of the hall.

Edmund licks his lips, and the lady on his left immediately signals for his cup to be replenished, never taking her eyes off him.

'Thank you, my Lady,' Edmund says before drinking, fixing her gaze. 'You are most kind.'

'Anything for a well told tale, Sire.' Her voice is low and pleasant; the voice of an experienced woman who knows her ways. 'Especially one as riveting as yours. If you were not seated here by my side, recounting it yourself, I might be inclined to think you would not make it, but we both know that fortune favoured you that day.'

The hall is hot, the bench hard and the candles flicker and twist when servants open and close the side doors on their way on some errand or other. Though the hall is no match to the palaces, Edmund saw in London, it is vast, beautiful with its low ceiling and thick tapestries that stand out in bright splashes of colour. The floor is scrubbed clean with vinegar twice a day, and the lingering tart smell hides beneath the curtain of scented women and roasting meat.

'We do, my Lady,' Edmund agrees and feels Lady Mowbray grow restless at his side. 'Where was I ... yes, the arrows fell as a hard shower of rain, relentless, deadly, and I was so tired that I might have lost my sword and my head if it had not been for the bold nature of the Prince.'

'The Prince ...,' Lady Mowbray breathes. 'I hear, he is the most elegant of men.'

'He is, my Lady,' Edmund agrees and rewarded with another smile. 'Even in the midst of battle, he could not be shaken, he charged at the head of his most trusted knights and lords and brought vengeance to King John. When I had all but given up hope, I saw him in his glittering armour as black as the skies above, his hair a golden crown, his blade fiercely raised above his head, and I knew …'

Edmund enjoys the bated breath of the two ladies, one of whom is now clutching his arm with a fierce grip. Idly, he wonders if he can have her right here in the hall if he chooses, and from her look, he knows he can. Instead, he turns to Lady Mowbray.

'I knew that I must keep fighting for him. For him and for England. At that moment, the sun penetrated the clouds and lit our path to King John himself, illuminating his crown and sending us word where he might be captured.'

'You were there?'

'Sir Edmund caught one of the French princes,' Lady Mowbray says and bathes in the awe of the older woman. 'My husband told me so and Sir Edmund confirmed it. Did you not, Sire?'

'Indeed, my Lady, though you tell it as if it were an easy feat. Which I can assure you it was not.' Edmund draws a hand through his freshly washed hair. 'I thought he would kill me when suddenly Prince Philip lay down his sword and surrendered to me. And that was just as well, for I have no doubt that I would not have managed another blow. I was lucky. We all were.'

For a moment, Edmund forgets he is telling a tale to entice two women. The battlefield lies bloodied and horrible before him, he can smell the iron of blood and the piss of fear, can hear muffled screams as wounded men are given a merciful death.

'We were indeed, Sire.' The Baron's voice seems to come from a million miles away. Listless and tired. 'I beg your indulgence, dear ladies, but I must steal away Sir Edmund for a moment.'

'Must you? Cannot it wait until tomorrow?' The naked despair and urgency in Lady Mowbray's voice warms Edmund's insides.

'I am sorry to disappoint, wife,' the Baron says with forced kindness, 'but it cannot. Fear not, you will have plenty of time for him to recant his tales of woe tomorrow. Not that I can imagine why you would want to hear it again.'

She gives Edmund a last lingering smile and excuses herself. The lady at Edmund's left inclines her head and strokes his shoulder as she goes.

'You should be careful with that one,' Baron Mowbray says with a tired smile. 'She is a force to be reckoned with and used to get what she wants.'

'I should think her husband …'

'He counts his blessings, which are mostly made of gold and silver, that he was lucky enough to marry her all those years ago before her father and brother were killed in battle.' Mowbray reaches for the pitcher. 'He had a title but no fortune. When he married her, he got more money than he knew how to spend and so now, he lets her run rampant as long as he can keep the gold.'

Edmund accepts the Baron's offer of more wine and looks after the woman, her yellow silk dress easy to spot in the mix of people. As usual, Edmund is surprised how often the Baron and his wife host suppers that last all night, and how many guests always seem eager to come from miles away. Perhaps it is because they are one of the few young households in the area, but he suspects that cannot be all of it.

'A marriage of mutual benefit?' Edmund asks and raises his cup.

The Baron drinks and wipes his chin with the back of his hand. 'Are they not all?'

'Is yours, my Lord?'

'Yes. I was simply fortunate that Elizabeth is as beautiful as she is curious.' Mowbray harks a laugh at Edmund's surprised expression. 'For all these months, she hounds me when I bathe, for then I have no escape, and she pursues her inclination for more stories of war, even while I am getting dressed. For a woman who wants the war to be over, she is ferocious in her pursuit of knowing everything that goes on in the battlefield.'

The thought of Lady Elizabeth watching her naked man getting dressed annoys Edmund to no end. Of course, it is not uncommon for women to attend their husbands while bathing, but still, Edmund would rather be without that particular image. He forces the jealous feeling aside and smiles. 'Why did you not give her your tales?'

'Because you are far better at spinning a story than I ever will be. And besides, she does not want my account, for I was not in the thick of things.' Mowbray takes another draught. 'If it were not for your obvious talents on the field, I should not doubt you would make an excellent minstrel.'

'I do not play any instruments.' Edmund endures the Baron's laugh, for in its own way it is kind enough. 'My childhood was of a more practical nature, shall we say?'

'Some day, I would have you tell me where you came from, but it can keep.' The Baron gets up and signals for Edmund to join him. 'I have news that should be relayed behind closed doors.'

They push through the crowd, the Baron nodding here and there in greeting. When the door to the great hall closes behind them, the carpet of sound fades and Edmund shivers.

'I know you are tired, so am I. But this cannot keep.' Mowbray crosses the dark hall and steps into his study, now as cluttered as it was neat when they first arrived. 'I have had word from the Prince. It seems Grosmont is in need of aid.'

'When do we leave, my Lord?'

Mowbray gives one of his increasingly rare, boyish grins. 'I think you will have time to entertain a certain lady before you go, if you can be swift about it.'

'It has been a good while,' Edmund says returning the grin, though it has been but two days. 'If you give me an hour, I think I can manage four good turns.'

'Lucky lady.' Mowbray holds out a letter with the royal seal at the bottom. 'You have two days, perhaps you could be gentle with her, and then both of you can still walk in the morning.'

Edmund leaves the study with a wide smile on his face. He does not have to search long; she is waiting for him in the shadows, eager and willing.

## 23 April 1358 – Windsor

As Edmund crosses the field bathed in waning sunlight, he looks up at the many shields displayed before the main platform. There is the shield of the Duke of Lancaster, dominant in the centre, but not for long. Though he will never admit it to anyone else, when the Duke was injured in the mêlée earlier in the day, Edmund had all but shouted out.

It was an accident, of course, but no doubt the misfortunate knight who did the deed is dreading what comes next. The King had been furious, and the Prince had rushed from his seat to intervene and drag the Duke to safety.

Edmund had been at the opposite end of the mêlée amusing himself with three opponents who would never have come close to striking true, and yet, he had seen the Duke go down, had beat aside the knights who fought to take Edmund's sword with ease and been by the Prince's side in seconds. By then, the Duke was unconscious and, for all Edmund knows, he still is.

Outside the barber surgeon's tent, Lords and knights pile around the opening. Some are patched up after the mêlée, others are no doubt only present in the hope that some piece of juicy gossip might slip from inside the canvas. There are always those who deal in secrets of course, as Edmund has begun to learn.

No matter their reason for loitering, Edmund pushes them aside without a word or glance either here or there, until his face is bathed in the light that escapes the fluttering flaps. Several of the finely dressed Lords give him an angry glare, but most of those glares fall from their faces when they see who he is. The Prince's companion. The great knight of Poitiers. He has no time for them. 'How is he, my Lord?'

The King's second son, John of Gaunt turns from the tent and looks up at Edmund. 'They are working on him now. Would that it did not look like a slaughterhouse in there, but they have just amputated an arm, and the blood is still dripping from the saw.'

'Did you see what happened?'

'We all did. It was an accident, I have no doubt, but …' Gaunt turns a suspicious face to the crowd. 'Come with me.'

Edmund lets Gaunt lead the way from the tents towards the stables. Though he has long since grown accustomed to the fineries of court and the splendour the royal stables, to see all of these magnificent beasts lined up, being prepared for the joust still takes his breath away. He loves horses, and always has, and he sees several on the line that he wants. If only …

'I hear you are not to enter the joust?'

'My name is not fine enough.' Edmund tries to make light of a situation he despises.

'My father-in-law's shield is still up,' Gaunt says and steps into the darkness of the stables, 'perhaps you could represent him?'

'Is that allowed, my Lord?' Edmund asks and wonders why Gaunt takes an interest. But then Gaunt must be keen to see the Duke represented, and he is no great horseman himself.

'Let me worry about that.' Gaunt looks about and dismisses a couple of confused stable boys with a gesture. Then he leans in. 'As I said, it was an accident, surely you will agree with me, Sire, but there have been rumblings at court, signs of discontent concerning the Duke. I would not speak of it, only …'

Your spies have no news for you, Edmund thinks, and you hope perhaps I know more. How curious. Edmund makes a note that he must begin to employ his own spies at court that he might serve Gaunt better in the future. Baron Mowbray's warning to stay in Gaunt's good graces is something Edmund has not forgotten. Not by a long shot.

'I can make enquiries, my Lord,' Edmund suggests. 'But for the time being, I know less than you, for I have heard no such whispers.'

Gaunt shakes his head. 'Who would dare speak of it when you are around? You who are his crowning glory; the son he never had and the squire he raised higher than any other man in his service.'

You should learn to conceal your distaste, my Lord, Edmund reflects, and bows his head. 'I shall keep my ear to the ground all the same, in case something comes to light. Do you have any idea who might have a grudge against my Lord Lancaster?'

'Anyone in want of money.' Gaunt sniggers. 'Which is to say it might be anyone at court, my father included, for it is no secret that Lancaster has all the English wealth and my father all the appearance of it. But they are old friends and my father is preoccupied at the moment, as you might have guessed.'

A horse nuzzles Edmund's hand and he pats the enormous black head. 'I heard that your grandmother is present?'

'No doubt you know that there is little love lost between her and my father?' Gaunt steps back when the black beast bares its teeth at him. 'I sometimes wonder if our family is cursed to never like one another, but then I look at my father and I know that he is capable of liking, even loving, when he chooses to.'

Edmund knows who the King loves, and he fights an urge to goad Gaunt, instead, he pats the horse again and looks into the sunset, the horizon ablaze in gold, amber and blood. 'If I am not mistaken, my Lord, you are next in line for the Duke's estate?'

This time, it is Gaunt who bares his teeth and gives a hard laugh. 'Yes, Lancaster will eventually revert to me. And, unlike my father-in-law, I am not loved and revered by all of the English court. But I want Grosmont alive for many more years, for I need him in the battlefield commanding my father's troops and assisting my brother when he wins the crown of France for us. A dead soldier is no use to me.'

With a nod, Edmund accepts that Gaunt might be many things, but one to plot the death of such a vital part of England's path to victory, he is not. Instead, Edmund strokes the horse and asks: 'Who does this magnificent beast belong to?'

Now, Gaunt smiles in truth. 'To the victor the spoils. It is to be the prize of whoever sits longest in the saddle. Though I warn you, Sir Edmund, in a tourney such as the one that is about to begin, no one unseats another knight, it is all for show. However, you might be just the man to provide the best show. And then this devil can be yours.'

'You might be able to get me on the lists?'

Gaunt gestures for Edmund to follow him back to the surgeon's tent where, no doubt, Grosmont is still out cold, but hopefully he is mended at least. They walk up the length of the field where boys are stacking wood for bonfires.

'It will be a night like no other,' Gaunt says into the evening mist. 'When they light the fires and the knights take the field, it will seem as if King Arthur himself has deigned us with his presence.'

Edmund smells spring in the air, the daffodils closing their yellow petals against the cool hand of night. He looks up at Grosmont's shield, displayed at the opposite end, golden lions with blue tongues on a field of red. What he would do to earn the right to tie that shield to his arm tonight.

'I would have you ride in his honour,' Gaunt says, 'will you do it? Even though you know that you cannot unseat the men you ride against?'

'I will, my Lord.'

Gaunt turns away from the crowd in front of the tent, and ducks under the guy lines which are almost invisible in the shimmering grey darkness. A narrow slit in the side of the canvas reveals a second entrance to the surgeon's tent.

'I shall go in alone; no doubt my father and brother are there already, but it would seem strange if I do not attend my wife's father.' With a hand on the canvas, Gaunt pauses. 'You will take the field for him, go put on your armour and make sure it is buffed to a sheen. Tonight, you will ride under the banner of the Duke of Lancaster. Perhaps there is yet a chance that we might be on friendly terms, Sire.'

Edmund bows and when he looks up, Gaunt has disappeared. Friends with two princes, Edmund contemplates as he makes his way swiftly to his own tent, now there is a turn. He will have to help his squire clean his plate, but it is of no significance. For in a few hours, he will be mounted and riding against some of the greatest men in the land, he will be paraded in front of the royal family, and he means to put on a show they will never forget.

# CHAPTER 8

## 26 July 1392 – Westminster Palace

'I remember you on the field that night.' Gaunt's ring glittered when he moved. 'Who could not? You rode as only a man possessed would have. But your crowning moment was when you took off the helmet before the last turn.'

Edmund remembered the rush of surprise and the crowd cheering. It had been a fine evening, an evening of wonder and supernatural spectacle. He had won over England that night, in the licking light from the fires burning up and down the sides of the field.

'And you won the prize.' Gaunt turned his cup. 'Which I suspect meant more to you than anything.'

'You allowed me to compete under the banner of a man I admired,' Edmund argued, though Gaunt had the right of it, 'I was indebted to you. And yes, I won the day and the prize. It has served me well ever since.'

'I suspect you won more than that.'

The silver ring with the great opal in it twinkled as Edmund picked up his own cup. 'It had been a long time coming. In the end, it provided me with an heir.'

Gaunt tipped his cup at Edmund and sent a solitary, nasty smile. 'You have a son?'

'Though he does not know it himself, I do.' Edmund rubbed his arm. 'I keep him quite close. And you can lay the credit for my having an heir flat across the tomb of a Duke no less. Whose dukedom you hold to this day. Whose shield you use as your own.'

'You would have me worry that my own wife, snatched from me too soon, was at the heart of this ridiculous tale, but I know better.'

'Yes, you always kept her uncomfortably close.' Edmund smiled. 'And though she was fair, to be true, she did not allure me.'

'Well, you have already revealed that you had an English mistress.' Gaunt tapped his finger on the table. 'I am in no mood to waste time guessing, do not think that your sordid little secrets are that interesting to me. But if it pleases you, tell me about her.'

Edmund wanted to get up and pace the room, but Gaunt had packed the study tight with furniture and, besides, there was nowhere his pacing could take him but back to his tale. No doubt, Gaunt was playing slow to get Edmund to show his hand, and if that was the case, he was willing to join the game.

'As you know, your father-in-law recovered and was once more sent to France. I went with him, for I wanted to see true battle again, and I got what I wanted. It began before the Prince commanded me to go to France. And after Rheims, how could she prefer her feeble husband to me? She, who loved tales of war and glory above all else, and who was chained to a man who might wield some power at court, but had not wielded a sword against an enemy for the longest time …'

One look at Gaunt convinced Edmund that he had not guessed, and a burst of gratification raced through Edmund's veins. How sweet to know that some secrets could be buried so deep that even the greatest spymaster in the land had no inkling of what had happened.

Edmund raised his hands. 'I only ever gave her what she wanted.'

## 14 April 1363 – Nottingham, Framlingham Castle

She falls from him, her hair a golden halo around her rose-cheeked face. Edmund enjoys watching her pant from excitement and draws lazy circles around her nipples, waiting for them to go hard again, waiting for her to be ready. He has already had her twice tonight but it does not hurt to have a quick send off before dawn creeps over the horizon and she has to sneak back to her own bed.

When she moans his name, he turns her around roughly and takes her from behind, gripping her hair and forcing her head back so that he may enjoy her arched back and neck even more.

One of his women once told him that the more demure the woman the more she could be made to do in bed. She was right, it seems, for every time Edmund beds a noble lady, she has always liked the rough manner of his handling to that of her soft-handed husband. Or so they say while they squeal, moan and sigh under him.

Elizabeth is no different, except she gives as good as she gets. Just before he comes, she pulls away so hard that he is still clutching some of her golden hair when she turns and pushes him down, mounting him as she would a horse. The thought of her naked on a horse rouses him even more, and all she has to do is slide down on him before he lets go and groans. She licks his chest and bites his nipple and makes him cry out in joy and pain. 'Filthy woman,' he gasps and she laughs.

'You like me that way, do not deny it!' She gets up and takes his juices with her. In the fading light from the dying fire, her ass is ripe as an apple and suddenly, all he wants to do is bite into it.

'Stay.'

'Are you mad?' Elizabeth laughs again and bends to pick up her nightgown.

Edmund rolls off the bed and grabs her, pushing her forward. 'Stay. Just like this.'

For a moment, she leans in, her backside rubbing against him and then she pulls away with surprising force. 'You know, he always comes to me in the morning.'

'When he comes at all,' Edmund says and gets what he deserves when the flat of her hand hits his cheek. He snatches her wrist and kisses it. 'Forgive me.'

'There is nothing to forgive.' Elizabeth lets him lick and kiss his way to her armpit and then sighs when he bends to suck her nipple. 'What we have I shall never have with him. But he is my husband. And your friend as you are so proud to boast.'

Edmund lets go of her nipple and draws her close. 'It is he who boasts.'

'Either way, how would he feel if he knew?'

Elizabeth had asked him once before, in the early days of their secret affair, and he had dismissed her concerns as a woman's folly. He still does, though if he looks hard enough for it, he does feel a twinge of remorse when he has her in his bed. Every night.

'You want it as much as I do.'

When he kisses her, she gives way for a moment, and Edmund feels her tense against him. Then she pulls away and slides the gown over her head. She nods for him to tie the lace around her neck. Somehow this is the only time Edmund thinks of her as Lady Mowbray. It is the only time they feel intimate. Everything else is pure lust. For his part at least.

'I never said different.' She weaves a careless braid. 'From the very first moment I saw you; I knew I had to have you. Had to be yours. And I am. But he is my husband. My duty …'

'Duty, honour, what of it?' Edmund asks sharply. 'I care not for any of that.'

'No,' she says and something sad descends on her face. 'But you give off such convincing performances that everyone else around you think you the greatest, most noble and honourable knight they have ever seen. They say that is why the Prince favours you.'

'The Prince never saw a warrior he did not like the looks of. Stamina on the field is all he wants and I can give him that,' Edmund dismisses her and goes to the washbasin, a plain bowl and a pewter pitcher set near the window. He begins cleaning himself, removing her scent from his body.

Her arms slide around his waist, her hands take over and he leans back against her. 'I cannot wear you out, it seems.'

Rather than turn to her and rip apart her dress, as he has done in the past, he lets Elizabeth work, rejoicing in the combination of cold water and warm hands. Through the thin linen of her nightgown, he feels her breasts and her hair tickles him just below his shoulder blade.

When she has finished him, she pushes him aside and washes her hands, staring at them under the surface of the water. 'He will find out eventually.'

'Not unless you tell him,' Edmund says and knows that she never would.

It will destroy her reputation before it will do any damage to his. That is why this game of cat and mouse is so enjoyable to him. When he sits at the table just below the dais in a few hours, he will look up at her and see her sitting to the left of her husband, he will have the Baron smile down upon him with a content look about him, and Edmund will know that he has had Elizabeth thrice as many times as the Baron ever has.

'What if I get with child. And it is yours? He will know, if I birth a golden-haired child.'

'You have golden hair yourself,' Edmund is tiring of her words and wants her gone. He needs his rest before another day on the field training the new men. The Baron has been clever enough to give Edmund a task that takes him out of the house most days, and for that he is grateful. 'He will be pleased you have a child that looks like you.'

He sees Elizabeth's reflection in the window, sees her beautiful face grow angry and ugly and turns to embrace her. 'You have already had two girls by him. If you deliver an heir, do you think he will care what colour hair the child has?'

She begins to relax and then she draws away again. He does not care. They have had this conversation a hundred times, she has even run from his rooms in tears, but her stormy anger never lasts but a few days, and then she will be back, knocking on his door, offering no apology and expecting nothing from him but pleasure. Which he will always provide. She is as smitten with him as any woman he has ever had, and he knows that even the slightest smile will make her melt away in his arms once more.

'His heir will be dark of hair,' she whispers as if to ward off what evil she has herself begun the mention of. 'We have been enjoying ourselves for these past many months and no child has come. Perhaps you are unable.'

Though her words cut him deep, Edmund refuses to let her see it and smiles carelessly. 'All the better for me. I should hate to think how many bastards I have scattered all over, if I was able.'

'It is you who are the bastard!'

'How right you are, my sweet Bessie,' Edmund says and blows her a kiss. 'That is all part of the attraction, is it not?'

She turns and leaves the room without closing the door. Smiling, Edmund picks up the wet cloth she wiped her hands in and rubs his groin.

On the table beneath a pile of old papers, lies a command that will take him from Nottingham before the month is out. He cannot wait to be off.

Nottingham has grown stale and weary and Edmund desires a change of scenery and company more than he will ever admit.

On the horizon, the Prince's court in Bordeaux awaits. He is setting out to settle a strife between two Counts who have been warring for a long time. Why the Prince has turned a broker of peace, Edmund cannot tell, but perhaps it is the Princess Joan who is behind this sudden change of heart.

Theirs is the marriage that should never have been, not if the King had hoped to seal a treaty of perpetual peace with France, for when the Prince chose Joan, he foiled his father's plans to grab the French crown without more bloodshed. As it stands, Edmund is pleased that the war can flare up at any time, and no doubt that is the true reason, he is summoned to Bordeaux.

Either way, it suits Edmund and, in a few hours, he will tell the Baron that he is leaving and does not know when or even if he will return. That will teach Elizabeth to take him for granted as she has done these past couple of months. More than anything, it will teach her that he will not always be at her service, a toy she can cast aside and pick up when she wants to.

Let her make do with her husband and mourn Edmund's leaving every night when she cannot sleep. He lies down, one foot on the cool, bare stone floor, and falls asleep with a smile, certain that if he should return sometime in the future, Elizabeth will be waiting for him, spreading petals of apology from the door and right into his bed.

# CHAPTER 9

## 24 March 1366 – London, England

'I am glad that you are here.' Mowbray raises a glass to Edmund. They are secluded in the Baron's study in his London house, set near the river, it affords a sublime view of the sprawling city. 'Admittedly, you cannot refuse the royal summons, but still, I am glad you have time to stop here.'

Edmund drinks deep and looks at the Baron. It has been almost three years since they have last clapped eyes on each other and Mowbray has changed. Aged. There are new lines on his face; his eyes sit more deeply in their hollows. Vacantly, Edmund wonders if he too is marked by time.

'How is your family?' Edmund looks about Mowbray's study, noting some of the priceless trinkets that lie scattered around the room. Above the fireplace, the Mowbray crest is a splash of white, red and gold against the dark wood cladding.

'I know my Lady will scold me if I do not extend an invitation to come and visit.' The Baron puts aside his empty cup and rubs his calf, a gesture now so natural to him that Edmund suspects Mowbray does not even know, he is doing it. 'And she would be in the right. You must come to Framlingham. The whole brood is there.'

'How many now?' Edmund paints on a smile, he cares nothing about children, they are tiresome little beasts that demand attention from everyone in their presence.

'Four. Three girls and a boy.'

Edmund's smile turns genuine. 'A toast to your heir, my Lord!'

'So, you will come and see them?' Mowbray inclines his head when Edmund downs the wine. 'It has been long since I have had an old friend seated at my table.'

'I am bound to the Prince, my Lord,' Edmund says and hides his relief that he does not have to see Elizabeth again. Time has not washed away her face; it is burned into his memory. She haunts his nights and walks next to him in the daylight. When she once told him, she would be constantly by his side, she had been right. But her phantom presence is unwelcome; he cannot even forget her when he beds other women. It is exasperating. 'We will not linger long, I am sure.'

'I confess, I should rather leave with you to fight once more beside the Prince, than sit any longer in this wretched Parliament. It drags on and on with no end in sight.' Mowbray shifts in his seat, crumbling the purple, yellow and green cushion that offers comfort to his back. 'When news reached us that the Prince was to send a delegation to seek counsel from the King, we were surprised.'

'How so?' Edmund knows the Prince is less than eager to enter into the dispute between Peter, the King of Castile, and his bastard brother Henry of Trastámara, the usurper supported by the Pope himself. If not for a few choice words, the Prince would have turned away King Peter. Fortunately, Edmund still has the Prince's ear.

'Our King has long been an ally of King Peter,' Mowbray says and signals for his servant to pour more wine. 'At the last Parliament, a letter from Peter was read in which he asked for support from England. We granted his wish. And yet here you are, in the train of Sir Nigel, who is holed up with the King.'

'Negotiations.' Edmund turns away from Mowbray's probing eyes. 'The Prince is host to King Peter, but feels he cannot make a decision on behalf of England without his father's assent.'

'But why the delay? We are bound to honour our agreement; it is the chivalrous thing to do.' Mowbray sighs through his drink. 'The Prince must see this.'

'There are rumours about King Peter that weighs on the Prince's conscience.' Edmund bites the inside of his cheek. 'It is not my place to say why the Prince does what he does.'

'But he is worried. He does not want to uphold our end of the bargain?' More probing.

'Sir Nigel has the answers, my Lord; ask him. At any rate, I do not understand how his bastard brother has claimed the throne?' Edmund hopes to divert the Baron with idle questions, he already has the answers to.

'From what I understand, Henry has been spreading rumours that King Peter is too kind to the Jews who are not well liked by the Castilian population. I could not tell you why.' Mowbray kicks at an ember spit out onto the floor by the fire. It sears the rushes, burnt lavender assaulting the senses. 'This is not a case of right or wrong, it is a case of politics,' the Baron continues, 'England needs her allies to stay on her side, and to come to her aid if need be. In exchange for their allegiance, we support them.'

Edmund leans back in his chair. 'Then we must aid King Peter.'

Before they departed for England, the Prince had taken Sir Nigel aside and said; 'do not concede readily for I am afraid of what the world will think of us if we side with a villain.'

If Parliament has already agreed to send aid in the war to come, Sir Nigel is running a fool's errand and, no doubt, he knows as much. But then, Edmund thinks, we are all sworn to obey the orders of others. The notion tickles his pride, and he does not care for it.

'You sound not as a man glad to be going once more to war,' Mowbray remarks.

'Would you be?' Edmund knows it is wise to pretend he does not care for battle, especially in the presence of the Baron, but in truth, he can hardly wait to unsheathe his blade and smell his enemies' fear again. It has been too long and the odd chevauchee, with one of the free companies that roam the French countryside, is not enough to soothe his savage desires.

Mowbray rubs his smooth cheek. 'No. But we are made for war and must be ready to answer the call of our King and his Prince whenever they see fit.'

'My fortune is certainly forged in battle, my Lord, for which I have you to thank,' Edmund says. 'Soon, we depart for Aquitaine once more. I believe Sir Nigel has all but exhausted his options, and, if you are in the right, the King will decide on battle. It is only a matter of time, I suppose.'

'Then you must dine with me tonight.' The Baron signals for his servant to inform the kitchens. Once the boy leaves, they are alone in the room. It has a feel of old dust settled for centuries upon the furniture although everything is clean and spotless.

'Even if the King has decided, he must ask Parliament if he wants to send anything more than his blessing. Though I warn you, dear friend, that Parliament is reluctant to dole out money on something that does not directly benefit England. It may yet be some time before you can set sails and return. Where are you to meet the Prince?'

'The army is amassing at Dax. The Prince is in Bordeaux.' Edmund puts aside his empty glass. The wine is heavy and sits in his throat; he had thought that they would be leaving within a few days, but now he knows that is not to be. 'When will you leave for Nottingham?'

'Nothing is settled yet, but if the King has no further use of his Parliament once the accord to aid King Peter is struck, I very much expect it to be home in time to celebrate Easter. If I am not to fight, at least I will be surrounded by my children and my wife.' Mowbray glides a hand through his dark hair, which is flecked with white. He has aged before his time during this long Parliament. 'You may think me an old worrywart, but I am concerned that not all is well in Nottingham.'

I do, Edmund thinks and smiles benevolently. 'How so, my Lord?'

'I hear but rarely from my wife, even less since you left three years ago. She writes only to inform me about how the children are growing and what they are learning,' Mowbray says and rubs his calf again. 'I worry that she has gone off me.'

'Surely you have not been too lonely here in London,' Edmund says and, for once, he relishes in the vision of a naked Elizabeth when she steals into his mind's eye.

Mowbray snorts a laugh. 'It is hard to be lonely in London, but I have made an effort not to seek out the company of, shall we say, inappropriate women. Still, a man's bed must be kept warm, Sir Edmund. As I am sure you will agree. And once you are encamped at Dax, there will be no shortage of bed-warmers. There never is.'

## 10 November 1366 – Bordeaux

There is something quizzical in her green eyes as she serves him. Her long, brown hair is drawn back from her face with two twisted ribbons and it falls down her back, covering the laced bodice. Edmund enjoys the sight and awards her a smile when she turns her gaze upon him once more. Perhaps later …

'When'll we go, Sire?'

Edmund blinks and stares at the soldier sitting opposite him. All the sounds of the great hall thunder back into his present, and he resists an urge to slap his hands to his ears. Was it this loud just a moment ago?

'Sire?'

'As soon as Lord Gaunt arrives with our archers. And it is not long since the treaty was signed.' Edmund is aware that his men, all clad in the Prince's colours of red, blue and gold, are eying him with some concern. 'This is politics, we need not understand it.'

The solider opposite him burps and wipes his hands on the cloth covering the table. It is already greasy and stained. 'Good enough for me, Sire!'

'Is it true that King Peter has offered his daughters to the Prince?'

Silence steals down the benches and many turn their heads to hear what Edmund has to say. He weighs his words for a while. 'Yes, it is not uncommon …'

'Unnatural it must be, Sire! What good's it do?' Several of the men nod in accord and the man leans in. 'They're just girls!'

'They are as valuable to King Peter as any daughter is to her father,' Edmund says but he knows that, to Peter, the two pale girls are just bargaining chips. All Princesses are.

He has met King Peter a few times during the Prince's war councils, and Edmund does not like the cast-aside Castilian King. If rumours are true, Peter was not merely dethroned by a jealous half-brother; the people of Castile, who fear and hate him in equal measure, set him aside. To Edmund that means that King Peter has played his cards very ill, for it does not do to be hated. Even if Edmund makes mischief all day long, he still knows how to spark love in every man who serves him.

A united Castile will not be easy to defeat, even with the greatest commander at the helm of the English army. Though Edmund hesitates to call it an English army, because the Prince has had to find many his soldiers in other countries. And mercenaries rarely rally the same spirit as those sworn to protect their liege lord.

'If he loves 'em, it don't look it,' the soldier across from Edmund comments and others nod.

'The lives of royalty are often impossible for us to understand,' Edmund says and sees disbelief plain on the haggard soldiers' faces. He has to draw breath to avoid laughing out loud. 'I am the same as you, I grew up in the gutter, I had to work from I was very young. I had no more than anyone else.'

'That may be true, Sire, I'll not argue with you, but no one should bargain with their children,' the soldier remarks.

Edmund agrees with him, of course, he was himself a bargaining tool for a knight. But it was a bargain that earned him gold and glory. It forged his future and lead to great friends. Not all bargains are bad.

'But you're a knight now. No more poverty for you.' There is no spite or jealousy in the soldier's voice and yet, Edmund feels discontent steal around the table. He has to put it out right away.

'So can you all be.' Edmund leans forward, grabbing his pewter cup. 'I have it on good authority that the Prince intends to make many new knights before we fall upon the usurper Trastámara. Serve the Prince faithfully and you may well be among them.'

'That's how you came to be a knight, I know!' The soldier sitting next to Edmund nods and turns to face the rest of the table. 'I was there when Sir Edmund captured the French Prince after fighting with the strength of twenty men at Poitiers!' He pounds his cup on the rough tabletop, ale spilling over. 'He's no liar! Sir Edmund tells true!'

Edmund's men begin to pound their cups in unison, the sound ringing round the great hall. Soon others join in, although they do not know why, and the Prince searches the room as if to gather what causes the commotion.

Edmund seizes the opportunity, jumps to his feet and salutes the Prince. 'PRINCE EDWARD! GLORY AND HONOUR!'

'ICH DIEN!' the soldiers roar. 'ICH DIEN!'

The Prince nods to Edmund and raises his golden cup to the assembled men. 'ICH DIEN! SAINT GEORGE!'

'SAINT GEORGE!' echoes around the room and the roar lifts to the high timber ceiling. 'SAINT GEORGE!'

Next to the Prince, the ousted King Peter scowls and does not lift his cup when the Prince drinks deep and wipes his chin with a grin. But all the soldiers, knights and noblemen follow suit. Edmund is close enough to the dais to notice a little change in the Prince's demeanour. He turns to follow the Prince's gaze and sees Sir John Chandos, a renowned English warrior and the Prince's great friend, in the doorway surveying the brawling men who are now patting each other on the back, laughing and fooling about. Chandos has often enough pushed Edmund aside in council. Perhaps it is finally time for a change.

'CHANDOS!' The Prince's voice booms around the room and the soldiers fall silent. 'How good to see you at last!'

Chandos spreads his arms and walks briskly towards the dais. 'Your Grace! I come with great tidings of many more men joining your cause.'

'Later.' The Prince signals for a servant who forces a big chair in next to him.

King Peter is pushed further down the table, his fingers talons on the table edge, his eyes narrow and angry. He is a fish out of water, and the more Edmund sees of him, the more he understands why the Castilians do not want him back. Compared to the illustrious Prince of England, Peter is a sallow, sad figure who cannot hope to command the love of thousands. Edmund wonders what will happen when they take Castile, and the Prince rides into the capital with King Peter in tow. Who will they cheer? Their King returned – or the golden English Prince?

The Prince looks straight through his guest at Chandos. 'Come join in the feast. You must be famished.'

Smiling, Chandos looks about as the soldiers settle in at the tables and return to their meals and conversations. As he sits down, he leans in. 'Tell me how is your lady wife?'

Edmund strains to hear the Prince's answer, notices his face grow weary and his shoulders hunch. 'She is unwell these days.' The Prince skewers a piece of meat. 'We live in hope, my friend.'

As soon as the Prince and Chandos disappear through a side door, no doubt to discuss the final stages of the planning, Edmund too rises. Several of his men are drunk and none seem to notice him slip away. He has a little matter of his own to pursue.

'Sire?'

Edmund turns to see the woman with the startling green eyes linger in a doorway. 'Yes?'

She looks about to reconsider, but then she steps forward. 'You are leaving?'

Is that dismay in her voice? Edmund smiles, it is as he thought. 'The men have no need of me, and I would rather be away from the noise of the hall.'

'You do not sound English.'

The comment is so out of place that Edmund laughs, the sound hard and loud in the quiet hallway. 'No, I suppose I do not, although I never really think about it.' He looks her over again. Her dress is too fine for a servant, and she wears pearl pendants in her ears. 'Why were you serving tables tonight, my Lady?'

She looks down for a moment, her dark-brown hair spilling over her shoulders. It is silken in the waning light. 'There is a bout of fever in the kitchens; many of the maids have been taken ill. But they are recovering, Sire.' When she looks up again, her green eyes glitter. 'I offered my services as the Princess has no use of me this evening.'

'You would pose as a common serving wench?' Edmund smiles at her sharp glare. 'What if the men had decided to serve up you? They do sometimes, my Lady, when they are deep in their drink.'

'I am certain it would not have come to that.' She seems to steel herself. 'There are plenty of knights who would never let the soldiers overstep.'

'There are plenty of knights who like to drink,' Edmund says and bows, half in mockery. 'But I am not one of those knights. I heard the Prince comment on his wife's health?'

'Much hope rests upon her condition.' The woman tugs at her sleeve, the fabric covered in little embroidered birds. 'One son in the nursery …'

I see, Edmund thinks, this is what it is; she is with child. He smiles at the thought. 'That is good news.'

'It is too soon to spread the word,' the woman steps closer, her eyes fixed on his. 'I would prefer …'

'My lips are sealed my Lady,' Edmund says and adds as an afterthought, 'if you tell me your name.'

She seems to consider if this is a bargain worth making, but Edmund is certain she will concede; after all, she lingers in the hallway, no doubt waiting for someone to come out that she might speak with. Perhaps even waiting for him? Edmund takes pleasure in the notion. He uses the wait to inspect her; she has regular features, nothing out of the ordinary except those bright green eyes. Her rich brown hair sets them off. Her dress falls in wide pleats around her waist, the embroidered birds look to be nestling in the creases. The wide sleeves hide her arms, and her hands are slender, the long fingers unadorned.

'I am Pascaline.' She looks about. 'Will you help me light the torches, Sire?'

Edmund nods and, for a while, they carry out the task in silence. He is ever aware of her proximity and, every now and then, he catches her glancing up at him, as if trying to appraise him. Turning so that she may do so in a more forgiving light, he lights the last torch and twirls burning twig between his fingers.

'They say you fought with the Prince at Poitiers?'

He pretends that her clear voice startles him. 'Yes, I … Yes, I did.' Edmund walks to an empty hearth and throws the smouldering twig into the darkness. It gives off a defiant glitter against the darkness before being consumed by it. He lets his silence wash over her.

'But you try to forget it?' Her sleeve brushes against the back of his hand, as she too throws her twig into the darkness.

It will not be long before these hearths are lit for the night, for November is finally upon them. The cold seeps through every crack in the walls and around the windows, making the castle cold and clammy. For a moment, Edmund wishes he was in Dax in his tent where the brazier is always lit and the cot is lined with fur to keep him warm. Castles have their uses, but in winter they are iced over hell holes. He looks at Pascaline, she looks warm.

'We are taught that battle is chivalrous and to be admired, but the truth is it is grizzly, horrid and best forgotten.' Edmund paints on a sad expression. 'Except that I never will forget it. And now, here I am, ready to go into battle for his Grace once more.'

'You are brave.'

'Sometimes I think I am just stupid.' Edmund looks down at her, takes in her presence. 'So very stupid.'

'We all are, sometimes,' Pascaline says and takes a step back. 'Without a little stupidity or perhaps innocence, where would we all be?'

'War is never innocent,' he says. She turns her head, and Edmund thinks she looks forlorn. Perfect.

'Perhaps not, but if our minds are not innocent, we take to the field with malice.' Pascaline gives him a calm look. 'And surely that cannot be a good thing.'

Edmund offers her his arm, and without a second glance down the corridor that leads to her mistress' rooms, Pascaline takes it.

## 28 November 1366 – Bordeaux

'I knew you were a bad influence!'

'No more so than you, my Lady,' Edmund teases and nibbles her neck. 'Lurking in the shadows, waiting for a stranger …'

'You were no stranger.' Pascaline turns her head. 'The Princess had told me about your heroics and how the Prince favours your company.'

Edmund smiles languidly; here is the truth, she is his kind, looking for an opportunity. He cannot help but admire her brazen manner. Not very ladylike, but then if he wanted a swooning woman, he need not look too far. No, this is better, Edmund decides, this is an equal match.

'Did she?'

'I am no fortune seeker, Sire,' Pascaline says with dignity, but Edmund catches the flash of embarrassment that flees across her face.

'Then what are you?'

'I was looking for a good, honest man. Disloyalty runs deep in any court, not least this one; it pays to be careful.' She fingers her long braid.

Edmund looks at the two pins adorned with pearls that hold the braid in place. 'You do not look to be in need of financial aid, and so I shall trust you speak true when you say you were looking for a good man.'

Maybe someday you will find one, he adds in thought, but not tonight.

'I see how the Prince relies on you.' Pascaline gasps when he slides a hand up her dress. 'Except perhaps I was mistaken. Perhaps all you look for is someone with whom to pass time before the next raid.'

You should move away then, Edmund muses, but you do not. He smiles at her, his hand resting comfortably high on her thigh. He can feel a vein pulse beneath his palm. 'What if I am?'

'Then I shall go.' But still, she does not move.

Edmund's smile deepens. 'How would I act if I were a good man?'

'You would stop.'

He tilts his head, looks deep into her bright green eyes and squeezes her thigh ever so slightly. 'I have.'

She looks a little rattled, Edmund likes that; she should not know where she has him, not yet anyway. He will win her over, it is only a matter of time, but he enjoys the chase almost as much as he enjoys making war, and so he will not be insulted if she does run from him. A cat catches the mouse it needs.

Then he slides his hand away. 'What if I harbour the same concerns about you, my Lady? What if I do not want to waste my time with a woman who is only in it for a bit of pleasure?'

'I think you mistake me for a common whore.' Pascaline's eyes have turned hard, but she has not moved away from him, she even looks a little disappointed when he clasps his hands behind his back. 'Well?'

'Whores are rarely in their trade because they enjoy it, my Lady, or so I have been told. I have never had the need, or the inclination …'

'You mean; you have never had to resort to a whore, because there are always women willing to spread their legs to a knight?' Her voice has taken on a shrill undertone scratching Edmund's ears.

But she is also a fine woman, fierce and combatant. He will enjoy taking her. Will enjoy seeing her yield. He will have sport first though. 'Not at all. I left behind the love of my life. I came here to forget her, and I have looked upon no woman as I ever did her. Until I saw you.'

'Why did you leave her?' Pascaline's question attempts to veil a newfound urge to be special. 'If you love her as you claim to?'

'She was promised to someone else.' Edmund turns away. It is only a half lie, if you do not count the part about love. He never loved Elizabeth, but she is someone else's. 'I could no more claim her for my own than I could pluck a star from the sky and offer it to her. I was nothing compared to the man who had her name on a piece of paper.'

With a wily look, Pascaline steps back. 'You are a knight, high in the favour of the Prince. If you wanted to, you could have had him intervene. Change matters.'

'No one can change the decision of a King,' Edmund mutters at just the right pitch for her to lean in. 'Not even a Prince. I knew I was beaten, and so I came at my Prince's command to live out my life in his service.'

'Noble.' She looks a little more at ease now, but not yet convinced.

She has good sense, Edmund admits to himself, she has rare insight. It only makes him want her more, but he does not show it. No cat ever shows a mouse it is hunting for it before it is too late.

'It did not feel noble, it felt as if I was letting her down, letting myself down.' Edmund sits down on a bench and gives a wistful sight. 'All I could think was that if I stayed, I would have sullied her name as well as my own and that I would not do. Better to be safely tucked away in a distant corner of the kingdom than to watch her being paraded around by a man, I believe to be unworthy of her.'

Pascaline yields and sits down next to him, taking one of his hands in hers. 'I do not doubt that you were doing this to be chivalrous, but I think she must have been disappointed that you did not fight for her.'

'It was pointless. Win or lose, she would never be mine. It was better to declare defeat in advance and turn my attention, my energy, my whole soul to another cause.' Edmund almost smiles at his own performance; he could have been an actor. But then he would not get to hold a sword, forge his future in battle, slay enemies and collect gold in reward for his services. Instead, he looks askance at Pascaline, as if trying to decide if she is having him on. The effect is immediate.

'How long has it been since you have seen her?'

'Nearly three years.' Edmund sighs again. 'But I see her every night in my dreams. Or I did.' Her grasp firms around his hand, and he pretends insecurity. 'Until I saw you, I never thought I would forget her. I thought I would be tormented by the loss forever, that only on the battlefield might I, someday, be released from my chains.'

'Death is not the only solution,' Pascaline whispers. 'But if you think I am this easy to sway, you are much mistaken, Sire.'

Edmund squeezes her hands and then places them firmly in her lap. 'I know. And now you know that, tonight, I shall not be haunted by a love that can never be mine, but by the promise that I might love anew.'

He walks away without looking back. He does not have to. Pascaline's green eyes burn into the back of his head, and that is enough for now. Besides, he will not be alone tonight, providence has already seen to that. But it will be the last night that his little, fiery, redheaded friend warms his bed, of that he is certain.

# CHAPTER 10

## 16 December 1366 – Bordeaux

Laughing, they stumble into Edmund's room and he pulls her down on his lap, kissing the nape of her neck. The snow in her hair melts and it sticks to his cheek. He brushes it aside sending a shiver down her spine from the sprinkling of cold water.

Pascaline turns to straddle him, pulling her snow-soaked skirt up and then rearranging it. Her legs are warm and silken and when she leans in, he feels the strain of his hose. His breath turns jagged as he tries to control himself. He has fantasised about this moment for so long that if he were a lesser man, he would be unmanned that it has finally arrived. As it is, he looks up at her, a smile on his face.

Edmund has courted her for weeks, patiently waiting for her to surrender. Had it been any other woman, he would not have waited so long, but he has enjoyed the chase more this time. She is intense, she is clever and she is the first woman he thinks of as a worthy adversary.

They kiss with greed, her hands claw at his shirt, which peels away as a reluctant second skin. The heavy snowfall they got caught in has left him drenched, and he hears the slop when the shirt hits the bare wooden floor.

For a while, Pascaline stares at him, seemingly unable to take her eyes off his chest and Edmund straightens his back. There are wounds and bruises, some old and faded others fresh from the constant training with the other knights and soldiers. The Prince himself dispersed the big black bruise across his ribs with immense force not two days ago, and laughed when Edmund repaid him in kind. When she lifts her hand and traces his muscles along the side of the bruise, his skin tingles under her warm fingertips.

'I want to see you.'

Edmund lifts her from his lap. She steps in behind him, wrapping her arms around his waist, her wet sleeves prickling against his skin. The soaked leather straps resist her efforts, but Edmund stays still. Every graze boils his blood; he closes his eyes and waits. Pascaline sighs when the straps finally yield.

He kicks off his boots and his hose fall down and aside, reduced to a pile of wet leather and thin wool. For the first time, he is conscious about his nakedness. Pascaline invokes something within that no other woman ever has.

Stepping around the discarded boots, she stands before him, her hair curling at the ends as it begins to dry before the low burning fire. 'I have wanted to see this since I first clapped eyes on you.'

She steps close and her skirt brushes against his thigh, turning him hard. Her eyes blaze every time the flames flicker. Absentmindedly, Edmund wonders if this is what inspires minstrels to write ballads.

Slowly, he reaches for her and glides his hands over her back and up the front, caressing the tops of her breasts. Keen to get her out of the wet clothes for a look of his own, he pulls on a cord and she gasps. Her hands guide his to another cord and when he tugs, the bodice unravels. The linen underneath is see-through in some areas and her nipples are dark beneath the soft garment. Crossing her arms, she pulls down the thin fabric and turns around.

'There is a hook for the skirt.'

He lets his fingers wander down her naked back, exploring the shapes, following the dip of her spine. She is curvy, more so than her clothing reveals, and he is pleased. Let the other men have the skinny women, he favours a woman to be made of solid flesh; it makes her a better match for him somehow. When the layered skirt flows to the floor, she steps out of it with ease, straightening her back and craning her neck to look into his eyes.

Rather than rush forward, Edmund turns and stirs the fire, jamming a couple of logs into the embers. Not that he is cold, but the wet clothes need drying out and he wants her to wait for him, as he has waited patiently for her. After all, it has been more than a month. Longer than he has waited for any other woman.

Pascaline strokes his back, her hands gliding across his buttock before crawling around to his crotch. She pushes her body against him, and he can feel her hard nipples prick at his back.

'You are sure?'

'Never ask me again.' His words come out in blows, his pulse picks up its pace as he lifts her up and carries her to bed.

When he puts her down, her arms stay locked around his neck. She offers an indulgent smile as she spreads her legs and draws him down on top of her.

The room fades away in her soft, wet, warm embrace.

## 6 January 1367 - Bordeaux

The halls are decked out in seasonal greenery; ribbons and candles lend charm to a room filled with tapestries and carpets, the walls plastered white and painted in careful patterns. When the Prince and Princess took up residence in Bordeaux, they brought with them all manner of beautiful ornaments and furnishings all of which lend a distinctly English feel to the palace. Edmund is not quite sure, he likes it all that well.

Most of the dignitaries assembled are filing across the courtyard and into the semi-darkness of the church at the far end. Edmund detaches from a large group of young men and hangs back, stepping out of the way when James of Majorca walks past, followed by Richard of Armenia. Last is the king who has sought out the Prince for aid in regaining his throne, Peter of Castile. The most hated man in Christendom, if there is truth to the whispered rumours Pascaline delivers every night.

'How befitting, do you not think, Sir Edmund, that three kings should bear witness to the christening of a Prince born on Twelfth Night?'

Gossip has filled the halls and corridors, chambers and parlours of the palace ever since the Princess gave birth to a boy. Surely, the birth of another heir to the glorious Prince of England is a good omen for the forthcoming campaign. Still, Edmund cannot imagine that the birth of a child will in any way change the fate of thousands of soldiers, but he knows better than to say so.

'It certainly lends greatness to the ceremony,' Edmund says, careful of his words. 'You will stay long, my Lord?'

'As long as it takes, though my brother wishes me to remain here.' Langley stares after King Peter in whose wake two girls trail along, their heads held high. 'Did you know that King Peter plans to leave his girls here?'

'Not freely, I am sure.'

'Are you?' Langley breathes deep. 'I suppose it shows that you are kind-hearted, Sire. But I rather think, the King has offered the two girls up as a guarantee of his honour.'

'I did not know he had to prove his honour, my Lord.' Edmund is far from delighted to be called kind-hearted. But certainly, there are worse things to be accused of.

Grinning, Langley clasps a hand around Edmund's elbow for a moment, leaning in. 'Is that so? Well, you will soon be on your way, marching to ensure that Peter can once more sit on his throne. And believe me, he did not sit there very honourably from what I hear. I do not presume to know much of kingship, but I will say this, he had better redeem my brother for his great kindness. Or there will be hell to pay.'

'I leave in two days' time. The army is mustering. It will not be long before all the troops are gathered at Dax, and then we march for Castile.'

'I know. When her Grace came in to change for the dinner, she told us that the Prince could delay no further.' Pascaline rolls onto her back, her brown hair spilling across the rumpled bedding. 'Is it really necessary to go in such force?'

'A King goes to reclaim his throne. Would you send him off with a couple hundred soldiers and some old nags for mounts?'

She plays with the corner of a sheet, slowly twisting it. 'Let him crawl back on his hands and knees for all I care. He should never be allowed to return at all. He is no king, he is a madman.'

'Many madmen have served as rulers.' Edmund runs a hand over her chest. 'They do not govern alone.'

'Are you telling me that if, some day, our beloved Prince grew into the beast that is Peter, you would be able to control him? You would be able to stop him sending thousands to the slaughter?' She smiles, but her eyes are cold, calculating. 'Then I say; stop the Prince now. For I believe it will end in slaughter. Tell him to stay here with his wife and his sons. Tell him that there is no honour and glory to be won fighting for a King whose own people turned him away.'

Her passionate speech makes Edmund want her all over again. Her words may carry no real meaning, but to have a woman so fiercely defending her own ideas inspires deep desire in him. Still, he smiles, his hand resting on her breast. 'I have no such control.'

'You do.' She pushes his hand away. 'You are simply spoiling for war.'

'I am a knight, a soldier. What am I without fighting?'

'Fight the right war, the one that will secure all of France for England,' she breathes into his ear. 'Fight the war of King Edward, not of some fool who could not even keep his seat when a few men rose against him.'

Edmund keeps on smiling at her. 'The whole Castilian army rose against him; that is hardly a few men.'

Reaching for the wine pitcher they both know is empty, because they knocked it over in the heat of the moment not five minutes ago, Pascaline shakes her head. 'You have the right of it; the whole Castilian army rose against him. That means something, Edmund, do you not see? Are you so blinded by the idea of spilling blood that you do not care what it might mean?'

'And what is that, my Lady?'

Edmund knows she hates being called a lady. She is a bastard, same as him, born out of wedlock and, most assuredly, she has ascended well beyond her station in life, as he has. Now, one of them serves the Princess and the other the Prince of England.

Her lips curl back to reveal her even, white teeth. One is chipped, because when she was young, her father tried to have her, and when she knocked him out with a hammer, her stepmother spared no effort to return the favour, swinging a pot at her face. Lucky the pot did not do more damage, Edmund thinks idly, or we would not be here right now, and I would know much less of the man we are to fight for. Leave it to gossiping women to know more than all of the Prince's council combined.

'When the Prince marches his forces from this castle, he leaves us with nothing but a skeleton crew to ensure our safety.' She sighs and sits down on the bed, curling one leg under her. 'He will leave his wife and sons virtually defenceless.'

'Do they have anything to fear?' Despite his eagerness to go to war, for yes, Edmund does miss being on the field more than anything, something about her words makes him uneasy. 'What do you know?'

'You sit on the Prince's council and you do not know of the unrest in his own lands?' It is her turn to smile at him with cunning in her eyes. 'He lets no news slip to you of the many small rebellions in towns not far afield? Can I make of this that I am more important than you, for I know more of what is truly happening these days?'

Edmund crushes her laughter with a hard kiss and then holds her out. 'You are keeping secrets from me, Lady Pascaline.'

'Perhaps you had best punish me, Sire.'

He turns her and takes her roughly with little care if she enjoys it or not. When he is done, she turns and gives him an inscrutable look.

'Tell me what is happening.'

'Take a ride one of these days, Edmund, you need not go far to find out.' She shakes out her hair. 'They are not yet at the castle gates, but once you are gone, they will be soon enough. The people grow weary of men in power who care nothing for them. And when the weariness peaks, rebellion follows. It is as it ever was; no man is satisfied to be in chains.'

'None of the Prince's subjects are in chains.'

Pascaline begins to braid her hair, her fingers work without effort, her breasts lift when she tugs at stray strands. 'You have lived too long in luxury. The chains need not be real to be felt.'

For a moment, Edmund regrets telling her about his humble origins. He only did so to curry compassion but, now that he has her, he regrets many things. 'I forget nothing. A man makes his own fortune, as I have done. Any man can – and any woman, as you are a perfect example of.'

'Perfect?' She smiles at him as her hands secure the braid with pins of pearl and silver. 'If that is how you see me then I must be content; is that how it is? Edmund, do not be a fool. The Prince needs to turn his attention to his own people, not scamper off to fight another's war.'

'It is not his decision.' He is tiring of her, of their constant return to the same subject.

'No, it is the King's. But he is not here. He does not hear the rumours, feel the mood when he walks outside the walls.' She pulls at her shift, which is lodged beneath his leg, but Edmund does not stir. Annoyed she sits back down. 'I have to go; it is almost daybreak.'

'What would happen if the Prince did take a walk outside the walls? Do you think the people would approach him? Do you think anyone would dare speak up against him?'

'No. But you could make them speak,' she says and puts a hand on his cheek. 'With no effort at all, you could have them sing to you as birds do on a summer sky. I do not fear sending you into battle; you have proven yourself many times over. I fear for what will happen here when you are gone.'

This time, he lets her have her shift, and she leaves the room pulling it on. In the void she leaves behind, Edmund allows for his mind to wander. He expects nothing from her; this has been a fling. A way to pass time while the lords of the world decide when to play war. But now that the war is here, her words weigh more heavily on him than any thoughts of bloodshed ever have. Edmund opens the window and lets January caress his naked skin.

When I return, he resolves, I shall walk beyond the castle walls and learn for myself whether she is right.

## 5 February 1367 – Saint-Jean-Pied-de-Port

'You will go first with the vanguard.' The Prince nods to Gaunt and Chandos. 'I will follow with the main host and King Peter. Armagnac will bring the rear.'

'In this weather …' Chandos looks out of the window at the flurry of snow.

'It can be done.'

There is no room for discussion in the Prince's words and Chandos knows this well. So too does Gaunt, and yet he clears his throat. 'What if we are cut off?'

'We will assemble in Pamplona.' Fury lurks beneath the measured words.

'The snow …'

'The weather here is famous for its fickle nature, my Lord,' Chandos intervenes. 'We must simply endure what comes our way. I am certain that if your brother could find a better solution he would have, but this is our only option.'

Gaunt turns to his brother; the anger that flashes across his face is barely contained when he speaks. 'I would have a private word.'

'Very well.'

The men in the room disperse. Edmund steps out into the whipping wind and turns his face to the sky. The snow that assaults him does not come from above; it is last night's snow, which is thrashed about by the incessant storm. Perhaps Chandos is right, perhaps this is the only way.

His thoughts turn to a fortnight past when two royal Princes had spent almost an hour in agonizing silence staring out over the crowd while their men ate. The Prince had looked fierce and Gaunt haggard.

When Edmund had seized his moment to slip away, the two royal brothers had caught him in the shadows of the outside passageway between the hall and the stairs leading to the courtyard. In the narrow gallery, their great tempers had sparked and clashed.

'You have no idea what this might do! It is folly!' Gaunt's voice had been laced with impatience. 'I have told you time and again that this is no just cause! The stories they tell about the King are abominable. Why would you support him?'

'You of all people should appreciate that my motives are purely political!' the Prince had fired back. 'Besides, it is father who made the decision for me, so why cannot you support me? What on earth possessed you to go around the hall telling everyone that it was a mad idea?!'

'You are twisting my words! I said nothing that I have not already said to you!' Gaunt had lashed out. 'Father may have made the decision, but he has not offered a single coin to pay your soldiers, has he?! And nor will he! You are in it alone, and up to your neck in debt!'

'It is not a matter of money, not everything is, brother,' the Prince had seethed. 'Sometimes, I think that is all you care about! I undertake this venture for reasons you will never understand!'

'Low blow, your Grace, even for you.' Venom had coursed through Gaunt's words. 'Fortune does not always favour the brave!'

'No, but you will support me in future - and no mistake. And while you are here, you will do as I bid. Or I will send you back from whence you came with a letter to father telling him that you were of no use to me.'

'Father did not send me here to be another flatterer!' Gaunt had growled. 'God knows you have too many already. Father sent me here to make sure you did not act rash, but all I see is more of your notion that you are undefeatable.'

'Only because I am!' The Prince had begun prowling the narrow passage, and Edmund had had to push himself against the wet wall, the rough-cut stones jagged on his back. 'You were with me at Poitiers, you know what we can accomplish together.'

'No, I know what you can accomplish while I look on. But not this time.' Gaunt had stepped into the torchlight long enough for Edmund to make out concern and fury playing across it. 'I full well understand the politics, but I also know that we cannot hope to come back victorious when we are to pay all of your men as well as the many mercenaries you have enrolled. They will not settle with being let loose in the Castilian countryside.'

'And why not, brother?'

If Gaunt had picked up on the ice in the Prince's voice, he did not let on. 'Because it offers much less than the ripe French villages they are used to plundering.'

'I will make the payments. I have discussed it with King Peter, and he …'

'Will say and do anything to ensure you support his cause,' Gaunt had spat, stepping into the torchlight once more, his eyes black. 'Trust me when I tell you this, brother, I know a liar when I set eyes upon one. I know a man bankrupt who will make promises of gold and riches he has never possessed - and never will.'

'Know one, or are one?'

The Prince's words had cut like a knife, and Gaunt's face had hardened. 'No matter what you may think of me, know this, I understand good politics and good business. And this endeavour is neither!'

Before the Prince could retort, Gaunt had turned and plunged into the darkness of the passageway leading to the bedrooms. The Prince had run a hand through his dark-golden hair, distress clear on his handsome face. It was the first time Edmund had ever seen the Prince look doubtful, concerned even. He had his orders direct from the King and had no choice but to keep his word, but Edmund had sensed that if the Prince had been cut from a different cloth, he might well have acknowledged the truth in Gaunt's words and reneged on his promise. As it stood, the Prince would rather sacrifice all his men than his honour. And he had been successful in the past with numbers much smaller than these.

After a while, the Prince had calmed down and leaned against the railing, staring into the darkness, the moon a sliver on the horizon. 'How much did you hear?'

Edmund started. He had believed himself unnoticed. What to say? How to explain without giving away his own secret.

'Everything.' Edmund of Langley had stepped into the torchlight further down the corridor, his slender frame casting thin shadows.

'He grows ever more restive.' The Prince had turned to face his younger brother. 'Can I send him home?'

'Father would be displeased. You know what that is like.' Langley had leaned against the railing next to the Prince. In the flickering light their mirror images were only marred by the years parting them. 'Best keep him with you for the time being; he has been of use before and will be again. If nothing else, he is an obedient son and will carry out our father's orders, even if he disagrees with them. There is truth in his angry words, as you well know.'

'I cannot recant on my promise.' The Prince had once more run his hand through his hair. A tell-tale sign that he was more deeply upset than he let on. 'There is no other way but to move forward. Ever forward, brother. For Saint George and for victory.'

'And to put a vain and dreadful man back on his throne,' Langley had said and yawned. 'How I wish all of you would look beyond your own follies at the people whose lives hang in the balances.'

'I do.' The Prince had clasped a hand on Langley's shoulder, his face kind. 'I truly do, dear brother. But father is convinced that we cannot afford to let a usurper sit the throne, no matter the cost.'

'You can find the money to pay?'

'I will borrow against all that I have.' The Prince had begun steering Langley into the shadows away from Edmund. 'After all, Peter has placed his two greatest jewels into my possession. And there they will stay, until he has repaid his debt to me.'

'Gemstones made of flesh and bone – a poor substitute to the real thing.' Langley had given a little laugh.

The Prince's voice had floated back to Edmund from the darkness. 'Perhaps, but I have a mind to hand them over to someone who will know how to make the most of them. A true merchant.'

Blinking at the memory, Edmund turns towards the camp, his body aching in the cold. There can be no rest until the Prince has won his battle, but for his part, Edmund agrees with Gaunt; this is not a noble cause. Dangling a couple of girls in front of the Prince is a poor way to repay him for the sacrifice he is about to make, and for the Prince to dangle the girls before someone else is even worse.

Outside, the storm lessens, the flurry of snow recedes and, in the milky dawn, it seems at least God is on their side. Edmund rides in the vanguard and makes it across with ease.

But the rest of the army is less fortunate. Much less fortunate. And when they finally re-assemble, it is only to be cast even further into the abyss.

# CHAPTER 11

## 26 July 1392 – Westminster Palace

Pouring water into their cups, Gaunt looked long and hard at Edmund. 'No more wine for either of us, though I suspect that, before you are done, we will both yearn to be drunk beyond remembering. But that will not do.'

'I agree. I would tell my tale sober for it is a sobering tale, or at least it was for me.' Edmund washed his mouth in the cold water and looked out at the moonless night. The sounds from the tourney field had finally died down. 'Do you believe that we are born to a destiny that none of us can change?'

'How long have we known one another?'

Edmund grimaced. 'Too long for me to care to remember, my Lord.'

'Then you will know that I believe we forge our own destinies. What lies between a man's beginning and end is hardly given by God, it is what we make of it. What we chose to fight for, and what we do not.' Again, Gaunt rubbed his shoulder. It seemed to be a constant nuisance these days. 'Do not mistake me, Sire, for I pray daily and I have raised a pious son of whom I am proud. But when it comes to success or failure, I prefer to hold the reins myself, for who knows what will happen if I do not. You and I have both seen what happens when you put your life in the hands of destiny.'

'Much might have been different if only your brother had the same view of destiny as you do, my Lord.'

Gaunt laughed, the sound hard and without humour. 'Yes indeed. I have often wondered what might have happened if we had not gone to Castile. What kind of kingdom we might have today.'

'It would have been very different, I think.'

'Do you?' Gaunt swirled the water in his cup. 'He is the son of a man for whom God and destiny were one and the same. I do not think the common man would have felt the difference.'

Edmund wondered at this for a while, Gaunt labouring silently at his shoulder.

'If the Prince had taken your advice, chances are he would still be alive.'

'No. Chances are he would have gone on some other hare-brained crusade, killing, hacking, burning and bullying.' Gaunt's words came out without regret. 'It was who he was. Peace and government were ill-suited to him.'

'Perhaps you are right.'

'The French would have rebelled sooner or later,' Gaunt said and finally let his shoulder rest. 'Castile was simply an excuse too good for them to pass up. Had you been in their place, you would have thought and acted as they did. My father warned my brother, I warned my brother, that the free companies harrying the French countryside should have been managed, kept under control, given other tasks to do or, better yet, disbanded altogether. Of course, the French would know that the only places to avoid the constant abuse were my brother's lands. Any idiot would have worked that out.'

Edmund shook his head. 'I was far away and had my own concerns to deal with.'

'Your woman told you, before we left for Castile, that the population was rebelling, and you did nothing.' Gaunt stroked his beard. 'That should have been your sole concern, Sire.'

Edmund buried a sneer. 'We all left, and not all of us returned the same men we were, before we went.'

## 4 April 1367 – Nájera, Castile

The barber surgeon draws the red-hot blade from the fire and Edmund turns his head away. The wood between his teeth is marked by hundreds of dents, and yet it is smooth to the touch. Not even the strong wine he has gulped down helps him when the blade sears his skin. He bites down so hard that his world darkens and the bite only serves for him not to gnaw off his tongue. He groans like a wounded animal.

'Once more, Sire.' The coarse man in the leather apron dips the blade back into the fire, blood sizzling in the flames.

Edmund snorts; at least the barber enjoys his work.

All hope that he is immune by now to the work of the blade burns away when the barber presses the glowing steel into his skin. In a flash, the blinding white pain crumbles into a soft black blanket that wraps itself around him.

Edmund opens his eyes and stares into the darkness. Around him, men groan and whimper. There may be honour in battle, but there is none in the aftermath. The Baron and Lord Gaunt were right; we should not have come.

With a grunt, Edmund rolls onto his side and tries to get up; what little relief sleep brought him vanishes in the glittering pain that engulfs his arm. He falls back, flexing his hand. Thank God it still works, his fingers are thick and useless, but they bend to his will and move a little.

His left arm is bound tight to his body, and Edmund gropes around with his free hand until he feels the wooden frame of the cot. He swings his leg over the side and, with a tug, he manages to get up, even if the dark explodes in white spots before his eyes. An acrid taste lines his mouth.

He sits still until his head stops swimming; his eyes closed against the dark. Ghosts whisper at the edge of reason.

A flickering light glows orange behind Edmund's eyelids. With an effort, he shakes off the dreamscape and whispers: 'Water?'

A hand offers him a cup to drink from, but what runs over his tongue is so foul, Edmund spits it out with a hoarse groan. He curses at the taste and the pain running through his wounded arm.

'It's all we've got,' a cross voice barks. 'If you'll not have it, there's wounded all around who will.'

'You cannot give this to any of the men,' Edmund protests, but the flickering light vanishes and he is left in darkness once more. 'Is anyone there?'

## 10 April 1367 – Burgos

Time has turned to dust. Edmund licks his dry lips and looks about, but in the darkness, all he can make out are cots and contorted shapes on top of them.

The tent flaps open and a soldier with the Prince of Wales' black and white emblem on his chest looks in, his presence illuminated by a torch. 'Sir Edmund?'

'Yes.' Edmund swallows back a taste of copper.

'The Prince is asking for you. Are you able to ...?'

Trying to get up makes Edmund's head swim and he reaches out for support, angry at his own feebleness. 'Anywhere but here. If the Prince requires my presence ...'

The soldier offers a shoulder, and Edmund leans on him. 'It'll keep, I'm sure.'

'Being crushed by a horse is not something that passes in a day, as the Prince well knows,' Edmund says, his legs are weak and his feet are clay. 'Nor is the slash of a dull blade. Best get it over with. I can rest later. The Prince must be told that the water offered to the sick should be thrown out.'

'What's the matter with it?' the soldier asks as they move from the tent, creeping through the warm darkness slow as two drunken toads.

'It is foul.' Edmund can still taste the putrid warm fluid, which bore no resemblance with water, but he cannot tell if he tasted it an hour ago or a week. 'None of the men should have to drink it.'

'It's all we've got,' the soldier says. 'Some say, the Castilians poisoned the wells.'

Grasping for a sense of time, Edmund's brain is slow to work out what he hears. 'What?'

'Bouts of sickness've broken out, men shitting themselves half to death. What spouts from them's more red than brown.' The soldier points into the darkness with the torch. 'We keep 'em out there, away from camp.'

Something in the soldier's voice gives Edmund pause. His brain tries to re-fire. 'What day is this?'

The soldier skirts a tent and turns right. 'We've been here a week, at least, but I've lost track of the days.'

'Where is here?'

'Burgos. The Prince's waiting for King Peter to pay his debt.' The soldier stops before a massive tent illuminated by several fires and signals for the grim guard to step aside. The moment Edmund is forced to stand on his own, he groans at the weight of his wounded arm and his unsteady legs. He has to pause for a moment before he can walk on.

He bends his head and takes a tentative step into the bright, roasting light. It takes a while for him to adjust to the brilliance in the tent. The loss of blood and lack of proper water has weakened him more than he realised. The idea that he has been in the carts that carry the wounded bites into his pride and makes him shake.

It takes a while for Edmund to take in the sight. 'Your Grace.'

In the corner, Gaunt sits on a low stool, his fingers steepled under his chin. His gaze never leaves his brother's face. 'Sir Edmund.'

The Prince lies on a feather mattress, his back propped up with cushions. He turns his head, and Edmund sees sweat beading on his brow. His blue eyes are dull.

'Sire.' The Prince coughs. 'How fare you?'

'The surgeon says I will live. I can certainly feel every bone in my body.' Edmund totters and looks around for something to steady himself on. He hates to feel weak and, even more, he hates for others to see his weakness. It is a blessing that the Prince looks even worse than he does himself. 'And you, your Grace?'

'I suffer with my men, but without complaint.' There is finality in the Prince's words. 'You may have heard that our ally is struggling to repay us for our services?'

'Sir Edmund has been carried in the sick wagon,' Gaunt observes, 'I doubt there was much talk of our financial woes among the dying.'

The Prince harks another cough and wipes his brow. His hand shakes. 'It makes little difference. Half the men are shitting themselves to death! Peter is a lying thief who has taken money and men from me and offers nothing in return! As soon as I can get up, I shall bring my justice to him in the form of a blade.'

Gaunt rises and snaps his fingers to summon a servant. 'Beware the fever does not cloud your judgement, brother.'

'You must be pleased, John, it is as you foretold!' the Prince growls. 'Peter deceived me.'

'Us,' Gaunt corrects and turns to the servant. 'Wine for his Grace.'

The servant's eyes flicker between Gaunt and the Prince. 'There is none, my Lord.'

'What do you mean?' The danger in Gaunt's voice makes the servant duck. 'No wine for Prince Edward of England? My ears must deceive me.'

'No wine for anyone, my Lord. There's water but it's …' The servant shivers when Gaunt takes a step forward.

'There is no clean water,' Edmund says, well aware how thin his voice sounds. He clears his throat, forces power back into his words. 'What I tasted might have been cold but it was also putrid. It should not be served to anyone. Fetch some but have a care that the Prince does not drink it.'

'Too late.' The Prince grabs his stomach and groans.

'You will fetch wine, ale, anything that can pass as drink for his Grace!' Gaunt sneers at the servant, 'or I will have your head for a bedpost ornament!'

The servant dashes through the tent flaps, and the Prince gives a weak laugh. 'How do you presume he will accomplish that when all we have is sullied water?'

'You are royalty,' Gaunt says and resumes his seat. 'There is always something to be done for royalty.'

'The water could be boiled.' Edmund sinks to his knees; he has no strength to stand, even shame cannot keep him on his feet. 'The cook in the kitchens where I grew up did so when clean water was scarce. Maybe it will help, maybe not, but if it is all we have …'

Scratching his cheek, Gaunt looks at the Prince whose fever-ridden eyes drill into Edmund's soul. 'It cannot get any worse. Try it.' The order is for

Gaunt and he rises reluctantly. 'Oh, and brother, have a care to ensure there is enough boiled water to give all the men, not just the royal ones.'

Edmund watches Gaunt slip from the tent and tries to stand up, but his legs do not obey. He is so angry with himself for looking weak that he could scream. Instead, he turns his attention to the Prince. 'You summoned me, your Grace?'

'Not for a discussion of drinks.' The Prince forces a pained smile that brings fresh beads to his brow, 'although, had I known you were such a fountain of wisdom, I should have kicked you awake myself.'

'I cannot guarantee that it will make a difference, your Grace. Not once the sickness has taken hold.'

'I must send word to my father.' The Prince winces as he turns in the bed; his face is tinged green in the candlelight. 'I have despatched messengers before, but this I cannot risk putting into anyone's hands. My message must be brought directly from my mouth to my father's ear.'

Edmund gestures towards the tent flaps. 'Why not send your brother, your Grace?'

'Too many reasons. For one, I need him to continue putting pressure on Peter to honour our arrangement. No one does that quite as well as John.' The Prince tries to readjust himself and sweat pours down his face. 'Can you sit a horse?'

'I think so.' Edmund wills his legs to obey; his whole body shakes, but he manages to rise. 'If you tie me to it.'

'Good.' The Prince beckons him to approach, sweat streaming down his face. 'You will have men at your disposal, some provisions, though God knows we have little enough to spare, and money to change horses along the way. My message must be relayed only to my father, no one else.'

'Yes, your Grace.'

'And pray that your boiled water does not kill even more men.' The Prince may be in the grips of death, but his eyes have turned hard and cold. 'Now, this is what I want you to tell him …'

Edmund has to bend close to the sickbed and swallows back bile. The sweet smell of death on the Prince's breath and Edmund's own feeble body is colluding to prove that he cannot undertake the royal command. He reaches out to steady himself on the bedpost but misses it and sinks to the ground once more. Fortunately, the Prince does not notice, and Edmund is close enough to hear the whispers. When his gaze falls upon the Prince's bedpan, he snaps his eyes shut. The sides are red and brown, the liquid as thin as water.

It is some time before the Prince is done and falls back onto his pillows. His eyes shut themselves against the world, and Edmund crawls to the end of the bed where he manages to haul himself up. When he turns, he knocks his bandaged arm into a small table and is winded. He stands there for a while, his eyes closed against a swimming world. When the feeling subsides, Edmund scuttles to the opening, clutching his arm.

'What did my brother ask, Sire?' Gaunt is standing outside the tent, a sweating servant by his side carrying a vat of water, a small side of ham tucked under his arm. Gaunt turns his head and hisses, 'Go inside and attend his Grace.'

Compared to the burning heat in the tent, the air is cool and it kisses away some of Edmund's fevered thoughts, but he is far from himself. 'That I ride with news to the Princess.'

'Any messenger can do that.'

'And the Prince chose me, my Lord.'

Stroking his uncommonly stubbled cheeks, Gaunt looks about. 'What did he really want, Sire?' Oppressed anger seeps into the question.

'He wishes to reassure the Princess that he will recover and return as soon as King Peter pays his debt.' Edmund's words sound muffled. How difficult it is to lie, with mud for brains.

'Which he will never do. Hell may freeze over, purgatory turn to dust and, even then, King Peter will never repay his debt. He has no funds, he never did.' Gaunt's practical tone is almost unbearable. 'I said as much to my father and brother, but they always know better. How wonderful it must be to know better.'

'His Grace told me to look to you for provision, men and horses.' Edmund fights to keep velvet faintness at bay. His eyes refuse to stay open. 'And money.'

Gaunt laughs and clasps a hand on Edmund's bandaged shoulder. 'Does he now? Well, then I had better hop to and fulfil his every wish! You mean to ride out now, in the middle of the night?'

'At dawn, my Lord,' Edmund whispers through the fresh pain. If Gaunt can unman him with but at touch, imagine what others might do right now.

The alarm that soars through his body awakens Edmund. He cannot abide being weak. 'I am to ride at dawn.'

'I too have a message that you can carry.'

Gaunt steers Edmund towards the heart of the camp where smouldering fires waft mouth-watering promises of fried meat. If he could only have a little sustenance, he will feel more himself. But Gaunt pushes him on relentlessly.

'This message you may deliver to my father. For surely that is your true destination, and you would do better than to lie to me, Sire, when I might be all that stands between you and certain death.'

# Part 2

# Reunion

# CHAPTER 12

## 9 June 1367 – Westminster Palace, London

'It sounds impossible, Sire, that my sons should be in such dire straits.' The King glares at Edmund. 'The last news we had was that Edward had won a great battle and reinstated King Peter. Now, you will have me believe that my son lies sick from some strange ailment, and King Peter has reneged on his promise?! You would have me doubt the word of a king?'

The roaring silence that ensues rattles everyone in the room. Edmund bows low and pushes back a flicker of anger that the King does not adhere to his son's own wish that Edmund's message be spoken in private. He is well aware that to displease the King is dangerous to say the least.

'I am but a messenger, your Grace.'

'Messenger? Ha! Not only have you relayed my son's predicament in a way that I refuse to accept, you also wish me to believe that his wife has to muster her own army to keep MY dominion safe?! What madness is it you travel with, Sire? Has the battle unsettled your wit?!'

Scattered laughter tells Edmund that while the King might not trust his message, most of the other men in the room find his tale all too easy to believe. Since he left Aquitaine, thoughts of the distraught Princess and the sick Prince have haunted his days and nights alike. He fears in earnest that England will lose its most promising heir before long, and that the Princess cannot stall the fierce French attacks on the Prince's supremacy. If only there was some way of convincing the King that all of this is indeed the truth. But more than anything, the King's dismissal of Edmund's account leaves him angry.

'Well??'

'Your Grace, I fought in this battle, I saw with my own eyes the usurper Trastámara flee before the Prince. I do not deny that we won a great victory that day, nor that, the very next day, the Prince reinstated King Peter.' Of course, Edmund had not seen the end of the battle, nor the Prince ride into the capital as victor and conqueror. Edmund had been busy dancing with death and, at times, he still feels death waiting for another turn.

He shakes his head and looks at the King. 'But since then, there has been no word from King Peter, though Lord Gaunt harries him every day. Even his efforts are fruitless.'

Edmund sees dismay in the King's eyes and something else that he cannot decipher. 'The Prince's army has fallen sick, and many of the men spared in battle have lost their lives to a sickness that is too degrading to speak of.'

When the King's glare turns hot, Edmund stands his ground; he has defeated death, he can withstand a mortal King's rage. 'I have no reason to lie to you, your Grace. Why would I? I saw the Prince glistening from sweat, pale and sick; he could hardly sit up, let alone drink or eat when he sent me from his camp with his plea. To be taken straight to you.'

'If indeed you were to take it straight here, Sire,' William of Wykeham says and earns a benevolent nod from the furious King. The newly appointed Chancellor of England is quick to proceed, 'how is it then that you also bring news from the Princess?'

'The safest route to England sent me through Bordeaux. Her Grace knows not that her husband is ill, he was adamant that only you should know, my King,' Edmund says and seethes inside that the upstart Wykeham, who has no doubt never seen battle, should be allowed to question Edmund's actions. 'But somehow, the French have caught word that the Prince is held up in Navarre, and they grow ever more restless. Whatever you may imagine, I say you can multiply it by ten if not more. The situation is growing out of control.'

'You are saying that I cannot keep the peace in my own lands?' The quiet tones are more unsettling than the roars, and Edmund shrinks back a little when the King makes a fist. 'You are saying I am impotent?'

'I only relay what messages I was tasked to deliver. Your Grace.' Edmund earns a couple of nods from the nobles standing around him. 'King Peter is on his throne but will not – perhaps cannot – pay his dues to the Prince. The soldiers' camp is overrun with sickness and foul water, food is scant and many have abandoned the cause since it became known that the Prince cannot pay them. They will not stay for a pauper.'

'Who can begrudge them?' someone shouts at the back of the room and several other men nod.

'I CAN!' the King rumbles, and the room falls silent.

Edmund's blood thunders through his veins, the King must be made to understand, to believe the Prince's predicament. He must send assistance, men or money to support the Princess in her struggle to keep English sovereign land safe. Not for the first time on his journey to the English court, Edmund curses the day he decided not to pay heed to Pascaline's warnings before the army left for Castile. To have lost out to a woman only makes the sting worse.

'Sir Edmund is an honest man,' a familiar voice says. 'What cause has he to lie to you, your Grace? We must believe him, we must act. With rebellion at the Princess' doorstep, and the Prince taken ill, we cannot sit idly by. It would be to own defeat before battle commences.'

The King's head snaps around. 'Is that so?'

'I can muster five hundred men within a week and send them to aid the Princess, if needs be,' Baron Mowbray says ignoring the King's glare. 'We can levy taxes to pay for the protection of Aquitaine and Bordeaux. To pay the Prince's troops.'

'No.' Baron Latimer steps forward. 'No taxes are to pay for this war. That was the agreement, your Grace.' He bows low to the King who nods.

'Latimer has the right of it; you agreed that the Prince was to support our ally in reclaiming his rightful throne. But England cannot pay for this war. That must fall to King Peter, for services rendered. I am sure the wording is not lost on any of you, after all, it was your Parliament who drew up the agreement.'

While many of the men in the King's reception room avert their eyes, the King leans back stroking his beard. 'You all believe Sir Edmund?'

'I speak only for myself. I know Sir Edmund to be loyal and honest.' Baron Mowbray puts a hand on Edmund's shoulder. 'If he says this is how it is, then I believe that the Prince is in trouble. I have heard rumours that his men have begun absconding. It is well known that warfare in the south can bring illness. And if the rumours have already reached our shores, I dare not imagine what the true state is. It also means that the French know what has befallen our Prince.'

'He will recover,' the King says, but his voice betrays him. 'Very well, I call upon Parliament to decide what is to be done. You will say that we cannot levy taxes in England, but perhaps we can in the Prince's dominions.'

'Only the Prince can do so, your Grace,' Wykeham objects and is silenced by a glance.

'The Prince is indisposed and, as King, I have the right to act as I see fit. In all my dominion.'

Edmund clears his throat, today, duty weighs heavily on his shoulders. 'The Prince levied taxes before we left.'

'And?'

'If it was a mere matter of money, your Grace, the Princess would have levied more taxes to fund her own soldiers.' In the face of the King's white-hot fury, Edmund finds new strength. 'There is no more money.'

'No more that they will give,' the Baron chimes in.

'No, my Lord,' Edmund says to Mowbray, 'there simply is no more money. If we are not careful, the Prince's own people will be forced to join the French uprising.'

'A rebellion?' The incredulous words seep around the room. 'You fear a rebellion.'

'I believe it is at the Princess' doorstep.' Finally, Edmund sees a little defeat in the King's expression and he is pleased. 'If you leave her to fend for herself, I fear that the French will overrun her and take her and the two boys prisoner. They will be the bargaining chips the French have been looking for to erase the debt they owe to England.'

The King lifts a hand. 'Latimer! Call for Parliament to convene. I will have this resolved quickly!'

While most of the men gathered still struggle to understand the enormity of Edmund's words, Baron Latimer half-runs from the room to the notes of hushed, incredulous voices.

'Leave us!' The King rises and his advisors bow as they leave, most with disbelief painted on their faces.

'Baron Mowbray, Sir Edmund, stay.' A few stragglers stare at the Baron for a moment longer before leaving, but if Mowbray is unsettled, he does not show it.

In the silence that descends when the doors close behind the last courtiers, the King's face grows old, and he slouches heavily on the throne. 'I regret now that I did not do as you asked, as my son asked. He was right to want to keep this between us. But he was wrong that I might aid him without the backing of Parliament. Though I confess that, perhaps, it is better this way, now that they know what has come to pass, they must want to send aid to my son – money, men, provisions.'

'I fear it will not be as easy as that, your Grace,' Mowbray says quietly. Without the other noblemen to fill the big reception chamber, it feels suddenly vast and cold. None of the tapestries can hide the chill that emanates from the walls. Mowbray continues: 'I know that many of us will muster for the Prince, but for a united Parliament to go back on the agreement we sent to the Prince before this happened …'

'The Lords of England will not support their Prince?' The King strokes his long beard, worry dancing on his cheeks. 'You think I was wrong to say that he must assist King Peter.'

'We were all taken in by the King of Castile.' There is something smooth and unbearable in Mowbray's courtier manners. 'Perhaps Parliament was wise to decide to support the campaign, but not send money.'

'Wise?!' Some of the King's rage stirs and he gets up. 'It was the most unwise thing any of my Parliaments have ever done! He is an ally. We cannot afford to lose allies.'

Mowbray inclines his head. 'Had this been a battle to secure the crown of France for you, Parliament would have sent money too, your Grace, but to take back the throne for a man no subject will ever grow to respect … It was impossible to endorse with English gold.'

Pacing the dais, the King falls silent once more, and Mowbray nods to Edmund. Time to leave the King to his thoughts, perhaps he can unearth some solution that has not yet presented itself to anyone else. But Edmund doubts it. The Prince is broke and broken, the Princess faces rebellion alone and, if the Baron is right, once Parliament convenes no one in England will lift a finger to assist either of them.

'There is one more thing, your Grace,' Edmund says and produces a crumbled letter patched with sweat. 'A message from my Lord Gaunt.'

'John?' The King stares at the letter, reluctance gleaming in his eyes. 'What is it?'

'I do not know, your Grace.' Edmund hands the letter to a royal servant. In truth, Edmund had slept while Gaunt's pen had scratched its way over the paper. 'He asked only that I deliver this to you – and that you read it without delay.'

'He fought with Edward?' There is curiosity in the King's question.

'As you commanded, your Grace.' Edmund picks at a loose thread on his tattered cloak. Against the splendour of court, he looks like a beggar. The realisation sours his next words. 'And he has been by the Prince's side ever since. Badgering King Peter to pay, seeing that the Prince is fed and his fires tended.'

'Not sick too, then?'

'No, your Grace. Although I cannot attest if he has not been. I was injured during the battle and was forced to ride in the sick carriage for some time.' Edmund feels the heat of shame. 'But I have heard nothing to suggest that Lord Gaunt had been ill. And he was in good health when I left.'

The King breaks the seal and reads, his eyes narrowed to make out the tiny script. 'Leave me.'

As they bow low, Edmund notices the King's hand tremble.

❧ ❧ ❧ ❧

'While I admit that your news has unsettled me, I am glad to see you.' Baron Mowbray leads the way through the maze that is Westminster Palace. 'That you survived another battle and are safe here in England is a great relief to me.'

'Thank you, my Lord. I too am glad to see you.'

Not once on his long journey did Edmund consider what it would be like to return to England. Or even wonder if perhaps he would see the

Baron again. After all, they parted on good terms, so why does the thought of what Mowbray might say next suddenly weigh heavily on Edmund?

He shakes off the unfamiliar feeling and clears his throat. 'How is your family?'

'I have been here so long, I hardly remember what my own home looks like,' the Baron admits as they cross a small courtyard, a tingling fountain the only ornament besides a plain wooden bench. 'The King has had many troubles these past months, and Parliament has been hard at work.'

Edmund sits down next to the Baron and relishes in the quiet of the courtyard after the hiss and growl of the throne room. 'This has not been a pleasant journey. But now that my task is fulfilled, I find I am no more at rest than when I left the Prince.'

'Is he very ill?'

Leaning the back of his head on the sun-kissed wall, Edmund closes his eyes and once more sees the Prince before him. 'I fear that he may never recover. For all I know, he may have died well before I arrived here.'

Baron Mowbray sighs and jostles beside Edmund. 'Tell me everything.'

'The battle was much as the one we fought together. As luck would have it – if you believe in such a thing – Henry of Trastámara had learned nothing from the Frenchmen's disastrous attempts at Poitiers. You were right when you said that, as long as the enemy continues to underestimate us, we will win.' Edmund smiles; the enemy's retreat had been appalling and amusing at the same time. 'Perhaps he thought he was unbeatable, but he was not. He escaped with his life only through the resourcefulness of some of his advisors.'

Edmund rubs his injured shoulder. 'I was crushed beneath a horse and took a lance to the shoulder. It had to be burned, but infection had already spread and for almost a week I was unconscious.'

Out of the corner of his eye, Edmund sees the Baron fold his hands. 'Go on.'

'By the time I came to, camp had been set up near Najera. Half the men were shitting themselves to death.' Edmund finally looks at the Baron. 'When I woke, I thought I had gone to Hell. I had not thought to find Hell here on earth.'

'What happened?'

'Some say that Trastámara had poisoned the wells, but you know as well as I that food and water runs out quickly. The water they offered me was foul.' Edmund sneers at the memory. 'I told the Prince that a cook once explained to me that foul water could be drunk once it was boiled.'

'And you believe it to be true?'

Leaning forward, Edmund clasps his hands around his knees, his left arm feels thin and scrawny, but at least he has use of it once more. 'Whatever they have done since I left, they must have moved camp. There was no food, the land was trampled down and, since we went back the way we came, any spare provision that might have been, we had on the way out. The woods were hunted bare, the fields burned.'

The Baron stares at the fountain, 'How many will be left behind, I wonder.'

'They were dying by the dozen even before I was sent away.' Edmund cares not for the flash of remembrance. It is raw against the serene backdrop of this quiet little garden. 'They wasted away, the stench, the despair, I know I have to go back, but now that I am here, far away from it all, I cannot help but wish I might somehow be spared.'

'I am going home soon. Come with me.' Rising slow to spare his old war injury, the Baron looks at Edmund. 'The King can do without you for now, and I know that a visit to Nottingham may put many things right.'

Elizabeth, Edmund thinks, she must not have said a word. Hiding a smile, he rubs his eyes. 'But can the King spare you? When he has just summoned Parliament.'

'However much I wish that Parliament will convene swiftly, I know that it will be at least a fortnight before enough members have assembled to make a decision. Until such a time, the King has already granted me permission to travel north, and I shall prevail upon him the necessity of you going with me. Until we have made a decision, there is nothing for you to do here,' the Baron says, 'unless you prefer to stay at court?'

'With an angered King and a whole host of nobles who do not care to be reminded of the Prince's situation?' Edmund laughs. 'Perhaps some other time.'

The Baron holds open a door to a narrow passageway and steps in behind Edmund. 'The King is not the man he used to be. Perhaps I should not speak thus, especially in this vipers' pit, but there it is. He is heavily burdened, and I think your message from the ailing Prince has made obvious to him how much he relied on his son to come and rule beside him.'

'He has spoken of this?'

'He has little choice now,' the Baron mutters as a couple of servants bustle by. 'He has to regain his power over all of his land, and soon, or we will be lost.'

'Perhaps what Lord Gaunt wrote will settle some of the King's grievances.'

Stopping under an archway, the Baron looks at Edmund with earnest curiosity. 'You truly believe than any message from Gaunt will bring solace? For I do not.'

# CHAPTER 13

## 14 June 1367 – Framlingham, Nottingham

'Edmund!'

His sudden urge to curl her up into a hard embrace that will last forever shocks him. In the sunlight, her hair sparkles golden and her cheeks are flushed. Beneath Elizabeth's beauty lurks something new. Edmund bows low to her, and a whisper of dismay runs across her face.

'What news?'

'The Prince won back King Peter's crown.' He clears his throat, now that she is so close; his body reacts to her scent and old promises made in the dark. 'You husband will join us here as soon as can be, and then you will know more. Parliament …'

'Oh? That is kind of you to convey when a letter from my husband would have been sufficient. He has been long detained by Parliament and so I did not expect him.' She gestures towards the great hall. 'Nor did I expect you returned to us, but I am well pleased that you are here. Will you eat with us? The meal is about to begin.'

He bows again, and she leads the way into the great hall. It is as if he has stepped into the past. The coats of arms soar high above his head and the trestle tables are filled to the last inch, men sitting shoulder by shoulder. A servant skirts him and half-runs towards the dais where Elizabeth takes her seat, surrounded by her girls. The little golden angel at the end of the table glances up and sends him a brilliant smile.

'Sire!' A few of the Baron's men look up and raise their hands in greeting. 'How was the war?'

'Grizzly.' Edmund sits down some way from the dais. Elizabeth only glances in his direction once before turning to her daughters. The one in the middle gestures wildly, her brown curls bouncing around her face.

'Where's M'lord?' A broad-chested, red-haired man shovels thick stew onto his plate. 'Wasn't he to come home?'

'The King had some last-minute assignments. But he should arrive in a day or two.' Edmund tucks into the food, the long journey to England had afforded but meagre meals and even though he had fed well during the crossing, the ghost of famine still lurks in his stomach. 'His Grace has also called Parliament to assemble in all haste.'

'Why?'

Edmund realises that the hall has gone quiet and looks up. 'You have had no news?'

A couple of the men shrug and others shake their heads. Edmund wonders how none of the gossip at court has found its way to Nottingham. Though it came with him, he lingered in London for a couple of days, waiting for the Baron to join him. Edmund only journeyed north when he had word that Mowbray would be delayed. The rumours have had plenty of time to get here well before he did.

He accepts a cup of wine and steals a glance at the dais; Elizabeth is staring intently at her children. 'The Prince won the battle …'

The red-haired man scratches his belly. 'But not the war?'

'King Peter's cause has nothing to do with our war.' Edmund turns and looks at Elizabeth; she knows, he is sure she knows. 'The Prince has fallen sick.'

A thick, heavy silence descends upon the hall, the sweet and spicy smell of the stew evaporates, and all Edmund can smell is fear. The Baron should have been here to make the announcement, Edmund thinks, a fine thing that he left this task to me.

'How sick?'

Looking down the table, Edmund recognises Elizabeth's cousin Ranulph FitzAlan, who has grown into a slender young man of almost seventeen. His eager eyes betray his indifferent air, and Edmund nods at Ranulph.

'Half of the Prince's army was sick when I was despatched. The Prince suffers the same malady.' He looks around at the tense faces. 'My Lord Mowbray will be here on the morrow. He will explain all.'

'You are here now, Sire,' Ranulph insists with a hiss. 'And since you were in the camp, surely you know more than my Lord Mowbray does. Will the Prince die?'

Edmund is caught short when Elizabeth's voice rings from the dais. 'You heard Sir Edmund. The Baron will be here soon, he will make all clear to you that is necessary.'

Ranulph looks at her, his eyes little glittering triangles. 'As you wish, sweet cousin.'

The noise in the hall is slow to resume, but in the end the men tuck into their meals and Edmund relaxes a little. The stew has lost some of its flavour, but the homey feel and the faint smell of summer and roses that waft through the open doors lends a little ease. Edmund allows himself a moment to close his eyes.

'Daydreaming, Sire?' Ranulph squeezes down next to Edmund and reaches over for the wine pitcher. 'Let me serve you.'

'Just as in the old days,' Edmund remarks and is rewarded with a small smile.

Ranulph was named squire to Baron Mowbray only a year after Poitiers. Since then, the boy had hounded Edmund, hungry for tales of war and bloodshed. The more gruelling the better. Though he is now a young man, it seems his tastes have not changed. Edmund recognises much of himself in the young FitzAlan, except of course that Ranulph is rich and has little wit.

Leaning in, Ranulph lowers his voice. 'My cousin may not want to share the news with the entire hall, but surely you can confide in me, Sire.'

'You are kind to take an interest, Master Ranulph.' Edmund accepts another cup of wine and inclines his head towards the dais. 'But if your cousin wishes to wait for the Baron to return, we ought to obey her.'

'She is far too used to having things her way,' Ranulph sneers and hides his displeasure poorly with a wide grin. 'But then you would know, Sire.'

Edmund has never taken to Ranulph who has a constant look of superiority and entitlement about him. Once, the Baron called him a ferret, and Edmund has to agree. Ranulph's eyes are small and dark, his nose long and narrow and his plain brown hair stands on end. His last remark hangs as a nuisance in the air.

'I have been away for some time. Things change.'

'Come now, Sire, surely you can tell me.' Up close FitzAlan's breath is sour. 'I promise not to let slip anything until the Baron is home. But you must not forget that I have a personal connection with the royal family.'

Some things never change, Edmund thinks and takes a little sip of wine, deciding how much to divulge. Knowing Ranulph, anything Edmund says is bound to make its rounds before the sun rises.

'The Prince was gravely ill when I was sent to England. Lord Gaunt was with him, but the conditions in the camp were terrible. I can only pray that they have marched on to find a better place. I was charged to go before the King and plead for assistance.'

'And?'

'As I said, his Grace has called for Parliament to assemble.' Edmund is tiring fast of FitzAlan.

'That may take weeks or even months.' Ranulph fails to hide his smirk. 'I remember how it is from my days serving the Baron at court. And how long did it take you to get to England, Sire?'

'Weeks.' Edmund grinds his teeth. 'Parliament will act swiftly; I have no doubt. The Baron will have news for us as soon as he arrives. For what it is worth, I do not expect to be long in England.'

'Why waste time coming here then, Sire?' Looking about the room, Ranulph licks his lips. 'If you are bound to return to the Prince as soon as can be? Which is what I assume you are trying to say?'

'It was Lord Mowbray's wish that I come here.' Edmund makes a fist under the table. The snot-nosed little brat Edmund used to know lurks just below the surface. If it were not for Ranulph's distant relation to the King, Edmund would drag him from the room and wipe the smile from his face right now.

'Sir Edmund!' A couple of the Baron's men pass the table and Ranulph glares at them, but they take no notice. 'Is there naught you can tell us?'

'My Lord Mowbray will return and make all clear.' Edmund leans back content that he is the centre of attention. 'Now, let me put some food in my belly.'

'You look a ghost, Sire,' one of them says. 'You're better off going straight to the kitchens and let cook sort you out!'

They laugh as they walk away, and Edmund smiles at their backs. The homely feeling increases as he looks around at the benches that are worn to a shine; the tables that glisten beneath the bowls of stew, squares of stale bread and plain cups. He is a little surprised at how pleased he is to be here.

Next to him, Ranulph shifts and his sleeve brushes across Edmund's hand. 'Any message for my Lady?'

Long ago, when Ranulph first joined the Baron's household, his own father had taken the Baron aside and, with a stern face, warned him that Ranulph was no easy lad. Best to be wary of all he says and does, the Baron later told Edmund over a game of chess. Sound advice if ever there was any.

'No.'

'Is that so?'

'What message would I bring your cousin when her husband is coming here himself?' Edmund says with disinterest. 'What he needs to tell his wife is between the two of them. It is no business of mine – nor of yours, Master Ranulph.'

Wiping his nose on his sleeve, Ranulph's eyes skirt the dais. 'Two girls who are the spitting image of my cousin's husband and one that looks nothing like him. Funny that.'

'In what way?' Edmund looks at the little golden girl, who is yawning. 'She looks like her mother.'

'If you say so.' Ranulph licks his lips. 'If you say so.'

Ranulph stands, a little unsteady on his feet, and makes a mock bow to Edmund before he leaves the hall, a couple of boys trailing in his wake. Edmund decides to tell the Baron that his cousin by marriage is reaching above his station. There is a fine line between being a favourite and being trouble; Edmund knows for he has often enough balanced on that line.

Once more, he looks at the girls on the dais. The two eldest have the dark looks of their father, no one can doubt their lineage. His eyes linger on the youngest. There is something vaguely familiar about her, but he thinks it is merely that she has the rosy cheeks and big eyes of all little girls. The longer he dwells on it, the more fear gnaws at his innards. Surely, Ranulph knows nothing; surely, Elizabeth has not been so foolish as to tell her fickle cousin about them?

When he looks up, his eyes meet Elizabeth's and she gives a small nod. Edmund gets up and leaves the hall without looking back.

ᏈᏍ ᏈᏍ

A light knock stirs the air in the room and, before he can answer, the door opens and Elizabeth slips in. 'You are alone. Good.'

Edmund rises to offer her his seat, he is in his old room, which is even more sparsely furnished than when he lived here. He knows why she has come. 'My Lady.'

'Come now, are we not friends?' She stands on tiptoe and brushes her lips against his cheek.

'Yes, we are.' Edmund is pleased that she has not gone off him. 'Elizabeth.'

The smile she awards him would melt even the thickest ice. He cannot help but smile in return and lets her grasp his hands when she says, 'I have missed you! I have been so lonely, so worried!' Her eyes dart over his face. 'But you are not happy.'

'I have been to Hell.' Edmund releases her and runs a hand through his hair; it is still wet from the water he poured over it when he returned to his chamber. 'It is hard to be happy, even here, knowing what I left behind.'

'Are you hurt?' She seems to struggle to keep her hands clasped before her, not to reach out and run them over his body. 'Were you hurt during battle?'

'I took a lance to the shoulder.'

She gasps when he opens his shirt a little and reveals the rugged, red scar on his shoulder. It scores a canyon of raw flesh across his collarbone. 'It is still healing.'

'Anywhere else?' Hunger seeps into her voice, he knows it only too well, and he recognises her satisfaction when he shakes his head. 'Good. That is good. Is half the army really dead?'

'Yes. A degrading death. No battlefield glory, just …' Edmund does not want to discuss the disgusting feats of war, but some of it might just render her even more willing, and so he satisfies her curiosity. 'I still hear them in my dreams.'

'My love …' Her words reach out to embrace him, her blue eyes blaze. 'Oh, how sorry I am. How awful it must all have been. And to have to go back. Why cannot you stay here? Here where you are safe!'

'It is not my decision to make.' Edmund sits on the chest beside his bed, just out of reach. 'I pledged my sword to the Prince. I have to go. I want to go.'

'I see.' Her voice turns cold with dissatisfaction.

'I told you as much when we parted,' Edmund says and watches her cool exterior crumble.

'Have you seen the children?' Her voice has a new pleading quality to it; she tries to smile. 'They have grown! And you have to see our youngest, Thomas. He is such a little angel.'

'Perhaps I can visit them tomorrow.'

She nods at his brush off and rises. 'We can go together. I always go to the nursery after breakfast. Which I assume you will be taking in the hall with the other men?'

'Of course.' He fixes her eyes and smiles. 'As I always did, Elizabeth.'

'Have you found someone else?'

'Does it matter?'

She loses no time considering, has probably made up her mind long ago, and so she simply grasps for him, her mouth searching for his. The depth and despair of the kiss sets his whole body on fire and, for a moment, he is surprised that she can still inspire such desire. But then it has been long since he has had a woman and, right now, he cannot imagine anything sweeter than that soft embrace.

Her hands claw at his shirt, the seams scream beneath her fingers, and Edmund lets her pull it over his head before he unfastens the small buttons down the front of her gown. Where she is ravenous, he exerts discipline, every movement calm, calculated. She breathes raggedly as she shrugs off her dress and clings to him, forcing her kisses until they are both out of breath.

When she traces his scar, her touch is cool on the red, rugged edges, and he closes his eyes against the exquisite pain. Elizabeth kisses his neck, his chest and he sits down hard on the bed, drawing her with him. Her soft, golden curls caress his arm and he buries his hands in the rich silky waterfall.

Edmund lets her push him back onto the bed, and when her hands begin working his breeches, he does not show her how much he wants her. With Elizabeth it is better when she thinks he is disinterested. It makes her work harder. And Edmund wants her to work very hard this night. He wants the lady of the house to stagger back to bed, worn and weary.

He wants her to fall asleep with nothing on her mind but him. Naturally, he gets his way.

ശ ഇ ശ ഇ

## 5 June 1367 – Nottingham

'Do you remember Sir Edmund?' Elizabeth's light voice rings through the nursery. The room is bathed in sunlight, the tiled floor freshly scrubbed. A few baskets and shelves hold some toys and other paraphernalia no doubt necessary to the nurse who tends the Mowbray children.

Margaret, dressed in a plain, blue dress held up with a slim, silver belt, is the spitting image of her father, her eyes grey as a thunderstorm. 'Yes, Mama.'

'Then greet him accordingly,' Elizabeth laughs and pushes the six-year-old towards Edmund, who is still standing just outside the door; he dislikes children. 'Do not linger, Sir Edmund, come in.'

Curtseying, Margaret eyes her mother with a mixture of wonder and dismay. 'Where is Father?'

'He is still in London, my sweet.' Elizabeth turns towards the crib and coos at a dark-haired baby. 'And this, Sir Edmund, is Thomas.'

'He is new,' a small voice whispers beside Edmund's calf and he looks down at a brown-haired girl with big dark eyes. 'He cries much.'

'Joan,' Elizabeth says as she lifts the baby up. 'What a silly thing to say.'

'But true.' Joan never shifts her gaze, and Edmund is unsettled by her intransigent behaviour.

'How old are you then?' he tries to divert the little girl, dressed in shades of green, with a question, but she is not perturbed.

'Four.' Joan looks at Margaret. 'Where is Nor?'

'Eleanor!' Margaret over-pronounces the name and earns a stern glance from Elizabeth. 'She has to learn.' There is something unnaturally adult about the girl that sets Edmund on edge. Now, she curtsies insolently. 'I shall fetch her.'

'She is such a clever girl,' Elizabeth says and hands baby Thomas to the wet nurse. 'But disquieting at times.'

Edmund looks into the other crib where a bustling boy is clamouring the side. 'This must be John.'

'Every inch his father.' Elizabeth pats John's head and kisses his little fat hands. 'Are you not, my darling, every inch your father, only I must teach you to stay at home rather than roam about the land.'

The obvious disapproval in Elizabeth's voice makes Edmund smile. 'He truly is the very image of my Lord.'

Elizabeth's golden hair is done in an elaborate braid and fastened to her head with jewelled combs. Edmund is a little annoyed. He likes her better when she looks like a common wench, her hair loose and her ways too.

'This, is Eleanor!' a truculent voice announces behind him and Edmund starts.

Joan laughs and skips around the room, twirling and clapping. 'Nor, Nor, pretty, pretty, Nor!'

'E-lea-nor,' Margaret sighs and pushes a startling miniature of Elizabeth towards Edmund. 'Joan, you must learn.'

'She will, in time,' Elizabeth says and pats Margaret on the arm before hoisting up John to rest on her hip.

Edmund feels Elizabeth's gaze on his back as he hunches down to greet Eleanor. When can he leave this hellhole and return to the great hall, to real life and proper conversations? 'Hello, little one.'

The girl stares at Edmund with avid, blue eyes, her face inscrutable for a moment before she beams a smile so bright, it almost knocks Edmund over. She reaches out for him and tips over, and Edmund catches her just before her head meets the hard tiles on the floor.

Joan laughs again. 'Always does that, Nor. Silly, Nor.'

Margaret seems to have given up trying to correct Joan for she turns to her mother with a pout and goes to stand beside the chair Elizabeth has settled in. With John on her lap and Margaret by her side, she looks every inch the mother she is, and Edmund's interest in her wanes.

'He's mighty thirsty today, M'lady,' the wet nurse observes with a squiggly Thomas in her arms. 'Mayhap …?'

Elizabeth nods and puts John back in his crib, unlike his baby brother, Baron Mowbray's eldest son and heir is quiet, calm. Elizabeth gestures, 'Come along girls, Nurse has to tend to the little ones.'

Eleanor still hangs in Edmund's arms, her eyes fixed on his face, her little plump fingers gripping his sleeves. There is a distinct charm in her smile and while she seems quite content to be surveying him, he is uncomfortable. Edmund looks up at Elizabeth who smiles too. 'She has taken to you.'

'What do I …?' Edmund watches Elizabeth walk out the door, Joan and Margaret either side of her.

'Bring her, if you can carry her. She wriggles all the time when my Lord husband picks her up. Perhaps you will have better luck.'

Edmund looks back into those big, blue eyes, the trusting face. With a sigh, he jostles her into a better grip, her yellow dress crumbling around her legs, and carries her out the door. Eleanor settles in his arms, pops her thumb in her mouth and does not move at all.

'I knew it!'

The girls have been fetched away by their governess for an hour of fresh air. Elizabeth is seated in the windowsill, looking out over the garden where the three girls romp about. From time to time, Edmund can make out the cheerful laughter of Joan and fragmented reprimands in Margaret's piercing voice.

Elizabeth turns away from the view. 'I knew it.'

'Knew what?' Edmund stands a few paces from her, his hands clasped behind his back. He longs to be in the training field with the other men, his weakened left arm needs practice, but she has asked him to stay, and he cannot in full view of the house deny her. Two servants are setting up trays of fruit and preserves while one of Elizabeth's ladies oversees them.

'Leave us.' Elizabeth waves the servants out and nods at her lady-in-waiting who closes the door with a little snap. 'John has never been able to hold Eleanor for more than a moment or two before she twists free. But she sat quite still on your arm.'

'I am a stranger, perhaps she sensed I am not practiced in carrying children.' Edmund holds up the carafe of wine and Elizabeth nods. He pours and offers her a cup. 'It is full natural that a child will be more at ease with her father than a stranger.'

'Exactly!' Elizabeth takes the cup and caresses Edmund's hand. Then she looks up at him. 'She is much more at ease with you.'

Edmund loses the grasp on the carafe and it clangs against the silver tray, tottering before coming to rest. He does not like where this is going.

'She is yours.'

The matter-of-fact way Elizabeth delivers the news leaves Edmund cold. Cold and annoyed. He is about to deny her when shouting in the courtyard disturbs them.

'What is this?' Elizabeth rushes to the window and then her shoulders slump. 'He is back.'

The Baron. For the very first time, Edmund feels a fool for having carried on an affair with Mowbray's wife right in his own household. He also feels something else, an emotion so foreign to him that he cannot even name it. She turns from the view.

'He knows nothing,' Elizabeth whispers, extreme urgency in her voice. 'He was so happy that one of our children should look like me. He suspects nothing.' She succeeds in grabbing his arm, her fingers cold. 'Please.'

Steps in the gallery reveal the imminent arrival of Baron Mowbray, Elizabeth's husband, Edmund's master. With stiff fingers, he releases her grip.

'You will have me lie to him?'

'What is one more lie?' Elizabeth steps back. 'You will take me to bed without hesitation, but this changes everything?'

'You should have taken more care.'

'Hypocrite!' Her eyes flash blue ice. 'You cannot have been so blind as to believe that there would be no outcome? No offspring. I thought you would be pleased, but I was mistaken, as I so often am when it comes to men! If you tell him, if you betray our secret, I shall claim that you seduced me, forced yourself on me and I dared say nothing because you are such a great friend to him. He will put you to the whip, he has to if he wants to save his honour.'

The Baron barges into the room and Edmund steps aside, a biting response dying on his lips. Elizabeth has shown her true colours. Naturally, she will attempt to save her own skin, and likewise naturally, she expects the

Baron to believe her. But Edmund is less certain, actually, he might just be able to make his case more persuasive – as he has so often in the past.

'You are home!' Elizabeth dashes past Edmund, the hem of her skirt whipping against his boot, and reaches up to kiss the Baron's cheek. 'I have prayed that, this time, you would not be in London for long, and my prayers have been answered.'

'The summons for Parliament spread across the country as we speak.' The Baron looks slightly taken aback but slides his arm around her back. 'Edmund, I have a message to you from the King.'

'I shall leave you to it and ask the kitchens to prepare all of your favourite dishes.' Elizabeth turns in her husband's embrace and looks at Edmund. 'Tonight, we celebrate your return, my darling.'

Edmund returns her stare without word, and she gives a hard smile before she leaves.

As soon as the door closes, the Baron throws up his hands in wonder. 'This is a turn.'

'She has missed you, my Lord.' Edmund lies easily. 'She hoped you would return soon. It seems she is tired of your many trips to London.'

'As well she might be, but she has never showed such … enthusiasm.' Striding to the window, the Baron strokes his stubbled cheek. 'When did you arrive?'

'Yesterday, my Lord, we could have ridden up together after all. I only told the household what you commanded me to say.' Edmund joins the Baron and looks down into the bustling courtyard. 'Though Master Ranulph did press me on the subject. He has not grown less tiresome in the time I have been away; I find. Rather the opposite. Is it necessary to keep him here?'

The Baron smiles. 'I fear so. My wife would never forgive me if I sent him away. She has only very recently forgiven me for releasing you.'

'Then I would be weary of him if I were you, my Lord,' Edmund says. 'For he is trouble if ever there was any, and I should know. But enough of him. If the summons has already gone out, surely it will not be long before we must both return to London?'

'Keen to leave, Sire? Although you have only just gotten here?' The Baron smiles at Edmund and shouts out the window. 'Pierce! Make sure the horses are rubbed down before they are fed!'

'It is uncommonly hot,' he says to Edmund who nods. 'And the roads were crowded, even for the season. Did you not notice?'

'Yes, it has been long since I have seen that many people and wagons out this time of year. I counted at least two carriages which had thrown their wheels, and one wagon upturned right before me, the oxen so tired, they simply lay there still in harness.' Edmund pushes his irritation with Elizabeth aside; no woman should be awarded this much of his attention. He shakes his head. 'It took me an extra day to get here because my horse threw a shoe, and the smith was busy with all the extra trade.'

'Mayhem. You should have insisted he service a knight before the peasants. There were times when I wondered if we would have to break for a second night, but in the end, I resolved to rise early and get here as soon as possible.' The Baron nods when Edmund offers him a cup of wine. 'How I have longed for proper wine! The taverns and inns serve cat's piss at best!'

Edmund washes down his own drink and watches the Baron take a chair near the window. A weak breeze ruffling his shirt collar. 'You said you have a message for me, my Lord?'

'Order,' the Baron says and shrugs off his heavy travelling coat. It looks out of place in the pale parlour with its white flowers and frail furniture. As a splash of dirt on a clean kitchen table. 'The King orders that you return to the Prince's service. Which is no more than we expected. It seems he has finally taken your message to heart. Perhaps you were right, perhaps it was the letter from Gaunt that swayed him. I still find it almost impossible to understand that our magnificent Prince lies wasting away on the border of Castile, simply because one of the worst kings in all of Christendom is a pauper as well as a tyrant.'

'You and I both, my Lord.' Edmund sneers at the memory of King Peter on their march, always complaining, always pathetic. 'Did the King say when I am to return to the Prince?'

Setting aside his cup, the Baron produces a letter bearing the royal seal. 'It is all set out in this, which will also act as a charter of safe passage, in case you encounter any difficulties once you reach the mainland. Which I assume is more likely than not from what you told me, and so too does the King if he thinks it necessary to put into writing in his own hand. Ah, to think that all that we accomplished as young men has brought nothing but trouble. I was so certain that the French could be brought to heel. So too did the King. But then, he has tried to gain the French crown ever since he set aside his father. I was so certain that the moment the Prince took on his principality, he would bring about peace. But then he was always a man spoiling for battle, was he not? Even when we were young.'

Edmund notices a glimmer of dismay in the Baron's expression and suppresses irritation. Of course, the Prince is spoiling for a battle, all real men do. 'The King will send reinforcements? Money?'

'Some reinforcements for the Princess.' The Baron leans back and sighs. 'He can do that on his own accord without sanction from Parliament. But no money and though I tried to prevail upon him the need for more men, he will not ask us to muster. Parliament will not levy any more taxes on the English. When I return to sit another Parliament, the result will be the same. They fear – and rightly so – that it will cause more than simple discontent. And more than anything, the King needs to keep England happy.'

'This has never been a problem before?'

'Not in our King's time,' the Baron agrees. 'But the past is a different matter.'

'How so, my Lord?' Rather than perch on one of the feminine chairs in the room, Edmund remains standing, feeling as a giant among the delicate tables and little, decorative boxes.

'I sometimes forget that you are not born in this land, nor have you grown up with its history,' the Baron says and shifts in his seat, rubbing his calf. 'In the time of King John, the English noble families rose against the Crown because of the taxes levied – and because they had issues with the way the King spent what they believed to be their money. As it was. The rebellion forged the Magna Carta, to which all Kings have been held accountable ever since. It must be upheld to ensure the balance between King and nobility – and all his subjects. The King does not reign supreme, although it may seem so. Above all else, he must ensure that peace is kept within the realm.'

'And if the King wishes to send aid?'

'His wishes are nothing to the peace of the land, as he well understands. While he supports his son's endeavours and even sanctioned King Peter's cause, he cannot send any money without Parliament.' The Baron pours another cup of wine. 'He has none.'

Edmund knows that the Prince has no funds of his own any more, but to know that the King too is a pauper fills him with loathing. 'None, my Lord?'

'England teeters on the cusp of bankruptcy. Which, of course, you did not hear from me. However much the King shouts and curses – which he did, but to no avail – he cannot afford to send any money to the Prince. I doubt there is anyone left who will lend him money, and Parliament was reluctant to sanction the Castilian battle, as you might recall. Now, it sees only that it was right to do so. When we meet once more it is for show. The decision already made cannot be altered.'

Edmund feels the room close in on him, the brightness of it mocking him. 'Did you vote for or against?'

'King Peter's cause?' The Baron once more strokes his cheek. 'Against.'

Why would you vote against battle? Edmund thinks, have you completely forgotten what it is to be on the field, serving harsh justice to your enemy? Never mind who we back, I did not go forth for King Peter, I charged for the streaming banner of the Prince. But the memory is bitter, tainted by his own failure, his injuries and resent shame.

Edmund finds his voice. 'Why, if I might ask?'

Beckoning Edmund to sit, the Baron draws breath. 'While our King and, indeed, the Prince are forces to be reckoned with on the battlefield, shrewd and strategic, they are also headstrong and, at times, politically blind.'

'You sound like Lord Gaunt,' Edmund says and earns a half-smile. Certainly, the Baron is right, but that is beside the point. 'And you force me to repeat what the Prince said in his defence. We did win the battle.'

'Yes, the Prince won another great battle, but at what cost? I rather fear he lost the war.' Mowbray skirts the table and comes to sit opposite Edmund. 'I can tell from your expression that you agree. See here, I understand – better than most – your desire to be always loyal to the Prince. My admiration for him as a strategist and warrior has not diminished through all of these years. But this time, he backed the wrong side, and reluctantly too, for I know he was not pleased when the King decided to keep his end of the bargain with King Peter. A man who is far from beloved in his land. You said it yourself; Henry of Trastámara escaped. He is the people's favourite. If we know this in England, surely so must King Peter, for though he has no love for his people, he must hear their discontent cries. Even a Prince of England cannot change that. But a usurper cannot be left on the throne; it opens up all kinds of opportunities for those of lesser standing and means. Which, in turn, threatens all the royal courts of Europe. Not least the English. No; the usurper had to go. We simply chose not to pay for it.'

Edmund rubs his shoulder, the wound throbs all the time, but he is becoming accustomed to it. It is another testament to his prowess on the field and, in time, he means to make it work in his favour. What happened during the battle may yet be told different, spun to a tale that will make a King want to reward a loyal knight. But first, the Baron must be set right.

'I heard that there were hardly any people in the streets cheering for King Peter when the Prince rode with him,' Edmund says. 'The people cheered the Prince but not their own King. The battle might have been well managed, but we did put a man back on the throne who does not belong there, my Lord, I agree. What is done is done. Surely, Peter must be made to pay?'

'It is our luck that Peter has left his two girls as ransom, because the money he will, in all likelihood, never return. The King has been made to see this; that is how Parliament will eventually prevail that no more money should be sent. The original agreement must stand; it cannot be different. And besides, we have the Princesses and can make the most of them.' The Baron gives a grim nod. 'It is all politics of course. The Princesses will know this too. They knew long before their father set out on his campaign. Perhaps even before he brought them to the Prince's court.'

'Pawns in the game of Kings.' Edmund is not interested in the Castilian Princesses; they can rot in a hole for all he cares. But he feigns dismay. 'Poor girls.'

'They will marry well and perhaps, in time, if God is willing, they will found their own dynasties. Maybe even birth sons to succeed Peter on the Castilian throne.'

'Let us hope they bring up boys who are more inclined to listen to reason. Perhaps even listen to their mothers,' Edmund says and the Baron barks a laugh. 'Or it will all have been in vain.'

'So much war is,' the Baron agrees. One of the silver candleholders spreads the sunlight around the room. 'You and I know that well enough.'

Edmund cracks the seal and reads the short message. 'He orders that I return to London within a week.'

'Ah, I suspected he would make short process. He was not pleased with his council, not at all. And he must expect that soon, enough of his Lords have convened to form a Parliament, which can make decisions.'

'There is nothing to be done then?' Edmund folds the letter and tucks it under his shirt. The second page he must read again when he is alone.

'Would that there were, for you know how well I love the Prince. If it were up to me, my men would be mustering as we speak, setting out to aid the Prince, but that is not the will of the King – or the Parliament, I imagine.' Mowbray rubbed his calf again. 'Many enough of his noblemen will refuse to pay for the Prince's misfortunes. And the King needs his noblemen. That is all there is to it.'

'What will happen to the Prince then? He too is bankrupt.'

'As I said, if it were up to me, men would be mustering. But it is not.' Reluctance steals across the Baron's face and his eyes skirt Edmund's steady gaze. 'No other orders?'

'The King demands that I come to London first,' Edmund says while the vipers in his stomach writhe. He wants the Baron to ignore politics and muster his men, but politics must prevail it seems. How did a King ever lose his power, is what Edmund would like to know. 'He wishes to bestow upon me my own estate.'

'Finally!' The Baron rises. 'We must toast your good fortune, my friend. How long you have waited for this moment. How long we have all waited.'

Yes, Edmund thinks and holds out his cup for the Baron to replenish, it is high time, for I have served the King even better than I ever did the Prince. I made sure the Prince understood the importance of backing King Peter, even if my sweet words are fouled now.

'Thank you, my Lord.' Edmund raises his cup. 'I hope to prove worthy.'

'You already are, Sire, and the King knows it. The Prince would never have sent you if he did not trust you with his life.'

But what will he do when I return with the news that England will not aid him? Edmund thinks and finds the wine bitter. What will happen then?

## 9 June 1367 – Framlingham

'Why are you so determined to go?' The hint of fear betrays the anger in Elizabeth's voice. 'Why cannot you be satisfied here? With your family?'

'If the King commands me, it may not be my own decision where I go,' Mowbray says. 'Truly, Elizabeth, you must understand …'

'NO!' She flares. 'I understand absolutely nothing! And you!' She rounds on Edmund. 'You will go too? To that hell hole from whence you have just escaped?!'

The Baron is leaning against a pillar in the middle of the room, his face a study of contemplation, but Edmund knows him well enough to know that he is battling his own temper and only winning by an inch.

Gritting his teeth, Edmund returns Elizabeth's angry stare. 'I have no choice, my Lady.'

'How strange that you are so happy to take orders, no matter how foolish they are,' Elizabeth fires back. Her anger seems to swallow up all light in the room, bathing it in gloom. 'What does the Prince possess that your English lord does not?'

The Baron clears his throat to gain her attention. 'If I have little choice, my dear, Sir Edmund has none at all. He is neither at my disposal nor at my command, he has not been for these past three years. He is pledged to the Prince. His entire life is in the hands of those with favour.'

'Of which you are one, last I heard,' she snaps and turns a pleading face to the Baron. A face Edmund knows well, has seen on his pillow on many an occasion. 'You say, he is such a great friend of yours, and yet you will send him back to what can be but a certain death?'

'If it were in my gift to command Sir Edmund to stay here, I would.' Clearly, they have had this conversation before, because the Baron looks tired and annoyed and it seeps through in his words.

'But to London you must journey now. To do the King's bidding.' Her sullen face is unappealing. 'Again.'

'It is a long sitting Parliament, wife,' the Baron says with a touch of resentment. 'But until I am released by the King, it is not within my own power. All I can do is lament that the King has not seen fit to call for a muster and aid his son. But that too is out of my hands.'

'And you?'

If the Baron is tired, Edmund has long since grown weary of her demanding disposition. She has changed these past three years, she has grown dull and wilful, but with none of the shrewdness that Pascaline has in abundance. He keeps his own council, but he will not answer her.

The Baron speaks up instead. 'Sir Edmund leaves with me on the King's command. He is to return to the Prince. Without delay!'

At the mention of the Prince, all three of them fall silent. Edmund remembers the Prince's sweat soaked hair, his feverish eyes and hollow cheeks. Every day, he wonders if the Prince is still alive, what will happen if he dies, if the Princess manages to ward off the French? If only he could remember what the Princess said to him all those weeks ago, but then he hardly remembers the days journey from Najera to Aquitaine. His men had set the course and lashed him to his saddle until he could sit the horse himself.

'Do you think he will live?' Elizabeth's hushed question brushes his cheek as a soft kiss. Her anger has subsided into a musing discomfort that ill suits the airy study.

'He is a strong man,' the Baron says. 'If anyone can conquer disease, it will be him.'

But having seen the Prince, Edmund is less certain. 'If they have moved camp, if he is with the Princess again, perhaps …'

'Is it true that the French took up arms against her the moment the Prince left?' Big blue eyes stare into his; she is short of breath. Edmund understands that the Baron has told her all. 'That she mustered her own army?'

'She is resourceful,' Edmund says, he is not inclined to discuss particulars with her, but he knows he must answer her in full. 'And the French did not attack right away. But somehow, they caught wind that the Prince was away for longer than anticipated and that he brought more men than what was first agreed. The French managed to rally the locals into rebellion. It is nothing the Princess cannot combat with aid from England.'

'It may not be as easy as all that. Parliament grows weary of these demands from overseas. They do not understand why we are to send our money and able men to fight what many believe to be a foolish war. There will be no money, not even for her.' The Baron settles behind his desk, shuffling the papers idly. 'We have had ample opportunity to take all of

France to ourselves, but for some reason – politics, chivalry – we have never succeeded. So many opportunities missed, and now …'

'Lord Gaunt warned the Prince against accepting King Peter's request.' Edmund has not told anyone until now; he has been waiting for the opportune moment to disclose his knowledge. To make the most of it.

The Baron glances at Elizabeth. 'Please leave us.'

Her dress whips around as she turns and leaves, the door slamming shut behind her. Above the oak door frame, the Mowbray crest shines blue, red and white, colours accented in the luxurious carpet under the Baron's table, and the cuffs of his garb, studded with rubies and sapphires worked into the white lace.

'Tell me.' The Baron leans back, his hair dark against the limewashed wood of his chair.

Edmund sits down on a low stool. 'I overheard them. In Bordeaux before we left for Dax. I hid in the shadows; I was making my way … back to my rooms.'

The Baron rubs his forehead. 'What did Gaunt say?'

'Lord Gaunt was troubled, he did not believe King Peter was in a position to repay the Prince his debt.' Edmund recalls Gaunt's angry face, the savage thwarting he suffered on the icy passageway. 'Rather, he cautioned the Prince and said not to trust a fickle ally.'

'And the Prince?'

'Would not hear of it. I understand that politics may force you to take the side of an ally. However fickle this ally might be. But …' Edmund digs his fingers into his thigh.

The Baron plays with the inkwell on his desk, the silver lid snaps open and shut, open and shut. 'But you think Gaunt was right?'

Edmund nods. 'From how King Peter acted while in Bordeaux, I believe he knew full well that he would never be able to pay the Prince. He took him for a fool.'

'And was proven right.' The Baron snaps the lid shut and glides a finger over the intricate silverwork. 'The Prince was never more at ease than on the battlefield. He must have been hungry for war.'

'I was most surprised that the King did not send reinforcements,' Edmund admits and remembers how he too spoiled for war. So much so that he delivered the final push. 'Though now, I know why.'

The Baron wipes his hands on an embroidered handkerchief; they leave vague, grey stains. 'I have had word from a few of my friends.'

'Will they grant it this time, my Lord, to aid the Princess?'

Pushing back his chair, the Baron fixes Edmund's gaze. 'No.'

# CHAPTER 14

## 7 July 1367 – Westminster Palace, London

Edmund hovers at the back of the great hall. He has been waiting for weeks for orders to stay or go. Parliament has been going back and forth on the subject, no doubt in part due to Baron Mowbray, who pledged his undying loyalty to the Prince and expressed his determination to send aid to the Princess, causing several of the other Lords to re-examine their own allegiance.

The passageways and gardens teem with noblemen and knights, a servant ushers in farmers, cobblers and tailors all of who gawp at the splendour that is King Edward's court. Edmund has never seen so many petitioners in the King's palace before. How small and insignificant they are in these hallowed halls decked with tapestries, gold and silver as far as the eye can see.

It has taken him a long time to shirk the frustration of Elizabeth's claim that he had fathered one of her children; his mind keeps circling back to it, angering him when he is finally at ease. How dare she? Does she really think, he will believe that she has only ever bedded him other than her husband? What is to say she did not take more lovers, perhaps even had some when they were first involved? He despises her, and he loathes children. He is no father; he never will be. She has no claim on him. Nor does the little golden girl.

Edmund looks up at the sound of approaching footsteps. 'Sir Edmund.'

The crowd parts for Edmund as he follows one of the royal servants who hurries across the hall. 'The King has little time to spare I'm afraid, Sire, best get about it quickly.'

Edmund nods, and the doors to the royal reception room swing open. The King is on his throne with a few of his advisors standing about. Edmund bows low and waits to be addressed.

'Sir Edmund. I wish the circumstances of your presence here today might have been different.' The King's words are laced with dismay. 'Come.'

Walking past the courtiers, Edmund notices their strained expressions and surmises that the King is in one of his moods. 'Your Grace.'

'You still have your letter?' The King nods when Edmund produces it. 'Good! Tell my son that I am sorry that the English are not more generous or kind to their future King. Tell him that I tried in vain to change their wayward minds and that my reminding them of their obligation fell on deaf ears.'

The air turns to glass; any word or breath threatens to splinter it. 'Yes, your Grace.'

'There is the matter of my gift,' the King says and looks about the room. 'On that we can all agree. When John wrote to me, he deigned to mention your achievements on the field and your obedience to your Prince, even though you were in no fit state to travel. Such loyalty must and shall be rewarded.'

The nobles and courtiers mumble in agreement and one or two even give encouraging smiles. Edmund bows his head to hide the smug curl of his lips. 'I thank you, your Grace.'

'I gift to you the seat of Beauworth.' The King rises and walks down the dais steps. 'It is currently held by one of my brave, old friends, but he has no issue and so there is no one to claim it upon his death. Until his time comes, you will remain in the service of my son and naturally the Baron Mowbray, should he choose to invoke his prerogative upon your return.'

'I am grateful, your Grace, for such fine a gift,' Edmund mutters to hide his disappointment. To be awarded a house that he cannot take at once. What kind of gift is that? No gift at all. The other men in the room mistake his manner for deference and look pleased that he should not think too highly of himself.

'The papers are drawn up and signed,' the King continues. 'The property and lands will pass to you when Sir William dies. On your next return, seek out one of my lawyers and all formalities will be attended to.'

With the King standing right in front of him, Edmund is reminded of his oath to his first master the Duke of Lancaster who told him that while the King of England could be brusque and even brutal, he always favoured those who proved their loyalty to him. Now, it was Edmund's turn to see for himself the truth of the Duke's words. Though perhaps the Duke would not deem what Edmund has done as a proof of loyalty.

'If it was in my power,' the King says in hushed tones, 'I would have awarded you something more. Perhaps some of the lands of the late Duke of Lancaster, for I know he was fond of you. But I fear John would never forgive me.'

Edmund looks into the King's blue eyes, a spark of youth in his aging face. 'I would never …'

'No, and that is why I wish it might be different. But mark my words, Sir Edmund, serve both my sons equally well and you will never want for anything. It is a rare thing that they agree on something, and rarer still that they find favour for the same man.' The King gives a sad smile. 'I fear that they are often at odds and that there resides some deep rivalry but, of course, John understands his role; he is there to offer advice. The kind no one wants but everyone needs; it is his greatest force. He is far too clever to attempt anything else. Perhaps that is why he asks what he asks in his letter.'

'Your Grace?'

The King steers Edmund to the far side of the room, away from the windows overlooking the gardens. The other men pretend at conversation, and Edmund basks in their envious glances. 'He asks to be made ward to the two Castilian Princesses who cannot now imagine they will ever be allowed to return to their father. It seems he intends for my son Edmund to marry King Peter's eldest daughter, Constance.'

Edmund bows his head; he likes Langley and wonders what he might think of married life.

'John is ambitious, for that I cannot blame him, and his thoughts when it comes to his brother are clever to be sure. If he were free, I know that he would marry the eldest Princess himself, but he is not, and so he must make other arrangements.' Something dark enters the King's voice. 'Still, I favour that he covets another crown and that we may have done with it all as soon as the marriage is completed. I bid you deliver this letter into John's hands, let no one else see it, not even Edward.'

'Yes, your Grace.'

'At sunrise tomorrow, you ride for Plymouth. From there you must make your way to the Princess as quickly as you can and deliver the troops I send for her reinforcements. I have had to muster men in my own name, and I do it gladly to aid her. If the Prince is not with her already, move on until you find him and bring him back to Bordeaux. Bring all my sons to Bordeaux and there give John this,' the King produces a letter and presses it into Edmund's palm. 'But not before.'

'Yes, your Grace.'

'Go with God, Sir Edmund,' the King says and now his voice echoes round the room. He turns to Edmund and adds, 'for I fear you ride with the Devil at your heels.'

## 26 July 1392 – Westminster Palace

'You were there when I returned,' Edmund said. 'You were there in the sickroom with your brother and the Princess.'

'The sickroom you put him in, Sire,' Gaunt replied, his voice free from emotion. 'I knew all along that someone had gone to him, poisoned his thoughts and made him rear for battle. But I confess, I never thought it to be you.'

Edmund felt pleased with himself. 'I never thought I fooled you, my Lord.'

'Me as much as any, though I care not to admit it, for I pride myself that I can see through any mischief and unveil any troublemaker.'

'As you have done, my Lord.' Edmund rinsed his mouth in what water was left in his cup. 'You saw through the ruse of Thomas Mowbray.'

'By your aid, Sire,' Gaunt growled and tapped his fingers on the armrest of his chair. 'But we digress.'

'I believe you got something you wanted that day though, my Lord.'

Edmund lifted the empty carafe and Gaunt snapped his fingers, a servant emerging from the shadows to snatch the carafe and whisk it away.

'If my father had known then what we know now, I wonder if he had perhaps chosen differently when it came to accepting that the two Castilian girls be put into my care.'

'You said that you thought it would be easier to secure the Castilian throne for your brother than for the Prince to forge a realm made up of England and France.'

'That was when I still believed he would live,' Gaunt said with a grudge. 'In some ways, we were still but children back then, innocent of what the world would offer. My brother was the strongest man I ever knew, of course I would expect him to live, and live long. I would expect him to get the English Lords on his side, as Joan did, to send financial aid and men to wage a war. We all did, you too, Sire.'

Neither caring for nor wanting to discuss policy, Edmund rubbed his eyes. 'It matters not now, my Lord, for we know what happened. I believe my name-sake would have been happy to marry the heir to the Castilian throne, but then you got not only two wards to play your games with …'

'You swore to never again mention what you saw that day.'

'And you believed me?'

☙ ❧ ☙ ❧

## 4 September 1367 – Bordeaux

'No more!' Edmund wipes his mouth. 'I must return to the castle.'

Langley laughs. 'You may well have a child in the crib and a woman waiting in your chambers, but are you not still free? We must make what we can of life before it is taken from us!'

In the dim light of the tavern, Edmund can just about make out the men at the nearest tables. Two of them glare at the young prince who is boisterous and liberal with his words. Ever since his return to Bordeaux, Edmund has felt that the city is not the same any more, nor is court. It is as if the once solid core of English supremacy has turned liquid and ebbs and flows with the tide. Langley has taken to prowling the taverns and brothels, and Gaunt has ordered Edmund to accompany him to ensure he does not overreach. An unnamed beast is lurking in the shadows.

'I believe this is what it is to have a family, my Lord,' Edmund says, tasting the strange word for his current situation. 'Shall we return?'

'Why should I go with you?' Langley's eyes swim about. 'When there is more wine to be had and most certainly more agreeable company to be found!'

Edmund throws his cloak over his shoulder. 'Your brother …'

Langley leans back, and tips his cup. 'Which one? The sickly hero or the silver-tongued politician?' He downs the strong wine and hiccups. 'For you know, they both ask something of me that I cannot give them.'

'My Lord …' Edmund is far more sober than Langley and wonders, for a moment, if he will be forced to carry him back to the castle for the third time this week. The more trouble Langley is, the more Gaunt owes Edmund. And he likes to be owed.

'Oh, come now, Sir Edmund!' Langley releases another roaring laugh. 'It is such a strange occurrence that you and I should share a name when we are so different, is it not?'

He swings the cup around and smiles at the other guests. Some nod their heads with bewildered looks on their faces; most just pretend that the young prince is not there at all.

Langley steadies himself by leaning on the wall and looks at Edmund. 'One more!'

They have been playing this game all day and Edmund is tired. He has spent much money on drink and has had little enough. Being Langley's reveller is no mean feat and many of the other men at court have dodged his company of late. Edmund nods at the barmaid and sits down.

'One.'

Langley taps his finger on the table and Edmund sighs. 'My Lord.'

Appeased that he has his way, Langley leans forward with conspiracy in his eyes. 'Should we offer these fine people a drink on us? What say you, Sire?'

I say that you have been spending money as if we have them; Edmund thinks and knows he will have to speak to Gaunt about Langley's latest tab. But it is not for him to deny the pleasures of a prince, and he rises to have a quiet word with the barmaid. When he returns with two new cups of wine, Langley is staring into the shadows.

'Last round, my Lord.' Edmund's words do not seem to rouse Langley. Turning to the darkness, Edmund catches a glimpse of a royal servant's garb. 'Who is that?'

Langley slips his fingers around the cup and licks his lips. 'My brother's spy. No need to ask which brother.'

Nodding to Langley, Edmund feigns a drink and over the rim of his cup, he watches his companion drink deep. If only he could discover why Langley seems so out of sorts, but when he asks, Langley just laughs, a piercing undertone to the warmth.

'Tell me once more about your visit to London.'

Langley makes it sound as if it is a pleasant outing and not a bitter task that Edmund has performed. He shakes his head. 'I have told the tale so many times, you know it better than I do, my Lord.'

'I need diversion, Sire!' Langley taps his fingers on the table again. 'Tell me about the Baron then.'

'He is hoping to go on a journey.' Not knowing how to proceed, Edmund drinks and pulls a face. The wine is not only strong but also bitter. 'A crusade perhaps. He is ever restless when he is in one place too long. He longs for new adventures, and I fear that sitting a long Parliament is about as far from an adventure as you can get. He wants to experience new things. Who can blame him?'

Sniffing, Langley wipes his nose on his sleeve and looks up, his blue eyes bloodshot. 'He reminds me of my brother. Bedridden and defeated. I still cannot believe that my father would do nothing for him. For us. Are we to stay here forever? For quarters are too tight, I find.' Langley pushes away his cup. 'You were right, Sire, I should not have accepted this last drink. Let us return to the castle.'

Outside, the weather is as grey as Edmund's insides. He has lain with Pascaline every night since he returned, awake and listening to her steady breathing once they are done. Every morning, he gets up at dawn and sits with the baby. He traces her little, round face with his fingers and wonders if she is really his. He does not care for children, they are tedious distractions. Try as he might, Edmund does not care for this one either, pretty though she is.

Of late, Pascaline has grown to bore him, and Edmund idly wonders if it is time to change bedmates once more. He will miss her knowing ways and clever conversation, but it is nothing that firm tits and a willing demeanour will not make up for in more ways than one. If he wants to discuss the lay of the land, all he has to do is attend council, he does not need her.

'… so I think he should stay out of it!' Langley's voice calls back Edmund. 'What say you, Sire?'

They walk through the gate and Edmund is puzzled how they got to be there when just moments ago; they left the tavern. Has Langley been speaking all this time?

'I am sorry, my Lord …'

'Sir Edmund.'

Langley and Edmund turn towards the light voice. A small boy, his hair jet-black, stands before them, a vacant expression on his face.

'Yes?'

'My Lord Gaunt requires your presence.' Without waiting for acknowledgement from Langley that Edmund is excused, the boy turns and walks briskly towards the far end of the castle.

Langley closes one eye and looks at Edmund. 'We can speak later, Sire. Unless you can spare one of you and just send the other to my brother?'

'I am afraid there is only one of me.'

Staggering, Langley turns towards the main building. 'So am I.'

Edmund makes his way to Gaunt's rooms where the servant is waiting for him, the same vacant expression as before. He opens the door and Edmund steps past him.

'Wine, Frank.' Gaunt looks up at Edmund at pauses. 'No. Water.'

Looking down at himself, Edmund straightens his garments and brushes back his hair. The smell of the tavern he can do nothing about, but then it is Gaunt's fault for sending him with Langley in the first place.

'My Lord.'

'I have heard rumours that my brother is leading you astray.' Gaunt signs another document and pours sand on the wet ink. 'Or is it the other way around?'

'I am just doing as you bid', Edmund says and lets his eyes wander around the room. It represents an oxymoron unlike any other he has ever come across. The room is bright and the décor bold, rampant lions and lively colours everywhere. In the middle of the room, Gaunt looms as a dark presence on a field of light. Rumour has it that Gaunt has smuggled in a woman to warm his bed, but if there is truth to it, Edmund can find no evidence. For all its beauty, the chamber is devoid personal ornaments.

'My wife wishes that I return soon,' Gaunt says without pre-empt. 'She asks that I be back in England before Christmas.'

Edmund does not know what to say. They have never spoken of Gaunt's wife before, nor of her expectations for his return. In truth, the pale beauty of Gaunt's spouse does not interest Edmund. But if Gaunt is looking for conversation, he is full well able to carry it out without assistance.

'When I return, I shall once more press upon my father the increasing need to send aid. As you know, my brother is still not well and, now that it has been so long, I fear that his days on the field defending the English claim are past him.' Gaunt pauses as the door opens. 'On the table, Frank.'

The servant executes his task with a skill preceding his years and bows low before closing the door once more. Edmund wonders if he stays outside and listens at the door, or if he is just as disinterested as he appears to be.

'You will continue to keep an eye on my younger brother when I return to England.' Gaunt pours a glass of water and offers it to Edmund. 'He seems pleased with your company.'

'Lord Langley is pleased with anyone who will drink with him, my Lord.' Edmund feels the cold of his words seep through the glass and into his bones.

Offering a seat by the windows, Gaunt goes to sit behind his desk, all of his documents and correspondence piled in neat little stacks. He fidgets with his quill and snaps the lid of the inkwell up and down, a tireless march.

'He is to marry the Princess Constance. My decision has not been an easy one, Sire,' Gaunt says and releases the silver filigree lid to click shut. His thumb is stained blue. 'He does not yet know, but as he is no fool, he suspects that I have made arrangements for him.'

Perhaps that is the cause of his current mood, Edmund thinks, but Langley has been in a state ever since the Prince and Gaunt returned from Najerá, though no one knows why. 'Yes, my Lord.'

'You are not to tell him. Before I leave, I will inform him myself.'

'And the Princess?'

'My spoils of war.' Gaunt rubs his brow and it comes away shaded in blue. 'To do with as I please, I believe was my father's exact wording in his letter to me. King Peter may come clawing for aid sooner than we would like but, this time, I believe my brother will not be so foolhardy as to accept another ill-fated campaign. Nor will my father for he believes he has honoured his agreement with King Peter and will not do so a second time.'

Edmund shakes his head and watches Gaunt with keen interest. Their conversations are always very one-sided, and he knows that Gaunt prefers it to be so. He has no need for a prying knight to ask questions, he has but need of a knight to do his duty and obey orders. As long as Edmund knows when to keep quiet, he will get more information that way than by being forward. And Edmund does enjoy information very much. But every once in a while, Gaunt must be assisted in divulging the right kind of information.

'They say Princess Joan would have his Grace return to England?'

'My sister-in-law wills many things, but in this she has no say.' Gaunt closes his eyes. 'Why do I tell you anything, Sire? What is it about you that makes me confide when, usually, I keep my own counsel?'

Edmund takes another sip of water, letting the cold snake down his throat. He is never going to tell Gaunt his secrets; he is never going to show anyone else how to spin the royal family to your own benefit. Why would he? When he is the one to gain.

'I need to know that I can trust you to keep faith with me, Sire. Even after I am gone.'

'I serve the King and all of his kin,' Edmund says with ease. 'I shall keep faith with you, my Lord.'

'Good.' Gaunt returns to his piles of paper; the quill scratching and dipping, scratching and dipping. Edmund turns for the door.

'One more thing, Sire,' Gaunt says without looking up. 'I have seen you roam the castle at night. I advise you face whatever demons haunt you and have it out. Too many secrets can kill a man.'

## 15 November 1367 – Bordeaux

From the battlement, Edmund watches the caravan of soldiers and knights file out of the courtyard. A little while ago, the Princess had blessed her brother-in-law before he mounted his horse and sent her a flourished wave. Now, Gaunt leads his men on the winding road, his eyes firmly set on the horizon and his return to England.

'Did you see what he has packed away in his carriage? Like a shirt,' Pascaline huffs.

'I saw only bundles of clothes,' Edmund says. 'Of what do you speak?'

'Oh please, if you cannot make out the difference between a bundle of clothes and a swaddled babe, I rather pity our darling girl. You might confuse her with your dirty linen and ask a maid to wash her in boiling water.' Pascaline turns from the view and sits on a low bench flanked at both sides by arrow slits. The eerie silver light of heavy clouds lends an otherworldly frame to her.

As soon as he returned from England, Edmund told Pascaline about Elizabeth, hoping that might end their affair. He had expected her to shout and scream, but instead she held up a red-haired little girl and claimed it was his. Now, every time he looks at the child, he looks for something familiar in her features, but sees none of himself in her. Even the girl's eyes are the wrong colour: green. If not for Pascaline's insistence, he would not believe her to be his at all. Still, a man must have his bed warmed, and Pascaline does that so well that he keeps her around. Of late, she has even grown a bit more interesting again.

Edmund feels her probing gaze and clears his throat. 'A babe?'

'Lord Gaunt has been busy.'

'But surely …' An amusing and unsettling notion surfaces and Edmund pauses to smother a smile.

Pascaline gives a knowing smile that has a hint of triumph in it. 'Not to worry, he has not ravished his little Castilian wards. I have it on good authority that the child is of a different lineage.'

'But why would he bring home a child?' Edmund mutters and then rises when the Princess arrives with two ladies in tow. 'Your Grace.'

Princess Joan greets Pascaline and whispers a command that takes her and the other ladies away. Settling upon the bench, the Princess bids Edmund join her. 'John is gone and good luck to him. I do not envy him a journey through such troubled lands as these, though I confess that if I could, I would take my husband this instant and go with him.' The Princess shakes her head. 'But unrest in the land forces us to remain.'

Edmund had been present when the Princess tried to convince the Prince that they should return to England with Gaunt. Though the Prince has never recovered from his sickness, on that day, he was his former self and formidable in his omnipotence. She might rule him behind closed doors as so many women do but, in the presence of his court, he was swift and firm in his actions.

'At least you have the good company of Lord Langley,' Edmund says. 'Though I had thought that Lord Gaunt would also remain here now that he has wards to attend.'

'We were all amazed that John be given wardship of the two girls, but I suppose that for politics it was the better choice. Whatever the reason, I know that my father-in-law will applaud John's plans,' the Princess whispers and grabs Edmund's arm. 'By marrying your namesake Edmund, Lord Langley, to the Princess of Castile.'

'What says Lord Langley to that?'

Ever since Gaunt told him of his plans, Edmund has been watching Langley ever more closely. He drinks heavily and beds anything that moves; clearly, he is not best pleased, though no one has commented on this.

'He is the son of a King. What can he say?' Staring into the gloomy sky, Princess Joan sighs. 'Fortunately for our King, his son is of a merry disposition and quite happy to marry whoever he is dictated as long as he is granted permission to enjoy life. In that he takes after his older brother, Lionel, whom we still mourn.'

Edmund has never met the Duke of Clarence, but has been told that the Prince and he were so alike that, sometimes, ambassadors would mistake them for twins and that the Prince is famous for having said that his brother was the most handsome. But Edmund can no longer conjure up the Prince that once was, let alone enhance him, for all he sees these days is the Prince's haggard and grim features.

'Lord Langley will be content then?'

'I should think so. Princess Constance is a pious and serious girl, and no doubt Edmund would be happier with her younger sister, but there we are. Perhaps he is just the man to breathe life into her dreary bones and liven her up,' the Princess smiles. 'I rather believe that Edmund will have the long end of this particular stick. Make no mistake, Sire, I do believe John gave the matter much thought before making his decision. He too loves his brother and would not offer him up to the Castilian harpy for anything less than a chance at a crown. You know, I do believe that if John were free, he might pursue Constance himself, and perhaps even begrudges Edmund his freedom.'

'He will not remain free.' Edmund says and enjoys the Princess' smile.

'No, but he will be in line for a crown.' She draws her shawl closer around her shoulders. 'And John is still the richest man in England – by marriage. The inheritance from the Duke of Lancaster must be enough to satisfy even him.'

'I knew the Duke very well,' Edmund says. He is still annoyed that, in the end, for all his services he received very little when the old man died. 'It was in Grosmont's service I first met the Prince, and through him I was transferred to the service of the Baron Mowbray.'

'The Duke was a kind man and ever on the look-out for ways in which to improve the lives of others.' Looking over her shoulder through the arrow slit, the Princess rubs her hands together. 'We cannot sit here forever, but I have something … a question, I suppose. And I do not know where to direct it.'

Edmund longs to be inside by a fire, but if the Princess can stand the increasing cold, then so too can he. Thus, he buries the ache in his shoulder deep inside and offers: 'Might I be of service?'

'That is what I hoped for, I confess.' She smooths her dress. 'John made the most curious request, one which I could not deny although it has perplexed me ever since.'

'Now you have sparked my curiosity, your Grace.' Edmund is careful not to smile.

'He asked for a maid to accompany him.'

'A maid?'

'One who is skilled with children.' Clasping her hands together, Princess Joan catches Edmund's eye. 'I do believe she was then asked to find a wet nurse.'

Edmund awaits the Princess to continue, it is best not to put ideas in her head or words in her mouth, she is not as easily influenced as her husband. At least now, I can use what Pascaline told me, Edmund thinks, once more her gossip serves me well.

'Pascaline helped John pack. I believe he asked for her in particular and had perhaps hoped she might be the maid to accompany him to England but, of course, we both know that was impossible,' the Princess says, her breath a puff of white. 'Since she is so preoccupied here and completely irreplaceable in my household. I sent with him Bernadine. I have never quite been able to make her at ease, so I believe she was well pleased to be sent to England.'

'Then it was a good decision for all parties involved, your Grace.'

Edmund is still waiting for her to ask whatever it is she wants. If the favour is grand enough, he might even be able to profit from it himself. Otherwise, it never goes amiss to have someone in the royal family owe you a debt.

'I want you to speak to Pascaline, see if you can find out why John would want to import a wet nurse when surely there are plenty of women in England equal to the task. I know that Lady Blanche was with child, but her household is already equipped with all the women she might possibly need. She has that young governess too who is, by all accounts, well-liked by everyone, including John. A rare thing.' The Princess stops to draw breath. 'In short, find out what you can and report back to me. It is just a woman's curiosity you need satisfy; the Prince must not be burdened with such trivialities.'

Edmund inclines his head to the Princess who is looking around. 'What a dreary place this is, even with the view. I do believe Constance might like it very well. It will match her constitution.'

'You do not care for Princess Constance?'

'I like my ladies merry.' The Princess rises and walks towards the stairs. 'As do you.'

Pascaline is waiting for Edmund at the bottom of the stairs. They watch the Princess and her ladies walk down the hall, laughter ringing back to embrace them.

'You are not sorry to be left behind?' Edmund wants her by the Princess' side, in her chambers, not here where she is of no use to him at all.

'The Princess is kind to let me make my own choices these days,' Pascaline says and gives his arm a quick squeeze. Where her touch lingers, little buds of warmth bloom on his skin. 'Of course, it cannot continue, but I mean to make the most of it while I can.'

A couple of servants scurry by with trays of fruit and sweet meats, carafes with steaming hot wine and sugared ale, all things that the Princess has decided will cure the Prince of his ailments. Edmund watches them go, careful to keep his distance to Pascaline. Theirs might be the worst kept secret at the Prince's court, but it always pays to be vigilant.

When they are alone again, Edmund walks down the hallway, ducking under a low arch. 'You told me, you helped Lord Gaunt prepare for his journey.'

'Yes.' Pascaline is walking just behind him and he can hear her dress brushing against the floor. It is a bothersome sound. 'Why?'

Something in her voice makes Edmund glance over his shoulder and give her a quick smile. 'Do you know if he employed extra servants before he set off?'

'For the child you mean?'

They turn a corner and Edmund throws a hand behind his back, signalling to Pascaline to keep quiet and fall back a little further. In front of his door is his namesake, Edmund of Langley, who turns at the sound of voices.

'There you are!' Langley gives an easy smile. 'I was looking for you when John left, but I did not see you, Sir Edmund?'

'I was on the battlement, my Lord, with the Princess,' Edmund says. 'What may I do for you?'

Glancing over Edmund's shoulder, Langley bites his lip. 'Can we go in?'

Edmund opens the door and Langley steps through. Stealing a glance in the direction from which he came, he sees the hem of Pascaline's dress disappear around the corner. She is clever enough to know that she cannot loiter in the hall waiting for Langley to leave. God knows what he wants or how long it will take. Once more, Edmund is pleased that he convinced Pascaline that the child could not stay in his rooms, nor hers for that matter. Sputtering with malice, Pascaline found room and board for the girl somewhere in the city and came back in a temper. It took a few days to sort her out, but now she hardly mentions the babe at all. Out of sight out of mind.

'Wonderful view,' Langley remarks from the window. 'Far supreme to mine. I have but a view to the courtyard and the corner of a turret blocks almost all view of the village beyond, not to mention the woods in the distance.'

'I certainly cannot complain, my Lord. Shall I call for refreshments?'

'No, no need, I have promised Joan to attend my brother tonight.' Stroking his sleeve, Langley looks at Edmund. 'Lord knows she needs some time to herself. Time with the children, free not to worry. Even if it is only for an evening.'

'You must tell me what I might do for you, my Lord?' Edmund is curious but also knows that there will be no trips to the taverns and brothels tonight, and so he is not very interested in Langley.

Langley's wide smile returns with something of a smirk to it. 'How good was the view from the battlement, Sire?'

'Very good.'

'You saw all of my brother's train leave?'

'Yes.' Edmund knows where this is going. Every single member of the royal household are gluttons for gossip, and all the better if it is about one of their own.

'He took with him a very special, shall we say, item.' Langley's eyes search Edmund's face. 'He is full of secrets, my brother. Just the other day, he told me that I am to marry the Princess Constance. But to bring a child on such a journey is truly a mystery to me.'

'Lord Gaunt told you of his plans?' Edmund asks, hoping Langley understands the question to mean the forthcoming marriage, not the child, but Langley is no fool.

'Not as such. I came upon him and the servants when they were preparing the carriage. The wet nurse was already inside, but the child was carried out just as I rode into the yard. A happy accident you might say. For me, if not for John, you should have seen his face.'

Langley always rides out early in the morning and returns to break his fast with the rest of the house. Gaunt must have known that his younger brother might find him out, but for some reason he had decided to risk his endeavour. A few hours later, and Langley would be wetting his mouth with the first cup of wine in whatever tavern he wanted to frequent. Except he would not do so today; to turn up drunk to attend the Prince would earn you a night in a cell, no matter your relation and title.

'Do you know why he travels with an infant?'

Edmund feels the ropes of royal demands tighten around his chest. Whom to serve first? Langley who keeps Edmund in supply where wine and women are concerned? Or the Princess who has direct access to the Prince and thereby Edmund's future? The choice is easy; women he can get on his own.

'No, my Lord. This is a great surprise to me. I do not enjoy the confidence of Lord Gaunt.' Not anymore, Edmund adds in his thoughts, which is most unfortunate for I worry that he has found me out.

'I think you underestimate yourself. John would never have recommended to Edward that you be sent to England with the petition to send money and men if he did not find, he could trust you.' Edmund knows this is not the truth, but he knows better than speak up, and Langley continues. 'I own that he was not pleased with your results upon returning to us. I do not doubt that you did all you could, Sire. Edward should have known that our father could not suddenly change the mind of Parliament, but John had hoped you might somehow sway people with your tale.'

'Thank you for your kind words, my Lord,' Edmund says. He has often enough gone over his journey to England and his inability to sway anyone other than Baron Mowbray to his cause.

'You were successful in securing what John wanted though,' Langley says and pats his shoulder to offer reassurance. 'And now, I may be in line for the crown of Castile. Perhaps some secrets are better left alone.'

'Your upcoming marriage is a great match, my Lord.' Edmund steers the conversation away from the mystery child Gaunt has tucked away in his carriage. With any luck, Langley will forget about the child, and all the better for it.

'Is it though? She is so very serious, she does not like music or dancing, she finds little pleasure in good food and fine wine. No matter what I attempt to entice her with, she turns up her nose at it. If I were free to choose, I should rather prefer her sister. She laughs, smiles and enjoys life as I do.' Langley makes for the door. 'I do not mean to sound uncharitable, only I want an easy life. I am not ambitious as John, or groomed for kingship as Edward. I am at the service of my family of course, and I understand my duties full well, but …'

'You may come to like the Princess in time,' Edmund ventures and smiles at Langley's grimace. 'Or perhaps not.'

'Luckily, there are always ways to enjoy life, Sire,' Langley says and opens the door. 'As I believe you well know.'

# CHAPTER 15

## 26 July 1392 – Westminster Palace

'A truth for a truth is that not fair, my Lord?'

Gaunt kept on twirling his lavish quill; the peacock feather glittered and sparkled in the candlelight. 'What truth?'

'That day on the hunt in Bordeaux, when my Lord Woodstock …,' Edmund began.

'Gloucester he is now, or have you forgotten?' The bitterness in Gaunt's voice was unmistakable. In his view, his youngest brother should never have been elevated by anyone, did not deserve such a kindness, and Edmund marvelled anew at the rivalries within the royal family, all of which had served him so well.

'As you say. But back then he was Woodstock and no more than a lad fresh out of his swaddling.' Gaunt harked a laugh and Edmund continued, 'the hunt we went on, where he was almost killed. What happened there?'

'How would I know?'

'You had an air of disillusion about you that day. I know we were together, but I still found it odd …' Edmund gave Gaunt a hard look. 'And you were hunting with bow and arrow.'

'So were we all, Sire. And as you say, we were together, you and I.'

Edmund shook his head. 'I did not bring a bow, nor did your brother.'

'He would not know one weapon from another,' Gaunt said impatiently, 'if you gave him a sword to hold, he would most likely end up cutting his own throat.'

'Is that what you meant for him to do?'

Gaunt's twirling quill stopped moving. 'I think we both know that he can do that just fine without my help.'

## 28 October 1368 - Bordeaux

Gaunt is in the yard making preparations to return to England. Why he is leaving on the day of the hunt, Edmund cannot say, but Gaunt is adamant that he must be away and nothing can stop him. Around them, carriages rumble past and the Master of Hounds is coaxing his pack into a big cage that will take them to various places around the forest.

A thunder of hooves makes Edmund turn his head. It is coming from the wrong direction. One glance at the guard in the tower tells him that everyone is on high alert, but only moments later, a big party emerges from the shadow of the gate, the royal standard snapping above the head of the first rider.

'Thomas!'

A lithe golden-haired youth jumps from the saddle of a big brown gelding and runs to the castle doors where the Prince is overseeing the preparations.

Next to Edmund, Gaunt growls and snaps his fingers away from his saddle. 'Cursed!' Little droplets of ruby blood drip from his hand. 'What is he doing here?'

'Brother!' Thomas all but jumps into the Prince's open arms and is awarded with a hard hug before he is pushed away. He looks up with a wide smile. 'I see now that they tell lies in England; for here is the greatest Prince that ever walked the earth as healthy and well as I have ever seen!'

The Prince laughs and tousles the youth's golden curls. 'And you are most welcomed here, when you bring such honeyed words. What a great pleasure it is to exchange one brother for another.'

Over Thomas' head, the Prince locks eyes with Gaunt, who takes a few reluctant paces towards the doors. Edmund sees a range of emotions flash across Gaunt's face before he pulls himself together and gives a tepid smile.

'Thomas. What brings you here?'

'Father thought it was time I come here and see for myself the English lands across the channel.' Thomas of Woodstock bows his head to Gaunt, in what Edmund takes to be mock submission, before he turns back to the Prince. 'If I had known how vast they were, I would have come sooner to help you govern them, brother!'

Unlike Gaunt, the Prince has a genuine smile on his face. 'If we had known you were coming, we would have arranged a grand welcome. As it is, you have the good fortune to arrive on a day of hunting, and we have need of all the able men we can find.'

Next to the Prince, Woodstock beams, his features so like his older brother that they might be father and son. Edmund has only seen Woodstock a few times around court and has never paid much heed to the youngest of the King's many children. Perhaps it is high time he does.

'What says mother?'

'She was uneasy to let me go, but then her affection for me is such that she can never be long without me.' There is something gloating in Woodstock's voice, but under the watchful gaze of Gaunt, it falters. 'She commands that I return with you, brother.'

'Then your good fortune runs out before it begins, Thomas,' Gaunt grumbles and swings into the saddle with a heavy thud. 'For I leave now.'

'NO!' Woodstock's eyes go to the Prince who is watching the sibling rivalry with a faint smile on his face.

The Princess' constant care and vigilant insisting that the Prince only come outside in the sunshine, is always clad in warm clothes and never without attendants has at last mended her ailing husband. At this very moment, he looks almost the same as the first time Edmund met him. But behind his good looks is the whisper of sickness and his stance is not as steady as it once was.

'If it is mother's specific command that you return with John then you must do so.'

'Why Thomas, what are you doing here?' The Princess emerges from the castle, a thick silk cloak around her shoulders, her hair tied back from her face and held in place by a golden net that sparkles in the sunlight. 'Did we know?'

'He has come to escort John home.' The Prince's words waver for a second.

'Surely not! He is only just arrived.' The Princess looks at Gaunt, stiff in his saddle. 'John?'

'Mother's orders.' Edmund hears the sneer in Gaunt's voice and so does the Princess for she awards him a wintry glare.

'Well then, you must stay two more days. We cannot turn away our own blood at our threshold, this you must see.'

'I am not returning for frivolous activities, your Grace,' Gaunt spits, 'but to bury my beloved wife.'

The Prince and Princess exchange a brief glance and then the Prince nods. 'Two days, John. You decide if you wish to stay here or if you wish to go ahead and then wait for Thomas at the docks. Some of the arrangements you can make from here, I have no doubt. I put to your service my fastest and finest messengers and freshest horses.'

'There,' the Princess says and tucks Woodstock's hand in the crook of her arm. 'The hunt is almost ready, but we have time for a little refreshment. I must then wait here for news that you have returned with the biggest stag as your prize.'

The Prince nods to Edmund but before he can move, Gaunt's gloved hand clamps around his wrist. 'A word.'

'My Lord, the Prince …'

'Let that little monkey entertain him, what are you to him?' Gaunt hisses and sends Edmund a burning scowl. 'I have need of your services now, Sire. What say you?'

'At your service, my Lord.' Edmund fights an urge to wrench free. It is not Gaunt's words that annoy him, but the underlying implication that Edmund is no longer one of the Prince's favourites. Surely nothing can be further from the truth.

Gaunt dismounts and nods to a stable boy who leads his horse away. 'Leave the saddle on. Now that I am to stay here for two more days, I shall participate in the hunt.'

Crossing the courtyard, Gaunt aims for his own quarters and Edmund follows in his wake. Lamenting that to be pinched between the two princes is no man's desire, Edmund's natural curiosity has already won the day. Even if Gaunt had given him the option to return to the Prince's side, Edmund would have come with him. He is certain that he can spin a tale that the Prince will lap up without blinking.

Gaunt slams the door shut and breathes deep. Edmund can smell his rage and dons a carefree smile to show Gaunt when he turns to face him. Though Gaunt is at least a head shorter than Edmund, at this very moment, he looks every bit as formidable as the Prince once did; pure loathing fuels Gaunt.

'What the hell is that little brat doing here? He belongs behind my mother's skirts! Pampered, insufferable little snake!' He paces the room and not even the white wash on the walls and the bright fabrics can withstand the black hatred oozing from Gaunt. 'Did you know he was coming? Well?'

'No, my Lord.' But I should have, Edmund thinks, I must have words with my little informants. Since discovering how valuable spies are, Edmund has constantly increased his own count. It always pays to have ears and eyes everywhere.

'I thought perhaps Baron Mowbray had told you something.' A little of the rage has gone from Gaunt's voice. 'I would have been far less surprised to see Mowbray here than that little ...'

'I have not had word from the Baron since his letter detailing his journey beyond the seas.' Edmund pours a little pathetic undertone into his voice. 'I have no other means of information from England.'

'Is that so?' Gaunt runs a hand across his eyes. Now, there is only fatigue in his words. 'Forget what I just said. I am distressed by the death of my wife and eager to return home to ensure she is entombed in a befitting state. I am contemplating that she be lain to rest in St. Pauls.'

Edmund bows his head to hide a wolfish smile. For a long time, Pascaline has been singing her songs about Gaunt's interest in the new governess employed to care for his girls. And even longer since stories from the English court filtered back to Edmund that Gaunt was distressed when his pale wife could only mother living girls and dead boys. He wonders how much of Gaunt's yearning to return to England is due to obligation and how much is desire. To see the governess, perhaps persuade her to warm his bed. Edmund resolves that if he ever sees this Mistress Katherine that everyone tells tales of, he must bed her, even if she is as ugly as sin.

In the end, we all turn to dust, Edmund muses inside, and I for one plan to make the most of my life before I die.

'Remember the spot in which we saw the buck?' Gaunt draws Edmund back from his joyous plans.

'Yes.'

'I saw it again this morning.' Gaunt gives a slow nod. 'I ask that you ride with me for the hunt today, Sire. And that we go without squires. They always chatter and will ruin any chance we may have of taking down the beast. I am determined that one of us shall bring back the best prey.'

'Yes, my Lord.'

A knock on the door sends a flicker of anger across Gaunt's face, but he calls for it to open. His black-haired servant-boy appears and gives another of his exaggerated bows. 'My Lord. His Grace the Prince requires that you and Sir Edmund attend him in the great hall.'

'Duty calls, Sire.' Gaunt brushes past Edmund and walks down the gallery without looking back.

When Edmund walks past the servant, he looks up, his grey eyes big. 'Is it true the Prince will ride today?'

'Yes.' There is something eerie about the boy, but Edmund cannot tell what it is, which is even more unsettling than the boy himself. 'What is that to a servant?'

'Nothing, Sire,' the boy says. 'Only I fear for the Prince. Dark clouds amass in the horizon. Have you not seen it, Sire?'

'I pay no heed to omens, boy,' Edmund says and gives the boy a stern look, 'and neither should you.'

The boy bows his head a little and his distressing, grey eyes vanish under his long lashes. 'It is only what they say in the taverns, Sire.'

'You are far too young to visit …'

'Sir Edmund!' Gaunt's angry voice ricochets off the bare stone and tiled floor. 'I will not be the reason my brother cannot start his hunt! And neither will you!'

When Edmund looks down, the servant is gone.

'He said what?'

The cloth covering his mouth muffles Gaunt's voice. He and Edmund are alone in the small clearing that Gaunt is so certain will afford them the best trophy of the hunt. Edmund cannot help wondering if Gaunt is right. In his own experience, deer roam far and wide and rarely return to the same spot several days in a row. But Gaunt is adamant and here they are, though Gaunt was late to arrive having been caught up in the Prince's train.

'That they speak of it in the taverns,' Edmund mutters and strains his eyes. The sunlight plays through the foliage, and the whole world is speckled gold and green. If the deer are here, they are well protected by nature.

'Omens?' Even in the low tones, Edmund hears Gaunt's disbelief. 'Dark clouds? Nonsense, is it not?'

'You know as well as I do, my Lord, that unrest mars the Prince's domain.' Edmund enjoys poking and prodding the dormant English lions, although he rarely points the finger at the Prince. 'Even though the Prince is back and in his element, nothing is as it once was. The French do not forget that he took all their able men and came home with a skeleton army. Though the old folks and the women work the fields they cannot produce as much food as before and they are disgruntled.'

'I have seen the problems.' Gaunt turns and plucks an arrow from the quiver strapped to the back of his saddle. 'The harvest will be meagre. And most of it must be given to my brother.'

Edmund nods inside but does not move. He has spotted something in the shadows on the other side of the path and is waiting for whatever animal it is to break through the undergrowth. His short lance hangs limp from his hand, there is no point to raise it until it is time to skewer his prey.

The bushes break apart and Edmund turns his lance at Gaunt just in time to bring him out of balance as he releases the bowstring, his arrow missing its mark and drilling into a tree.

'What the HELL?!'

'You could have KILLED ME!'

Edmund stares at the boy on the ground, his golden curls adorned with leaves and twigs.

'Thomas.' The name comes out as a weak hiss and Gaunt jumps from his horse, almost tangling his foot in the stirrup. 'What are you doing?'

Recognising the fear in Gaunt's harsh words, Edmund too dismounts and kneels beside the frightened prince. 'My Lord Woodstock, where is your horse?'

Woodstock blinks and rubs his face with a dirty hand, the glove sliced open at the thumb. 'The stupid beast was scared by a boar and bolted. I tried to hang on, but …'

Gaunt pulls his arrow from the tree, his back turned to his brother. Edmund can tell that Woodstock is scared out of his wits, and he also knows how close they came to disaster. But something in Woodstock's eyes stays Edmund's hand when he reaches out to help.

'Would that you had shot the stupid horse, John,' Woodstock gulps and gets up, brushing his hose with great vigilance. 'For I shall never sit it again! If it bolts so easily, I have no use of it.'

'Perhaps the problem is its rider and not the horse.' Gaunt puts the arrow back in the quiver and looks at Woodstock. 'If a boar set your horse running, what set you running?'

Woodstock looks from Gaunt to Edmund and then at the ground. 'Nothing.'

Edmund turns to take his horse aside, but Gaunt stays him. 'Come now, Thomas. Sir Edmund is well equipped to keep secrets and so you can entrust yourself to us. In return, you must promise not to breathe a word of what happened here. Then we will all have secrets to keep.'

Kicking the ground, Woodstock seems to take stock of the situation. 'I could tell Edward that you tried to kill me. I could tell him that you do not care for me and so you seized …'

Before Edmund can move, Gaunt has his hands around his brother's neck. 'I could tell him that you wrung your neck on a branch!' Coming to his senses, Gaunt gives a shaking laugh and looks at Edmund. 'And since Sir Edmund is the most credible of all of us, he will tell Edward what truly happened. Come now, Thomas, what sent you running?'

'A pheasant.' Woodstock's cheeks burn red as he looks at Edmund. 'Not a word.'

'A very big pheasant no doubt.' Gaunt takes Woodstock by the arm and leads him to the horses. Edmund can tell that Gaunt is entertained even if his jaw is set. 'Perhaps the Devil had taken hold of the poor bird. For surely that is the only reason you did not just scare it off.'

'I hit my head when I fell from the horse.' Woodstock's eyes are brimming now, and Edmund can tell that he is ashamed and humiliated, but Gaunt will not let up. Edmund bites his tongue to keep from laughing.

'Oh, I see. Are you bleeding?'

With a blank expression, Edmund holds out his reins. 'Take mine, my

Lord Woodstock. If you are hurt, you must return to the castle and have your injuries seen to.'

'No one can mend a bruised ego.' Gaunt gives a cold shrug when Woodstock begins to shake and sob. 'You are too young to be here if you cannot handle the thrill of the hunt. You should never have come.'

With tears streaming down his dirty cheeks, Woodstock steps into Edmund's folded hands and is hoisted into the saddle. From there, he looks down upon Gaunt and anger creeps up Woodstock's neck and into his eyes. 'Beware, brother, that you do not speak out of turn. For I know something that you do not wish for anyone else to find out.' Woodstock turns Edmund's hunter and kicks it into a canter. 'And keep your dog there quiet too!'

Edmund expects Gaunt to follow Woodstock, but instead he stands stock-still and stares after his youngest brother. In the crushing silence, the sounds of the forest are slow to resume and Edmund can almost taste Gaunt's rage. Deciding not to be the first to speak, Edmund picks up his lance and checks that his dagger is still in its sheath.

Flexing his fingers, Gaunt turns and freezes. Without a word, he notches an arrow and inclines his head ever so slightly towards the spot where not many moments ago, Woodstock tumbled through. Edmund sees the buck and by reflex, he stops breathing. The bowstring sings a single note and the buck disappears before Edmund can release his short lance.

Gaunt curses beneath his breath and notches another arrow. He nods to Edmund who lets go of his lance and creeps forward. He reaches for the branches and jumps aside just in time. The wounded buck leaps into the clearing and there collapses at his feet, soaking the ground in blood.

'Good kill.' Gaunt hunkers down by the buck and pulls out his arrow. 'You should have brought your lance but, as it stands, the kill is mine.'

Edmund tries to smile through his own disappointment. 'You had it killed already. My lance would be for show.'

With a tired sigh, Gaunt shakes his head. 'Remember what my servant said to you earlier? Dark clouds are gathering. If this is not an omen, Sire, I know not what to make of it. No deer should act as this one has. Why was it not startled by Thomas flailing about, crying like a girl?'

'I cannot say, my Lord.' Edmund admits to himself that he wondered the same thing. Wild animals are never this predictable.

'Because something is wrong in Bordeaux,' Gaunt says and tries to clean off the blood that streaks his boots. 'Very wrong.'

'You believe in omens, my Lord? A moment ago, you dismissed them so easily.' Edmund pulls back the buck's head and slashes its throat. Warm blood courses over his hand and wets his blade, the pleasant iron smell tickles his nose. He lets the buck bleed out onto the ground before he begins gutting it.

'Not as a rule. But tell me, Sire, what might induce deer to stay so near a path that reeks of man? To circle back to the same spot time and again even though we ride here every day? Our Master of Hounds even takes his dogs here at least once a week. It makes no sense.'

Edmund can hear Gaunt walk around the clearing but keeps his eyes on the buck. 'Kids.'

'Not this late in the year. At least, they are big enough to roam with the grown animals. And what buck ever cared for his kids?' Gaunt's voice is further away now. 'I am riding back. There is someone I must speak to. Wait here for the wagon. I shall point them in your direction if I see them along the way.'

'Yes, my Lord.' Edmund curls his lip in disdain.

'Be well pleased, Sir Edmund! Tonight, we will toast your good fortune.' Gaunt turns his horse about. 'For not only did you aid me in bringing down the buck, you also stayed my hand and averted crisis!'

## 28 October 1368 – Bordeaux

'Do not send me home, brother, please.' Woodstock's words fill the great hall. 'We can decide that I came by another road and did not see John. That way I can stay.'

'If it is mother's will that you return home with John, and when you got here, he had already left,' the Prince says, 'then I would be obliged to send you back directly. It cannot be helped. And she must have known that John would leave for England soon after you arrived. Be content that she let you go at all.'

Woodstock looks to his left where Gaunt is hovering, a dim outline against the bright tapestry of a naked Eve being offered an apple. As ever,

Gaunt is dressed in plain black clothes. Only now, he has omitted any chains and other symbols of his status. In mourning, he seems swallowed up by darkness.

In striking contrast, Woodstock wears bold red and blue clothes and over his shoulder hangs a thick cloak of bright green silk. He wears all of his chains, pins and rings and it hurts Edmund's eyes to look at him. He seems determinately indisposed to pay homage to his brother's recent loss, although Edmund knows that Woodstock has at least one whole chest filled with exquisite dark blue garments. It was all the talk in the Princess' chambers last night, as Pascaline told him when she returned from her duties. Some of her tales are more useful than others, Edmund thinks, but I like to know all that goes on, and for that alone, I shall continue to bed her. A smile steals across his face.

The Prince has the presence of mind to dress in dark purple to honour Gaunt's loss and, next to him, the Princess is wearing a plain dark brown dress and a thin string of black diamonds around her neck.

She looks at Woodstock with a mixture of motherly concern and fierce determination. 'My mother-in-law commanded that you return with your brother. John is going home to see to his wife's funeral. His beloved wife. You will do as you are bid, Thomas.'

A change of tune, Edmund reflects and sees Woodstock look away, his cheeks as flushed as they were yesterday in the woods. Edmund wonders if he will speak out of turn as he threatened to do. Here is a rash young man used to having his way, Pascaline had said when they settled in for the night, and Edmund knows she has the right of it. Still, he is surprised at the Princess' change of heart over a single night, and he suspects Gaunt's whispered words last night at the feast may well have something to do with it. Not to mention the words he exchanged with the Prince right before leaving.

Woodstock draws breath, but the Prince holds up a hand to silence him. 'We will speak no more of it, brother. You are most welcome here, to be sure, but mother must have her way, for we all know that no one can soothe her as you do, and she grieves for the loss of a great favourite. We all mourn for Lady Blanche – even you – and you will return with John when he leaves this midday. I appoint you as my representative at the funeral, since I cannot go myself.'

Bowing his head, Edmund can tell that Woodstock's cheeks are glittering with tears. But he says nothing.

The Prince walks to him and puts a hand on his shoulder. 'We will be together again soon. I shall ask that you be granted leave to join my court for the next year. It is about time you see what governing can also be. There, let that be a boon.'

Edmund does not have to look at Gaunt to know that he is snorting derision. Edmund is surprised that the Prince wants to take part in the education of Woodstock, but then he needs to be taught how to master his temper and put the needs of others before his own. How else will the Prince settle discord and keep his brothers in check when the time comes for him to rule England?

At the very back of the room, Langley hovers with an inscrutable look on his face. It is no secret that his prolonged engagement with the Castilian princess has taken its toll on him and, most days, he is heavy in his drink. Aided by Edmund whenever he can. But since Gaunt learned that his wife had died, a new sombreness has stolen over Langley and, for once, Edmund does not know what to make of it. When last he tried to discuss it with Pascaline, she just laughed and said she was well pleased that he not be always in a tavern drinking with the prince. She prefers Edmund to be home and at her disposal. Though said in jest, Edmund still thinks she is also quietly rejoicing in knowing where he is at all times, and that does not sit well with him. What right does a woman have to rule a man?

'Come brother, you are young and have your life ahead of you. What is another few months when you know what adventure lies ahead?' The Prince beams at Woodstock and he is quick to return the smile. 'There! Now, are you all packed?'

'No, he is not,' Gaunt seethes at Edmund's side. 'Why am I forced to take this peacock when staying here is exactly what he needs? I will not have him parading about for my wife's funeral. But then, I should have known better than to think I could change my brother's mind.'

Gaunt signals for Edmund to follow when he turns to leave the great hall, courtiers, knights and ladies parting before his determined stride.

'When Thomas returns here, if my mother allows it, make sure you keep an eye on him.' Gaunt pulls on his thick riding gloves and looks out into the courtyard where horses wait for their riders and the last of the wagons are being loaded. 'He is an ambitious little prick, and I will know all that he does.'

'You do not plan to return, my Lord?' Edmund hears relief in his own voice and hopes that Gaunt does not. Though he does not care for Gaunt, it has been useful to be in his favour these past months and Edmund has wondered many times if he will be able to anticipate the Prince's decisions and steer them in his own direction without the knowledge Gaunt has freely given. Still, Edmund prefers to have one Prince to deal with at a time.

'There is much to do in London. I am speaking not only about my wife's funeral but also about the estate she leaves me. I must ensure all is as it should be, and I must visit all of my lands.' Gaunt rubs his hands together against the wet grey gloom. 'She was well-loved by all.'

'I am sorry that I never met her.' A little gallantry never goes amiss, Edmund thinks and follows Gaunt to the mounting block. 'I saw her a few times, but I never met her properly.'

'I know that I am asking you to serve two masters, Sir Edmund,' Gaunt mutters as they wait for his horse to be brought. 'But I find I have no one else to trust here.'

In the back of Edmund's mind, the King's praise that he is the only man the Prince and Gaunt ever agreed on rings, and he gives a comforting smile, careful not to look smug. 'I serve the Crown and England.'

'But my brother before all others.' Taking the reins, Gaunt looks at Edmund. 'As you should. I ask a favour. If it goes against orders from Edward, you must heed him. I do not expect much by way of communication, only that you keep an eye on troublesome Thomas and report back if he grows too big for his boots. But I doubt that my mother will consent to him going. She loves her baby-boy too much.'

Gaunt gets into the saddle and his squire jumps to, arranging the thick travel cloak and ensuring that the stirrups are the right height. Edmund watches Gaunt ride to the edge of the courtyard, rearing to go, his eyes scanning the throng of men in search of Woodstock no doubt.

'I will not go!'

The doors to the castle swing open, and Woodstock's adolescent voice bounces off the walls. Even with his back turned, Edmund knows that everyone is looking at the scene for just a moment too long before the noise and rumble resumes. He steps back and watches the Prince guide

Woodstock to the mounting block, a firm hand on his brother's narrow shoulder. From Woodstock's face it is obvious that he is being forced ahead, but the Prince smiles and makes no show of his irritation.

'They all wear masks.' Pascaline says at his elbow, looking at the Prince and Woodstock. She nods to the door. 'He is furious that Lord Langley does not have to go too.'

'He is a child.'

She sighs. 'He is a prince first.'

'Why does he get to stay?' As the Prince pushes Woodstock up the steps to the mounting block his mutter reaches Edmund. 'If I go, he must go too. Make him!'

The Prince squeezes Woodstock's shoulder once more. 'His place is here. I will make arrangements for him to join you for the funeral, if I see fit. You are in the care of our mother, whom we all revere and love. She wishes you back in England, and so you will go.'

'You take orders from a woman?' Woodstock's question comes out in pants, pain vibrant on his face.

'No. I take orders from my mother.' There is both warning and amusement in the Prince's voice. 'And you would do well to heed her word too, for she is a fierce and clever woman. As I say, we shall see each other again soon. What is a few months in a young man's life?'

'An eternity,' Woodstock sneers and is all but thrown into the saddle by his brother. A final squeeze to Woodstock's leg silences him on the topic.

'FAREWELL!' The Prince raises his hand, and Gaunt nods before spurring on his horse.

'There is one I am not sad to see the back off.' Pascaline lingers when the Princess turns from the stairs and returns inside to the roaring fires and mulled wine. 'He is trouble.'

'He is young, he will learn the ways …'

'Not him.' Pascaline sends him an unreadable glance. 'Lord Gaunt.'

# Part 3

# Decay

# CHAPTER 16

## 26 July 1392 – Westminster Palace

'Your French woman never warmed to me,' Gaunt said, 'I knew as much. Still, she was wrong about me, was she not, Sire? In the end, my dear brother Thomas was more trouble than I. And I am surprised she called me out that early when she had nothing to speak up against until later.'

'Limoges might have been avoided.' Edmund felt his balls harden and retract. He had few regrets in his life, but this was one of them.

'You looked to be as disgusted by the slaughter as I was,' Gaunt said with a faint trace of sadness in his voice. 'I begin to think, I have been mistaken about that all these years.'

'I spoiled for battle, yes,' Edmund agreed and, for once, bile rose in his throat, 'but it was no battle. There was no glory, no true adversaries in our actions. What can be gained from murdering innocent women and children?'

'Your display in the square?'

'My honest attempt to stem the madness within,' Edmund said flatly. 'I truly believed I could dissuade your brother of his intents.'

'Intents you put in his rattled brain to begin with,' Gaunt hissed, his hands splayed on the table trembled. 'It was you who launched the attack, you who ensured …'

'I might have played some small part in your brother's plans, but … I still hear them in my sleep.' Edmund could not bear to shoulder the responsibility of that day. Would not be held accountable for an ancient mistake. 'I called for his greater goodness, what had once been his finest piece of armour.'

'That armour was buried along with the rest of his immortal soul on the field outside Najera. If you had any sense, you would have recognised that he was beyond caring by the time you whispered your poison into his ear.' For the first time that night, Gaunt's voice trembled even more than his hands, his eyes were sleek pits of tar. 'You mean to persuade me now, after all these years, that you honestly tried to stop him?'

Something inside Edmund splintered; little fragments of horror streamed out and began to seep into his blood, into his thoughts. He cleared his throat, reached for his cup and then abandoned the notion. He straightened his back and looked at Gaunt, he would not give the mighty Lord even a single glance at his discomfit. 'Yes.'

'From what you have told me thus far, Sire,' Gaunt spat with disdain, 'I choose to say you are a liar. Well-rehearsed no doubt, but a liar nonetheless. I have been around many enough to call one out, though you had me fooled too. I should have trusted my first instincts, but you weaved a web of comfort that blinded me. Now, the web is torn asunder.'

Edmund turned his thoughts inward, evaded Gaunt's palatable anger, sought some form of redemption but found none. For all that Edmund loved battle, Limoges was never a battle, it did not even count as an act of war. It had torn apart the last shreds of a sane mind and, try as he might, Edmund could not even convince himself that he had played no part in the events that had come to pass.

'Why did you tell my brother to sack the city?'

Gaunt's whisper came from far away, and Edmund shook his head. 'I did not, my Lord.'

'Is that so?' Gaunt drew breath and leaned back. Edmund could tell he was forcing down his temper. 'For of late, I have heard a different tale. One that I dismissed because we all know what an admirable knight you are. I called it slander. Now, I would say it is closer to the truth than anything I have ever heard.'

'No one could account for your brother's descend into madness, not even I.'

'You were two of a kind, you admitted so yourself.'

'We were, my Lord,' Edmund said with true deference this time. 'But he went into lunacy alone.'

'You pushed him.'

'I tried to pull him back …'

'You pushed him.' Gaunt's voice fell an octave. 'You and you alone pushed him.'

## 18 September 1370 – Limoges

'This war is far from over.' The Prince coughs and falls back. His forehead is slick with sweat, his hair drenched. 'You mark my words! All of you!'

'Brother, you know that I would go anywhere with you, to Hell and back if need be,' Gaunt says, 'but this is madness. You are sick. You should not be here. None of us should be here. This is a task for savages and harriers. It has nothing to do with government.'

'No. It has to do with punishment.' Though the Prince looks weak and frail, his voice booms, as strong and fierce as ever. 'The punishment of traitors should never be left to men of weak beliefs. It must be administered from the seat of power. Or have you forgotten everything our father taught us?'

Gaunt grits his teeth, and Edmund smothers a sneer. He is tired of the brothers' constant bickering, and he is hung over after a night of drinking with Langley who lingers in the shadows, dark circles around his eyes; Langley is still not wed and the torment of waiting has him wrapped in invisible chains.

'No, I have not,' Gaunt says. 'But he also taught us patience and deliberation, and that is what I would have you think on now.'

'Get out.' Somehow the poison in the Prince's whisper drives fear into Edmund's tired mind. The Prince pushes himself up in a stronger seat; sweat springing from his temples at the exertion. 'Get out! Get out you filthy COWARD! GET OUT and take all of these whimpering fools with you!'

Gaunt's eyes flash as he pushes past Edmund and storms out of the room; the open door serves as a toothless mouth that has just swallowed up a prince.

'GET OUT!' the Prince roars once more and all of the other men in the room jump, pushing against the doorframe and wincing when they catch on the big hinges.

Edmund turns as one of the last, stepping aside to let his fellow drunk precede him. Langley sends him a weak smile of equal gratitude and pain before the darkness outside eats him too.

'Not you.'

Pausing with his hand on the handle, Edmund looks back, expecting someone else to still be there. But he is the last. 'Your Grace?'

'Close the door. I can take no more folly today.'

Edmund does as he is bid and then waits for the Prince to speak again. But he just lies there with his eyes closed, slowly sliding further down under the piles of hides and blankets that the Princess has no doubt ordered he be slathered in. His fingers are claws on the white linen shirt, clutching his chest.

'He will be the death of me.' The words come out so quiet that, for a moment, Edmund thinks he might have dreamed them. But then the Prince speaks again, his voice an awful whisper. 'I swear to you, all he wants is to undermine my authority and then plead with our father that I am too weak to undertake my responsibilities and that he should replace me.'

'Your Grace, I am certain …' Edmund begins, but the Prince keeps on speaking as if he is oblivious to Edmund's presence.

'He has coveted my position since he was born. He will never be content to stand behind me, to advise me and take orders from me.' The Prince turns his fever-ridden face. 'Did you not hear him today, Edmund? How dare he second-guess my decisions? In front of my men, my knights and my council? I will tell you why. Because he is certain that, in time, our father will cast me aside for him. A sick cripple exchanged for a healthy heir.'

'He is concerned, your Grace.' Edmund wipes his brow. The air in the room is cluttered, sickly and infected, and all the braziers burning are still not enough to keep the shivering corpse that is the Prince warm. 'It is just that he is the only one …'

'The only one who dares speak up? Who dares defy me to my face, is that it, Edmund? Do you disagree with me too?'

Edmund is still trying to decide how to spin this situation to his own benefit, but in the heat, it is hard to see a clear path. 'It is not my place …'

The Prince coughs and the whole bed rattles beneath him. When he finally catches his breath, he opens his eyes and gestures for Edmund to help him get more comfortable. Handling him is like touching a living cadaver. Edmund arranges his face and ignores the sickly stink. It is unworthy for the Prince to be ill, and it is unworthy for Edmund to have to serve him as a common groom.

'I am making it your place,' he groans as Edmund puts his arms around the Prince's hollow chest and heaves. 'I am in dire need of counsel, and I would have it from someone who loves battle as much as I do. Someone who is not afraid to take a hard road if needs be.'

'What if you do not like my advice, your Grace?'

'Then I will ignore it,' the Prince croaks a laugh, 'but you have never failed me in the past and, therefore, I do not concern myself with such trifling.'

Edmund steps back and turns around, the scent of the Prince imprinted on his clothes and his skin. He reaches for the pitcher of water and pours a generous cup, which he offers to the Prince whose hand shakes as he grabs it, but he manages to drink from it with some effort. 'Go on. Advise me.'

'You must strike fear in the heart of these rebels,' Edmund says with emphasis, trusting his instincts to guide the way when everything around him is opaque. 'They must learn once and for all that you are their master. The time for patience and diplomacy is long past. Nothing will work with them but to be put to the sword and forced into obedience. You must set an example that will be spoken of in every tavern and market from here to the border.'

'See that is advice which is sound and just,' the Prince says and coughs again. 'Would that my brother could see things as we do. Or better yet. Would that you could exchange places, for nothing would please me more than to have you at my side in matters such as these. You would make a far better brother than he ever has.'

'You flatter me, your Grace.' But of course, Edmund knows better.

The Prince waves; a feeble and weak gesture. 'I speak as I find, as I have ever found. You and I are more alike than you may ever know. That is why we understand each other so well. Strike fear into their hearts, you say. Make a statement, I say.'

'What do you have in mind, your Grace?'

'Kill them all and burn the city to the ground.' The feverish glare of the Prince's gaze chills Edmund to the bone. 'And so it will be.'

It is his decision, Edmund thinks as he closes the door, his decision alone, I had nothing to do with it. But for once, a little doubt leaks out and stains his thoughts. After all, they are about to sack the city of his bedmate, the mother of his child. Something dormant stirs in the pit of Edmund's stomach, and he all but runs to find Langley intending to drown his concerns in a bottle of strong wine.

He hopes that the Prince will change his mind; that he will call for his men to turn around and march for Paris. If nothing else, Edmund hopes that Gaunt will revisit his brother's chambers and talk some sense into him.

Tomorrow, Edmund thinks, we shall be gone from this place. Even if I have to dissuade the Prince of his mad endeavour myself. We shall be gone from this place in search of true battle.

Still, it sits uneasy in his mind and no amount of wine can wash away that little bead of doubt.

# CHAPTER 17

## 19 September 1370 – Limoges

'Keep your men in line!' Edmund shouts. 'Lord Warwick, are you ignoring a royal command?!'

Warwick turns his horse around and glares. 'No! I am carrying out a royal command!'

For just a moment, Edmund is struck dumb but then he recovers. 'How so?'

'The Prince ordered that all men, women and children be killed, did he not?' Warwick's haughty face is almost more than Edmund can stomach. Bloody fool! Now, Warwick even smirks. 'I merely passed on that order to my men.'

'Along with a carte blanche to rape and pillage as they see fit?'

'How much do you pay your men?' Warwick leers. 'Oh no, you have no men, is that not so, Sire?'

Before Edmund can reply, Gaunt careers in between them, spooking Warwick's horse. Despite the dire situation, Edmund almost laughs, but the screams all around him paints such a terrible picture that his laughter dies on his lips.

'Sir Edmund! Lord Warwick! Why are you bickering?!' Gaunt glares at them. 'Warwick! Gather your men and keep them in check!'

'What might that mean, my Lord?' Warwick draws out his last word and Gaunt colours.

'That you seem to have mistaken your orders!'

Warwick waves his hand dismissively. 'Kill everyone. Those were the orders, were they not my Lord? As I see it, if my men have a little sport first, so be it. Or are you offering to pay them? I hear that your coffers are brimming with gold and silver.'

Edmund can tell that it is taking all of Gaunt's willpower to keep from charging. He pulls the reins tight and spits: 'No. That, I believe, falls to the man who musters troops to fulfil a royal command. And yours was to kill, not rape and plunder. The Prince is requesting your presence in the square.'

'Best I do not keep his Grace waiting then,' Warwick says with a wide smile.

'You too, Sir Edmund.' Gaunt turns his horse around and leads the way, wiping the smile from Warwick's face.

'Lockley!' Warwick barks and a young man appears as if out of nowhere.

'My Lord?'

'We are wanted on the square. Find Sir Alan and bring him to me.'

Without waiting for the squire to answer, Warwick spurs his horse and follows Gaunt around a street corner. Edmund looks at the youth; there is something dead about his eyes, something strangely lethal about his person, something he recognises but at this moment wants to deny.

'You are new?' Edmund is trying to place his face and fails.

Lockley looks up at Edmund and gives a stiff smile. 'Yes, Sire.'

'And Sir Alan, would he by any chance be Alan Coxcombe?'

'Yes, Sire.'

Edmund nods and Lockley turns about disappearing as quietly as he appeared. Coxcombe has not been long in Bordeaux, but already he has made a name for himself. He is skilled on the field, though he sits his horse a little heavy and holds his lance at a strange angle. Edmund has witnessed Coxcombe unseat many good knights and has heard Langley speak well of him. It made Edmund want to seek out this upstart and smother him in his sleep, but that would not do. Rather he be killed here, today, perhaps under the pretext that someone tried to defend their home.

Surely Warwick has it wrong when he names him a knight, for the Prince has not knighted any men before they left for Limoges. And since

Coxcombe has yet to prove himself in true battle, he cannot be a knight, it would not be right. In the back of Edmund's mind, Grosmont's voice reminds him that there are many ways to become a knight, but only those knighted on the battlefield can truly claim the title.

The sounds of sobbing women, crying children and pleading men return to Edmund's world. He turns his horse and heads for the town square, it is easy enough to find, all he has to do is follow the increasing inferno of voices. His stomach churns, try as he might, he cannot turn a blind eye to the English soldiers dragging girls and women past him into dark alleys. The screams tear at his ears until he is convinced that they will bleed.

A soldier in Warwick's colours stands with his back turned to the street; he has a girl pinned against the wall. Her wide brown eyes and open mouth frozen in a stifled smile sends Edmund over the edge.

'LEAVE HER BE!' He jumps from his horse and draws his sword. 'I told you to leave her, soldier!'

The man turns and Edmund's sword slides in his grip. 'Coxcombe?'

'Sir Alan, I think you will find,' Coxcombe says in such a conversational tone that, just for a moment, Edmund thinks he has misunderstood the situation. But then he looks down.

'Spurs can be lost, Sire!' Edmund hisses and raises his sword once more, the tip floating only a hair from Coxcombe's chest. 'Leave the girl!'

'You have no authority over me.' Coxcombe winces when Edmund's sword flips. So, the rumours are true, Edmund thinks, you are afraid of me. Coxcombe gulps. 'None what so ever.'

'But Lord Warwick does,' Edmund growls, relishing in the fresh surge of power that runs through his body. 'And we are to present ourselves at the square. Now!'

'He tells truth, Sire,' a young voice pipes up.

Edmund turns and faces Lockley. Although the squire looks uncomfortable, there is something hungry in his grey eyes that are half hidden by his black hair. Why is he so familiar to look at?

'You are quick on your feet, boy.'

'Carryin' out an order, Sire.' Lockley tugs at his boiled leather vest, it is short on his lanky frame. 'Sir Alan, my Lord Warwick wishes to see you urgently. In the square.'

When Edmund looks back at Coxcombe his hand has not released the girl's throat. 'For the last time, let her go.'

'Just a little fun before she dies,' Coxcombe says and flicks his wrist. 'Now, you must live with the knowledge that you deprived her of a moment's joy in her sad, pathetic, rebellious life.'

Edmund watches the steady stream of crimson run down Coxcombe's hand, it is a mesmerising sight. He grabs Coxcombe by the collar. 'Time to go, Sire.'

The dead girl collapses as soon as Coxcombe releases her and, for some reason, it makes Edmund sad. A strange and unwelcome feeling. Lockley patters to the nearest corner, his shoulders hunched. Edmund realises that the youth is much taller than he first thought, and he wonders why the squire tries so hard to appear insignificant.

'Lead the way, squire.' Coxcombe rearranges his clothes, and Edmund grabs the reins of his horse. 'You disappoint me.'

'I have no desire to impress you,' Coxcombe says with such ease that Edmund tugs at the reins and his horse chews the bit. 'Maybe this is who I am.'

'I doubt that.' For I would know a ruthless man anywhere, Edmund continues in his thoughts, after all, I am one. But even I have a conscience it would seem.

'Refuse all you like, Sire. Our lives take such twists and turns that no one can help but change.' Wiping his bloody hand on his cape, Coxcombe gives a cynical smile. 'Although I believe that, often enough, we are helped to change by our masters.'

'I must have had better masters than you.' Edmund smiles in return and Coxcombe's face falters a little.

'Of that there can be little doubt. But let me ask you this, Sire,' Coxcombe says and leans in, one hand on his saddle, 'have you ever disobeyed an order?'

'I have never had cause to.' Edmund kicks his horse and leads the way. The distant screams grow louder.

'What might make you refuse?'

'Your interest in my thoughts is as immaterial as it is unwelcome, Sir Alan. Let us focus on the task at hand. We are here to punish the French for their rebellious thoughts and insubordination,' Edmund sneers over his shoulder and sees Coxcombe cringe. 'They have harboured men who seek to destroy the Prince and his household, they have plotted and schemed – and for that they must pay a price.'

'Death.' Lockley's voice cuts across the increasing rumble coming from the centre of town. He looks up at Edmund with a serene expression. 'They must pay with their lives.'

A single glance from Edmund sends Lockley running, one hand on the short blade in his belt. Edmund rises in the stirrups and looks ahead but the city streets are narrow and curved and all he can see is English soldiers pushing men and women before them towards the clamour.

'I would not trust that boy,' Coxcombe says from behind Edmund's back. 'Though Lord Warwick does. With his life if rumours are to be believed. A position that was once mine.'

'What is that to a knighted man?' Edmund tries to shut out the increasing noise. Out of the corner of his eye, he sees two soldiers beating an old man; it does not invoke the same rage that Coxcombe's hand around a girl's neck did. Edmund leads the way. 'You are elevated.'

'I still live on his mercy.' Coxcombe pushes his horse even closer and forces Edmund to slow down. 'That boy is trouble. Showed up out of nowhere and will not say from where he hails, nor who is his kin. Nothing. We know nothing about him.'

'If my Lord Warwick is satisfied with his services, who are you to complain?' Edmund's hand creeps to the hilt of his sword. They are in the throng of people now and must be weary.

'He is hiding something, you mark my words. And why is Lord Warwick so eager to accept his services? What has he got that no one else seems to have? When have you ever known Warwick to trust anyone?'

Although he does not like to admit it, Coxcombe has a point. Edmund has had but a passing encounter with Warwick and he seems to be a careful man. But before Edmund can decide what to say next, they turn the final corner and find themselves at the fringes of a large crowd.

Could this be the gateway to Hell? It finally sinks in, what he has done, what it has come to, the concern he drank away yesterday comes back in a roaring torrent and Edmund gasps for air.

'A joyful crowd assembled to pay homage to their ruler.' Coxcombe's voice spills over with contempt. 'Those must be tears of pure bliss.'

As Edmund pushes through the crowd, dirty bloody hands claw at his boots, begging voices attack his ears. A child no more than four or five is thrust in Edmund's path and he almost tramples the boy. When Edmund looks down, he sees Lockley's hands shoot out and grab the boy by his narrow shoulders, a short dagger glittering between his fingers.

'Move!' Lockley's voice makes Edmund's blood run cold. The boy is shoved back into the crowd and Lockley looks about with pure hatred. 'Undeserving, filthy vermin!'

'Enough!' Edmund tries to keep calm, but the unadulterated horror from the crowd seeps into his bones. Their fear becomes his fear. This is no battle, this serves no purpose, it fights no war. This is vengeance pure and simple. Edmund would know it anywhere, for he has often enough served the god of vengeance, though not on this scale. It must be stopped.

Catching Gaunt's eyes, Edmund realises that he is not the only one who dreads what is about to happen. Gaunt's face is white but his cheeks burn red. Is it caused by righteous indignation or pure terror? From this distance, Edmund cannot tell. To his left, Coxcombe elbows an old woman and then nods to Warwick. Lockley has once more disappeared. Something about the squire makes Edmund's hairs stand on end. He grabs the pummel of his sword and the backdrop of sobbing and screaming subsides for a moment, only to return as a bolt of lightning that squeezes every muscle in his body.

'Mercy, noble lord, mercy!' The frightened choir rises up to the skies, as the Prince stares down at the people grovelling at his feet, their faces grimy from soot and dirt, many bloodied by the soldiers circling the square. 'MERCY!'

The voice of God himself will not make the Prince spare you; Edmund shakes at the realisation and an image of the frightened brown-eyed girl floats before him. The Prince's blue eyes are dead and cold as he slips his sword from its scabbard and raises it to the throat of the terrified mayor kneeling before him.

'Why should I show mercy?' His voice is low and yet every word feels as a thunderclap. 'When you have harboured my enemies, wined and dined them, schemed and plotted, laid out traps and famished my lands.'

The Prince raises his eyes above the crowd. 'MY LANDS!'

'My Lord,' the mayor begins but is cut short by the Prince's blade pressing at his throat, piercing the skin.

'You deserve no mercy.' The finality of the words washes over the crowd, and women begin to scream and cry, men shout curses and children try to flee.

A soldier spears a young boy who tries to run away, and Edmund seizes the moment: 'YOUR GRACE!'

The Prince turns slowly towards Edmund, who rushes forward and kneels, holding out his sword with both hands. This will be his crowning moment; this will be when he wins over even the most reluctant of the Prince's followers to his side. He can undo what he has done.

'Please, your Grace, my Prince, I did not offer up my sword to you to spill the blood of innocents. The blood of women and children. Reconsider your Grace, I beg …'

Pressing the point of his sword into the side of Edmund's neck, the Prince leans forward and fixes him with a fierce glare that seems to burn away some of the Prince's illness. 'Innocent? You believe, Sire, that these villains are innocent? That the women did not bed the invaders with pleasure, that the men did not drink with them and plan a rebellion? Against their Lord – against the King of England?'

Edmund blinks, understands in an instant that it is too late. Inside him, something fragile cracks, leaks. He turns his gaze to Gaunt, who is even paler now, his eyes black. But there is determination in his look too.

'This was your idea, Sire,' the Prince whispers; droplets of fever net his brow. 'I simply refined it. Now, witness our mutual triumph.' The Prince's voice rises to boom around the square. 'You would lay down your sword to protect them and believe I would be appeased!'

Edmund feels a trickle of warm, sticky fluid make its way down his throat and vanish beneath his armour. 'Your Grace, what choice did they have?'

'Every choice!' He applies more pressure to the sword and makes Edmund sneer, but the Prince does not see it, he is looking at the gathered people. 'They had but to call upon my aid and I would have granted it, but they are weak, spineless creatures waiting only for a reason to turn their backs on their rightful master and curry favour with the French King. A usurper! A despot!

'An imposter sits on the throne that rightfully belongs to my father; these people rise against the Crown – the Crown that you swore allegiance to.' The Prince snaps the sword away, leaving a shallow cut that reaches from his jaw to just below his ear. The look Edmund receives is riddled with hatred. 'And you would have me spare them?'

'The women and children at least,' Edmund knows he has gone too far, but he cannot let the Prince kill everyone in the city. For some odd reason, he simply cannot.

Turning his back, the Prince raises his hand. 'Kill them all!'

Edmund's sword falls to the ground. The square becomes a red torrent, screams and cries stifled by cold steel. When he looks up, his knees soaked in blood, Edmund sees Gaunt pale-faced beside the Prince and Langley crying, tears coursing down his cheeks at the sight of all the carnage.

The Prince pushes a woman towards Edmund, a cruel smile playing at the corner of his mouth. 'Prove your loyalty, Sire. Prove to me that we are two of a kind!' Edmund crawls back shaking his head, but the Prince is relentless. 'PROVE IT!'

Gaunt gives a slow nod, his eyes wide with stunned shock. Edmund knows that if he resists, he will be lucky to die by a soldier's blade but, more likely, he will be brought back in chains and left to the unspeakable abilities of whatever gaoler, the Prince sees fit to punish belligerent knights. Langley wipes his face and turns away.

I could fight him, I would win, Edmund thinks, as he gets to his feet, his stance unsteady. But instead of following the advice of his treacherous thoughts, he bends down and picks up his sword. Then he looks at the Prince, the man he owes everything to and nods. Do what must be done, and he will call me brother before all others. So what if a woman dies at my blade, I will be richer than ever, I will be able to claim anything once the deed is done.

The Prince has a hand loosely around the woman's neck and every time her legs give way, he tightens his grip and she staggers to her feet. Edmund can tell that she is frightened witless, she does not sense that the square has gone quiet as a tomb. That all her townspeople have died around her. All she sees is an armoured man stepping forward, the terrifying glitter of a sword in his hand; she is paralysed by fear and does not even try to escape when the Prince lets go. Her blue dress is a stark contrast to all the red around her feet and her pale face. Her lips move in silent prayer, but Edmund knows that God will not save her; he will not favour the weak, for all of the people in the square have already died. God should have struck down the Prince the moment he raised his hand, and God did not.

Nor did I, Edmund thinks, and now I must pay for my sins.

Looking at the Prince, Edmund wields his great sword and brings it down in a hard thrust, the sharp steel cutting through skin, muscle and bone, the woman sighing her last breath. He stares at the Prince without blinking, disdain mingling with burning, blinding hate. If not for Gaunt stepping forward and pushing him away, he would have drawn out the sword and plunged into the Prince's black heart.

Here stands no hero, Edmund sneers inside, here stands a Godless man, uncouth and uncontrolled. He curses Gaunt and Langley for their paralysis, for their inability to speak sense to the Prince, he curses himself for having lost control for a moment, for the Prince lying to him about his true intention.

I loved you as a brother, Edmund thinks, but I love you no more. You are no champion, no true warrior, I mistook you for my kind, but now my eyes are opened to the truth.

'My Lord!' A soldier runs through the square, blood spraying from his leather boots at every step. 'My Lord, there are more people in the churches. They have barricaded the doors.'

The Prince sends Edmund a last look. 'Burn them!'

'My Lord?' The soldier looks uncertain.

'Burn them ALL! Burn the churches, houses, huts! Burn this HELL-HOLE TO THE GROUND!'

The soldier runs from the square, looking back just once as if he cannot understand what has just happened. But he knows what will happen to him if the order is not carried out. Oh yes, Edmund thinks, he knows, we all know. If we do not bow to our monster, we will die in this square and birds will pick our eyes from our decaying faces. He pushes away the thought that, only yesterday, he fed the monster with poison words. This is no fault of mine; this is not what I had in mind. These are the actions of a deranged, sick man.

Gaunt puts a hand on Edmund's chest. 'Come with me.'

Instead, Edmund's hand curls tight around the hilt of his sword. What is more knightly than to slay a monster? Even if it wears a crown. Every man, woman and child in this city will revere him as a hero. Except they are all dead.

'Come with me right now, Sire, or I will take your head!' Gaunt warns him. 'Is that what you want?'

'I can save them, my Lord.' Edmund's words come out hard and without feeling. 'I can right this wrong. The people want a hero, I can give them one.'

Gaunt steps close and Edmund feels the point of a dagger slide between the shoulder plate and his armoured arm. 'Killing your Prince, your liege lord, will not make you a hero. This city will perish whether you put a blade in my brother's back or not. Do not mistake me, Sire, I will kill you to protect him. Even the man he is now. It is my duty!'

Hauling Edmund from the square, Gaunt shoots him a grim stare. 'What my brother did today will haunt him for the rest of his miserable life. It will haunt all of us. But it is done, and nothing you do can undo it. Tomorrow, he will call you to his side, and you will stand there, so help me God, even if I have to put you in chains to ensure it happens.'

'You will have to do more than that.'

'I know you for what you are, Sire,' Gaunt spits, 'I have known you for what you are since the first time I saw you. You may call yourself a true knight, but you are no hero and you never will be. You are the dark side of my brother's coin, and you have released the darkness within him. Now, you will suffer the spectacle of what happens when you unleash madness.'

Edmund growls when Gaunt pushes the tip of the blade through the boiled leather and pricks a tiny hole in his skin. But it is not the blade that pains him; it is that Gaunt has called him out; has torn the mask of chivalry from Edmund's face and exposed the devil within. It must be contained, stamped out. 'This is no doing of mine.'

'And no doing of mine,' Gaunt retorts, 'but we will work hard to put it right, will we not, Sire?'

'How? He is burning the city, putting every soul to the blade.'

'We will remind him of this day until his last day.' Gaunt's voice is strained, anguished. 'We will ensure that nothing such as this ever happens again. And you will stop poisoning his thoughts. That is what we will do, Sir Edmund. I will be watching you! Do you hear me? From this day and until the last day, I will watch you as a hawk.'

Finally, Gaunt removes his dagger, and Edmund breathes a sigh of relief. He looks about. Sees what he has done as if for the first time. And is repulsed.

In front of them, a company of soldiers march along the street, two carry torches, the rest have drawn their swords. A little girl peeks out from a narrow alley and one of the soldiers spots her. A roar cuts through the air and three soldiers run at the petrified girl who is nailed to the ground staring wide-eyed at the men. Two of the soldiers grab the girl and the third soldier thrusts his sword clean through her scraggy body, bones crunching beneath the horrid soft squelch. The soldiers toss her bloodied body aside as if it is nothing and re-join the rest of the company of which two busy themselves setting fire to the thatched roofs of the poor, clay huts.

A pig squeals by engulfed by flames and, briefly, the air is saturated by the stink of burnt bacon. Gaunt pushes Edmund against the wall of a hut, crouching beneath the spreading fire above. It is obvious that he is appalled by the butchery commanded by his own, glorious brother.

Edmund's face is wet though he cannot tell if it is from sweat, blood or tears. When he wipes his brow, the gauntlet scorches his skin. He lets himself be guided by Gaunt through burning streets, a cacophony of distant screams accompanying their muffled footsteps.

'We were to set an example and put fright into all of the other cities in Aquitaine, to ensure they do not fall prey to the French usurper's sugared words. We were to administer harsh justice, punish those who are guilty of treason.' Gaunt's voice is raw. 'This is not justice.'

'Did you expect him to be lenient?' Edmund pushes away his own part in the bloodshed. 'To pardon them for their treason?'

'Innocents burned alive,' Gaunt whispers as if he has not heard Edmund. 'Children, women. Burning God's houses. There will never be a place for us in the kingdom of Heaven! We are damned! My brother has damned us all!'

The barrier inside finally breaks, crumbles and falls away. Edmund turns aside and retches. When his vision clears, he sees that he has vomited on the little girl, her golden locks now coloured red by blood, her dress covered in his sick. He falls to his knees and takes her head in his hands. Big blue eyes clouded by fear and death stare back at him.

A dull realisation hits Edmund and makes him smile grimly.
*I am Death.*

# CHAPTER 18

## 2 December 1370 – Château de Castelnaud-la-Chapelle, Dordogne

On impulse, Edmund scales the wooden stairs and crosses the wet grass of the inner garden. He looks up at the window again; the light is still there, a beacon calling him to shore. If only he could trust that shore to be safe.

Gaunt's door opens, a servant appears and sets aside a washbasin. He disappears into the gloomy depth of the room and returns with a pitcher. Looking about, he bends to retrieve the basin and walks away from the still open door. Edmund watches the hall swallow up the servant and then walks through the door before he can change his mind.

'My Lord.'

Gaunt starts and looks about. He is a pitiable sight, his clothes in disarray, his eyes are red and his face sags.

'Sir Edmund.' The dry words stretch thin, struggling to reach Edmund by the door. 'Enter.'

'Thank you, my Lord. I saw the light …' Unsure how to proceed, Edmund is grateful for the seat Gaunt offers near the fire and shivers at the cold draft from the shuttered windows.

'No rest for the wicked, Sir Edmund.' Gaunt ties his shirt and runs a hand through his dark hair. It is streaked with premature grey. 'That is what my mother used to say when my brothers and I could not sleep. Mind you, she never slept much either, so she must be an authority on the subject.'

They share a weak smile, and Edmund feeds the hungry flames. 'Sleep eludes me these days.'

'You are not to blame. No more than I am.' The weight of Gaunt's words presses down on Edmund. 'I know what I said that day, I know what I accused you of, but I have had time to think – too much time, perhaps. In this affair there is but one culprit, one executioner. The Prince. It was his black heart that lay waste to the city.'

'I do not think he would agree, my Lord.'

Gaunt stiffens as the door opens and a servant comes in carrying a pitcher on a tray. Confusion spreads on the servant's face when he sees Edmund and he mutters something that only Gaunt hears.

'Go.'

Waiting for the door to close, Gaunt pours steaming liquid into a cup and hands it to Edmund. The spices of the mulled wine attack his senses and lend promises of sweet delight, he drinks deep and rejoices in the burning sensation as the wine rushes through his body and paralyzes his mouth.

'They call him the black Prince,' Gaunt says. 'Apt, I think.'

'Who?'

'Whispers that come back to me.'

'Ah …'

'Do not pretend that he is without blame. Distribute harsh judgements, carry out the sentence quickly,' Gaunt mimics his older brother's voice. 'Those were his words before we set out. You heard them as clear as I did.'

'His county lay wasted.' Edmund defends the Prince with a mix of loyalty and disdain.

'He was not in the right!' Gaunt slams his cup onto the table and rubs his forehead. 'He was not. It was a Godless act. I have told him as much. I have written to our father.'

'What do you hope …?' Edmund cannot finish the question and it floats into the crackling fire, consumed by despair.

'At the time, all I wanted was a weight lifted from my shoulders. But I know full well that my father will commend the Prince on his decision. They are two pieces cut from the same cloth. I sometimes wonder where I fit in. I am to advise the Prince, but not speak against him when he is foolish. I am to stand by him, no matter the madness that engulfs him, and now …' Gaunt raises his cup with an unsteady hand, it is only now that Edmund realises that Gaunt is drunk. Has probably been drinking for most of the night. He gives a mock salute. 'Now, I am to accept that I shall be as much to blame as he is.'

'I have heard a rumour that the Prince is leaving?' Edmund asks to divert Gaunt from his rant.

'On the Princess' orders.' Leaving his seat behind the desk, Gaunt walks around the room, cup in shaking hand. 'He is not getting better. The sickness that broke out during our ride has left him weakened. You remember him being carried into the city on a stretcher, he could hardly stand in that square, and yet, he did unspeakable … never mind. The Princess believes it is from exertion and blames me for letting him go to Limoges. We of course know the truth.'

Edmund watches Gaunt take another turn. 'He is being eaten up by guilt. Or he would be if there was any justice left in the world – but I rather doubt it.'

'And you?'

'Plenty of guilt for me too.' Gaunt empties his cup and flings it into the fire. It spits a protest of embers onto the dry rushes and Gaunt stomps them out.

'You are leaving too, my Lord?' Edmund tries to assess what is happening. He has not been called for the Prince's council since they returned from Limoges, and Pascaline is reluctant to relay news from the Princess' chambers. Edmund is clawing in the dark.

'We all are, Sire.' Gaunt hiccups. 'To Bordeaux and the Prince's stronghold for the time being. But it will not be long before we are packed up and shipped back to England.'

'I cannot …'

'Cannot leave?' Gaunt slumps on a chair; his elbows on his knees, his hands dangling. 'You will find that it becomes ever easier. Leaving the woman, you love. I should know.'

Edmund leaves Gaunt to his cold and unforgiving chambers. No, Edmund thinks as he prowls the dark galleries and hallways, it is not that I cannot leave. It is that I cannot now follow the Prince and pretend to be a loyal knight in his service.

But of course, he can. He must. If he is to continue on his path to riches and glory, he must march in the Prince's wake and carry out whatever orders he is given. And he must do so with a smile on his face.

## 5 December 1370 – Château de Castelnaud-la-Chapelle

'You must be mad!'

'Pascaline …'

'MAD!'

Edmund ducks as she throws a mirror of polished copper across the room, it clatters on the floor. 'This is not for you to decide …'

'You are a beast!' She turns a tear-streaked face to him. 'How can you command me to bundle up our children and leave here? Follow the heartless Prince and his pathetic advisors?'

'Would you rather be left behind?' Edmund grabs her hands before she can pick up more ammunition from the small table. 'You are bound to the Princess as I am to the Prince. We are not free to do as we choose, we are servants.'

Loathing bubbles in his veins, he hates to be a servant; he hates her for being one too. At least one of them ought to be free and, given the choice, he will choose freedom for himself.

'You knew my sister lived in the city,' Pascaline whispers, trying to draw away from him. 'You knew and you did nothing.'

'You were not there. Do not presume to tell me what I could have done.' Contempt laces his words and he pauses to regain control. He knows he cannot afford to be responsible for the Princess losing one of her most trusted ladies in waiting. 'If I had another choice, I should gladly grasp it, but there is none. The French are rallying, they are fuelled by the … inflamed memory of Limoges.' Edmund clamps his arms around her struggling body. 'They will not understand that you are blameless. They will see only someone who is in the employ of the English court, and they will kill you just as the Prince ordered us to kill his subjects.'

When Edmund feels sure she is calm, he lets go, her tears cold imprints against his skin. 'Think of your children.'

'So many secrets.' Pascaline's voice holds no feeling. 'One even has a child at its heart.'

Edmund watches her pick up his dagger, fingering the ornate hilt. With an effort, he keeps a sneer from his voice. 'We agreed …'

'I helped Lord Gaunt bundle up his bastard boy and send him to England. I convinced my sister – my sweet sister, Edmund! – that it was for the best. That the boy would be well attended and provided for. He would grow up to be a Prince of England.' She pulls the blade from its gilded scabbard in a slow careful motion. 'I promised her that, one day, she would see her boy again, give him a mother's blessing. That she would be proud of what he had become. But he is just the bastard of a monster. A liar. A man without heart! I pray now that the boy never becomes a prince of England, for I know what that is and I want it not for him!'

'We must trust that she is with God.' He has long since convinced Pascaline that it was Gaunt who talked the Prince into the slaughter in Limoges; he is not going to change his story now. Taking the dagger from her requires little effort and Edmund puts it aside. 'And I do not think Lord Gaunt is entirely without heart.'

'They whisper about him,' Pascaline hisses. 'They say he spurred the Prince on and that now, the Prince is ill and cannot defend his lands because of his brother's immense ambition!'

'Let them say what they will.' Edmund is aroused by her furious glare. 'I was there; I know what truly transpired. Whatever else, you cannot lay blame only at his feet. And what of the Princess? Would you abandon her?'

Pascaline's face falters, new tears brim in her eyes. 'I find my love for her has wasted away. She does not reproach the Princes for their deeds.'

'She is his wife, she cannot be seen to quarrel with her husband in public,' Edmund says and thinks, what she does in private is another matter. The memory of passing by their door a few days ago listening to the raised voices and the Princess' harsh words still lingers in his mind.

'And if we go to Bordeaux?'

Sighing, Edmund sits on the bed and rubs his hands together; he knows that he has won her over. 'We will be safe at least. We will decide what to do there. But we cannot stay here, my sweet, I know you want to, but we cannot. It is not safe.'

'Before we go you must marry me.' She lifts his head with a finger under his chin. 'Prove to me that you are, first and foremost, loyal to our children and me. Marry me and I will do as you bid.'

Edmund caresses her face. 'That is what you want?'

'Yes.' Pascaline seems appeased. 'It is all I want.'

There will be no wedding, the departure has been moved up, Edmund knows this even before he talks to Pascaline. He feels nothing when she glares hatefully at him as he helps her into the Princess' carriage. Marriage is not for me, Edmund thinks as he mounts his horse, I will be free all of my life.

The Prince's standard unfurls, and Edmund is one of the first knights to move out, riding in front of the Prince's litter. The Prince is too weak to ride and so, it is Edmund the people salute, his smile they tuck into their memories. He likes the idea that they revere him as they would the Prince. He likes it better than anything. He is a force to be reckoned with; even the people who cheer him on know that. And he has no doubt that they love him better than the Prince. After all, it was not he who ordered an entire city put to the sword.

Edmund's smile widens. There is yet glory to be won. All he has to do is reach out and grab it.

# CHAPTER 19

## 26 July 1392 – Westminster Palace

'Whatever did happen to those girls after your mistress died?'

'They were taken on by some nobleman or other who could not father children of his own.' Edmund shook his head. 'He must have been desperate to take on two girls, but everything seemed to sort itself out. The Princess insisted on giving me details about their progress, but in the long run, she too lost interest in them.'

Gaunt sighed. 'Where are they today?'

'I could not tell you; they were Pascaline's girls, who is to say they were really mine? As you said, she was my mistress, not my wife, and so …'

'You got what you wanted.'

'After a fashion,' Edmund agreed and smiled; the Princess might have stopped enquiring after his girls, but Edmund had kept tabs on them. 'Though I admit it took a long while to make amends with your brother and ensure his busybody of a wife did not interfere.'

'Then you are lucky my father too was taken with you.' Gaunt folded his hands. 'I often wondered how you managed to win back my brother's favour.'

'All I had to do was stay close. And take an interest in his boy.'

For a moment, Gaunt almost smiles and then his face falls back into its accustomed neutral look. 'I would have thought that would appease Joan too.'

'She was a cunning woman; I could not hope to win her over forever.' Ever since the Princess discovered that Edmund was not at all interested in his presumed offspring, she had been wary of him.

'Are you freely admitting that not all women fall for your charms?'

This time Edmund's smile widened. 'They all fall initially, but only the truly clever ones wise up. Which is more than can be said for almost all of the men I have ever met.'

'Save me?'

'Perhaps. But then we are here, are we not, my Lord,' Edmund said. 'And you are still listening.'

Gaunt harked a laugh and poured more water. Outside the hour was getting late, the bells had chimed twice already and, in the distance, Edmund could make out torches being put out, night stealing ever closer to the castle.

'My father certainly never knew what you really were.'

'I am surprised you did not tell him, now that you claim to have known all along.'

'I never claimed such a thing; I too was taken in. I confess, Sire, that of all the men I have ever known to play the courtly game, you are the greatest adversary and the most able actor I have ever come across.' Gaunt drank deep. 'My father was a wilful man, even if I had aired my budding concerns about you, he would never have listened. He saw too much of himself in you.'

'Can you blame him,' Edmund said and earned a curt nod.

'I knew he was blinded by you from the moment you told me about the estate he granted you.'

'It is a most beautiful house. I freely admit that when I first clapped eyes on it, I could hardly believe my luck. And to think I would be training soldiers all day long; nothing could have pleased me more.' Edmund grabbed the pitcher and looked with dismay at the clear liquid flowing into his cup. 'But then, no one had bothered to tell me that to take on the role of master would have me chained to a desk.'

'You must not have been paying attention when we were in council with my brother,' Gaunt sneered. 'Then you would have known.'

'I think we can both agree that, once I got the hang of it, I rose to the occasion.'

'I would have been disappointed if you had not.' Gaunt resumed tapping his fingers on his desk. The sound drove Edmund slowly mad, and that was most likely why Gaunt did it. 'You got much more than you deserved, far too much.'

'For all my services, I believe I got my just deserts, no more no less,' Edmund said with spite. 'I had to endure court, I had to endure listening to lesser men for hours on end and, more than anything, I had to contend with Kings who did not know what they were about.'

'If you want me to thank you for what you did, you will wait forever. You got a wonderful house, yes, but you also got all the adjoining towns, fields, woods and much more to boot. You have wanted for nothing all of these years. For God's sake, even my own father-in-law left a small fortune to you in his will. Not to think of how much the King doled out for you.'

'I served a child on bended knee; I earned my keep.'

'We all served a child,' Gaunt says dismissively. 'Though I own that you kept very close to him.'

'He was surrounded by the wrong people.'

'Some say he still is.'

Edmund shook his head. 'We rooted out most of them, and you have me to thank for that.'

## 4 May 1375 – London

'I owe you a debt of gratitude.' The Princess' words come out hard and without feeling. 'Richard is terribly fond of you.'

'He is a fine boy.'

'He is, Sir Edmund, and I would keep him that way.'

Edmund looks about the room; at the far end, three of the Princess' ladies-in-waiting sit demurely, sowing near a window. Two more are practicing a new dance accompanied by an old man playing the lute. The brunette twirls, the sunlight catching her dress, and she smiles at Edmund. He rewards her with a half-smile before turning his attention to Princess Joan once more.

She is eying him with a pensive expression. Edmund notices, for the first time, that she has aged; she is no longer the beauty who caught a prince in her net. Actually, she has grown fat; her dress looks to be pinching in all the wrong places. She looks old compared to the young beauties she surrounds herself with. If she had any sense, she would call upon ugly girls to serve on her in future, before anyone else notices that she is well past her prime.

'I have little enough reason to trust you, Sire,' Princess Joan says, 'but what happened in the past ought to stay there, if at all possible. We have been through many an ordeal and you have ever been loyal to my husband, even if I find fault with you in other areas.'

'The Prince has my undying loyalty, your Grace.' Edmund is careful to keep his voice level, carefree. 'Whatever his command, I shall endeavour to fulfil his expectations.'

'And now, he has asked you to care for my child?'

'He has merely voiced his concerns that he no longer is able to go riding with Master Richard. He also wishes his heir to be accomplished at the tilt and, in time, be as great a warrior as his father.' Edmund looks down at the plump Princess. 'If you disagree, your Grace, please let me know.'

She purses her mouth and then exhales. 'Of course not. We all want Richard to be a strong boy and capable …'

Her voice trails away and her eyes glaze over. The Prince and his wife have never fully recovered after the death of their firstborn son. And even a blind man can tell that Richard is a poor substitute for the big, burly boy who died at the age of six. Truth be told, the Prince has quite given up attempting to raise a future King and so, between them, Edmund and Gaunt are trying to amend what tasks Richard's father is reluctant to perform.

'He will be, your Grace,' Edmund says smoothly, 'if you can find it in your heart to trust me. I know full well that I disappointed you in the past, but I was distraught, I was not myself. Allow me to love the Prince as I can never hope to love my girls, whom you were kind to find a good situation for.'

Princess Joan looks somewhat appeased, her shoulders are a little less tense. Still, she hesitates and Edmund knows he must work tirelessly to be allowed close to her son, to be permitted direct access without reluctance. But he has plenty of time to work his way back into her good graces and, until then, Richard is a quirky boy in dire need of a real man to teach him how to behave.

The door opens and Richard tumbles in followed by the slender, dark-haired Thomas Mowbray. Edmund does not care for Baron Mowbray's brat who is a bad influence on young Richard. Impressionable, he is easy to lead astray and if anyone is to do so it ought to be Edmund, not some eight-year-old boy.

'My Lord.' Edmund bows before thin, sickly-looking Richard who gives him a severe nod.

'Mother.'

Princess Joan puts her hand on her son's head for a quick blessing before he pulls away. 'What are you doing?'

'Exploring, your Grace,' Thomas Mowbray says, his voice silken. 'My Lord Bordeaux was hoping we might be permitted to go to the stables and see the new horses?'

Edmund can tell that the Princess cares little enough for Thomas, and yet she keeps a happy smile on her face. 'Of course, as soon as you are done with your studies, which I cannot believe you are. Now go, your tutors await.'

'I do not want to study today, mother,' Richard objects but blushes under his mother's stern glance. 'Every day, we slave away with letters and books, I want to be out and about. Cannot Sir Edmund take us for a ride?'

With a smile, Edmund turns to the Princess. 'You must do as your mother bids, my Lord, for she knows best what is important. If she will permit, I shall take you to the stables this afternoon, unless your father has need of me.'

'He does not,' Princess Joan snaps; the smile strained now. 'If your tutors are happy with your progress, you may go to the stables with Sir Edmund and Sir Simon later. Mind you keep to the church hours though, Richard, God watches you.'

The two boys bolt from the room, Richard's high-pitched voice carrying over the hustle and bustle of the busy court corridors. The Princess bites her lip and looks out of the window. 'It may well be that my husband trusts you with his life, Sire, but I will be keeping a close eye on what you do with my son.'

'You would do wise to show the same courtesy to Thomas Mowbray, your Grace,' Edmund says while he follows the brunette as she crosses the room, the dancing done for now. 'I have a bad feeling …'

'Are you certain it is not just petty jealousy, Sire?'

Edmund drowns his constant irritation at her meddling manners and maintains his deferential smile. 'Master Richard should surely be surrounded by boys of his own age, but I have known the Mowbray children for all their lives. The older brother John is a more sensible choice of companion for Master Richard, your Grace, that is all I am saying.'

'Is it?'

'I merely ask is that you do not let your dislike for me cloud your good judgement when it comes to your son's companions, your Grace.' Edmund bows to excuse himself. 'As Baron Mowbray, John is a perfect companion for a future King; he is wise beyond his years, kind and intelligent.'

'And Thomas is not?'

Edmund hears doubt in the Princess' voice and knows he has won her over, for now at least. 'Thomas is cunning and by no means lacks cleverness, but there is something about him that does not sit right with me. I am not alone in my concerns, my Lord Gaunt told me just yesterday …'

'I should have known that John was behind this.' Once more Princess Joan's voice is strained. 'He takes an uncanny interest in my son.'

'He has a boy of similar age,' Edmund says easily, 'perhaps we must trust that he knows a thing or two about boys too?'

'And now, he wants Henry to be best friends with Richard?' She turns towards the door. 'Tell me, Sir Edmund, do you see the two royal cousins ever being on friendly terms? For I confess, I do not. Henry is raised to be his father's mirror image. I should prefer Richard to mirror Edward. If you can help achieve that then perhaps, in time, I might trust you again.'

Her ladies-in-waiting are quick to arrange themselves behind the Princess as the door opens and she leads them from the room, but the brunette turns her head one last time, and in her eyes are a promise of future delights. Edmund watches the women leave with a contemplative air.

Inside, he acknowledges that the Princess has a point. Like her, he does not think Richard and Henry will ever take to one another. Neither does Gaunt for that matter. But the games must be played. It is all any of them know how to do.

## 8 June 1376 – Westminster Palace

'Sir Edmund! Did you see?'

Edmund smiles at Richard who looks uncomfortable in the saddle of the big warhorse. His grasp on the short lance is unsteady and he rides poorly, but he cannot know.

'Very well done, my Lord. You grow stronger and better every day.'

A brown steed thunders past Edmund, the lean dark-haired boy in the saddle sits straight and strong, his lance steady and his aim true. Edmund sighs, it is unfortunate that Richard's cousin is not better governed by his father.

'Sir Edmund.' Gaunt stops next to Edmund; his hands come to rest on the rail. 'How are the boys?'

'As you see, my Lord.' Edmund gestures. 'My Lord Bordeaux is learning.'

'Slowly, by the looks of it.'

The smug tone in Gaunt's voice makes Edmund's temper rise, but he knows how to control himself. Gaunt watches as his son hits his mark and crouches in the saddle to avoid the heavy sandbag whizzing through the air.

'Master Henry is very able.' Edmund knows that flattery is what works best with Gaunt. 'You must be very proud of your son.'

'I am. He has skills in the saddle that I can only dream of,' Gaunt says with faint pride. 'I was ever groomed for politics and diplomacy, not for warfare and jousting. I left that to my brothers though I own that, beside Edward, the only one who truly made his mark on the field was Lionel. Now, one is gone and the other is lame, and I am still here.'

'Then I hope, your son favours you when it comes to luck in survival.' Turning his head, Edmund sees Richard sneer at Henry when the two cross paths. Richard's horse sidesteps and he makes a nervous sound. 'And that you will aid our Prince in matters of politics.'

'I live to serve.' Gaunt's face is taut. 'But I have my own crown to concern myself with these days, and so I fear that Richard will have to look elsewhere for lessons on diplomacy. My brother will be a poor example of how to conduct oneself in that regard. But perhaps you can make amends where such matters are concerned.'

Edmund watches Richard trot down the line, his lance wobbling in his grip. He has to work hard to keep a smile on his face when all he wants to do is snatch the tiny boy from the saddle and shake him until his head comes loose. Why can he not learn how to ride at least? Edmund has worked tirelessly for years trying to teach Richard the skills required of a prince, and he has failed at every turn. The boy seems completely unable to handle sword, lance, dagger and even mace; his stick-like arms make him unsuited for a bow. His horsemanship leaves a lot to be desired, and Edmund is at the end of his tether. But it will not do to become reckless or discipline a royal child in full view. And knowing the Princess Joan, discipline of any kind will never be permitted. Consequently, Edmund applauds dutifully when Richard reaches the board and the tip of his lance only just hits the bottom corner, moving neither board nor sandbag.

'I too live to serve, my Lord,' Edmund says slickly, 'if you deem my services in politics to be adequate for a future Prince, I shall do my utmost.'

'Future King,' Gaunt says quietly and earns Edmund's complete attention, the training boys forgotten. 'My brother is on his deathbed; you and I both know it. He has been for months. The physician says that the Prince will not survive the night.'

For the first time, Edmund looks properly at Gaunt and sees the dark circles under his eyes, the lines around his mouth. It drives a strange kind of fear into Edmund's heart, a fear he has never known before. 'He has conquered his illness in the past …'

'No more. His strength is gone, his will to live with it,' Gaunt says. His toneless voice snakes around Edmund's arms, his hands grow cold. Gaunt sighs, 'I fear for the future of England. What will become of us if we are left with a child king?'

'You must be mistaken …' Edmund shakes his head. 'What of your father …?'

'He is an old man.' Watching his own son blast past, his lance meeting the board with a loud crash, Gaunt seems to find his bearings. 'We must make preparations for the future, and my father is not part of the future.'

Stunned, Edmund applauds with Gaunt when Henry trots back, tipping his splintered lance at his father. The boy's face is a blur, Edmund cannot concentrate on what goes on anymore. A child king. No, surely Gaunt is mistaken, the Prince will rise again, he must govern England, for the boy who now clambers off his horse, his legs shaking and his face slick with sweat, is not ready to rule.

'Listen to me!' Gaunt's voice cracks through Edmund's thoughts. 'My brother trusts you as much as he has ever trusted anyone. My sister-in-law has reservations, but I believe they are waning and, at any rate, we cannot let a woman's fancies control what happens next. I want you to go to my brother as soon as your lessons here are over, go to him and declare your undying devotion to his boy. Make whatever promises you must to ensure he dies with peace in his heart.'

'Why not you?' Edmund's tongue sticks to the roof of his mouth. 'Why not …'

Gaunt grabs hold of Edmund's wrist and squeezes tight. 'I tried. In vain. He does not trust me; he does not trust anyone anymore. The sickness has warped his mind. Except that he does trust you, he loves you as a brother. For all that you have done, for all your faults, I order that you prove yourself to be a brother to your Prince, and prove to me that you will work with me to ensure England has a proper King.'

'Sir Simon …' Slowly, Edmund's brain begins to work once more. 'Sir Simon is a great favourite too. He will be the right kind of advisor for Master Richard. He will be …'

'I do not care about Sir Simon!' Gaunt's grip tightens. 'He is a tutor, no more. He is a great favourite only because Joan prefers him to any of us. Go to my brother and make your pledge, Sire. Do so now, or I will ensure that before my father passes too, you will have nowhere to live, no money, no horses, nothing at all. I will strip you of all you have, if you do not help me!'

The desperate note in Gaunt's words makes Edmund pause. They lock eyes and Edmund recognises despair and grief on Gaunt's face, but something else lurks there too, concern, earnest concern about something else. Something bigger.

'What do you fear might happen, my Lord?'

'I fear that you – and everyone else at court – have been far too eager to name me an adversary, while someone else has been allowed to reign free.' Gaunt stops and watches a grey horse speed by, another dark-haired boy sitting the saddle as if he was born to do so, wielding his lance with experience far beyond his years. Thomas Mowbray, the Baron's second son.

Edmund allows for time to pass, for the crash of a lance meeting wood to wash over them, all the while keeping his eye on Gaunt's face. They applaud when Thomas rides by with a big grin on his face. Wily, Edmund thinks, he is so wily.

'I am not the only ambitious man at court, Sir Edmund,' Gaunt says at length, 'and you would do well to remember that.'

Nodding, Edmund watches the three boys leading their horses from the field. Richard, thin and small for his age, his golden hair glistening in the sunlight; Henry of Bolingbroke, stout of frame and dark of hair, every inch his father; and Thomas Mowbray, lean and proud and ever so attentive to Richard. Will he be a good friend to a future King? Or will he only serve himself? Of late, Edmund has wondered often enough what kind of a man Thomas Mowbray will be. For all that he has the appearance of his dead father, Edmund's friend the Baron, there is something hungry and eager about Thomas that reminds Edmund of Elizabeth. As she was towards the end of their affair; artful and unreliable.

Edmund turns to Gaunt. 'I shall go to the Prince immediately, my Lord.'

'Beware of my brother Thomas,' Gaunt says still staring after the three boys, Henry last to pass into the stables, looking a little forlorn, excluded by the other two.

'I think we should beware of all these Thomas's at court these days,' Edmund says and earns a small nod from Gaunt.

'They do seem to be very greedy.'

Walking away, Edmund thinks, not greedy, but hungry. Hungry for power. The most dangerous kind of hunger.

## 1 October 1376 – Leeds Castle

'You must promise to keep faith with Richard.'

'I pledged myself to the Prince's son, your Grace,' Edmund says without a hint of the annoyance he feels inside at having to answer to a woman. 'I shall honour that pledge.'

'The vultures already circle.' Princess Joan wrings her hands. 'They think they can take charge when … I know full well it is treason to speak of a King's death, but my father-in-law is not the man he once was, you must agree with me on that, Sire, and I must ensure the safety of my son. He must come before anything else.'

Edmund leans against the wall and quietly enjoys the Princess' desperation. She has dogged him ever since Pascaline died years ago, she has never trusted him, not entirely, not even when the Prince did without hesitation. Part of him despises her for it, and part of him acknowledges a worthy adversary. All the more reason to savour this moment of triumph when she comes crawling, begging him to do her a favour. He has longed for this moment, yearned to have her owe him something, and now, she will. She will owe him forever for his fealty.

'I am sure there is nothing to fear, your Grace.' Edmund dons a sad smile. 'Your son must be loved and respected wherever he goes, as is befitting the heir to the throne.'

Princess Joan turns sharply, her eyes hard. 'You know my son's uncles better than anyone, God forgive us, you have shed blood with two of them and seen ambition in the eyes of the youngest. Tell me, Sir Edmund, do you think they will hesitate for even a second if they smell vulnerability?'

'My Lord Gaunt and Langley were devoted to your husband, your Grace,' Edmund says with ease. 'On his deathbed, they swore to protect your son, to provide him sound advice and ensure he becomes a just and beloved ruler.'

'And Thomas?' The Princess spits. 'What of Thomas? You are all fools if you dismiss him because he is young. He is the most cunning of them all, even John cannot match his self-serving and foul ways.'

Behind his calm expression, Edmund once more acknowledges that the Princess is a better judge of men than any other person at court. He shakes his head. 'I know too little of my Lord Woodstock to speak of him, but if you think he is such a foul creature, surely there are many who will seek to remove him from court if he misbehaves.'

'Oh no, Sire, for he has a way with people, he makes them trust him and pulls the wool over everyone's eyes.'

Everyone but you, Edmund thinks, and Gaunt; neither of you trust Woodstock, though you would never tell one another. He gestures an apology. 'If you wish it, your Grace, I shall do my very best to ensure that your son has the council he wants and deserves. But this is neither here nor there as long as the King lives, and I for one will not speak of his death when he is in good health.'

'Good health?' Princess Joan ogles Edmund her fists balled. 'Have you seen him these past many months, Sir Edmund? Have you spent time in his company? For then you would be the only one save that odious woman who has stolen away his Grace the King from matters of state.'

'I hear only that he is happy,' Edmund says and earns an angry glare. 'Certainly the King knows his own mind and what is good for him. If he prefers the company of a young, fair woman, who are we to question his decision?'

The Princess looks as if she has swallowed something rotten. 'I knew you could not be trusted.'

'And yet you ask me here, your Grace.'

'Yes, I am that desperate. I own that quite freely.' She turns to the window, no doubt watching her son loitering in the garden. Drawn away from the books Edmund knows Richard secretly loves. The Princess sighs. 'You and I will never be friends, but my husband trusted you in all important matters, and so, I put my son's safety in your hands.'

'The loss of the Prince was a great wound, your Grace, one that will never heal, I fear.' Edmund joins the Princess at the window, resting his hands lightly on the sill. 'He was cut down in his prime enforcing his father's wishes. He never recovered from the blow dealt him by King Peter, and I hold him solely responsible for the loss we have now suffered. You and I have had our differences, it is true, but I loved your husband as a brother.'

The Princess allows Edmund to hold her hand for a moment before she draws away. 'Then bestow the same love upon my son that a true uncle would. For God knows, he cannot expect any love from the uncles he has.'

'Love is a powerful thing, your Grace,' Edmund allows, 'but I have no real power to wield in the face of his uncles. Lord Gaunt I might be able to work with, and Langley has long since bestowed his friendship upon me, but Lord Woodstock … Him I can do nothing about.'

'No one can.' The Princess turns from the window, her shoulders heavy from the burden of grief and fear she now carries. 'Except perhaps John, whom you know so well.'

You are trying to exert power over me, Edmund observes to himself, and for a moment you almost had me, but then you spoke out of turn, or perhaps you simply did not notice what you did. She is by no means a broken woman, although age and loss have taken their toll on her. Perhaps she can yet be overcome.

'It is true that I have often enough served Lord Gaunt,' Edmund admits and watches her with intent, 'but he is no friend of mine, as I have already said. He is the King's uncle; I am but a knight.'

'My husband's favourite knight, and so I must trust that Edward knew what he was about when he decided to single you out.' Princess Joan looks up at Edmund. 'Serve my son as you served his father, and I will forget our differences, I will even allow that my son be permitted to see you as a true knight without my interference.'

'It is difficult to be a favourite,' Edmund says and earns a nod, 'but if it will set your mind at ease, then your wish is my command, your Grace.'

'Perhaps I have been mistaken in my reluctance to trust you.' She inclines her head. 'Serve him well, and I shall ask no more. Fail him, and I shall take everything you have from you, Sire.'

'I shall not fail, your Grace.'

Edmund kneels before the Princess and knows she will be watching him as a hawk. Perhaps it is time to introduce a few more young men to the future King's service, some that might take her mind off Edmund. All he has to do is make sure he can control them.

## 4 October 1376 – Leeds Castle

'Why do you linger here, Sir Edmund?' Gaunt's face is tired and lined. 'You must be eager to get back to your own lands. I suspect there is more than enough for you to contend with.'

Edmund chews the fresh bread, relishing in the smooth churned butter and the chewy crust. 'There is, my Lord, but I have not been released.'

'Who is left to release you?' Gaunt sits down and scowls at the man beside him who is quick to leave. 'Your services revert to my father and he has no need of you. Not here in any case. Soon, we shall all be back in London, and I have a mind not to stay too long there either. Go home, Sir Edmund, go back to Beauworth and there, make a name of yourself among your men. '

'They are your father's men, my Lord.' Edmund wipes his chin and looks at the dais. 'Why will you not stay in London?'

'I have a crown to claim.'

'I thought it rested on the head of Trastámara once more.'

'Do not remind me of that usurper!' Gaunt sneers and ducks when the Princess looks at him 'I should like to stay and serve my father, but his little concubine will not allow for him to see his sons. Only Thomas.'

Edmund grabs another piece of bread and reaches for the butter, but Gaunt pulls the bowl away. 'You do not understand, do you Sire? It matters not if I stay or go, my father does not want so see me.'

'I hear he is looking once more to the north.'

Reluctantly, Gaunt pushes the bowl of butter towards Edmund. 'He does. I have tried to dissuade him, but he will not listen. He claims that he must bring the Scots to heel before he dies, even though it cannot be done. We have neither the men, nor the means to manage a war on two fronts.'

'The King is a hungry man.' Edmund finds he has lost his appetite but chews the buttered bread nonetheless. 'I thought he had abandoned his claim on the crown of France?'

For once, Gaunt smiles, a dark, devious grimace. 'Never. If he could, he would rather die on the field, sword in hand, cutting his way to the golden circlet than in his own bed. But he is too old.'

'So, he needs to send someone young to fight his battles for him?'

'I know what you mean, Sir Edmund, but no,' Gaunt says angrily, 'I will not submit to my father that you be let loose in France once more.'

'Send me north then,' Edmund suggests and smiles at Gaunt's glare. 'Come now, my Lord, you know as well as I do that I will be of more use to you on the field than behind a desk at some house or other. I was born for the glory of the battlefield.'

'And yet you have promised Joan that you will guard her son.' It is Gaunt's turn to smile at a glare. 'She may not care for me, but that does not mean she does not trust me, Sire, and you would do well to remember that.'

'For what it is worth, my Lord,' Edmund says, 'there is one she trusts even less than you or I.'

'I know.' Gaunt pulls Edmund's discarded bread towards him. 'That is why I am sending him north.'

Conceding the cleverness of Gaunt's scheme, Edmund drinks to disguise his reluctant admiration. Sending Woodstock north is a grand idea;

it will keep him away from Richard and the King, and it will keep him occupied for the foreseeable future.

'Will Lord Langley come with you?'

Gaunt sprays bread over the table when he laughs. 'I must leave someone here to ensure things do not get out of hand. You know as well as I do that if I leave my father to his mistress' whims, we will all be ruined. She is a greedy little wench and must be bridled wherever possible.'

You will go south, no doubt to your own mistress, Edmund thinks and allows himself to revel in the image of Gaunt's young beautiful governess whom he has bedded and made a mother several times over. But also to reinforce your father's claim on the French throne, no matter if you say you are going to Castile nor not. You serve your father first, you always have. Your youngest brother will go north, no doubt the Princess will be grateful to you for this gesture, and I must be too. Which leaves behind the only brother I know trusts me without hesitation.

This time, Edmund smiles in earnest, for he is best pleased with Gaunt's plan. He is playing right into Edmund's hands.

# CHAPTER 20

## 16 July 1377 – Westminster Abbey

'He will be a fine King,' Thomas Holland says. Although he is only a maternal brother to the King, he is styled as a royal prince in a cloak of red and ermine, gold rings on all his fingers. 'My brother is just the kind of King we need after that old …'

'Best not say too much, my Lord,' Edmund says and looks around to find his squire. The boy was at his side only a moment ago, where has he got to now? Children are vexing and that is the truth. 'But yes, he will be a great King.'

'He is very fond of you.' Holland's voice grows cold. 'Then again, our mother has been kind in her many mentions of you.'

'I owe her and the King my good fortune, and I shall not forget, my Lord.' Edmund finally finds his squire in the crowd and waves him closer; he wants more than anything to get away from Holland who is a tiresome brute though fortunately not very clever. 'I suspect we shall meet again at the feast?'

Holland puffs out his chest. 'Certainly, but I shall be close to the King and you – well – somewhat further away, I suspect. Though the King has asked that you come early and visit him in his chambers.'

'A great honour, my Lord, I shall be there in plenty of time for his feast.'

'He will have to rest first,' Holland says, 'to think Sir Simon took the liberty of simply scooping him up and leaving the ceremony.'

Edmund smiles, the boy had hung limp in his tutor's arms, a little spittle dripping from his open mouth. He lets his eyes linger on Holland's face and says, 'It was a long ceremony, and he had already been anointed. No doubt you will fill Master Richard in later, and he will have plenty of other ceremonies to attend.'

Holland shoots Edmund a haughty glance. 'Beware your intimacies in the future, Sire, he is a Prince no more, and you have not changed your position at court.'

'Naturally, my Lord,' Edmund says and watches the back of Holland disappear in the throng of people leaving the abbey. 'You puffed up peacock!'

'Peacock, Sire?' Robert de Vere appears next to Edmund, a smile on his handsome, young face. 'I did not think they let those roam the streets.' There is mischief in his voice and eyes.

'Some they do. My Lady Countess,' Edmund says and bows low to de Vere's wife Philippa, the King's cousin. Now there is a marriage most advantageous for the young Earl, no doubt it has come about through his close relationship with the King. A friendship the royal uncles do not approve of. A friendship instigated by Edmund himself, but de Vere is growing unruly and that will not do.

'Sir Edmund,' Philippa says and smiles generously. 'What a happy occasion. Although many of us thought he would be years from the crown, if not for …'

'Best not speak of it any more, my dear.' There is little love in Robert's stern voice. 'Now, we have a young King with many years on the throne ahead of him, and such a favourite with the people already. The Londoners are hard to please, but he has achieved it by merely falling asleep at his own coronation.'

'We must allow that he is young.' Philippa takes her husband's arm. 'We shall see each other tonight, Sire?'

Edmund bows low to the couple and watches them walk away; Philippa is of an age with the King and de Vere only five years older. The new court will be filled with young people, all but children themselves, and Edmund wonders if perhaps it is time to let the old ways die down and let youth replace them. As long as he has control of the King's young friends, he will not care either way.

As he turns, Edmund spies John Mowbray standing at the very edge of the crowded room, he looks to be deep in thought. Here is a young man whom Edmund can never hope to rope into his little display of friends for the King. Although John is a great friend of Richard, he is far too measured and controlled to be of any use, and he has too good a mind for Edmund to do anything with him. When John Mowbray, who inherited the title of Baron Mowbray from his father at the tender age of five, looks at Edmund, he inclines his head and receives a smile in return. Except it is not a trusting smile, it is a courtly smile.

Next to John, Thomas Mowbray appears, his role in the ceremony at an end. He is the one to watch. As the second son to the Baron, Thomas has to curry favour with all the right people at court, since he has no claim to either lands or titles. And Thomas is much more inclined to fall prey to flattery and soft words designed to ensure he keeps faith with whomever takes a liking to him. Not that Edmund likes him particularly, there is something very familiar about Thomas, something that nags Edmund and makes his skin crawl. Perhaps it is simply that for all that he looks like his father, he has the disposition of his dead mother, as well as a hankering for secrets and gossip. How fortunate that John does not pay heed to his headstrong younger brother or there would be trouble brewing all the time.

Edmund makes his way through the crowd, smiling here and there at men he knows and women he has bedded in secret. Most of the ladies blush and one or two even send him licentious smiles, but Edmund keeps his smile light and his feet moving. It will not do to get distracted at this important time. He has business with the King, once he is awake and, before then, he has to examine more closely the letter he received from Lady Blanche of Wake, aunt of some sort to the Mowbray children.

What can she possibly want with me, Edmund considers as he steps into the bright day, she is as old as Methuselah and has been away from court these many years. But then the past has taught him never to ignore a woman's call, she might just know something he can spin to his advantage. Besides which, he is curious about the lady who now watches over the Mowbray family. It is better to win her over to his side than to have to stand back while the Mowbrays take over court. Thomas is already too close a friend to the King, Edmund will have to change that if he is to stay in control. After all, he has promised the King's mother to keep him safe. What better way to do that than to ensure that he does not fall prey to Thomas Mowbray's wily ways?

Edmund turns right and walks along the wall towards the King's chambers. Not long ago, they were reserved for an old man. Now, they harbour a child. He will have to work doubly hard to ensure the boy knows him only to be a loyal servant and great friend. Otherwise, things might just get out of hand.

That afternoon, Edmund receives a summons from the new King to serve him for the feast and stand by his side throughout the evening. Edmund does so with a smile on his face and a sword by his side, bending often to make a remark or laugh at the King's timid observations.

The King has made his choice and, further down the hall, the Holland brothers sneer at Edmund.

## 18 July 1377 – Westminster Palace

'Sir Edmund.' The childish voice rings high above the rumble of the courtiers.

Edmund bows low and walks through the crowd that parts reluctantly around him. He is well aware that most of the men in the room are here to seek advances for their children, many of whom are of an age with the King. And a vast number of them find Edmund to be an unwanted addition to their company; he is in all regards beneath them, no one of consequence. Except, as they are about to find out, to the King.

'Your Grace.'

Sir Simon Burley is positioned behind the throne to the left; from his vantage point he watches the King's every move. If anyone knows how delicate the King's situation is, it is no doubt his tutor, the old knight whom the Queen Mother has appointed guardian and advisor to the King; a role Edmund had wanted for himself, but now that he has seen what Sir Simon does, he is pleased to have escaped. Looking around the room, Edmund notices that Gaunt is not present and hides a spell of surprise. He had thought Gaunt of all people would circle the young King, either eager to secure a position for his son or for himself. His absence is no doubt noticed by all present here today.

"I have heard many tales of your valour.' Such a sweet, innocent voice, so pure and kind.

'Indeed, your Grace?' Edmund asks adding surprise to his expression.

'Yes,' the King says and looks at Sir Simon before continuing. 'I should like for you to tell me of your adventures with my father.'

'If that is your Grace's wish.' Edmund finds it hard to be deferential to a child and only succeeds because he knows that he owes all to the King, his position, his household, everything he has is in the King's gift.

Edmund suspects that all the other men present struggle as he does to pay due homage to the new King. Still, he hopes no one voices concern or asks that a regent be appointed until the boy comes of age. That would be devastating, a blow to Edmund's plans he will find hard to recover from. No, leave the child vulnerable and let me be always close to him in his hour of need, Edmund thinks while he smiles at the boy.

The King is ten years old, he should be studying and riding in the fields with his friends; God knows he needs the practice, for he is still uncomfortable in the saddle and lacks all skill necessary to become the man his father once was. Not to mention that no one had thought to teach the boy how to govern, a skill he so desperately needs, and one that does not appear overnight.

Kingship does not lie in the drop of holy water, which just two days ago anointed the gangly, pale boy now sitting on the massive throne once dominated by a great warrior. Edmund counts his blessings that he knows how to disguise his vexation that all his future fortune is in the hands of a child.

'You may leave us,' the King says and smiles at the gathered men. 'I shall call for all of you in time.'

Sir Simon bends his head and whispers; there is urgency in his manner.

'Oh,' the King says and stays everyone leaving, 'I thank each of you for your gifts and congratulations. They warm my heart and steady my hand in my new position. You are all quite invaluable to me.'

His confident words and bright smile relieve some of the tension harboured in the nobles and courtiers. Edmund notices that a few even leave with smiles on their faces. But not all are so easily appeased.

'Who does he think he is?' Woodstock hisses as he passes by Edmund. 'Why is my brother not here to set him straight? What the hell is wrong with John these days?'

'I suspect he is brooding somewhere in the north,' Warwick replies and earns a wolfish grin from Woodstock.

'He had his eyes set firmly on that seat! I should wager all my worldly goods he will never come to terms with having a child King!'

Woodstock vanishes from Edmund's peripheral view and all he hears is a roar of laughter from the two men as they pass through the doors and into the reception rooms beyond. The door swallows up any further nastiness from the King's uncle when it closes, and for that Edmund is grateful.

'Come closer, Sir Edmund,' Sir Simon says with a smile.

When Edmund is at the foot of the low dais, he can see that the King is struggling to keep still. His right leg jitters constantly, and he seems unable to stay it even when Sir Simon gives him a harsh look.

'Sir Edmund!' The boy's voice climbs a couple of octaves. 'Sir Edmund, you must have such great tales to tell!'

'Indeed, your Grace,' Edmund says and returns the expectant smile; he is amused that this is the first time, Richard has kindled any interest in tales from the past. The King's eyes flicker constantly between Edmund and Sir Simon as if he is attempting to decode the unspoken language of grown men. 'What would you like me to tell you?'

'Sir Simon says I must not tire you,' the boy lets slip and grins when Sir Simon bows his head in short-lived displeasure. 'There, see? He is impatient that I be kingly, but I have already a crown upon my brow, a throne beneath my arse, what more can he hope for do you think, Sir Edmund?'

Edmund cannot suppress his bubbling laughter; the boy is as quick and keen as ever. He remembers the King as a small boy, constantly struggling to keep up with his older rowdy brother. What he lacked, and indeed still lacks, in physical skills, he makes up for with his wit. All he needs is someone to govern him subtly and without opposition.

'Your Grace,' Sir Simon says. 'Can I leave you for a moment? I shall return within the hour and bring with me that which you requested.'

'In that case, you have my permission to leave, Sir Simon.'

While boyish in his manners, he makes a good show of being King, Edmund thinks and nods to Sir Simon.

'Let me think,' the King continues. 'I should very much like to hear of the first time you met my father!'

'It is so many years ago, I feel quite old,' Edmund says.

'You are!' There is a note of grudge in the King's voice. 'You are grown, and so is Sir Simon and all my uncles and everyone here! And do you know, Sir Edmund, that I have recently lost my good friend Thomas? Sent home! He does not even have a real home, just an old aunt who is such a bully!'

'Is that so, your Grace?'

The King scratches his nose. 'Yes. I am stuck here with my cousin, Henry. Who is so very dull. All he wants is to ride horses and swing swords.'

'Perhaps you merely need to know each other better?'

'I wager you had many happy hours as a boy and grew up with so many brothers that you were never short a playmate!'

That goes to show how little you know me, Edmund thinks and shakes his head. 'No, your Grace. I was quite alone.'

'All alone?' The King jumps from his throne and scales the steps to stand beside Edmund. The boy does not even reach his chest. 'Sit, sit.'

Edmund sits down on the bottom step, and the King plops unceremoniously down next to him. 'Were you really so very alone? You are not just saying so to comfort me?' The King eyes him for a moment. 'No, I see that you speak the truth. What a sad way to grow up. For all that I do not care for cousin Henry, at least he is my age and we can sometimes find something to do together. But I do miss Thomas.'

'Is that Thomas Mowbray by any chance, your Grace?'

The King's face lights up once more. 'Yes! Do you know him?'

Edmund is nonplussed by how quickly the King's mood seems to change, but then he is just a child, and must be allowed to change as the wind blows; at least that is what women say.

'I have known Thomas since he was in his cradle,' Edmund offers. 'I served his father, Baron Mowbray, and it was in his service I first met your father.'

'All those fathers gone,' the King muses, suddenly pensive. 'What luck that you are still here!'

He smiles at Edmund who is dubious of the boy's shifting moods. Perhaps tempering the young King will be harder than Edmund anticipated. It seems putting a crown on his head has changed his nature, Edmund thinks, he is quite different from the boy I saw tilting less than a year ago.

The King fidgets. 'Tell me where you met the Baron and my father.'

'To own the truth, I first saw your father while I was squire to the late Duke of Lancaster.' Edmund pauses when fragments of memories begin to flitter about. 'My master knew the Duke from somewhere, and he took me on when he passed through the region in which my family dwelled.'

'Your master must have been an important man.' The King's eyes shine with expectation.

'He was certainly well-connected.' Edmund evades. 'The Duke was called to rally to your father's side before the battle of Poitiers. The first time I saw your father, he was hacking away at the Baron's shield.'

'But I thought they were friends?' Now the King sounds upset, his voice quavering.

'They were, the greatest of friends,' Edmund says careful to add feeling to his words that they may soothe the boy. 'They were sparring. It can sometimes look as if men hate each other when they are on the sparring field with their swords drawn and visors down, but it is all sport, I assure you. And besides, your father was undefeated, he was never in any danger.'

'Not then,' the King says, his face solemn.

'No, not then.' Edmund takes a deep breath. 'A few days later, the Baron picked me to spar with him, perhaps at the Duke's initiative, and he was pleased with my skills. The Baron approached the Duke to ask that I join his men and fight with the Prince while the Duke was sent to protect the port of Calais.'

The King stares wide-eyed at Edmund, his mouth has dropped open a little and the fine white teeth are showing. 'How old were you?'

'Fourteen, I believe. It seems a lifetime ago.' As ever, the memory of the young Baron in all his finery petitioning the Duke to release Edmund brings back memories of better days, of days on the field with blood on the blade. 'When the Duke agreed I felt as the luckiest man in the whole world. I also felt sick.'

'Sick?'

'To go to battle must never be taken lightly, your Grace.' Edmund puts on his mask of seriousness. 'At the end of every enemy sword and lance awaits death, eager and hungry.'

'I shall never ask you to go to war for me,' the King says with great conviction. 'I favour peace.'

'Sometimes war comes to us,' Edmund says and sees the King's eyes narrow. 'While I too favour peace just as you do, your Grace, your enemies may see things differently. They may bring war to you.'

'Because I am a child?' There is danger in his words.

'No, your Grace, because we cannot control our enemies,' Edmund says and thinks, you cannot even control your friends, if you do not know them. He continues, 'We can only control ourselves and that is not always enough. Your grandfather made powerful enemies and when he died, you inherited them.'

The King nods slowly as if attempting to unravel what he has just heard. 'Then I shall have to make a powerful peace.'

Such adult words in the mouth of a boy, Edmund thinks, but nods agreement all the same. Peace is all the King can hope for; at least until he comes of age, and that is a long way away. If Edmund can help it, he will ensure that the King sees battle before he is a man grown, for Edmund is spoiling for war, not peace, but it will not do to begin this new stage of their relationship by disagreeing with the boy.

Instead, Edmund smiles. 'In that I cannot argue, your Grace.'

Appeased the King claps his hands. 'Go on! My father?'

So hungry for tales of his father, Edmund thinks, I wonder why his mother has not told him more. But then, sorrow has taken its toll on the Queen Mother and, since the Prince's death, she has deteriorated, grown fat and lax. It now rests on Edmund to fill in the gaps and paint a picture of the Prince that his son will be proud of. Thank God that is an easy task.

'As you have most certainly guessed, your Grace, the Duke agreed and, the very next day, I became part of the Baron's men. He did not need a squire who was the same age as he was, so he made me a soldier. I thought for certain that fortune had smiled upon me.'

'And it had, Sir Edmund, for I know that the Baron was a great man.'

'He was,' Edmund says and for a moment allows the Baron's fair wife, Elizabeth, his onetime lover, to dance before his eyes. To his great regret, she never strays far but for now Edmund pushes her aside. 'Every once in a while, when we put up camp somewhere on the way to Poitiers – the French King kept changing the place of battle – makeshift sparring fields would be fenced off and your father would pick a couple of men to train with him.'

'One day he picked you,' the King breathed. 'My lady mother told me so, and I have been curious about you ever since. But she would not tell me anything.' A frustrated shadow races across the young face. 'Now, neither she nor anyone else can tell me that I am too young to hear the stories of battle – or to ask that you tell me about my father!' Triumph replaces frustration.

'That is only too true, your Grace, though I believe your mother did it to protect you.' Edmund knows she also did it because she hoped to be rid of him but here he is at her bidding. He adds severity to his voice. 'Battle is grizzly business and should never be taken lightly.'

'I am afraid of nothing,' the King declares staunchly and shakes his head, his golden locks dancing about his face. 'I shall have my stories now!'

Moderated though, Edmund thinks, or your mother will make good on her promise to kick me out. He continues his tale: 'Your father did indeed pick me out, and I like to think I gave him good battle. Though he won in the end.'

'Because he was the Prince, heir to England and France.' The King's words sound more as a well-rehearsed line in a play than a trusted truth.

'Because he was strong and had much more experience with a sword than I,' Edmund objects and wins a brilliant smile from the King. 'And yes, because I was sure to be hanged, drawn and quartered if I killed the Prince on the cusp of battle! How would that have looked?'

The King laughs, a strange tingling sound more reminiscent of a young woman than a boy. 'Badly. But you would not be worth such a punishment. Most likely they would have just hanged you and moved on.'

Edmund shakes his head in mock disbelief. 'I should like to think that the death of a Prince would bring about a more spectacular death than just a hanging!'

Now, the King is clutching his knees while laughter shakes his thin body. When he is past the worst fit, he wipes his eyes and stutters; 'but … but you would … surely you would be hanged. So … so I must thank you.'

'You should, your Grace,' Edmund says with an appeasing smile. 'For you were yet to be born, and then we would have been denied this pleasant conversation in which you are determined to make me the villain.'

Something sly creeps into the King's eyes, but he nods all the same. 'You sparred with my father and spared him?'

'It was the other way around. He spared me. I think he primarily chose me for my size. There were not many men as big as I, and your father ever desired an adversary who could outmatch him in sheer size,' Edmund says with a tinge of pride. 'But none matched him on the field. By the end of that first day, my bruises had bruises. I was blue and yellow all over, and I could hardly lift my arm high enough for the bread to reach my mouth that night.'

'What happened then?'

Impatience is no virtue in a King, Edmund thinks, but it is the mark of childhood nonetheless. No doubt, Sir Simon has to work hard to wrestle the King from his childish behaviour. But perhaps Edmund can use it to his own advantage.

'Well?'

'Forgive me, your Grace, I needed a moment to gather my thoughts,' Edmund says and earns a curious glance from the King. 'Finally, the French King could postpone no more and sent emissaries to declare that the battle would take place at Poitiers. By then we had ridden halfway across France and back again, hot on the heels of the French army.'

'Poitiers …' the King breathes, momentarily lost in what appears to be a reverie. 'It sounds to be such a perfect place for chivalry.'

Hardly chivalry, Edmund thinks, when memories of his very first battle trample through his brain, but it did whet my blade and my appetite for war making. It showed me what I am born to do, and I will continue to do so every chance I get. It is the ladder I climb every day, and I intend to get to the top without interference.

'Yes, and as you know full well – or Sir Simon has failed his duty to you and he never would – we won. Your father devised such a cunning plan that it completely stunned the French soldiers, noblemen, knights and King alike.'

'Was it horrible?' The King twitches with glee. 'Did many die?'

'Many died, yes, but all on the field and all with honour.' Enemy screams echo in Edmund's mind and he relishes in the horrors of that day for a moment before he continues, 'Your father captured King John, aided by your uncle Gaunt and the Baron. I captured one of the French Princes. But before then, the French army fell to pieces and many fled.'

The King turns a dark face to Edmund. 'Cowards.'

'They feared for their lives, as well they should, your Grace,' Edmund says but quietly agrees with the King. 'They knew that only death would find them if they stayed on the field. Though there is no honour in flight there was not a single English soldier who did not understand their actions. And besides we hunted them all down.'

'You would flee from battle too?' Horror screams from the King's wide eyes.

'No, your Grace,' Edmund says with conviction. 'I never would. I am sworn to the English Crown and will defend it until my dying day.'

'Good man!' The King grasps Edmund's arm with little strength. 'I wish that all the men surrounding me were as straightforward as you. I shall have to teach them what true loyalty is.'

'That day, we were all loyal to your father,' Edmund continues. 'He was able to bring back King John in shackles and demand a ransom the like of which was never seen before.'

'Not that they ever paid it,' the King pouts. 'I find the French are inferior to us on all accounts, but still I cannot say that I wish to continue the listless war my grandfather pursued. I shall have to direct my councillors to find other means to protect my French dominions.'

Either the boy is excessively shrewd, Edmund thinks, or his teachers are whispering words in his ears. These are hardly the words of a ten-year-old, these are the words of men thrice his age and driven in the arts of politics and war. And Edmund, for one, would prefer the King to pursue his grandfather's quest for the French crown, for that would mean more warfare and more glory to be won.

'If I appoint you to my council, how would you advise me, Sir Edmund?'

'As best I can, your Grace,' Edmund says with surprise, this is better than what he could have hoped for. 'I should never presume to know a thing about being King, but I shall attempt to give fair council on matters of war, which is all I have ever known.'

The King studies Edmund for a moment before beaming another affable smile. 'That is all I ask. I shall have true council from all who surround me. I shall find my own advisors and make sure they swear fealty only to me. I shall not make mistakes of asking the advice of those who seek only to promote their own causes, those who are frightened of what a new reign might mean for them.'

'You have much family to rely on, your Grace.' The fiery glance the King shoots Edmund makes him wish he could smile in earnest, but he has to play the game. 'I only mean …'

'I need no more ambitious men always in my chambers, Sire,' the King says. 'I have said as much to my uncles and all those affiliated with my family. If the English families were not so very intertwined in one another, I might find more ease in choosing the right men to guide me.'

In an attempt to steer the conversation back on safe ground, Edmund nods. 'You are the King. Your word is law.'

'And so it shall remain,' the King chimes in and rises. 'What happened when you returned to England?'

'Your father went to London with the prisoners; the Baron was awarded time to visit his wife and brought me with him. It was the very first time I set foot in England.' Edmund smiles when the King resumes his seat on the dais steps and turns eyes full of wonder at him. 'I was born and raised in France, albeit a part of France that was under English rule. I thought you had been told my surname; La Fontaine.'

'La Fontaine …' the King seems to ponder something. 'I like that better than Sir Edmund. And besides, it confuses me that so many men are named the same; I have an uncle Edmund already. In future, you shall go by the name La Fontaine when you are here at court.'

Edmund bows his head to hide an overbearing smile. 'As you wish, your Grace.'

'We shall always be great friends, La Fontaine; I feel it. I rely on Sir Simon for my education of course, he is a brave and intelligent man. But for council on matters of warfare, I shall turn to you in future.'

'Might I suggest you take into your confidence your uncle, Lord Gaunt?' Edmund sees at once that the King is suspicious and continues, 'He may well be the most ambitious man in England, your Grace. He is also the only one who went on all your father's campaigns and helped him win them. While your father was a great strategist, Lord Gaunt is a politician first and foremost. His skills will be a welcome addition to your council.'

'You vouch for him?'

'I believe he will serve you faithfully.' Edmund wants to be instrumental in the King granting Gaunt a seat on his council that he might owe him future favours.

It is no secret that Gaunt has coveted the English Crown more than anyone and that his drop in the succession when the Prince had his sons with Princess Joan was a great personal disappointment. But Edmund also knows that Gaunt can do much more for England on the King's council, a confidant and ambassador for the young King, than from afar. And besides, Edmund prefers to have Gaunt in London and in the midst of court where he can keep an eye on him. All of Gaunt's past attempts to secure the Castilian throne have failed, and Edmund wants Gaunt to know that his greatest mistake was not to take Edmund with him when he went to seize his crown. Perhaps the future will shape up differently, all that is needed is to stay patient, and no one masters the patience of time passing as Gaunt does. In time, Castile will be his.

'He will be a great champion of your reign, your Grace,' Edmund says, 'and a great ally once Castile yields to him and his wife.'

The King's leg begins to bob up and down again. 'Then I shall consider your suggestion. But I will hear nothing more about uncles! I want a young court, not a bunch of twitching old men!'

'Yes, your Grace.' Edmund hears the King's grandfather in those defiant words and knows now is the time. 'Perhaps you will permit me to suggest a few young men for your personal company?'

The King is about to reply when the door opens and Sir Simon appears with two servants in royal livery in tow. Edmund is quick to hide his irritation at being interrupted and turns to Sir Simon with an easy smile.

'Your Grace,' Sir Simon bows low and approaches the dais. 'I bring the gift.'

The King rises and brushes imaginary dirt from his trousers. When Edmund looks at him, he sees that eager obedience and desire to do right has returned to the King's face. What power Sir Simon wields, unknowingly I hope, Edmund thinks.

'Kneel before your King,' Sir Simon says to Edmund who is quick to bend his knee. 'Do you swear eternal fealty to the Crown of England and our sovereign King Richard?'

'I do.' Edmund's spine tingles, although they are all but alone, he feels the monumental promise raise him up and battles the regret that his pledge has not been witnessed by all the court. But it does not matter, he has the King's trust, and soon he will have the King's ear too.

The King draws the ceremonial sword, the hilt and pommel enormous in his small hands. He totters slightly under the weight before he lifts it high enough to rest it on Edmund's shoulder. What should be a light touch, is a prolonged rest of blade against cloth.

'Today, Sir Edmund – La Fontaine to your King – I bestow upon you a gift to bind you to me in perpetuity,' the King's young voice sings out, a note of greatness in it. 'From this moment, these are your coat of arms.'

Sir Simon draws away the cloth covering what the servants carry between them. Edmund looks at the shield. The rim is hammered copper, the base has inlay of mother of pearl and filigree of silver. The unicorn prances, horn to the stars upon a bed of dark blue.

'What an honour, your Grace!' Edmund's mouth goes dry, what is this childish folly?

'My mother always says you are a unicorn,' the King says with a wide smile. 'She says that while the other men around my father were thoroughbreds and dray horses, you stood out. You might mix with them with ease, but you are one of a kind.'

'She is most kind, your Grace.'

Edmund wonders what might have prompted the Queen Mother to speak thus and whether it is a veiled threat of some kind. But when he looks at the King, his eyes glitter from honest glee as he nods and the servants offer the shield to Edmund. The silver tray upon which it rests glitters in the daylight streaming in through the high, narrow windows. Edmund reaches out and runs a hand over the smooth surface. He feels the minute dents of the blacksmith's hammer and recognises how much effort has gone into crafting the shield.

'I have never had anything so fine, your Grace.' Edmund grits his teeth.

Behind him, the King claps with childish glee. 'Then you are pleased? You accept? You are mine?'

Something in the wording gives Edmund pause, but he looks down at the King's contented face, and offers another docile smile. 'It will be my honour to serve you, your Grace.'

# CHAPTER 21

## 13 June 1381 – Carlisle Castle, the Western March

'Why are you here?'

'The King sent me.' Reluctantly, Edmund thinks and tries to gauge Gaunt's face. It reveals nothing. 'With a royal command.'

'To stay put, no doubt. If only Richard had sent Thomas here when I asked him to, much might have evolved differently.'

'He is trying to govern; we must give him credit for that.'

Gaunt runs a hand through his thinning, greying hair. Although he is of an age with Edmund, he looks years older. 'He is trying to avoid problems. It is no secret that I am far from beloved in London – in England for that matter. The people care not for a Lord.'

'They perhaps do not know you.' Edmund knows his words are not true. They do know him. But flattery is easy coin to part with.

'Oh, they know me. Or so they think. Because I am wealthy, I must care nothing for England or her people. They forget that I have served this country since my birth, I have gone from impossible battle to impossible battle, I have served first my father and brother and now a child King and I do not complain. I do all of this to stay enemies at England's door. And what do they do in return?'

Rather than reply, Edmund shrugs off his cloak, it is heavy from the slow drizzle of northern England, the hem caked with mud and dirt.

'It is different for you, Sir Edmund,' Gaunt says. 'You are liked wherever you go. Men follow you willingly, not because you can pay them, but because they believe in you. You are much as my brother was in his years of glory, before he changed. But then we all did.' Gaunt waves a hand as if to disperse his memories. 'What are his Grace's commands?'

'To remain here.' Edmund sees dislike flash in Gaunt's hard eyes. 'To keep the enemy of the north at bay. The last thing the King needs is for the Scots to get wind of the rebellion and decide to make their move.' He licks his lips. 'Are you any closer to a peace?'

'No peace can be made with savages.' Gaunt throws away a spent quill. 'What can I hope to achieve that my forefathers failed to do? I may be skilled in diplomacy and policy, but even I know that to reason with the Scots is a bloody waste of time!'

'And yet it is what the King desires above all else.'

Gaunt takes the document from Edmund and breaks the seal. His face creases and then seems to fall in on itself. Meanwhile, Edmund looks around the room, it is as glum as Gaunt, the walls wet from damp, the windows so narrow that hardly any light creeps in. Though it rains outside, no fires are lit. Having known Gaunt for some time, Edmund assumes that it is either from neglect or because Gaunt likes the dark. It suits his unforgiving demeanour.

'I should have thought what he desires above all else is for his subjects to return to their fields and bow their heads in submission.' Rather than look Edmund in the eye, Gaunt stares at the order before him made out in the King's rounded, feminine hand. 'When he was first crowned, the people adored him. He was the golden boy of England, fair, sweet and kind. Since then, he has done little enough to prove them right. Perhaps this is his lesson that the people's love is not constant.'

'He can hardly be blamed …'

'Can he not?' Gaunt snaps. 'If he is to be the King he so desperately claims to be, he must know that his trusted advisors are flouring their own cakes. That his tax collectors are bought and paid for and put aside much of what they demand as royal taxes for their real masters. You will have me believe that he knows not what is happening right under his own nose?'

'You must know better than me, as many of the tax collectors are yours to command. But I should say that the King had no idea the people's opinion had turned against him.' Edmund shakes his head. The King is surrounded by yes-men and boys who know nothing about the ways of the world. Until recently, it had been a fine arrangement, but it has soured and Edmund has grown weary of his creatures. 'Who are these advisors you accuse of lining their own pockets with Crown taxes?'

'De Vere.' Gaunt breathes deep. 'He must be in the thick of things. He never leaves my nephew's side; his wealth grows at such a staggering speed that even I cannot believe it.'

'He is a merchant,' Edmund says dismissively. He will not own that de Vere has succeeded in setting him aside after having used Edmund's influence to rise at court. But he has ideas on how to change that.

'You like him no more than I do,' Gaunt replies. 'I can see it in your eyes. Tell me, Sir Edmund, why do you think you are here? When you would be of so much more use to the King in the south? Either protecting him in London – or better yet stamping out rebellion in your own region.'

As always, Gaunt hits the mark and Edmund has to work hard to look indifferent. 'I do not question the King's commands.'

'Perhaps you should. I have plenty of men at my service, loyal men who will do my bidding. I need no more knights to feed, certainly not a knight whom I do not know if I can trust.' Gaunt shakes his head. As usual, he is dressed in dark garb and only wears a single ring on his finger, his crest cast in gold. His hair has grown grey with age too, and he looks less and less like his brothers and his nephew, the golden King. Gaunt turns the ring. 'I am at a stalemate here. I cannot hope to win the Scots over with nothing but a raggedy army and trinkets.'

'I heard that you sent most of your men to Lancashire,' Edmund says. He has long wondered why Gaunt had done such a thing, and he is not alone in his contemplations. It was all the court could speak of, until the rebels rose in the south.

'Can you blame me?' Once more, Gaunt runs a hand through his hair.

'No. I sent my men to Hampshire.' Edmund's soaked boots render his feet cold. He longs for the crackling of a well-built fire. 'I would have gone with them.'

'But the King would not let you?'

Edmund hears the incredulity in Gaunt's words, they mirror his own feelings when the King sent him north not south. 'No, he would not. He insisted this message be delivered in person.'

'Do not think that I accuse the King of wanting rid of you, Sir Edmund,' Gaunt says with a sly smile. 'I believe he holds you in the highest regard. But that only marks you for animosity. Much as my blood marks me. The King surrounds himself with advisors who would not hesitate to climb over our bodies to get closer to the King.'

'You may not accuse him, but you do believe him to be blinded.' Edmund sits down and admits to himself that he has lost control with the young court. It must be rectified and soon, before Gaunt is allowed to return to London and sees for himself what has become of the King's council.

'And you do not?'

'I care not for de Vere; in that you are correct. He is perhaps too close to the King; last I saw he has even replaced the young Thomas Mowbray in the King's favour. A decision I am sure the King will regret in time.'

A decision I am already regretting, Edmund concedes to himself, for I would much rather deal with young Mowbray, whom I know much better than de Vere. The very thought of the young upstart married to the King's cousin makes Edmund's blood boil. He was a poor choice of companion for the young King, a very poor choice.

'Yes, Henry says that Thomas was most displeased to be sent from court.' Gaunt pushes the inkwell away. 'I might forgive you for coming here whatever the order, but not that you did not bring my son. You must have known; I have often enough requested he be sent here.'

'There was no time, my Lord.' Edmund knows that Gaunt will hold him responsible for any misery that might befall the Lancastrian heir. Better just say it. 'The King has moved his household to the Tower.'

All blood drains from Gaunt's face. 'The Tower?'

'On Sir Simon's counsel.'

'A voice of reason in a sea of ignorance.' Gaunt tries to regain his usual composure, but Edmund can tell that he is distraught. 'I wonder for how long.'

'Hopefully for long enough to stamp out the rebellion.' Edmund wants nothing more than to change places with Sir Simon who has also grown to be of too much influence. But in this one regard, Gaunt has the right of it, at least Sir Simon does not have a greedy bone in his body. What he does, he does solely for the love he bears his King.

'The Tower is the safest place for all of the court to be at this moment, my Lord,' Edmund continues, 'You would do well to make progress here, which is what the King desires above all else. If only you could break the Scots, the King would be free to govern the unrest. Your failure weighs heavily on his mind.'

'You have come all this way to provoke me, Sire?' Gaunt looks ready to snap, and it almost makes Edmund laugh, but then, he too has been sent north, and that is not amusing.

'We both need to be in London and the sooner the better. I care as much for the King's safety as you do, my Lord, and I want him surrounded by better advisors than he is today,' Edmund says, 'but until such a time as I can make my return, what would you have me do? Deny a royal command?'

In the silence, Edmund wriggles on the uncomfortable chair. In Bordeaux and even in London, Gaunt was surrounded by beautiful furniture, soft cushions, vibrant fabrics and white-washed walls, painted in lavish patterns. How the mighty have fallen, Edmund thinks and sniffs, the air is wet and tastes stale. He stocks the fireplace and grabs a candle to light the kindling. The wood spits and screams, but the flames catch all the same.

Gaunt rubs his right arm. 'How bad is it?'

'The people have had enough. The leader – some man named Wat Tyler – has rallied so many men that we cannot hope for a peaceful resolution,' Edmund says and directs his chair to the fire. 'Not unless every lord returns to his lands and reminds his people what they owe him. Which is why the King should have sent me south. And have called you back to London.'

In truth, Edmund admires Tyler for his rebellion, and he despises the King for denying him the pleasure of killing the rebel on a starless night. It could be easily done, but the King favours peace still. That is the real reason Edmund is sent north. Because the King wants to avoid bloodshed.

'You would call upon loyalty?'

'Compared to your estate, mine is of no consequence, but I know my people would never join the revolt,' Edmund says with a sneer. 'They may dislike the tax collectors, the court, perhaps even the King, but they will never disobey me. Can you say the same, my Lord?'

'If you were there,' Gaunt mumbles avoiding Edmund's question.

'Yes, if I were there.' Edmund sighs and looks about for a pitcher of wine, but there is nothing to be had in Gaunt's dreary chamber. At least, the reluctant fire is warming his feet. 'But I am here.'

Gaunt throws the royal order in the fire and watches the note crumble in the flames. 'For how long?'

Edmund does not intend to reward Gaunt with an answer, let him stew and wonder. Instead, he rises and asks, 'You will provide a room for me?'

'In this listless place?' Gaunt gives a cold laugh. 'How many men did you bring?'

'Not enough. Not enough by far.' Pushing the oddly warm wood of the door, Edmund can hear Gaunt begin to pace the room. 'You will have to bring the Scots to heel soon, if you are to be allowed to go south, my Lord. The King will not accept your return otherwise. And you cannot hope to receive reinforcements now that the King has a battle of his own at his doorstep.'

'Whose fault is that, Sire?' Gaunt growls.

'I should imagine it is my Lord Woodstock's fault,' Edmund retorts. 'Who else in England is as greedy and ruthless as your own brother?'

Gaunt's footsteps stop. 'I can name a man or two.'

'Really?' Edmund turns towards Gaunt and they eye each other. 'For I cannot.'

'Am I to understand that until I succeed with the Scots, I shall have the honour of your company?' Gaunt resumes his pacing. 'For that would be a great gift indeed.'

Edmund smiles at the slight. 'Fear not, my Lord, I am certain that your skills in politics are not yet spent. Perhaps you will feel obliged to try harder now that you know your lands are under threat from your own people.'

'I am at my wits end.' Gaunt's words are as hard as his footsteps. 'And I must have done some great injustice to warrant my nephew sending one of his favourites to this dark part of the country. How long did you say you were staying?'

'We are going around in circles, my Lord.' Edmund is tired and wants a drink. 'Why not focus on a swift victory here that we might all of us sleep more soundly.'

'You have nothing to fear from the Scots. Your estate is about as far south as can be.' Gaunt pauses, his footsteps stop. 'Come to think of it, the rebellion began in your part of England, did it not?'

You know me too well and yet not at all, Edmund thinks and fights an urge to give a spiteful reply. Instead, he weighs his words and wills his hand to stay away from the hilt of his sword. It may yet come to blows, but he will not be the one to initiate. Let Gaunt seethe and worry, it is nothing to Edmund. He knows when he is allowed to return to London and he has no reason to fear that the King has grown weary of him. Even de Vere has failed to change the King's mind about Edmund.

He pushes the door open and Gaunt calls after him. 'You owe me an answer, Sir Edmund.'

## 23 June 1381 – Carlisle Castle

'They did WHAT?!'

Gaunt's roar brings the messenger to his knees. The poor man looks as if he has not slept nor rested since leaving London, and Edmund shakes his head.

'Burnt it, my Lord,' the messenger whispers, his muddy cloak dripping with water.

Before Gaunt can act, Edmund steps in front of the crouching man and fixes Gaunt with a measured stare. 'Leave us.'

'There is a message for you too, Sire,' the messenger scrambles to his feet and pushes a crumbled document into Edmund's hands. He can feel the messenger tremble.

'Thank you. Go with Simmons, he will provide food and rest.' Edmund nods to the old servant hovering by the door. 'You are to stay here – for the time being.'

'Ordering about my servants, Sire?' Gaunt sneers behind Edmund's back.

'He is but a messenger and, by the looks of it, he has hardly had a moment's rest on his journey here. The horse he came on was on the verge of collapse.' Edmund pauses to ensure that the servant does not linger outside the door. When he hears the sound of footsteps disappear, he sits on the low stool by the empty hearth; Gaunt refuses to light fires although everything is damp and windy. 'It is far more important what the messages say than who brought them, would you not agree, my Lord?'

Gaunt cracks the seal and unfolds the document not pausing to smooth the crumbled paper. His eyes dart across the paper; Edmund can tell that he tries hard to keep his face still.

While Gaunt digests his order, Edmund slips the seal from his own letter and breathes deep before reading it. What is on the paper is almost too terrible to relay.

'What does yours say?' Gaunt is now seated at his desk. 'Well?'

'The King has crushed the rebellion.' Edmund tries to swallow his malcontent that he was not present when the rebels were thwarted. Nothing is going according to plan it would seem.

Gaunt nods grimly. 'What else?'

'I am free to return to my lands.' Almost, Edmund thinks, folds the paper and tucks it under his shirt. 'And you, my Lord?'

'I am to relinquish my frugal attempts to broker a peace with the Scots and return to London.' There is something raw in Gaunt's words. 'At least Henry is safe, if this letter is to be believed. You are willing to believe that the King rode into the midst of the assembled rebels and managed singlehandedly to ensure they did not take up arms against him? A boy of fourteen?'

'Same age as your son, my Lord.'

Edmund admits to himself that he struggles to believe the gangly King has it in him to act with such heroics. He has long since abandoned any hope of the King learning how to handle a lance, much less a sword, although he has finally learned how to sit a horse properly. Which is hardly enough to provide him with the ability to control a rebel army.

'Henry is different.' Gaunt looks uncomfortable. 'If the tale is true, everyone in England will be telling it in a matter of days. Which means …'

'Which means that once I travel south, I shall hear the King's praises being sung in every tavern and town I enter.' Edmund smiles, but inside displeasure bites into his stomach, he wants to be the hero of the commoners' songs. It burns.

'He will be a living legend.' Incredulous, Gaunt slips his order into a small chest on his desk and snaps it shut.

'He is the grandson of a great warrior – and the son of another.' Edmund knows that Gaunt does not like to be reminded of his inferiority to his older brother. It makes him feel better to rub Gaunt's nose in his own deficiencies.

'Do you think a fourteen-year-old can handle being treated as a hero?' Gaunt asks and does not wait for an answer. 'A boy who already believes divine destiny placed him on the throne. That God walks alongside him.'

Edmund has often contemplated the King's unfaltering belief that he has been chosen by God to rule England. But then, when thousands of people fall to their knees in adoration as soon as a crown is placed on your head, what would that do to any child? Besides, Edmund has worked hard to support the King's belief that his hand is guided by divine intervention. It keeps him mollified.

'He is still adored. Given what has just come to pass, I should not imagine he will change his mind about his place in the world,' Edmund says. 'He is the King.'

'And while the King has permitted you to go home, I am to go to London. Where the crumbing ruins of my former home await me. I shall gaze upon them, Sir Edmund, and curse all those who took part in the ruin of such a fine house.' Gaunt taps an ink-stained finger on the table. 'I will make them regret their actions.'

A lesser man would feel relieved that no one was hurt and that his son is safe, Edmund thinks, but then that would roam too far from your usual manner. Gaunt is many things, but sentiment is something he reserves for his estate and fortune, not something he disperses on his family. In that they are two sides of the same coin.

Gaunt slams open the door, shouting down the hallway: 'CAPTAIN! WE LEAVE AT DAWN!' He turns around and looks at Edmund. 'You may go.'

'I am to leave with you, my Lord.' Edmund rejoices in the effect of his words.

'Is that so? Am I to suffer you witnessing my defeat? The burning ruins of my home?'

Edmund breathes deep. 'I am to go directly to the King. So are you.'

Striding out, Gaunt growls. 'The King can wait.'

ᗢ ᗣ ᗢ ᗣ

## 10 July 1381 – Westminster Palace

Edmund leans against a column at the very back of the great hall watching the men and women of the court flitter about like confused little birds. Some of them look happy and pleased, others look concerned, some even a little frightened. No doubt those with the biggest frowns are the ones whose fate has yet to be determined. The King had little support from his court during the great conflict and he is almost certainly going to make examples of those who fled when the peasant army surged through the streets of London.

The big doors open and Gaunt strides across the floor, scattering people as if he had swatted away the last pieces on a chess board. The smouldering ruin that is Savoy Palace, once Gaunt's seat of power, seems to have become part of him, his very presence dark and ominous. Edmund is happy to acknowledge that he understands Gaunt's distress at loosing what is without question the finest palace that has ever been built. But in reality, it was not his to begin with, it belonged to his long dead wife, and her father before her, the Duke of Lancaster, Grosmont. For that reason alone, Edmund is a trifling sorry that it stands no more. The rubble will soon be cleared away, but it seems the palace will not be rebuilt. No doubt, Gaunt does not want to part with the money needed for such an endeavour. Or perhaps he simply does not believe he will be in London much, and so he will decide to revert the costs to some other castle of his instead. The rebellion has made many a Lord decide to reinforce his estate.

It bothers Edmund a little that he has been unsuccessful in his efforts to extract from Gaunt what exactly he plans to do now that they are both in London once more. No doubt, Gaunt will resume his seat on the King's council and much good may it do him, but it would soothe Edmund's mind if he knew at least a little of what Gaunt plans on doing while he is here.

'Sir Edmund,' Woodstock's soft voice curls around Edmund wafting through the air as bad perfume, 'imagine seeing you here.'

'I am always here, my Lord.' Edmund honeys his words; it does not do to put off two royal uncles in one go. 'I hear, you played a great part in the King's recent triumph.'

'I had words with my nephew before he chose to ride so callously into the midst of a mob,' Woodstock says, watching his older brother vanish behind the doors to the King's private apartments. 'I told him either to gamble all or do nothing at all. I am glad he decided to do the kingly thing.'

Are you now, Edmund thinks and nods, 'I can only imagine what great counsel you were for our young King, my Lord. How I wish I had been there too.'

'No doubt you would have cut down the rebel leader yourself, Sire,' Woodstock sneers, 'but as it were, I am glad it fell upon our mayor to do so. I also congratulate myself that I helped plot to ensure the city guard was not far away in case things went sour.'

'How fortunate they did not.' Edmund nods at a passing courtier and lowers his voice. 'I hear the King has great plans for the rebels?'

Woodstock laughs and pounds Edmund on the back. 'Freshly returned from the north, and you already know all that goes on. Some day, you must tell me how you do that, Sir Edmund, I would dearly love to know.'

Edmund watches Woodstock disappear contemplating how gaudy he looks in all his finery. The King must soon be warned that his uncle is not to be trusted. But before then, Edmund must address the problem of de Vere. In Edmund's absence, it seems he has grown in the King's favour and that will not do. The first order of business must surely be to ensure he is taken down a peg or two, and Edmund to be returned to his rightful place by the King's side.

The doors open anew and Michael de la Pole enters. Perhaps opportunity has just presented itself, Edmund thinks and inclines his head to de la Pole, who changes course and makes for Edmund. Perhaps this is exactly what he needs to put things right.

'Sir Edmund.' De la Pole's words are as creamy as freshly churned butter. 'You cannot imagine my pleasure in seeing you here. You missed quite a spectacle.'

'So I gather, my Lord Baron,' Edmund says. 'I hear the King was heroic.'

'Or foolhardy,' de la Pole whispers through a smile. 'But he dispersed the rebels and that is more than any of us could have hoped for.'

'You were not for putting him in harm's way, I can imagine.' Edmund keeps his eyes on the moving crowd. 'But then nor would I have been if I had been here.'

The Baron pauses as a group of young women bustle past, giggling and blushing when Edmund smiles at them. They are pretty in their soft coloured dresses, their hair hanging free, as signs that they are maidens. Edmund wonders if perhaps they are the ladies-in-waiting for de Vere's wife, she has the status to warrant a flock of fine hens.

De la Pole looks at Edmund. 'I should have thought you would have argued that he be forged in battle. That he must do something utterly reckless in the face of danger to secure his position and thwart any objections to his young rule.'

'The King is safe on his throne,' Edmund says without hesitation. 'I would not have him risk all just to silence a few disgruntled men.'

'A few!' De la Pole huffs. 'They came by the thousands, Sire, and I will have you know that no one charged the King to act as he did. In fact, we all tried to talk him out of it.'

'To no avail, I am happy to understand.' Edmund glances at de la Pole to determine what mood he is in. As a great friend to the King and high in favour with all the nobles, the Baron is not to be crossed unless necessary. 'I would have cautioned him too, my Lord. But he is young and not easily swayed once his mind is made up. Which we know only too well.'

De la Pole slaps his soft riding gloves into his palm. 'We are all lucky that no one released an arrow. Or you and I might be having a very different conversation right now, Sir Edmund.'

'I gather the King has some announcement to make?'

'The King granted charters of freedom to the rebels,' the Baron says and nods, 'but only to make the rebels disperse. It seems some of the more unruly insurgents cannot be brought to heel in Essex. The King is considering going there himself to ensure the last of the revolt is stamped out.'

'He is brave.' Edmund knows now that he has to be part of the army the King brings, must be allowed to play a part to prove he is still a force to be reckoned with. The King's most ardent defender. 'You must forgive me, my Lord, I have long been away from court, do you know who he plans to take with him?'

The Baron half-smiles. 'I am certain he cannot do without you, Sir.'

Edmund returns the smile. 'Especially if you were to back my submission to join his Grace. After all, you are his most valued counsellor.'

# Part 4

# Misfortune

# CHAPTER 22

## 29 July 1381 – Framlingham, Nottingham

'Yes, I must have more news of that tonight. But first, the boy, La Fontaine.'

Edmund smiles, since first meeting Lady Blanche, he has grown strangely fond of the old woman. Perhaps he should not be so loose with his words around her, but then, he must have an ally in the Mowbray house. For that reason alone, he is willing to take on the Baron's youngest son, whom Edmund has just left in the middle of a busy courtyard, the sun bouncing off the boy's golden curls.

'What do you think of him?'

'He looks a bright boy, and no doubt I shall make much of him in time. He has a strong build and if your accounts are anything to go by, as I know they are, my Lady, he will be quick to learn too,' Edmund clasps his hands behind his back. 'To own the truth, he reminds me of myself at his age. Not quite as alone in the world, but still …'

Blanche touches his arm and Edmund turns with her; he has already spied the boy's earnest face reflected in the windows.

'Argyle, come meet Sir Edmund La Fontaine.'

She beckons the boy closer, and he moves swiftly and with much grace. Up close, Edmund inspects the youngest Mowbray and finds his features to be regular and his frame to show much promise in the way of height and strength. Yes, he will be a fine squire and a good counterweight to the other two Mowbray brothers.

When Argyle bows, Edmund nods at him. 'It is a pleasure to make your acquaintance, Master Argyle. I have heard so much about you, and now that I lay eyes upon you, I feel reassured. Are you ready to become my squire?'

'Oh yes, Sire. I have been practicing, just as aunt Blanche has promised.' When Argyle splutters his answer, Edmund has to conceal a smile; here is a trusting boy. Argyle looks at Blanche and his voice trails off, 'Well, that is to say … Yes, Sire.'

As children go, Edmund likes the boy well enough and, fortunately, boys do grow up to be men. 'Good. We shall rest here for a few days if your aunt will have us. The area is pretty and charming, and my men need the break. This will give us time to settle the final details and perhaps for my men to hunt a little game?'

Edmund looks at Lady Blanche who nods her agreement, and he turns back to Argyle. 'Once we are done, you will come with me to London. We are requested at court.'

He catches Argyle's surprise and delight and thinks, I shall have to be careful with him at court, he is just the type of boy who might attract the wrong kind of attention.

'Off with you,' Blanche marches the boy out. 'Go help John in the stables and when you are done, change for the meal tonight. I want you to make an effort, Argyle,' she says just loud enough for Edmund to hear her, 'you will not disappoint, will you?'

'No, aunt,' Argyle says, his blue eyes wide and earnest. 'Never.'

'Well, there he is,' Blanche says once the door closes on the boy. 'Not much to look at to be sure, but I think …'

'He will be a fine squire and, in time, I shall ensure that the King himself knights him. After all, he is a Mowbray, and his brothers are already great friends of our young King.' Edmund arches his back and it crackles after the long ride. 'As a matter of fact, I own that I am very surprised to see both John and Thomas here.'

Blanche gestures for Edmund to sit down. 'The Queen Mother saw fit to send most of the boys in the royal household home once rumours surfaced of troubles in the south. But I gather that it has all turned out for the best?'

'Yes, my Lady,' Edmund says; he kept a watchful eye while the last of the revolt was stamped out in Essex.

What happens next is a different matter though, Edmund thinks and catches Lady Blanche's eye. She has the same concerned look that Gaunt had when they parted ways in London. The King's callous actions on Smithfield ensured that no more men lost their lives in the revolt than was necessary. But Edmund knows that the King plans to revoke all of his letters of pardon and distribute harsh justice to all who rose against him. Perhaps he will yet turn out to be his father's son in every way.

On Edmund's express advice, the peasants will be strong-armed back into their place, although it will hurt the King's popularity, which is what made most of his council voice concern about his plans. But Edmund is certain that the King will rally and the people forgive if not forget what he is about to do.

'La Fontaine?' Blanche calls him back from his contemplations.

'I am sorry, my Lady. It is as you said, you shall have the story tonight.' Edmund smiles.

'Good, for I have other business of a more pressing nature.' Lady Blanche summons a servant who brings a tray of delicious pickled plums, pastries and wine. They wait for him to arrange the food and pour the wine. 'You may leave us.'

'Other business?' Edmund picks up one of the dainty, costly glasses and toasts Lady Blanche. 'What might that be?'

'John and Thomas will soon return to court. Thomas in particular is very close to the young King, you are right about that,' Lady Blanche says and turns her beady eyes at Edmund, 'but he is being pushed aside by Robert de Vere. What make you of him?'

'He is married to the King's cousin and a great favourite.' Edmund still grapples to resume control over the wilful young de Vere, but he is confident that, in time, he will succeed. 'The King enjoys his company and his easy manners.'

'A true diplomat.' As always, her astute comments make him smile. She turns to the tray. 'I would like you to speak up for Thomas. He is rash, I admit it, and quite a handful, but I know he will serve the King loyally. He is dependent on him, since he is the second son and cannot expect to get anything of consequence. John will keep the Mowbray estates in one piece and marry a suitable girl – soon I hope – and Thomas has little interest in the church. Therefore, I want him to succeed at court. He is bright, even if he is not always interested in learning, and he understands how to play the games at court.'

'You make it sound as though I should be asking his patronage,' Edmund says. Her words spark a little concern but also an idea. 'I cannot imagine he needs my help?'

Lady Blanche shakes her head. 'As I say, he is rash. So far, John has managed him, at times even sent him here to get him away from trouble …'

'Yes, I heard about the incident with the horses.' Edmund gestures away Lady Blanche's displeased expression. They were but childish pranks, nothing more. He continues in a more measured manner, 'I shall do what I can, my Lady, as you well know I am …'

'Obliged to our house.' The Baroness picks at the tray of food and fixes Edmund's gaze. 'It is no use, my dear, I know it all.'

'All?' Edmund drinks deep. Here is the truth at last. 'I am sure …'

Lady Blanche folds her hands in her lap. 'Say nothing you may regret later, La Fontaine. Elizabeth spoke often and well of you. She was – shall we say – very intrigued by you.'

Edmund is momentarily torn between curiosity and annoyance. Why would Elizabeth invite an ancient woman into her confidence? When he had told her explicitly to keep her foolish fancies to herself. And why has Lady Blanche waited so long to broach the subject?

'I am sorry to be blunt, but there can be no other way.' Lady Blanche pinches a plumb between her fingers. 'She was fond of my nephew, I am sure, but he was away for long periods of time. And Elizabeth was ever a restless soul. When you joined the household on recommendation of the Prince, naturally, she was fascinated by you.'

Edmund's cheeks burn, but not from shame, as Lady Blanche no doubt thinks. They burn from anger that has to be checked. 'She never …'

'I visited, as you may remember, and since she had no mother to speak to, she turned to me.' The Baroness' calm voice is almost disconcerting; can nothing distort her worldview? Edmund looks up to see a faint smile on the old lady's face. 'I have lived long and seen much, my dear La Fontaine. Perhaps you forget that Lord Grosmont was my brother. With a man like him, you learn to take everything in your stride. As it stands, it takes much more than a passing fancy to rattle me, or I would have been a bundle of nerves with that brother of mine.'

'You read my mind, my Lady.' Edmund returns her smile, Grosmont was indeed a handful on his own. 'Lady Mowbray was kind to acknowledge me.'

'But she did so much more,' Lady Blanche continues. 'She singled you out.'

Elizabeth pops up in his mind, a sneer on her face, her eyes cold. Why could she not just keep her big mouth shut? What they did was no one else's concern, and all this while, he had thought it died with her.

'It happens.' The kindness in her voice feels as reproach. 'Most marriages are made for advances and alliances, with very little for either party to hope for but civility. I believe she was happy with my nephew, but they were children when they married. And you must know the power you have over women.'

Edmund knows better than to admit to the vanity of self-awareness and finds there is no need, for Lady Blanche continues without waiting for a response. 'Women like you. It is your build and your golden hair. But most of all, it is that you are unobtainable.' She holds out her glass, and Edmund rises to pour the wine. 'You were lovers.'

With his back turned, Edmund nods. He is annoyed that he must stand here, a man grown and make an act of contrition for a sin so old he had all but forgotten it. Or tried to.

'I believe Lord Mowbray was sent to Aquitaine in sixty-three,' she continues. 'But you did not go?'

'He came back later that year, and I went to the Prince's court in his place. But no, I did not join him there, I stayed here.' Edmund hands Lady Blanche her glass and sits down again. 'I was young.'

'You were knighted by then.'

Edmund drinks deep to hide his displeasure. 'Must we have this conversation?'

'So, you kept my niece company while she waited here, at Framlingham.' Lady Blanche ignores him and continues, 'A young mother of two, bored witless by living in the country and starved for stories from court.'

'It was innocent,' Edmund says, 'at first. I would relate battlefield tales, in which she took great interest. Then she wanted to know more about the

Prince, of whom I was happy to speak for he was such a hero. It was as if she was hungry for tales of war and heroics. Perhaps in the beginning, she merely wanted to build up her husband as a great warrior in her own mind. But she was also interested to know exactly how I came to be in the service of the Baron when I had a good place with your brother. Your nephew was kind to take me on.'

'Kind?' Lady Blanche laughs, the sound oddly young and tinkling. 'My nephew was many things, but I have never heard him described as kind before. Loyal, diligent, brave even – but kind? No. The Prince had no doubt spoken highly of you by means of my brother, and my nephew accepted your services in the hopes that the Prince might later repay the favour.'

Evasively, Edmund says, 'For whatever reason, I found myself in the Mowbray service, where I continued to serve until Reims and the Prince's wedding.'

Edmund still remembers the day the fair maid of Kent, Joan, had wed her cousin, how grand they had looked, the famed beauty and the mighty Prince. A perfect vision of royalty and kingship. How jealous he had been that day, but that was before he learned how easily greatness can be washed away.

'I first met Lady Mowbray in sixty-two. She and Baron Mowbray were a fine pair.'

'They were fond of each other, I believe, each in their own way,' Lady Blanche concedes, 'but there was not much love lost between them.'

'She bore him six children, there must have been some love.' Edmund still cannot believe that one of them is his. Has Elizabeth betrayed him on that score too? Is this the old woman's way of saying that he now has to take on guardianship of a tiresome girl?

'She bore him children, no doubt.' Lady Blanche sounds a little impatient. 'When did it begin – in earnest?'

'After the birth of Joan.'

Edmund remembers watching Elizabeth go into confinement and only weeks later reappear with a child in her arms and a smile on her face. Soon after, she had begun to request his presence at all times, and he had eagerly obliged.

'I think perhaps she was lonely,' Edmund concedes, 'and a little melancholic that Lord Mowbray was not at home to see the child. More than anything, I believe she was sad that she had not produced a male heir.'

'Yes, it did distress her. But later, she produced three in a row.' She taps her fingers on the armrest and looks at Edmund. He returns her look without concern and she lets time slip, no doubt waiting for him to say something, but he too can play the game of waiting.

'Although the third …'

'Killed her.' Edmund pauses as if distressed. 'I always felt, I should have done something …'

'You were called on by the Prince, and no one could know that she would not come out of the birthing chamber with another boy in her arms, as strong as ever.' She sighs. 'Too many women die in childbirth. But I interrupt your tale.'

Rubbing his shoulder, where the wound the Prince gave him lies as a rugged ridge, Edmund looks away. 'She sought out my company more frequently after the birth, and I confess that by then I was infatuated with her.'

'You fell in love?' Lady Blanche's casual question makes Edmund want to sneer. He finds his interest in this tedious conversation quickly dies down. But the old woman wants a tale, and so he will spin one for her.

'When I was with her, I forgot about everything else. I could pretend we were the only two people in the world. The nighttime brought such joy and the daytime such misery. If she suffered too, she did not betray such emotions to me.'

Lady Blanche merely nods, and Edmund continues, 'We were happy, I believe. We had to be careful, no one could ever know – and I do not believe they ever did. When my Lord returned to Framlingham, we never once looked at one another nor met in secret. His mere presence was enough to remind me where my loyalty should lie. Then I left for Aquitaine and …' Edmund stops, reality dawning on him.

'Elizabeth fell pregnant with Eleanor,' Lady Blanche says. 'Her beautiful, golden girl. The first of her children to take after her.'

And me, Edmund thinks sourly, she looks like me, even more so now that she is grown. He wants to bury the memory of Elizabeth once and for all. This has gone on for quite long enough and Edmund has to dig deep to keep up his pretence.

'Had you resumed your affair before my nephew was released from Parliament?'

'I was with the Prince fighting for King Peter's throne.' The garden suddenly looks dull, all the colour of the flowers washed away by the warm sunshine. It will be evening soon. 'When I was sent to England to inform the King …'

Lady Blanche studies his face. 'You came here?'

'I met the Baron in London. He insisted I go here to recover before being sent back to Najera.' Edmund feeds the fire another log. 'I went before him but only by a night.'

Drinking the last of her wine, Lady Blanche seems to contemplate something. 'I did not know you returned to Framlingham. How long did you stay?'

'Only a few days, before the King's summon called me back to London and from there directly to the Prince who was returned to Bordeaux by then. To see him waste away is the hardest thing I have witnessed in all my life.' Edmund draws a hand through his hair, it is sticky from the intense heat in the room; only an old woman, sensitive to cold, has a fire burning in July. He looks at Lady Blanche. 'After that, I never saw Elizabeth or the Baron again.'

'She died giving birth. To a wonderful fair-haired boy.' The Baroness leans back in her chair; she looks to be in pain. 'Argyle.'

'I only heard about her death after I took possession of Beauworth.' It is all in the past, and the past does not bear to be examined too closely. Edmund infinitely prefers the present and future.

'And now, I charge you to take in her son, to care for him and train him,' Lady Blanche says, slowly rising from her seat. She sighs at the effort and gratefully accepts the hand Edmund offers her, squeezing it before releasing him. 'She loved you too.'

'Why dredge up the past? When you knew?' Edmund knows he has to ask; he can tell from her expression. 'What good is it to rouse old ghosts?'

'Because I wanted to know if you were the right man to charge with Argyle's well-being.' Lady Blanche opens the door to the hallway and steps aside for Edmund to leave. 'But I ask that you consider this,' Lady Blanche stays Edmund with an old cold hand, 'Elizabeth had four children distinctly Mowbray, and two fair-haired, golden angels. How did that come to be?'

ꕥ ꕥ ꕥ ꕥ

Edmund splashes water on his face. It burns as the sun does through the high, narrow windows. The smell of dry wood on the floor mingles with the faint scent of roses wafting through the open window. He takes the pitcher and pours more water over his head trying to still his whirling thoughts.

When he stands, the water trickles down his naked back. Two golden angels. Eleanor and Argyle.

Argyle, my new squire. Edmund grabs a clean kirtle. Is this God's poor attempt at a joke? Is he to be strapped to a child he did not even know existed until a few hours ago? The idea sits uneasy with him, and he wishes that he could send the boy away as he did with Pascaline's two girls. But then, it is not certain that Argyle is his, perhaps he simply takes after his mother. It had to happen sooner or later.

As long as the boy does not know, Edmund will rest easily, he does not need the bother of a son, though he does favour the idea of a boy over the girls he has previously been claimed to have fathered. After all, a son might be of use to him. But better he is kept in the dark that he does not begin to ask for things Edmund has no intention of providing. He must ask Lady Blanche if the boy knows, before he leaves. This puts a different light on things to be sure.

Pulling the belt tight around his hips, Edmund pauses. Is he going to give Argyle the same kind of upbringing he had? Wondering about his parents, as Edmund always wondered about his. Especially, he has wondered about his elusive father, for if there was something to be got, it must have been with the father he never knew.

Walking down the stairs, Edmund runs his hands over the smooth stone, cool to the touch. How many times has he walked here with the scent of Elizabeth in his nose and the tingle of excitement that perhaps that would be the night he met the Baron coming home late from the nearby tavern. As nightly excursions go, the Baron had as many as Edmund, if not more. The privilege of being a lord are many, Edmund muses and smiles, he must begin to make more of his own privileges once he returns to Beauworth.

He pauses on the landing and looks out of the window; in the garden Eleanor walks alone, the late afternoon sun a blazing crown on her head. She is so like her mother, but Edmund hopes she is a more carefree spirit and much easier to please. Eleanor looks up from the garland of flowers forming in her hands and smiles. She holds out the garland and then drapes it around Argyle's mop of golden curls. He gives her an indulgent smile, and she dips a curtsey when he bows for her. He is already far taller than she, and yet he obediently takes her arm when she demands it. They turn to the house, Argyle's hand resting on his sister's narrow waist. She whispers something in his ear and he laughs, nudging her side.

Edmund watches them half-run across the garden and disappear in the shadows of the large balcony protruding from what was once Elizabeth's bedroom. The sight of the carved timber jolts Edmund's memories and he takes the steps two at a time relishing in the more pleasant aspects of remembering.

'Sir Edmund.'

'My Lord.' Edmund bows his head to John who stands at the bottom of the stairs, his hands behind his back. He is lean and dark, and perhaps a head or more shorter than Edmund.

'My aunt asks that you accompany her into the hall,' John says and nods towards the small parlour just off the main entrance. 'I admit, Sire, that I am most curious to know if you have any news from court, but I know it is not my place …'

'I am under strict orders from your aunt to relay what happened to her tonight.' Edmund notices the fleeting dismay on John's face, quickly replaced with a kind smile. 'If you listen carefully, you will know soon enough too. Though I am surprised you had no news?'

'Only what I have picked up when I visit the villages. The unrest was mainly in the south, I believe?' John looks up, his dark eyes scouring Edmund's face. 'Did you have to enforce strong measures on your lands?'

'I was sent north,' Edmund says, 'to aid Lord Gaunt in hammering out a peace treaty with the Scots. No doubt, you know how that ended. But my master of arms reports that what little unrest he experienced was put out before it got out of hand.'

'Your tenants are happy with their lord, I should think,' John ventures and earns a smile. 'That is what I was given to understand while I was at court.'

'I try to be just.'

John lingers before the parlour door, concern on his face. 'I try for that too, but I am so often away. And when I return, I feel always a child. How am I to run this estate, to advise the King, if I do not know what I am doing half the time?'

'Let your aunt teach you,' Edmund advises, careful to express no snideness. 'She has much experience and wants only what is best for you. You can learn a great deal from her, I am certain.'

'Sometimes, I wish I could stay here all the time.' John struggles to admit his desire. 'Only because I think my brother is much better suited to life at court than I. He and the King are such great friends. I am on the outskirts.'

'A safer place to be, my Lord,' Edmund says and gives John an encouraging pat on the shoulder. 'Never measure yourself against anyone else; it will only cause concern. You will be a great adviser to the King, as your father was to the Prince.'

John knocks on the door. 'I must take your word for it.'

'Come!' Lady Blanche's voice cuts through the wooden timber.

'You will know before long what happened at court,' Edmund says with reassurance. 'Let that be comfort for now.'

Opening the door, John mutters, 'it may suffice for me, but not for my brother.'

'Ah, La Fontaine, there you are.' Lady Blanche lifts her hand, and Edmund offers his arm. 'We must put on a show tonight, for there are so many come to see you. I do believe that half the county has come just for a glimpse of the great knight that once roamed these halls.'

'I shall be on my best behaviour, my Lady.'

Lady Blanche nods to John. 'As shall we all, is that not so, John? Are your brothers and sisters ready?'

'I could not find Thomas.' The grudge in John's voice is mirrored in his eyes.

'Well then,' Lady Blanche says pursing her lips, 'you must make another attempt. There is still some time before the last of our guests are here. I leave it to you, as master of this household, to ensure that all of your sisters and brothers are gathered in the hall by the time La Fontaine and I return from a short walk in the garden.' Lady Blanche nods to Edmund. 'It is a fine summer evening; it should not go to waste.'

'Certainly not, my Lady.' Edmund's stomach growls, but he knows he must put on a show of his own to appease the old woman and fasten a smile on her face. At least he is in for a long dinner, and for that he is grateful.

John walks off in pursuit of his lost brother, a frown on his brow, and Lady Blanche sighs. 'At times, I wonder if perhaps I should let you take Thomas instead of Argyle, for he is in much more need of discipline. But then I am reminded, in no small way by Thomas himself, that he is high in the King's estimation and must attend court to keep up his friendship. Is it true, La Fontaine, that Thomas cannot be spared?'

'The King relies on his friends.' Edmund steps out into the garden first and offers his hand to steady the old lady when she follows him down the few steps and into the garden. 'He has been through a trying time.'

'Having Thomas here has reminded me of my obligations to the children,' Lady Blanche says as the garden doors glide closed behind her. 'I must secure matches for Joan and Eleanor. Only the best of course. Perhaps you noticed that Margaret arrived earlier? What a fuss.'

Edmund tries to arrange his face in a pleasing manner; of all the Mowbray children he is certain none is as cunning and clever as Margaret. Something about her has always set his teeth on edge. 'I have not seen her for many years, so I would not know her anymore, I think.'

'Married and grown. I hope she will soon be with child. She needs the distraction that only a child can provide.' Lady Blanche picks a path that takes them from the rose garden and through a small thicket. 'Here we may speak more privately. I have a request that, tonight, when you talk about the events in London; please, do not overdo it.'

'I could not even if I wanted to, my Lady.' Edmund reaches up and holds a beech branch for Lady Blanche to pass under. 'I was not present.'

'Still, you must have heard everything upon returning. You were at Beauworth?'

'Alas, I was not.' Edmund wonders if he should tell her about the journey he made north, but decides against it. It is enough that he told John who had not commented on it. Perhaps he made nothing of it, but that would be disappointing and, for some reason, Edmund has warmed to the eldest of the Baron's boys. He would like to think John as resourceful and clever as his father.

'Good. Now, I wanted to give you time to think on what I said earlier.' She gestures to a stone bench, half buried in a bush of minute white flowers. 'I shall have to speak with the gardeners.'

Edmund brushes the dry foliage off the bench and offers a hand to steady Lady Blanche as she sits. She must be nearing seventy, but you would not know that to look at her face, only her uneven gait and dry, bony hands give her away. Arranging her skirts, she looks out over the oblong lake that stretches all the way to the woods. 'My niece used to prefer to come here when she was troubled.'

'It is beautiful.'

'Rugged. But I can only reprimand myself that it has not been attended.' Lady Blanche folds her hands. 'I confess that, these days, I do not often go this far from the house on my own. Well, we have little time, pick your questions carefully. If I can, I shall give you an honest answer.'

There is only one thing, Edmund really wants to know. 'Argyle?'

'Cannot be my nephew's.'

'How can you be so certain?' Edmund follows a pair of swans bending their heads to each other in the middle of the lake. He does not want to be a father.

'She wrote to me. It seems that since the birth of Thomas, my nephew had shirked his marital duties.' Lady Blanche's skirts rustle. 'As soon as I laid eyes on the child, I knew she had the right of it.'

'Have you told him?'

'To what end? I do not wish to take what little family he has left from him. He is such a trusting, kind and honest boy, La Fontaine. If I did tell him, he would feel obliged to tell his sisters and brothers. His whole world would crumble.' Her hands are still folded; Edmund can see her fingertips turn white. 'I only ask that you love him for who he is, but let him keep his family.'

Small favours, Edmund thinks, I do not have to tell the boy. As for loving him, I have better things to do. He turns to Lady Blanche and gives her his most comforting smile. 'I do not want him to grow up wondering.'

'As you did?'

Edmund can feel her looking at him, but he keeps his gaze on the swans, now floating apart. What does she know of his childhood? Other than what he once told her himself. But something stirs. 'Yes. All these years … Tell me what you do know, my Lady, I beg of you. I shall keep Argyle's secret, I shall happily take it to my grave, if only you would tell me.'

'My honour-bound promise was made to two people who are now dead.' Lady Blanche sighs and Edmund turns to look at her. She looks to be struggling with her conscience, a problem Edmund has never had. In the end, she seems to decide. 'I will tell you what I can. Do not think that I would not – with the greatest of pleasure – divulge it all if it were up to me, but it is not. And when you think upon it, I believe you will agree with me that it is for the best that some things are left in the graves of long dead lovers. I know you will.'

Harnessing his impatience, Edmund nods and Lady Blanche puts a hand on his, her brittle skin is an uncomfortable sensation. He thinks she does it to comfort herself, for surely, he is not comforted at all.

'The man who stole your mother's heart only knew of a child, not that it was you. It was imperative that he never be made aware of you. Especially when you came here. Henry and your master, who was also your grandfather, struck an ill-made deal, as I often enough reminded Henry. I believe that the moment he laid eyes on you, he should have gone back on his word.'

'His honour …' The words fall from Edmund's mouth before he can stop himself. Grosmont was a man of honour. But the most shocking reveal was not of the Duke's involvement in some sordid affair, it is that his hard-handed childhood master was his own grandfather. Grosmont's slip all those years ago had been the truth, spoken of only once.

'Was more important to him than anything.' Lady Blanche shakes her head and amusement glimmers in her eyes as the diamonds in her hair glimmer in the light of the setting sun. 'Unless it had to do with women. And horses. And games. Yes, he was an honourable man when it suited him, but there were times when I wanted to tug his ears as you would an ill-behaved child. So, you may thank Henry that I cannot tell you all.'

'A little will do.' Reluctantly, Edmund admits to himself that his interest is sparked. He watches the setting sun dance on the still surface of the lake.

'It must, for we have to return soon.' Lady Blanche pats his hand. 'Help an old woman to her feet, and I shall speak as quick as I can while we make our way back. Perhaps through the rock garden. It is new. I had to have one when I heard what was planned for Windsor.'

Edmund rises and holds out his hands to her. 'That I must see.'

'You care not for gardens, La Fontaine,' she chuckles and gathers her skirt to step over a low hedge.

'Since having my own house, I find I take a greater interest in many things that eluded me before,' Edmund says but does not mean it. If a rock garden means less work for the gardeners, it would be the only reason, he would even consider one. Still, it does no harm to flatter an old woman. 'Beauworth was in a fine state when I took charge, but the gardens … they would have put you off, I have no doubt. Now, I find that I want to make good on what Sir William – God rest his soul – neglected.'

Lady Blanche points to a small opening in the hedge, an arched trellised pathway leading to the right. 'You need a woman to tend to such things.'

'No more talk of women on this visit, my Lady, I beg of you.' Edmund keeps his tone light, but earns a concerned glance nonetheless. 'You have made your point.'

'Then I just have to let it sink in,' Lady Blanche says and takes his arm once more. 'But I will leave that for another time. You need to know that your father was already married when he met your mother. Happily married. Which is why his interest in your mother was such a surprise, and why I ignored it for too long. Not that we lingered with your grandfather and yet … What does it matter now? Your father had a family, sons of his own, and daughters too. If his misstep had been made known the ramifications … No one could have known what they might be, though I think they would have been small and easily stamped out. Only, he was not prepared to face them.'

'I see.' Edmund does not.

Short of breath, she pauses at a bend in the trellised pathway. 'You do not, but if you riddle it out, perhaps you will. He was of royal stock.'

Edmund does not remember how he got back to the house. He does not remember the rock garden. All he remembers is Framlingham coming into view and how he grit his teeth, straightened his back and took Lady

Blanche into the great hall at the head of the long Mowbray procession, Margaret's keen eyes burrowing into the back of his skull.

In a span of half an hour, he went from orphan and beggar to a child with a royal father, an abandoned mother and a grandfather who picked him from the gutter but never told him why or who he was. As deceit goes, this is more than even I could have dreamed up, Edmund thinks, and I have never wanted for imagination.

'Do not keep me at bay any longer, La Fontaine,' Lady Blanche says loud enough for Argyle and even Joan to hear.

Edmund can tell they are both spying on the conversation, though Joan has the good sense to pretend an interest in whatever Reynold Grey is telling her. John is unfortunate to be sat too far from the centre of the dais to hear what Edmund has to say, but no doubt the golden-haired boy sitting to the left of Lady Blanche will share the tale as soon as the dinner is at an end. He has that damned, open-faced look of an honest person. If I am to be burdened with a son, why cannot he be more as Thomas, Edmund reflects, at least he would be of some use to me.

'What news from court?'

Edmund swallows, plasters on a smile and relays the King's heroics, aware that Lady Blanche is watching him as a hawk. He does not mention his visit to the north, nor what happened in Essex. There is no cause to shock an old woman and a young boy.

Reality will sink its talons into Argyle's fair skin before long, and Edmund will be waiting for the boy to open his eyes and see the world for what it truly is. Perhaps then, Argyle will be of use to him.

# CHAPTER 23

## 18 August 1381 – Westminster Palace

The King looks over at the window where Argyle stands, his back turned to the room. 'He is nothing like his brother.'

'I thought you liked Thomas Mowbray,' Edmund says and earns a smile. 'But perhaps you are comparing my new squire to John?'

'John Mowbray is far too serious for my taste,' the King admits and picks at his elaborate sleeve. 'Though I do not doubt that John wishes to serve me well, his advice sounds too much like my uncle's to make me at ease. Which is why I missed you to guide me.'

'Then you should not have sent me north when the rebels were at your doorstep, your Grace.' It would seem that patience does not come easily to Edmund today. He pauses before continuing, 'No one was more baffled by your decision than I. Except perhaps Lord Gaunt.'

The King's loud laugh stirs Argyle for a moment, before he turns away again. Tapping his foot, the King looks at Edmund. 'I would have liked to see my uncle Gaunt's face when you arrived, and with orders that he make peace with the Scots. I must go there sometime and right the wrong my uncle did.'

'He did nothing, your Grace,' Edmund says with a sigh. 'The Scots are impossible to barter with, impossible to negotiate with and impossible to goad into open warfare. Your ancestor was twice defeated in Scotland and though he also won some battles, he never succeeded in forcing the Scots into submission.'

'The hammer of Scots, what a joke!' The King's face turns sour. 'I will go there sometime, La Fontaine, and with you by my side to guide me, I shall defeat them once and for all. I do not care if we have to kill every man, woman and child to succeed. I envision a united country. You will help me turn that vision into reality.'

Perhaps you are too much like your father in his later years, Edmund muses, and bows without agreeing. 'All of that is in the future, your Grace. I would prefer to know what you plan to do with your present predicament.'

'You mean the promises I made to a bunch of rebels and madmen?' The King stretches and, for a moment, his foot comes to rest; then it begins tapping again. 'I will punish them all. The men who rose, the women who let them. De Vere suggested that I hang them all.'

'I have already lost good men and women on his advice and your orders, your Grace. Before I left London to go to Nottingham, you had decided that they had been punished enough. I carried out your orders in Essex. I did everything you asked.' Struggling not to lose his temper, Edmund keeps his voice only slightly above a whisper. 'What am I to tell them?'

'The people rose against their anointed King. I cannot tolerate such insolence, and you cannot imagine that I will simply turn a blind eye to their insanity.' The King ignores Edmund's stern glance and fiddles with his throne's armrest. As with everything in the palace, it is new and glittering, matching the image the King wishes to imbue upon all who come to him. 'De Vere is right. I must be seen to exert power. I must be seen as a King of magnitude. I must be a force to be reckoned with. Surely you agree with that?'

Edmund watches as Argyle turns this way and that, looking around the garden below the windows. The King is right that Argyle is nothing like his brother, far from it. For the briefest of moments, Edmund is pleased with the notion, but there is an argument to be won and letting the King believe he has the long end of the stick will not do.

'Of course I do, your Grace, and I already hear the people sing your praises throughout the realm.' Edmund gives the King a concerned look. 'I fear that if you are too harsh in your retribution, the tales of heroics will sour and wither. I only wonder if you can afford to throw their love away at this crucial moment?'

But more than anything, Edmund thinks, I wonder how much longer I can live with de Vere being your chief advisor, when he gives such poor advice and is completely out of my control. I have to fix it, or find someone to replace him in your favour.

'For revenge, you mean?' The King shakes his puffy sleeves and the pearl beading rattles lightly when he gets up, pacing the dais. 'Why should my people stop loving me if what I do is just? I will not abide treason. They are all traitors to me.'

'Not all of them, your Grace,' Edmund argues careful to maintain his concerned tone. 'Most of the men and women all over England believe you are a hero. Brave in the face of adversity and generous in your gestures towards those who merely …'

'Merely tried to relieve me of all my friends?' A winning smile races across the King's face. 'Or my bad advisors, as they would have it.'

'The people believe it is your uncles who are to blame. Lord Gaunt for the taxes, Lord Woodstock for the tax collectors.' Edmund lets a measure of desperation creep into his voice. 'They would never presume …'

'But they did, La Fontaine,' the King whispers and slaps Edmund's back hard enough for Argyle to look around. Edmund smiles broadly and the boy returns a timid smile before his eyes dart on. The King notices too. 'He is a curious fellow.'

'He is young.' Knowing that the King is far clever enough to deduce his hidden resentment, Edmund moves on. 'The people wanted to save you from bad advice that much is true, your Grace. Once your mayor killed their leader it was only your resourcefulness that saved your men and yourself.'

'God favours the bold,' the King says and returns to his throne. 'As you well know, La Fontaine.'

'Yes, your Grace.' Trying to decide how to proceed, Edmund has to smother a smile when inspiration comes to him in a flash. 'If you must demonstrate your authority, imprison those who led the rebellion.'

'Spare the many?' The King's question heralds no response. 'I should be different than my father?'

'Your father had his moments, your Grace, but I can attest that the one time he went to extreme measures, he profaned his own memory. It was a dark shroud on all of us, and your father later came to regret his actions.' Edmund is still displeased that Langley told the King of Limoges, not that he should not be told, only that Edmund had planned to tell the tale himself and make much of his own heroic gesture even if it was not rewarded with leniency.

'Mother says he was never the same again.' The King bites into a plumb and spits out the stone. It clatters across the stone floor. 'I shall not repeat his mistakes.'

'That gladdens my heart, your Grace,' Edmund says. 'Truly it does.'

The King rises, restless as always, and begins to walk down the dais stairs. 'I shall not waver.'

Edmund bites down on an angry remark and follows the King who waves at Argyle. 'You will stay here a few days will you not, La Fontaine? I have chosen a bride.' The King offers his most charming smile, but Edmund notices that it does not quite reach the royal eyes. 'You will be ever so proud.'

'Your Grace.' With Argyle within earshot, Edmund decides against chiding the King into submission. There will be time to change his mind later. Instead, Edmund bows. 'We shall be honoured to stay for your announcement.'

The King turns his smile to Argyle. 'How find you the royal court, Master Argyle? While I know full well your brothers, you have never been here before, I believe?'

Argyle looks down and stammers a reply. Edmund pays no attention; let the boys speak of what they wish; he has more important matters on his mind, such as finding an ally who can help him change the King's mind and ensure he does not stray from Edmund's grasp.

## 8 September 1381 – Westminster Palace

'He is undermining every lord's authority. He will sink this land.' Gaunt is deep in his drink already, Edmund sees it in his blood-shot eyes and hears it in his slurred speech. 'How could he?'

'They say that the rebellion would never have come to pass if you had not agreed to levy heavy taxes on those who had nothing to begin with.' Edmund sighs. 'My Lord.'

'They say many things, Sire,' Gaunt sniffs. 'Do you believe all of it?'

'You are the most senior nobleman at court; you are the King's uncle. You are ruler in all but name.' Edmund glances around the room. With its vast, vaulted ceiling and luxurious carpets, silver candlesticks and abundance of glittering ornaments, it might as well house a king. Under the tang of heather, Edmund detects a hint of lime; Gaunt has recently had the walls washed white again. No doubt, he has commissioned the finest painters in London to come and decorate the white surface.

'You know as well as I do that the King was governed not by me, but by Sudbury, though of course he is now a head short. Too bad the rebels did not route out de Vere, now that would have put a smile on both our faces I dare say.' Gaunt snorts and draws the carafe close, sloshing wine into his cup. The silver sings against the frail glass. 'I may have signed the tax documents, but other men whispered into the King's ears, I promise you that.'

'And now that the King is about to turn the people of England against himself? To repeat the sins of his father?'

Though Edmund cares little enough for the common man, even he acknowledges that devoted people put in more of an effort to farm his lands and tend his woods. If he learned nothing else from his childhood serving the man who he now knows was his grandfather, it was to be just as well as severe. The only way to manage peasants is to keep them both occupied and content; at the moment, the King seems bent on doing neither.

'De Vere will prosper, you mark my words,' Gaunt says between gulps. He licks his lips but some of the wine still trickles down his clean-shaven chin. The ruff of his collar is already stained pink with wayward wine. 'The King cares little enough for his people. He will not care to lose their love.'

Edmund rubs his forehead. 'Then he is a fool. The people can make a King – they can also break one.'

'Dangerous words, Sire.' The strange amusement in Gaunt's eyes gives Edmund pause. 'But I agree. Surprisingly.'

Before Gaunt can drink more, Edmund snaps the carafe from the table and pours the rest of the wine into the empty hearth. 'You need a clear head, my Lord. The King is to announce his engagement tonight.'

'Oh, I shall be there. What do I have to return to in this wretched town but a pile of smoking rubble? Fear not, my mind is clear enough to survive a night in a young court. Actually, I believe I might enjoy the dinner more, if I am drunk.' Gaunt looks about for a servant, but none are present. 'I can crawl into the hall, give everyone something to talk about.'

'They talk enough as is, my Lord,' Edmund says and lets his irritation shine through. Why is it that the royal family can never dance to Edmund's tune when he needs them to? 'If we are to change the King's mind, you must be sober.'

Gaunt laughs and bangs a bejewelled hand into the tabletop. 'I would have more chance of turning back time than to change the King's mind. He has ideas that you and I cannot begin to fathom. He has inspiration of course, but some of these ideas are his own. Even Sir Simon cannot change his mind on this matter, Sire. What chance do you or I have?'

'I am to sit by while his executioners take away half the people living on my lands?' Try as he might, Edmund cannot abide the idea that the King might actually carry out his order. 'Just let him run mad? He will be executing innocent people. Even I will not tolerate such behaviour.'

'You and I are old men in a young court,' Gaunt says with a dissatisfied expression. 'It matters not what we tolerate. And are you willing to swear upon your honour – such as it is – that no one in your villages rose against the Crown? Not one man picked up a pitchfork or cheered on Tyler as he made his way north?'

'No one can, my Lord, not even I.' Edmund rubs his neck, he is not concerned about his people, he is concerned that he is losing his grip. Gaunt has to be brought round and lend his support. Sighing, Edmund says, 'but I have already doled out enough punishment to ensure they never misbehave again. I am satisfied that it will not happen.'

'The problem is, Sir Edmund,' Gaunt says and looks longingly into his now empty cup, no doubt wondering if he can summon a few more ruby drops of succour. 'The problem is that the King's friends do not have lands or people to worry about. The problem is that half the Lords or more care naught about their tenants.'

Edmund wonders if Gaunt counts himself among the lords he speaks about so dismissively. Certainly, the rebels thought so. They were so incensed that they did not even loot Gaunt's magnificent palace before they torched it. Somewhere in all the smouldering rubble, Gaunt could still find a fortune. But of course, that is neither here nor there. Rousing himself, Edmund asks; 'Have you punished your people?'

'Yes.' No hesitation in Gaunt's words. 'Of course. I cannot have any Lancastrian rise against my own family. They have been punished. The leaders turned into dangling corpses. The rest forced to look on. My orders are carried out even as we speak. I will not suffer rebellion.'

And you wonder why there is no love for you, Edmund thinks. But he has to admit to himself that Gaunt has proven his loyalty in a way that Edmund has not on his own lands, though he was uncompromising in Essex. 'Harsh punishment.'

'They took up arms against the anointed King. They stormed the Tower where my son was lodged, they burned down my home.' Gaunt waves an unsteady hand towards the window. 'There is my constant reminder. But worse than anything, they rebelled against my family, my blood.'

'You are saying that I must let this pass?' Again, Edmund's mind turns to the treasures that the rebels never thought to take from Gaunt's palace. Rumour has it that they did empty his wine cellar, so some of them must have had some sense, but to leave everything of value behind? Then again, if anyone was caught with a trinket from Gaunt's mighty Savoy palace, the culprit would be hanged before he could speak up. Perhaps they were wise to leave Gaunt's treasure to the fire.

'That is my advice.' Gaunt tries to get up and plonks back down on the hard wooden seat. He rubs his hip. 'Although not too many adhere to my advice these days. Still, if anyone could change the King's mind, my money would be on you. You have a strange hold over the boy and, for the longest time, I did not care for it, but perhaps in this instance it is a good thing? Who knows? And more importantly, who cares?'

Edmund fidgets with the brooch that holds his short cape pinned to his shoulder. The ruby and gold pin is a gift from the King; gaudy and irritating, but he wears it all the same. Just as he wears the smile that he now paints on. 'I must try. I have few enough tenants and workers as it is; I cannot afford to lose any more than I must.'

'Do not let me detain you,' Gaunt says with distaste. 'Go and make the most of your sway. Perhaps you will succeed where better men have failed. Although I suspect that by the end of the week, not only has the King announced his betrothal to a thoroughly unworthy girl, he has also alienated his people – the ones he has not had killed.'

'You do not wish to stay, Sire?' Argyle's question comes from leagues away, the quiet slosh of river water kissing the bank outside Westminster Palace returns with the boy's voice. Behind them, the windows are lit golden by hundreds of candles, shadows scattering the light as the feast draws long. Outside, the autumn air is refreshingly brittle, as if anticipating a turn for winter at any time. A few late roses still bloom in the hedges, but it will not be long before the lavish royal gardens brow barren and torches are lit to scare away ghosts.

Edmund tries to shake off his bleak mood and looks at Argyle. 'I think that this will do for the time being.' When Argyle gives him a curious look, Edmund continues, burying his exasperation of being stuck with a witless boy. 'Certainly, it is splendid news, and yet I worry that not everyone in England will be pleased with the King's choice of wife. There are those who would rather the King marry someone else.' Edmund signals for a barge, the lantern dangling in harmony with the bargeman's strokes. 'Then again, he has hardly to ask permission – even from his uncles.'

They step onto the barge and Edmund settles on the low bench, expecting Argyle's usual quizzical torrent and when the boy does not speak, Edmund gives him a sidelong glance. Reluctantly, he admits that Argyle looks like him when he was younger, only Argyle has the easy, natural grace of a child born into riches.

The steady movement of the barge, the little specks of light further ahead on the river and on the riverbank slowly begin to put Edmund's whirling thoughts into order. Gaunt's depressed and desperate state is disconcerting in itself, but even more so, Edmund is aware that the King's announcement of his forthcoming marriage to the Bohemian Princess was not met with the kind of enthusiasm he had expected. Edmund had seen it in the King's eyes, when he accepted congratulations; he had felt it in the air and in the King's hastily whispered words: 'How dare they?'

Next to Edmund, Argyle slumps, his arms now hanging over the railing. I shall make him a great warrior and a great courtier, Edmund promises himself; I shall ensure that he is raised to climb as high as his brothers in this world. I shall mould him in my own image and make him a ruthless man who is capable of conquering the world. I shall make him my true heir and have him serve me without question.

Edmund looks up at the tart smell of smouldering wood and cindering blocks. The Savoy, now a pile of blackened rubble. They say that it took several days of dousing the fire to ensure it would not spread, Edmund thinks. He wonders if the recovery of Gaunt's treasures has begun; he has heard nothing of such an undertaking, which is a strange thing. As with most other matters, some of the best gossip is about the Lords of the land, and for Gaunt's treasures not to be mentioned by even the lowliest of scullery maids or pageboys is a wonder.

The barge glides on, and the bitter smell of tar recedes, washed away by the other smells of London and the faint tang of salt. Up ahead, Edmund spies another barge; the standard furled, the canopy above the seating dark red against the night sky, only a lantern on the stern. As the two barges pass, Edmund thinks he sees a familiar face, but he is not certain.

'Here we are, M'lord,' the bargeman says and Argyle stirs beside Edmund.

'Pay the man,' Edmund instructs and steps off the barge, waiting for Argyle to fumble with the purse strings and climb onto the pier. Edmund is quietly entertained that the boy seems to have lost some of his grace after sleeping in an awkward position.

They make their way back to the house in silence, Edmund wondering if Argyle is so overwhelmed by the royal splendour that he has no questions to ask. But one look at his face tells Edmund that a host of questions bubble below the boy's complacent expression. His eyes betray him, Edmund thinks, Argyle must learn to hide his innermost thoughts if he is to be of use to me.

'On the morrow, inform the men that we leave for Beauworth in two days' time,' Edmund says and clasps a hand on Argyle's shoulder, 'it is high time I return to my estate, and you began your training.'

# CHAPTER 24

## 16 September 1381 – Beauworth

'What are you telling me, Warden?' Edmund is certain he has misheard.

'I heard it down the tavern,' Warden says and pauses when a horse careers past, kicking up a cloud of dust. 'They be raping girls all over the county.'

Edmund brushes sand off his collar. Even before they reached Beauworth, he had heard the first distasteful whispers of the tax collectors' vile behaviour. He had hoped it was merely gossip, called up as the country began to realise that their benevolent King would recant his guarantees and instate fierce measures. Taxes and even rebellion is one thing, Edmund thinks, but I will not abide rape, it is the pastime of repulsive brutes.

'You are certain?'

Warden nods, his face never betraying what he thinks. 'How's the new squire?'

'He is eager to learn,' Edmund says and thinks, and very curious, but I might yet make that work in my favour. He turns Warden's attention to business. 'How are the men?'

'Training them keeps me occupied. It keeps them occupied.' Warden pushes a clump of dirt from his boot with a stick. 'Are you expecting more to come, M'lord?'

'Not this season.' Edmund turns his back to the field. 'The King has appointed the men he needs for his … next campaign. And then there is the matter of the rebels. I think that you did well in keeping the peace on my lands. But even we cannot promise the King that no one took up arms to join the ragged army that marched on London.'

Walking from the field, Warden looks towards the forest. 'They say some of the rebels be hiding, biding their time. They say that the King means to dole out harsh punishment.'

'They speak true, Warden, and there will be nowhere to hide when the King is done. He means to have the rebels dangling from nooses. He wants to make a clear and bold statement that the common folks ought not interfere in matters of state.'

'Didn't he issue letters of clemency?'

Edmund picks up the pace, his long legs outmatching Warden's stiff gait. 'Yes. But such letters can be withdrawn.'

'Then it's true?'

'What I would like to know is if the rumours spreading far and wide are true,' Edmund says and looks at Warden, the fields behind him are bare once more, every sheaf taken in for winter. 'You say that you have heard it too. That the tax collectors overstepped their authority and carried out unseemly deeds. Though I would prefer to think it a blatant lie, I would know the truth before I act. If there is truth to the rumours then it must be put right.'

There is very little in the world that gets Edmund's back up. He has a hankering for war, he enjoys spilling the blood of his enemies, he rejoices in the spoils you can take from the battlefield and the loot that comes from harrying villages. He has yet to set eyes on a woman, he did not like the looks of. But he detests petty men with no backbone who reach above their station. And more than anything else, he loathes rapists.

'One of the girls'll talk to you, if you'd want, M'lord.' Warden scratches his neck; it is red from standing in the sun all summer, and this far south, the sun is still strong. He looks unhappy. 'She's scared but she'll talk.'

This is my chance to take down a spineless nobleman, Edmund thinks and smothers his dawning smile. Instead, he turns a pensive face to Warden. 'Fetch her to me.'

Edmund is standing by the window when the door opens. In the pane, he sees a girl enter, her dress a dull indistinguishable colour, her head bowed. She has the vacant look of a simpleton and, no doubt, she is as coarse in manner as she is to look at. Behind her, Warden reaches out and puts a blurred hand on her shoulder.

'Master Warden, I would have you stay outside the door.' Edmund listens for the door to close before he speaks again, 'Thank you for coming.'

She winces but stays put. 'M'lord.'

'My master of arms says that you have something to tell me.'

'I'll not want trouble, M'lord.' When he turns around, he can see tears rolling down her rosy cheeks. She has a childish sweetness about her, and he can almost taste her fear.

'There is nothing to worry about.' Edmund turns on his charm. 'Please, come closer child.'

Wearily she walks forward, clutching her sleeves and looking about in wonder. Edmund remembers what it was like to live in poverty and lets her have her fill. She will tell tales when she returns to her village, and he is happy to let her.

'What is your name?'

'Betty, M'lord.'

'Please, Betty, sit down.' She raises her wide eyes to him and he smiles, satisfied to see her shrink back a little. Perhaps she is not as witless as he first thought. He breaks eye contact and says: 'It is quite all right. Shall I send for someone to sit with us? One of my servants perhaps? Or I can call back Master Warden?'

'No, M'lord.' Betty stays standing. 'It's just … I's told that I'd not sit in your presence. It'd be rude.'

'Not if you are offered a seat, Betty, I assure you.' Edmund signals for her to sit on a low stool. She perches on the edge, her hands wringing in her lap. Edmund leans on his massive desk, the edge biting into his thighs. 'Please, tell me everything Betty, leave nothing out.'

She blinks for a moment before beginning. 'The taxmen come, it's – what – near on a year ago. Ours was the last village of the day. It was hot, I remember, ever so hot. When they arrived, they didn't set up their usual stall. They went to the tavern, booked rooms and such. My father's the local brew master, he'd been up since dawn waiting in line to pay his dues.

There's a bit of a ruffle when they didn't do as they used to, but then everyone's got places to be, and so they went on their way.'

Edmund notices that Betty's face is streaked with dirt and is slightly annoyed that she did not make an effort to clean herself up before coming to him. He gestures for her to go on.

'They'd be spoiling for sport. Bored, I 'spose. Drunk to be sure.'

'When they arrived?' Edmund does not think it sounds too worrisome. Being on the road all the time will drive many a man to drink.

'Yes, M'lord.' Betty's cheeks colour deep crimson. 'They came upon us when we was washing. The four of us. I'd gone in last. The clothes we'd hung on some branches by the brambles. We'd just have a quick dip 'fore going home, and so …' She hides her face in her hands. 'So, we'd taken off our clothes see, to not get 'em wet and such.'

'You were bathing?'

'In the stream.' Betty looks at him between her fingers. At first sight, she looked plump, but now Edmund sees that she is a slender girl, and he has little trouble envisioning her naked, her body pearling with water. She bites her full lips. 'I can't swim, so I's close to the bank, just 'bout to get up when they come barging through the shrubs.'

'What of the other girls?'

'They know how to swim.' Betty's cheeks pale and her eyes glaze over. 'I told 'em to go ahead. Go back to town and fetch someone. The men, they didn't seem interested. Just drunk. They'd push the clothes on the branches aside, but that was nothing to me. When I thought they wasn't looking, I made to get out of the water, get to me clothes. That's when …' She begins to sob.

Edmund lets her work herself into a state, she might be afraid of him, but if she is distraught, she will also welcome a little comfort, even if it is just a kind word. For now, he lets Betty cry until she is ready to get on with her story.

'That's when I's grabbed from behind! I'd not even seen 'im goin' round back. I'd been so focused on the men on the bank that I hadn't even heard 'im splashing into the stream. He's just there, all sudden.'

'What happened then?' Edmund knows that she is reliving a terrible day in her life, but it does not stop him being somewhat amused by her unrefined speech. He leans in. 'What did he do?'

'Grabbed me and hauled me out the water. I tried to cover meself, but it's no use. There's three of them. They're all around. The man behind me, he tears at me arms so hard I'm scared they'll come off!' Betty spills more tears. 'Then one of the others, he comes close, he pushes himself at me, grabs me …'

When she crosses her arms over her chest, Edmund enjoys the contour of her breasts against the rough spun cloth. She is a woman grown, although she does not think so, and judging from where her story is going, she is broken in too. No doubt, she will make some young man very content.

'It's not nice. It's not like when a boy you like … His hands're soft and all, but I've not invited nothin'. The man behind me laughs loudly, forces me to my knees. The man who grabbed at me, he pulls up his gown, he's not wearin' nothing underneath.'

In his vivid imagination, Edmund easily imagines what happens next. He must know how much happened, must hear her say the words. So far, what she experienced does not constitute rape.

'He takes out his … it's not big, but … it's right there. He pushes it at me, he wants me to … I turn me head, I don't want to. I think they're going to let me go, it's just a joke. Just a joke. But it isn't. The man behind me pushes me forward and now there's the last one. He opens my mouth. The … it pushes in. It throbs. It's disgusting. It's warm, soft … and then … I want to spit. I want it out!' Betty cringes and holds her stomach. 'They force me to swallow. I don't know why I didn't bite, scream, or nothin' …' Betty's voice trails away.

Edmund rises and kneels before her. 'Betty. That was not your fault.'

'No, I know, M'lord.' Betty looks at Edmund with steady eyes, her tears have dried out. 'Neither's what came next. But it happened none'less.'

Sitting back on his heels, Edmund returns Betty's gaze. The joy he felt at envisioning Betty with her mouth full of manhood flees before the idea that one of his farm girls was raped on his land. His land. He has to know: 'What happened?'

'They push me down on the bundle of clothes we'd left on the bank when we went in the water. It presses against the small of me back, so I try to roll over, and …' Now, her whole body is crying, but her eyes are dry. 'Then they do it. One at a time. Holdin' me hands over me head. The first's so big and heavy. But when he pushes me legs aside, I forget how heavy cause I'm screaming 's loud as I can. Louder still when … he takes me. He bites me breasts and breathes so hard, and then … it's hard, painful, I try to move, but I can't.'

Edmund gets up and walks to his desk. She is spoiled and he is disgusted. 'All of them?'

'Yes, M'lord.' Betty's voice quavers behind him. 'I couldn't …'

'I told you it is not your fault, Betty, and I stand by my word.' Edmund turns to her. 'Why did you not come to me sooner?'

'They said you'd not care, M'lord.' Betty turns her scared eyes at him once more. 'You'd want the same.'

Sighing, Edmund sits down on his desk. He has never had to force himself on anyone, nor would he have to with Betty, if he chose her for a bedmate. All it takes is a smile and a few words, and she would be undressing before him without a second thought. But he does not want her damaged goods. He does not need it. Edmund's blood boils at her story and the fact that someone dared question his own morals.

'No man should treat a woman this way.'

'I wasn't no woman, M'lord.' Betty sounds as a girl at confession. 'I's twelve.'

'Bastards!' Edmund punches the table hard enough to break the skin on his knuckles, for the inkwell to topple over, and for Betty to jump to her feet with a shriek.

'I'm sorry, M'lord,' Betty babbles. 'Truly, I am. I shouldn't have come. Me father, he shouldn't have said nothing. It's a mistake. I'll …'

Edmund cuts her short with a sharp gesture. 'No, it was no mistake. You were right to come. I am sorry for your pain and suffering. Warden!'

Warden pokes his head round the door. 'M'lord?'

'Take Betty here to the kitchens and make sure she is fed. Then come back here, I want a word with you before you take her back to her village.' He smiles at her clumsy attempt to curtsey and she blushes through her tears.

Warden bows and totes off Betty who leans her head on his shoulder. While he waits, Edmund feeds his fury. Twelve years old. The men should be hanged for rape, but since they wore the King's colours, they must have felt safe, they must have felt justified in their actions. Edmund is dissatisfied about the rape, but he is enraged that they dared do this on his lands.

This is what comes from the King sending me north, Edmund seethes, and I will make him feel the injustice and degradation of it before I am through with him. He and de Vere and all of the other young fools who traipse around in their fine clothes and know nothing of the world. But more than anything, I will make Woodstock suffer for I cannot imagine his taxmen would act in such a fashion unless they were given to understand that it was sanctioned from someone of standing.

'M'lord.' Warden steps into the room and closes the door. 'She's eating in the kitchen.'

'You were right to bring her here.' Edmund sighs and masters his rage. 'I only wonder how many other girls came home telling the same tale. Why did her father not send her straight here? Why were we not informed? You would have seen justice for her, I am certain.' Edmund reaches for the pitcher of wine and then puts it aside. This is no time to be drinking. He looks at Warden. 'At least we can send her home well-fed.'

'She hasn't got a home, not anymore.' Warden shakes his head. 'The last year or so, she's been living in the streets, begging and taking what little kindness others have to give. She comes once a month to the monks' abbey when they feed the poor. That's where I first learned of her tale.'

'What of her father? Her mother?'

'What use is a girl who's not a virgin? She's spoiled.' There is pity in Warden's words but also finality. 'Where's she going to go?'

'Have we room for another scullery maid?' An idea forms in Edmund's mind. She may yet be of use to him and so he presses the subject. 'A dairy maid?'

Warden makes a noncommittal sound. 'I'll have a look see, shall I? But what'd she tell you?'

'What the peasants told the King on Smithfield is true, I know this now. The royal tax collectors are overstepping their authority, raping women and even young girls.' Scratching the scar on his neck, put there by the Prince all those years ago, Edmund tries to think what to do next. 'We must keep Betty here. The crime happened on my land; I will not be seen as an ignorant monster. My people must be able to trust me, to rely on me to keep them safe.'

'And you do, M'lord,' Warden says, as ever, he looks oddly out of place in Edmund's fine parlour where the coloured glass casts odd shapes on the bare, wooden floor. Soon, rush matting will be put down and fires lit in all hearths, absentmindedly Edmund wonders if the kindling store is filled yet. He has to act on what he knows.

'Not if I let this pass, Warden,' Edmund mutters at the realisation that he will have to go to London and fight a cause his heart is not in. Still, it must be done. Without the love of his people, he is no one, Grosmont taught Edmund that a long time ago. He looks out of the window at the garden, the gravel paths being raked by a couple of skinny boys with bare feet. 'Who is to say that I shall not fail in future?'

'Cause now you know.' Turning to the door, Warden pauses. 'Now, you can do something.'

'You think highly of me, Warden.'

'Only 'cause I know you.' The door scrapes shut behind Warden and Edmund leans on the windowsill. You think you do, he reflects, and I like the way you think.

## 11 November 1381 – Westminster Palace

'You were trying to take money from people who have none!' In his fury, Edmund forgoes his usual carefree manner. 'Was it such a stretch of your imagination that you could not see what it might force the people to do?'

'They are peasants, they should know their place!' Gaunt says in a tight voice. 'Which our King has now shown them, and there they will stay if they have any wits about them.'

'What of your tax collectors, my Lord?' Edmund makes fists so tight his nails draw blood and looks at Woodstock.

He stares down the length of the table to fix Edmund's glare. 'What of them?'

'They must be punished too, my Lord.' Edmund breaks the silent war and looks at the King. 'Your Grace, the tax collectors have been raping women – and young girls, little children.'

The King exchanges a quick glance with de Vere, who is perched at the end of the table as a bird of prey observing the room, before answering Edmund. 'I believe that is a custom?'

'Just because it is a custom does not make it right, your Grace,' Edmund says tautly and once more regrets ever letting the King become so reliant on de Vere. 'They reached too high.'

'Indeed they did, your Grace, for such a privilege falls to the lord of the land.' Woodstock picks up the argument, his many rings glittering in the sunlight streaming in through the windows in a rare spell of fine weather. 'Perhaps that is why Sir Edmund is in a state?'

His acrid remark sends laughter roaring around the table, and Edmund feels heat crawl up his neck. He forces back a snide remark about Woodstock's own wanton wife; if rumours are true, she has recently been the cause of a most unfortunate affair that ended with a young man losing his manhood. Does Woodstock truly think that the scandal has not reached Edmund's ears? He smiles. 'I need force myself on no one. And any man worth his salt will retch at the thought of taking a twelve-year-old girl against her will.'

'Was she offered up?' de Vere asks in a bored tone.

'Excuse me, my Lord?' It does not sit well with Edmund to have to address de Vere as his superior. He is a boy, soft-handed and soft-headed. He will have to go, but first Edmund has to win this argument. 'Offered up?'

'I hear around the taverns that some men offer up their daughters or wives in exchange for not having to pay their total taxes due.' De Vere picks his teeth with his short-bladed dagger and looks at Edmund with outright disinterest. 'If that be the case, surely it must be the fathers and husbands who are punished? Which I believe they will be, by means of your Grace's demonstration of power.'

The King nods at de Vere's observation and raises an encouraging hand. 'So, they shall be, my friend. That ought to settle any disputes, surely?'

Most of the assembled noblemen look at their hands or fidget with their chains and ornaments. One or two shuffle papers about and a cup clinks when it is replenished. It seems Edmund is alone in his indignation, but he will not be brushed off as an irritating fly. 'Your Grace, I must insist that enquiries be made into the conduct of the tax collectors. At least those who were sent south to collect taxes in my county.'

'I was not aware you had a county, Sir Edmund,' de Vere mocks and earns a few nervous laughs. 'Is your estate so very big?'

'I was speaking on behalf of all those who own lands in the south, my Lord,' Edmund replies through tight lips. 'If it is a fluke and only happened in one village in all of England, is it not strange that one tale should spur on a revolt of such magnitude as the one our King fought down so valiantly?'

Some of the older advisors on the King's council nod in agreement. Edmund sees Gaunt stroking his smooth cheek pensively and exchange a glance with Lord Arundel, who lets his usual haughty mask fall for just a moment. If Gaunt can be swayed there is still hope that the King will call for an inquest. And if Arundel joins Edmund's cause, it will put further pressure on the King; together Arundel and Gaunt are the richest men in England, and since the King is in constant debt to both, he will be hard pressed to simply ignore their requests. But first, Edmund must secure the support of these two mighty Lords who think of him as a devil in a chorus of angels.

'Am I truly the only one to hear such tales?' Edmund locks eyes with de Vere, who is leaning in to whisper something in the King's ear. 'Or have you heard similar stories in the many taverns you visit, my Lord de Vere?'

'You make me sound quite common, Sire.' Being put on the spot makes de Vere colour, and he puffs out his cheeks. 'I can assure you that I am not!'

'But have you heard such tales?' the King pipes up. For all his bravado and boasting of divine insight, some days, the King is still just a child on the cusp of manhood and his voice has a habit of breaking when he is troubled. All the finery and elegant clothes cannot hide how heavily he still depends on others to rule.

De Vere looks around the room for support, but the lords at the table offer none. Reluctantly, he turns to the King with a soothing smile. 'A few. But I did not wish to worry your Grace.'

Charming scoundrel, Edmund thinks, I know what you do in those taverns, after all, I found you in one. I only hope that your young wife is not a victim of your strange fancies. Since the tide is changing in the room, Edmund decides to bide his time. Next to him, John de Montagu, filling the seat on the King's council for his father, the Earl of Salisbury, seems to make up his mind.

'I have heard similar stories, your Grace,' he sighs, his heavy chain jingling when his chest expands.

Edmund knows that the King holds Montagu in high regard and, therefore, he is one of the foremost subjects of de Vere's jealousy. It is no surprise that de Vere immediately leans in and whispers something that makes the King snort a laugh.

To the King's right, Gaunt stops stroking his cheek and glares at de Vere, Gaunt's eyes as black as his robe. 'Please repeat your words to the rest of the council, my Lord.'

'It was a private …'

'You are not in private, my Lord,' Gaunt says, his face reveals none of his thoughts, an expression Edmund knows all too well. It means he has set a trap and is waiting for it to spring. 'Repeat your words, please.'

'Your Grace …?' De Vere's eyes flicker from Gaunt's blank face to the King who is blushing as a maid, his delicate features underlined by rosy cheeks and red lips.

The King is much more adept at reading a room than de Vere can ever hope to become; he looks about and nods. 'Repeat it.'

Sulking, de Vere glares at Montagu. 'I merely noted that you are often found out of bed and that now, at least, we know where you go.'

'Certainly, the same can be said about you?' Gaunt says and de Vere's face turns a dark puce that ill suits his gaudy, yellow and orange gown. Without raising his voice, Gaunt continues: 'There is not a tavern in town that does not run a tab for you, I hear. And no, I do not frequent such establishments, my Lord, I have no need of them.'

Before the King can stop him, de Vere shrieks: 'And what of you, my Lord? A wife in one castle and a mistress with her brood in another! You think we are all ignorant to your ways? You believe that any of us condone how you openly disregard your duty? Do you think that Castile is blind to your flaws?'

The King's slender hand floats above de Vere's clenched fist. 'I will not have petty arguments on my council. Uncle, I will have you apologise to my friend.'

Even though five men sit between Gaunt and Edmund, he can feel Gaunt's inflamed rage, consuming all the air in the room. Edmund has to crush a sneer before it is born onto his face, he has to stay placid, for now, he is about to discover just how close the two young men have become.

'Please accept my apologies, my Lord,' Gaunt manages to say, his hands splayed on the table, knuckles white.

The King nods encouragingly to de Vere, who smiles with so much excess it seems his mouth stretches his face in an unnatural angle. 'I accept.'

Gaunt looks to the King for the order to be reversed, but the King does not meet his eye. This is the truth then, Edmund thinks, the King favours de Vere above all others. I shall have to forge a new alliance if I am to remove the King's lofty friend. Gaunt wants de Vere gone as much as Edmund does, but the act must come from another corner if it is to slide off Edmund's back like water off a goose.

'Let us return to the matter at hand,' Woodstock's rich voice cuts through the silence. 'The tax collectors.' If he feels Gaunt's harsh glare, Woodstock ignores it. 'I believe Sir Edmund was about to find favour for his complaint.'

There is something arrogant in Woodstock's voice that baits Edmund, but he manages a perfunctory nod. 'Thank you, my Lord Woodstock. I formally bring to the table the request that the southern tax collectors be questioned about their methods.'

'I second the request,' Montagu says and pounds his fist on the table.

Having recovered enough from the royal snub, Gaunt too pounds the table. 'I agree with Sir Edmund. The matter must be investigated. I will not suffer such actions from men carrying out royal orders.'

With his words, Gaunt forces the King to agree by prodding his pride. 'So shall it be. Scribe! Write up the order and I shall review it with my uncle later today.'

The King ignores de Vere's sneer and looks at his council. 'Any other matters that require my attention?'

It is evident to all that the King is bored and wishes for nothing more than to leave the dreary business of running a country to the old, tiresome men at the table and find entertainment with his young friends elsewhere in the palace.

'No, your Grace,' Gaunt says, no doubt eying the opportunity to get rid of de Vere when the King leaves. 'If other matters need your attention, I am sure they can wait.'

'Good.' The King pushes back his chair, sturdy and dotted with gemstones, and all of the men around him rise to bow their heads to him. 'You may carry on with other business if you wish to. Uncle John and uncle Thomas, you will no doubt visit my chambers later today?'

Before either uncle can reply, the King sweeps from the room, de Vere in hot pursuit.

'Insufferable upstart!' Montagu growls and catches Edmund's eye. 'He may well say what we all think, Sire, on certain matters. But it does not do that he sets himself above the royal family.'

'The King spoils him,' Warwick says from across the table while the rest of the council settle down on their benches. As one of the King's principal advisors, he too must feel the changing tides, Edmund thinks, and he will not like to be pushed aside.

Warwick sighs, 'He will be wise not to over-play his own importance.'

'De Vere or the King?' Montagu wants to know, but Warwick turns to mutter something to Sir Simon, the King's most loyal subject and mentor, sitting next to him and offers no reply. Montagu lowers his voice and says to Edmund: 'He is trouble.'

'Lord Warwick?'

Montagu nods with importance, his slightly underhung jaw tensing. 'Him too.'

'My Lords, we must return to the business of running this land,' Gaunt says at the end of the table, a stack of papers in front of him and an eager scribe behind him wetting his feather in ink. 'Unlike certain members of this council, we cannot all afford to attend only to the King's pleasures.'

Laughter quickly disperses when Woodstock rises, a cunning smile curling his lips. 'There is the matter of the Scots, dear brother. Still no results?'

Gaunt's cold eyes flash with anger, and Edmund knows how much the difficult situation in the north weighs on his shoulders. Woodstock knows this too, and he relishes in kicking his brother's shins. It is Edmund's fortune that the younger brother seems to have forgotten what happens to people who displease Gaunt.

'I might remind you, brother, that you shoulder the responsibility of the tax collectors,' Gaunt hisses, 'I recognise now that I was mistaken in awarding you such a great responsibility, when all you will ever be able to handle are small, insignificant matters. Now sit down and shut up, or I will have you out on your ear. You are ill-suited for government, so know your place.'

'And where is that?' Woodstock is rigid with indignation.

Gaunt snarls a smile. 'At the very end of this table, in quiet contemplation.' He turns from his brother without another word and nods at Warwick. 'I believe, you have a matter you wish to present, my Lord?'

## 13 November 1381 – Westminster Palace

Above the crowd, the King sits at high table, de Vere constantly bending his head towards the royal ear, his wife, the King's cousin, is reduced to a pretty ornament and completely ignored. Although Edmund is seated near the dais once more, in the company of the King's young companions, he is restless. He knows that he must keep peace with de Vere and the King's maternal brothers, all of whom are seated with the King on the dais. If only a few of them could be bent to Edmund's will without taking extreme measures.

Curiously absent are the King's uncles who only graced the meal with their presence for half an hour before they retreated. Now, Gaunt's seat sits vacant on the dais and his son Henry looks out of place at the very end of the table, a gap of two empty seats between him and John Holland, the King's favourite half-brother. As usual, the great hall of Westminster is filled with courtiers, knights, noblemen and the occasional noblewoman. Once the King marries, Edmund hopes more women will come to court; the nights are fiercely boring when the only leisure to be had is gambling.

'I would have a word, Sir Edmund,' Montagu smiles and gestures towards the side of the hall, where heavy, dark curtains ward off the strong wind whipping through London tonight. 'I would confer on a private matter with you.'

'My Lord?'

'I hear you have a set of wonderful coloured glass doors.' Montagu picks two cups of wine from a passing servant. 'I should like to know what might make you part with them?'

'They are part of the house, my Lord,' Edmund says with pleasure, it is one of the few things he is truly proud of in his house, mainly because no one else, not even Gaunt, can boast such lavish decoration. 'I cannot imagine anything might ever impress me to part with them.'

'Nothing at all?' Montagu sips his wine and looks about the room. 'We are in dire lack of women, Sir Edmund. Where are the sweet young things that should be dancing for our pleasure?'

'Perhaps the King's future bride brings with her fine women.'

Smiling inward of Montagu's voicing Edmund's own desire for more women, he acknowledges that he is also hoping to make a friend or two in the future Queen's quarters. Preferably women who can provide not only comfort and pleasure, but also some much-needed information. A court consisting of men alone is a coarse place indeed.

'Women from Bohemia?' Montagu looks at Edmund and laughs, a deep rumbling sound that makes his jaw jut forward. 'I doubt it. Rather he had chosen a French princess.'

'They are in short supply, I hear.' Edmund raises his cup to Montagu's and returns his smile. 'We may all yet be surprised. If nothing else, she must bring young women, and they are always fairer than old ones.'

'Have you seen the portrait of the Princess Anne?' Montagu asks.

'No, my Lord. Is she pleasing?'

'That and of an age with the King,' Montagu acknowledges. 'I wonder what de Vere thinks of this match? I wonder if he has encouraged it? Or if he is quietly fearing her arrival, in case she takes up the King's full attention. It happens sometimes in young marriages.'

Retreating slowly into the shadows near the thick woollen curtains, Edmund looks about before he speaks. 'After the display today, I should not wonder that de Vere has been instrumental in the decision, though I hear that our poor unfortunate friend, Sudbury, who is now a head short, played his part too. But that is not what concerns me, I am more worried that it seems the King is almost lost without his friend.'

'You noticed it too?' Montagu's worries seep through his words. 'I fear that our King, whom I love dearly, might do something foolhardy. Might even repeat past mistakes.'

'Past mistakes, my Lord?'

'Sometimes I forget, Sir Edmund, that you are not of English descent. I speak of course of the King's great-grandfather Edward the Second. A most tragic tale. You shall have it one day.' Montagu shakes off his apparent melancholy and smiles. 'Perhaps when I come to Beauworth to fetch my glass doors.'

Edmund laughs. 'Then I shall never have it, my Lord, for the doors were in the house long before it was bequeathed to me. They are part of its history while I am but a temporary custodian.'

'Glass and stone persist while man perishes?'

Nodding Edmund takes another sip of wine. 'I am but a grain of sand. When my time comes, I shall roll back into the sea, and all I can hope for is that someone is kind enough to remember me.'

'For a man heralded by Kings and Princes, you are most humble.' Montagu seems to assess how honest Edmund might be.

'I come from a humble background,' Edmund says. He even dresses the part when at court, careful never to outshine men whose fortunes far exceed his own. Men such as Montagu. 'Most of my current fortune I attribute solely to luck.'

'Skill more likely.' Montagu snaps his fingers at a servant and replaces his empty cup with a full one, the base of it dripping wine. 'The Prince thought highly of your skills with a sword, and the honesty in your council. I see now that he was right to do so.'

Right to the very end, Edmund thinks and smiles noncommittally. 'The Prince merely liked a man to spar with who did not flee from the field when he wielded his sword.'

Once more, Montagu's deep laugh embraces Edmund's ears. 'Well spoken! I once saw him chase off three soldiers with nothing more than a stare. He did not even need to draw his sword.' Straightening the chain of thick, silver links set with garnets and some kind of green gemstone, Edmund does not recognise, Montagu continues: 'His must in many ways have been a lonely life.'

'How can you say so, my Lord, when he was in the constant company of his brothers?' Edmund says, he needs to assess how much Montagu is willing to part with in terms of intimacy.

'Little love lost there. They all admired him for his prowess, but I for one think that of those left, only Langley truly loved his brother.' Montagu lowers his voice and Edmund has to lean in to hear his words. 'Gaunt wanted the throne for himself as you know well enough, and Woodstock … well, you heard him today. He loves only himself.'

# CHAPTER 25

## 26 July 1392 – Westminster Palace

'There was peace for a while after the rebellion. Though we were both proven right, my Lord. The English people's love for their King did dwindle, and they grew accustomed to his iron-fist rule. Meanwhile, I set about training my son to become my heir in every way.' Edmund stretched. 'I confess I enjoyed it more than I thought I would. To finally meet another who could match me, after all that time, was a blessing.'

Gaunt folded his hands. 'I have heard tell he was a disappointment to you.'

Smiling, Edmund shook his head. 'You have been listening to idle gossip again, my Lord, no doubt spilled from someone who has every reason to be unkind. After all, you cannot always be close to the King without attracting unwanted attention. Just as our friend de Vere did.'

'He was no friend of mine.' Another candle guttered and died, leaving Gaunt's face in half-shadow. 'He was entirely your creature, as I always suspected, until you could no longer manage him.'

'I created a new one,' Edmund said, 'one who turned out to be much more pliable, much easier to bend to my will than even my own son.'

Gaunt rose to fetch another candle. It dripped on the floor, leaving traces on the carpet. Once he had put it down on his table, he leaned against the back of his chair. 'Some would call Argyle Mowbray simple.'

'Only fools would do that.'

As Edmund reached for the pitcher of water, Gaunt pushed his cup towards him. 'I am no fool.'

'Neither is Argyle. When the deed is done tomorrow, he will be forced into a position that he will grow to despise.' Edmund poured the water. 'But he will play the game nonetheless, for that is what he has been taught. What he has trained for his whole life. Even if he does not yet know it. A reluctant hero is easy to love, and even easier to underestimate.'

'You believe that he will be able to outsmart his own brother?'

'That remains to be seen.' Edmund drank and wiped his chin; the cool water was a welcome refreshment in his throat and on his skin. 'But yes, I believe you would be safer betting on my son than his greedy, ruthless brother, if you are still inclined to such wagers.'

Gaunt smiled and shed a few years in the merciful candlelight. As time went on, Edmund saw more of his own traits in Gaunt's features, it was irksome. 'Are you quite certain, you have the right Mowbray picked as your son?'

'I will not deny that, for a long while, I favoured Thomas to Argyle and often wanted him to be my son.' Edmund put down his cup and locked eyes with Gaunt. 'But once I understood Argyle's true talents, I knew that he was to be preferred. In the long run, his kind will always prevail.'

'You have me enthralled once more, Sire,' Gaunt said, his words laced with disdain and a smidge of curiosity. 'Do tell.'

## 14 September 1383 – Beauworth

From his study, Edmund watches the caravan of people wind its way out of the woodlands and towards his house, standards flying above the riders in the front. It is rare for him to feel torn, but Edmund has pondered for days on end if this visit is a good omen or a bad idea that should have been stamped out. Whatever it is, it is too late to recant now. Besides, it has been too long since Edmund was last in London, the King seems to rely solely on his friend de Vere and a few other companions these days, and Edmund is starved for news of any kind. If only it came in the company of someone else.

When the line approaches, the standard flickers in the wind, and Edmund notices that it is Woodstock's banner at the head of Coxcombe's retinue. No doubt he is here on a special errand, for rumour has it that he dislikes Edmund even more than he dislikes Coxcombe, but Edmund has replaced that rumour with one that they are great friends, because it is easier to manage this far from court, except that he now has to be a generous host to a man he loathes; so be it. He has met Coxcombe only once or twice since Limoges, and Edmund did not know that Coxcombe had switched allegiances from Warwick to Woodstock.

Something is amiss, Edmund is certain of it, he can feel it in his bones. And yet, he must play host to this pathetic excuse for a knight, for such is the law of the land. Fortunately, Edmund is spoiling for sport, and if nothing else, Coxcombe can be sport.

The snake of riders progresses quickly, and Edmund watches Warden cross the courtyard, stable boys and squires scampering to carry out his orders. Yesterday, they moved a large part of Edmund's horses to the newly erected stables in the nearest village, forcing the local farmers to put their cattle back to pasture. It is only the middle of September and the weather fair this far south, but still, he is irritated that he has to make such changes all for a visit from a man everyone in London thinks is his friend.

Warden turns and looks up; even through the warbled glass, Edmund can tell he is needed in the yard. Making his way down the stairs, he is joined by Argyle who has been up since daybreak making his room ready for the squire who will be lodging with him. The house is ill equipped for a large number of guests and everyone must squeeze together to make room for the visitors. Another thing that annoys Edmund today, that he has an inferior house, a matter he had thought to rectify when next in London, only a royal summons has been wanting, and he has been unable to find an excuse to visit the King. It has to be more than to petition for more estates, for the King is not in the habit of just giving away his lands, unless your name is de Vere. Edmund bites off a groan.

'How long have you known Sir Alan, Sire?'

Edmund can think of no man less deserving of the title, but he has to play along. 'Some ten or eleven years.'

'Has he visited before?'

'No, this is a first, Master Argyle.' Edmund smiles at Argyle, though his constant chattering and questions sets Edmund's teeth on edge. If not for the boy's ease in learning to fight and his strong build, Edmund would have cast him out long ago. He continues, 'I have asked Warden to arrange some hunting while our guests are here. Perhaps this is the year where you take your first stag.'

'Would that I should, Sire!' Argyle's eyes gleam. 'But I suspect I shall be ordered about by Master Warden a good deal before we ride out for a hunt.'

With a loud laugh, Edmund pushes open the massive door and lets in a bout of air and a swirl of leaves. 'In that you are quite right, Master Argyle. Now off with you, make yourself useful! Tonight, you shall wait at my table but until then, I want you to assist Master Warden any way he sees fit.'

'Master Argyle!' Warden's gruff voice rumbles across the confusion in the courtyard. 'Attend our guests!'

Argyle runs off, weaving his way through the throng of stable boys and milkmaids to reach the gate just in time for the first riders to emerge into the fading sunlight. The unfurled banners look new, so do Coxcombe's clothes. When he reaches the stepping-stone, Edmund strides over. 'Sir Alan.'

'Sir Edmund!' Coxcombe swings out of the saddle, twitching a little. 'It is kind of you to offer shelter for me and my men.'

'It has been too long,' Edmund says unconvincingly and forces a smile. 'I hope you have time to participate in a hunt or two before you are off again.'

'We do.' Coxcombe looks about without bothering to return the smile and catches the eye of a gangly, ginger-haired youth. 'Stephen!'

Edmund nods to Argyle. 'Show Master Stephen to the stables and make sure Sir Alan's horse is rubbed down, fed and watered. No doubt, it has served him well on the journey here and deserves a rest.'

The two knights weave their way through the throng of people in the courtyard, Edmund leads his guest up the stairs and into the parlour that looks out upon the garden.

'To think you'd open your doors to me – freely.' Coxcombe looks at Edmund; malice he has previously concealed quite well now lingers in his eyes. 'But then we're all dependent upon others. And it's best that we play our part to perfection, isn't it?'

Edmund watches Coxcombe as he turns to the coloured glass doors. Although he manages to crush any outburst, Edmund can tell from the reflection in the glass that Coxcombe is overwhelmed. For a moment, Edmund has the upper hand and he is quick to strike. 'Now that we are alone, Coxcombe, I would know the true purpose of your visit?'

'My Lord Woodstock's attempting to reconcile with his brother – and the King.' Coxcombe clasps his hands behind his back, but his eyes remain on the glass. 'He's eager to prove that what's happened is all in the past.'

'I do not see what that has to do with me. Or with you for that matter. If it is all in the past, whatever it is, then surely there was no need for you to come south.' Edmund pauses when the door opens and a servant comes in with a fresh pitcher of wine. 'Some refreshment?'

Coxcombe accepts the silver cup and studies it. 'You have some fine things, Sir Edmund. How did you come about such an abundance?'

Edmund puts down the pitcher and turns to Coxcombe with a smile that can easily be mistaken for a smirk. 'The late King was most generous and bestowed upon me not only Beauworth but also all of its riches. Sir William – the last occupant of this fine house – had accrued much wealth in the wars waged when King Edward was a young man. Since Sir William never married – well …' Edmund drinks.

'I'm still awaiting the gift of a house of my own.' Coxcombe's grip on the silver cup turns his fingertips white. 'But then, we can't all hope to be as fortunate as you've been. Beloved not only by a Prince but also by a Baron, a Duke and various – other – people. Not to mention our King.'

'Does not Lord Woodstock have some house he can bestow upon you? Since you are such a great servant of his.' Edmund sips the watered wine and looks past Coxcombe into the garden.

'Nothing that will serve. And besides, I should prefer for the King himself to gift me with some property.' Even with great effort, Edmund can tell that Coxcombe hates being here as much as Edmund hates to be his host.

'For that to happen, you must first serve him. And war is not imminent.' Edmund manages to drown his smirk only by taking another sip of wine.

Coxcombe empties his cup and puts it down with a hard thud. 'War's always rising somewhere. If I can't earn my keep in England, perhaps I should look further afield. As you once did.'

'We both did.'

'Yes, but what difference in our outcomes, wouldn't you say?' Coxcombe rounds on Edmund. 'How is it, Sire, that the knight who openly defied his Prince was rewarded with such riches as these now present before my eyes. While I – I who did all that was expected, obeyed every order – I have nothing?'

The hiss sparks Edmund's rising temper. 'You went beyond the orders, I think.'

'And you were quick to rebuke me. But now, I know that you too reached above your station.'

They glare at each other while footsteps stop outside the door, someone is lingering, perhaps trying to hear what should not be heard. Edmund holds up his hand and waits for whoever is there to retreat. When the sound grows faint and disappears, Edmund lowers his hand.

'Beware what you say. Every house has ears. If you expect your visit to somehow affect the relationship of princes – although I fail to see how that is to come about – then we must all be on our best behaviour.'

'I struggle to be a good dog.' Coxcombe turns his back, his angry face reflected in the yellow, green and iridescent blue of the glass doors. 'I suspect you do too.'

'I have made my peace with the past. Some things are best forgotten.' Edmund continues in thought, to earn the truth, I hardly think of it at all. The past is tiresome, I care only about the future.

'And in such splendid surroundings, I can imagine everything is easily forgotten. I even hear tell that you're often at court, and that the King drinks up your every word. Although of late, it seems he has grown weary of what you serve.'

'I am surprised to find you in the service of Lord Woodstock.' Edmund decides to change the subject. 'I did not know that Lord Warwick had released you?'

'Beggars can't be choosers, as perhaps you'll discover someday.' Coxcombe looks ready to punch a fist through the precious, coloured glass. 'For me, entering into the service of Lord Woodstock is an advancement. If I had stayed with Lord Warwick, I'd still be training his men. After a while, such a task loses its lustre.'

Edmund picks up Coxcombe's cup and fills it again. 'Perhaps you would care to see the garden, Sire? Or I can provide fresh horses, if you wish to see the woods before the hunt tomorrow. It is a little late in the day, but the woods are not far off.'

'You think I want to sit another horse today? The journey from Pleshey was enough to satisfy my equestrian appetites. No doubt, you'll equip me with good men to help me find the best spots in the woods, and thus, I'll settle for the garden.' Coxcombe waves the cup away. 'We'll look as two old women prancing around beds of blossom, but fear not, Sire, I'll be ready for the hunt tomorrow.'

Opening the doors to the garden, which has improved vastly in the years since he took residence at Beauworth, Edmund breathes in the sweet autumnal scent of late roses and blossoming herbs. 'I am glad to hear it.'

'And as for your interest in my new employment, I'm sure the courtly gossip's far superior to anything I might add. No doubt, they've concocted some hare-brained notion that I failed Lord Warwick in my duties, or that I did something to give offence.' Coxcombe shrugs. 'It's of little matter. Working for one of the royal princes far exceeds what any other Lord might offer. Only men in the King's personal service can set their aims higher than I.'

Edmund tries to ensnare the calm of the garden, but Coxcombe's words bait him. 'Any man dependent upon the grace of another can never truly feel safe. Or free.'

'You'd know.' Coxcombe steps onto the gravel path that carves a line through the flowerbeds. 'The forest looks ripe with deer.'

'And so it is.' Edmund leads the way to the end of the path and points towards a flock of twenty deer headed by a magnificent stag. 'There is your proof. But you will see for yourself tomorrow, and as you say, I shall provide good guides to ensure you get the best position.'

'I hope to come away with a good kill … or two.' As Coxcombe passes, he gives Edmund what must be intended as a taunting glare. 'I might just settle for one extremely good kill. It's not the number of preys one takes down; it's the importance of what you hit. Don't you agree, Sire?'

## 15 September 1383 – Beauworth

Argyle's loud laugh rings through the noise in the great hall, and Edmund looks up to spy the youth in animated conversation with Coxcombe's squire, Stephen. He always makes friends easily, Edmund muses, at least he has that to merit himself along with a few other qualities that have been showing themselves of late.

'Fast friends.'

'That they are.' Edmund looks at Warden. 'How was the hunt?'

'Successful.' Warden seems to choose his words with care, bending close to Edmund. 'Sir Alan took three deer on his own.'

'The stag?'

'Not on the carts.' Warden nods towards Argyle. 'Although he had a clean shot at one point. But something spooked his horse.'

As if Argyle can feel Edmund's eyes on him, he looks up and flashes a quick smile, before turning his attention to the table once more. 'Good. I had hoped he would come away with a good kill.'

'He took five pheasants with bow and arrow, that's something. It's not his favourite weapon, but he's good with a bow. Anyway, he'll have better luck next time.' Warden looks to be weighing his words. 'Any reason you returned early, M'lord?'

'I was not in luck.' Edmund surveys the room. 'And now I should attend our guests.'

'Will they stay long?'

Rising from his seat, Edmund clasps a hand on Warden's shoulder. 'With any luck, they will leave the day after tomorrow.'

Argyle half-rises, but Edmund shakes his head. What he hopes to resolve is best kept away from the crowd. Instead, Edmund hails Coxcombe and gestures towards the glass doors, forms of guests, servants and maids dancing on the panes of blue, purple and deep red. Coxcombe takes his time rising from the group of young men who surround him. He tips his cup to them, and they drink while he walks away.

'I hear you were the man of the day.' Edmund opens the doors and Coxcombe steps into the parlour. 'Three deer. Thank you for filling my larder in such an impressive manner. Did you take them down with a lance or do you prefer the bow?'

'The biggest three deer. One could have rivalled that stag of yours, if it hadn't met with my lance.' Deep-seated smugness coats Coxcombe's words. 'But then a flock only needs one stag. And even the greatest beast can be brought to heel by a younger rival.'

The insinuation is not lost on Edmund, but he simply smiles. 'Wine?'

'Why not? It seems you've brought out your best casks for me.'

'Guests are always treated with every curtsey here at Beauworth.' Edmund offers Coxcombe a cup, the foot and stem is silver wrought to enfold the thin, amber glass.

'A lesser man would be in awe.' Coxcombe takes the glass and traces the pattern and exquisite craftsmanship with a greasy finger. 'But I'm not a lesser man. Though you've treated me as an inferior often enough.'

'I know a worthy adversary when I see one,' Edmund says without grace and sits by the window in his large, oak chair. 'You have helped me line my stores for the upcoming winter, and for that I am grateful. But still, I wonder …'

Coxcombe drinks deep and wipes his chin with the back of his hand. 'You could've stocked your own stores without my help.'

'Why are you here?'

'A knight can't visit his fellow warrior and reminisce of days past?'

'Ours would not be fond memories, and I would not want anyone to make the mistake of thinking you are a great warrior.' Edmund looks out into the garden; torches being lit around the paths. 'We have nothing in common, nothing to say to one another, and so, I feel justified in asking, once more, why you are here.'

Coxcombe's face curdles at Edmund's words. 'You truly believe that with a show of plenty and some well-chosen wine, my tongue will untie and I'll tell all?'

'I will attend court soon,' Edmund says with feigned disinterest. 'I can simply ask around when I get there. For surely, you would not have come here unless you were forced to do so?'

'It is as I say. Lord Woodstock's eager to ensure the King of his fidelity. Since you're one of the King's most trusted knights, it makes good sense to send me - one of Lord Woodstock's most trusted knights – on a courtesy call. It will also serve to prove to Gaunt that my Lord desires peace.' Coxcombe takes a seat near the empty hearth. In the flickering torchlight from the garden and the few candles lit in the parlour, his face is a dark mask. 'But since we're alone …'

Here it is, Edmund thinks, the real reason you deigned to journey south. Instead of speaking, Edmund nods for his guest to continue.

Coxcombe stares past Edmund into the darkening garden. 'Since the peasant uprising, the noble lords of England have been … on edge, shall we say?'

'It was resolved.'

'By a boy King, yes. And then the boy King decided to flex his muscles.' Coxcombe smiles. 'It's of little enough matter to you or I, since we're – as you said yourself – at the mercy of others, just as the peasants are. For my part, I confess, I found the King's actions entirely just though no one asked me. But it's of great matter to my Lord Woodstock.' Edmund offers more wine, and Coxcombe declines. 'It's of great matter to all those clever enough to acknowledge that what was done, was done with malice and childish spite.'

'Careful now, you would not want to speak out of turn. My tongue might slip when I am next at court and then where would we all be?'

Coxcombe rolls his shoulder and looks at Edmund. 'I say nothing that hasn't already been discussed on the Privy Council. As you well know.'

'The King is young, his attempt to assert his supremacy was – perhaps – rash, but it could not be helped. And it is in the past.' Edmund remembers the bitter discussions on the council all too well. Gaunt had been furious that his advice had been dismissed with the wave of a hand, Langley had tried to smooth over the differences and Woodstock had stormed out. 'What is done is done.'

'It could be undone.'

'You cannot bring back the dead.' Edmund has long since made peace with the fact that he was forced, in the end, to hang twenty of his good farmhands. At least, he got off cheap where other southern lords had corpses dangling by the hundreds.

Fingering the silver filigree, Coxcombe nods. 'Of course not. But other measures could be taken to ensure that the people are redeemed – in some small way, if nothing else.'

'Is this about the rebels – or about personal ambition?' The words slip from Edmund's mouth before he can stop them and Coxcombe's fingers stop moving.

'Your master and mine are cut from the same cloth,' he says in a smooth manner. 'I struggle to see how this might shock you.'

'The King …'

'Not that master.' Coxcombe glances at the door when a shadow passes close by, but it keeps moving. 'Your real master.'

Edmund decides to play dumb. 'I have sworn my sword, shield and life to the King. I will fall on my sword if he asks it of me, those were the words I said on the field at Poitiers before the Prince we all lost, and I repeated to his son when he took the throne. The King is my master.'

'He commands us all. But we're sworn to other princes, you and I.' Coxcombe's words flutter as silk across the quiet room. 'I wonder how you keep so many alliances at the same time. You mustn't sleep at all.'

'I sleep just fine.' Something inside Edmund's brain stirs, but he cannot catch it. 'And I serve only one man.'

'A man – not a boy?'

'A King.' Again that stirring, again it slips between his fingers. 'Perhaps you do not?'

Coxcombe sets the cup aside and leans forward, resting his hands on his knees. 'You asked my true purpose for coming here. What if it's to ensure that whoever you serve'll keep faith with the lords of England?'

'I am but one knight. What difference do I make?'

'I asked the same question,' Coxcombe says.

'And what was the answer?' Edmund demands discarding his attempts to be civil.

Shaking his head. Coxcombe interlaces his fingers. 'That I was to come here, strike up an old friendship – of sorts – and attempt to ensure your pledge that if, in future, the King tries something similar, you'll wield your power and ensure he's curbed.'

Edmund leans back in his chair, the leather of his boots creaking. 'I have no such power. No one can curb a King; you would do well to remember that.'

'Not so, according to the great men of this realm. My Lord Woodstock knows of your secret meetings with Lord Gaunt. What you discuss has so far eluded him, but then measures can be taken …' Coxcombe tips his head. 'The royal princes worry about the King's young friends.'

Edmund almost laughs, this is too good to be true, what luck to have the most powerful men of the land fight for his allegiance. It will make his future plans much easier to realise, perhaps even to have them endorsed. Now that would be a grand thing. He shakes his head in mock modesty. 'I may be in my prime, but my youth is well and truly behind me.'

'Still, you've the King's ear. That's what everyone says, and my Lord Woodstock would like to ensure it stays that way.'

'He really does trust you.' The wonder in Edmund's words makes Coxcombe jerk.

'Certainly he does! He's no reason not to! He knows what I am,' he hisses. 'What he doesn't know is what you are. Friend or foe?'

'You can tell your master that I am the King's man.' The stirring in Edmund's mind has turned to a nagging. What is he missing? 'When I am at council, I strive to advise the King in a way that serves his best interest. As do we all, for what else can we do? England thrives when the King is pleased.'

'If you want what's in the King's best interest, you'll be wise to intercede if his newfound friends from low places get above their station.' Leaning back, Coxcombe glides a hand through his hair. 'I'll say this, Sire, the King's moving down a dangerous path. He's young, and so he's in dire need of good direction … even you'll agree with that. He's not going to get that from just anyone. The question is, will he get it from you? If need be, will you oppose him?'

In a flash, Edmund finally grasps what is stirring and pulls it into the light. Duplicity. His favourite game. He turns a horrified face at Coxcombe. 'He is the King!'

'He is a King,' Coxcombe confirms. 'But is he the right one?'

'What is to stop me going to the King with your treasonous talk? What is to prevent me pointing the finger at your master and tell the King that his own uncle is plotting against him?' Edmund threatens although inside, he is brimming with glee. How well this is turning out. How easy it will be to remove those young fools who have lost their way and strayed from Edmund's grasp.

Coxcombe rises and looks at Edmund for a moment, cold disdain on his face. 'You know it to be true. The Crown sits askew on the boy King's head. He needs all the friends he can get, the right friends, true to him and to England. You know that his is a coveted position. You fear for him.'

Before Edmund can reply, Coxcombe opens the door to the hall. 'For all that you loathe me, Sire, you know I speak the truth.'

'You speak with the duplicity of a skilled courtier,' Edmund announces to the empty room, Coxcombe already at the foot of the stairs. Inside, joy surges through Edmund's veins. This is better than anything he could have asked for, this is a free pass to get a filthy job done, and done well. All Edmund has to do is seize the opportune moment.

# CHAPTER 26

## 26 July 1392 – Westminster Palace

'You were waiting for de Vere to make a fool of himself,' Gaunt observed with a whiff of acknowledgement accompanying his words. 'Unfortunately for you, he never did. Or am I mistaken?'

'Not at all, my Lord. It was not de Vere who brought about his own undoing, but rather our beloved King, or do you not agree?' Edmund stretched. 'He led his own dear friend to the slaughter and he did not even know it. To raise de Vere so far above his natural position was a folly only a young and ungoverned King might attempt. In the end, I did not have to do a thing to ensure that everyone wanted rid of the young upstart.'

Gaunt shifted in his seat. 'You had to bring up that despicable time?'

'Without it, neither you nor I would have had a clear path to our goal.' Edmund leaned back and closed his eyes. 'The King had to be put in his place and shown that, for all his young friend's merits, this was one place where he could provide no council at all. I only regret that the enemy did not see fit to pick de Vere from our march and put an arrow in his back. Or better yet, a knife.'

'To me it marked the dawn of a dark time for England.' Gaunt rubbed his temple with an ink-stained finger. 'Though I was surprised that you went against the King's orders in the end.'

'I knew that he would have to yield eventually,' Edmund said, reliving some of the endless marching they had done. He shook his head, 'and I would have him yield to me. No matter his orders, I would never put the city to the torch. There was no way he could have made me do so. As well you know.'

'You think too highly of yourself.' Gaunt spoke without censure.

Edmund opened one eye. 'And you continue to underestimate me – like many others who came before you. I wonder why learning is so hard for some.'

## 21 June 1385 – Carlisle

'My Lord de Vere, we raise you to Marquis of Dublin.'

Edmund feels a familiar tingling run down his spine as the soldiers and knights around him cheer the men who rise before the King, new titles bestowed to bring about good fortune before the dealings of war. Once the King's own birth was proclaimed a good omen. Then his father marched with Peter of Castile to reclaim a blood-stained crown, and in the end, it killed them both. Now here Edmund is again, embarking upon another mad quest for another power-hungry man. But this time, Edmund will stay in control of the situation.

He shakes his head as the crowd disperses around him, winding their way back to their campsites. Argyle falls into step with Edmund and he looks at the boy, now on the cusp of manhood, his face an open book for all to read. There is still much for him to learn.

On a whim, Edmund decides to give a lesson. 'The King was most generous today.'

Argyle gives Edmund a curious glance. 'Sire?'

'He raised his personal friend to Marquis of Dublin. Which brings de Vere on par with the King's uncles.' Edmund turns right and follows the makeshift fencing. On the field, his great grey destrier, aptly named Noble, and the other warhorses graze in peace, unaware of what has just transpired.

'Is that bad news?' There is an edge in the boy's voice that moves Edmund to slap Argyle's shoulder lightly. He grows ever quicker in mind.

'It may mean nothing at all.' He speaks without conviction and sees budding understanding in Argyle's blue eyes. Edmund continues. 'To be the

King's friend is a great honour, do not mistake me for I am proud to serve, but at times, he makes it difficult for us to do our duty. We are sworn to protect England and the Crown, and we are honour-bound to advise him before battle. Which might be easier if he were … more like the Kings who came before him.'

Edmund wishes he could exchange Argyle for Gaunt, but the great Lord has taken to avoiding him of late. Besides, it is time to discover if Argyle is as loyal to Edmund as he believes him to be. He wants to know if Argyle can be trusted.

'You mean like his grandfather, King Edward?'

'Certainly, he was a great man.' Edmund raises his hand to greet Reynold Grey, once Edmund's squire, Grey is now mustering men under his father's banner, the three red dots prominent against the blue and white stripes. 'But I thought more of his father. Now he would have made a fine King! I fought with him in France, as you well know, and I was much bereaved when he died an untimely death.'

While Argyle seems to be pondering something, Edmund quietly laments what the King has done this day. If only he had paid more heed to Edmund's council, or indeed even Gaunt's, he would not be walking blind into the bog of unrest his appointments will no doubt create. The King's reckless behaviour cannot go unchecked for much longer; Edmund hopes that someone else will broach the subject on one of the coming war councils. Woodstock perhaps, but Edmund has no control over him either. No, he must seek out someone more malleable, and soon.

'Why do people call him the Black Prince? The King's father?'

Argyle's voice pulls Edmund back to the present. 'Some say it is because he rode a black destrier, others say it is for his personality and others again that his standard gave him the name. I saw his banner unfurl at Poitiers, and he did indeed ride a black horse. But I shall always remember him as an amiable, strong man, destined to be the eternal pride of England.' At least until his mind broke, Edmund thinks and continues: 'Any or all of it may have brought about the name.'

'How did you come to meet him?'

Still curious, Edmund thinks and decides the best way to test Argyle is to tell him something that most of the King's young friends do not know. If it filters back to him somehow, he will know where it came from.

'I was part of a large retinue of soldiers fighting under the command of the Duke of Lancaster, your aunt's brother, mind you this was before Lord Gaunt inherited the title. We were successful for some time raiding in the south-west of France. I was destined to go to Calais with the Duke when your father intervened and had me transferred to his retinue. It was in his service that I finally saw true battle when we faced the French at Poitiers. If not for the Prince's great knowledge of strategy, and his brother's eye for tactics, we would never have managed to come out victorious.'

Edmund looks towards the sky; he remembers fighting under Baron Mowbray's banner. He remembers the bloodshed, but the colours of his memories are faded, the men faceless. What does stand the test of time is the Prince's blade on his shoulder the following day. His spurs won and his prisoner paid for handsomely.

'Is the King like his father?'

'Some say so.'

When Argyle makes to ask another question, Edmund holds up his hand and turns away. 'I must go to council. Go back to camp and make sure my armour is ready.'

'You think you'll get use of it?' a familiar and unwelcome voice asks.

'Sir Alan.' Edmund wrings a smile from his face and turns to Coxcombe. 'Better to be prepared, would you not say? If nothing else, it will keep my squire busy.'

'My Lord Woodstock wishes a word.' Coxcombe has a restless air about him. 'Now.'

Edmund watches Argyle walk away, slow at first and then with more purpose. When he is gone from view, Edmund gives a curt nod. 'If it cannot be helped.'

'It can't.' Coxcombe leads the way, careful to avoid the cesspits. His neck flames red. 'I'd think you'd be pleased to be called for council. After all, you're a great royal favourite. Even the King's young friends seem unable to push you aside.'

'Some things one should not covet,' Edmund says and sees Coxcombe's shoulders tense. 'And if you did not notice, I was not in the line of men awarded new titles today.'

'In here.'

Edmund looks up but does not see Woodstock's banner. The tent is plain, placed on the outskirts of the camp in the shade of the nearby woods. How curious that one of the most flamboyant men at court should prefer to reside in such a nondescript location. Coxcombe holds the flaps for Edmund but does not enter behind him.

'Sir Edmund.'

'My Lord Woodstock. You summoned me?'

Woodstock stays in his seat, the small travel table before him empty but for a single map. He taps it with a ringed finger. 'Scotland.'

'The greatest prize,' Gaunt says from the shadows. 'My father desired it. My grandfather ran from it. My great-grandfather brought all his might, but it would not yield. And now, a boy will attempt to take it.'

Laughing, Woodstock looks from Gaunt to Edmund. 'My brother jests. Of course, we hope that the King will succeed. Pay no heed, Sire, you know as well as I – perhaps better so – that my brother cannot bear to be upstaged. If we take Scotland, the King will wear more crowns than John, and that he cannot abide!'

'The Scots' crown is wound from thistles; I have no desire to be constantly stung by it. Let him have it, if he can manage. If only we could be certain that his success will make England stronger.' Gaunt scowls at his brother and something transpires between them that makes Woodstock turn his attention to the map. Gaunt looks appeased. 'What say you about the ceremony, Sir Edmund?'

'Grand, my Lord, as all the King's ceremonies are. And how lucky the men were to be awarded such high offices.' The words stick in Edmund's throat, but he spits them out all the same. 'It was quite a spectacle and must be a sign of the good things that are to come when the King is victorious.'

'It was an insult!' Woodstock flares. 'It is all good and well that we are made Dukes, after all you have been one for some time, dear brother, and since you stole the Castilian crown from our brother, it is high time he got something for his troubles. But for de Vere to become Marquis! He might as well have made Sir Edmund here a prince!'

'We can all agree that it was a surprise.' Behind Gaunt's measured words, Edmund hears disdain. 'Not three days ago, the King informed me that de Vere was to receive another earldom.'

'You should have paid attention and not just give in to his every whim! If I …' Woodstock stops mid-splutter when Gaunt gestures.

'Enough! I asked Sir Edmund a question, which I believe he can answer with more insight than he did. Why not let him?'

'The King is exercising his rule,' Edmund says and suffers a scornful look from Woodstock; how he hates this pathetic excuse of a man. He turns his attention to Gaunt the only worthy adversary on this joke of a quest. 'I am concerned that the King would all but hand over Ireland to de Vere. His influence has grown in these last few years, more so than I had noticed or imagined possible.'

Unfortunate, Edmund thinks, most unfortunate that he should become such a great favourite when all I ever wanted from the boy, he once was, was someone to distract the King and bring me the gossip I need. Perhaps I will have the good fortune to learn before long that de Vere has fallen prey to the Scots. The idea is enough for a small smile to play at the corner of Edmund's mouth.

'He is completely unchecked!' Woodstock pounds his fist into his palm. 'This would never have happened in our father's time! It should not be allowed to happen now. I have said this before, John, I believe we must take measures to ensure that de Vere does not over-stretch.'

Unlike his brother, Gaunt remains calm. 'He is of no concern to us. He will never be a match for us.'

'He is married to our cousin, and he is one of the richest men in England!' Woodstock sounds like a petulant child, too used to getting his own way. He was pampered by the late Queen, and it seems her constant doting has left him spoiled and in constant want for more.

'Not as rich as you – or I.' Gaunt looks at Edmund. 'What say you, Sir Edmund? Are we to be concerned with de Vere?'

'It does not hurt to stay alert, my Lord.' Edmund has yet to learn why he is summoned here, but so far, he is enjoying himself. To have the royal brothers battering each other as rams in heat is always entertaining. 'But for now, I agree with you, my Lord Gaunt, there is no cause for concern. He may have the title, but he has not taken Ireland for himself yet. When he does – if he does – then we might have to act. For now, let him play at being a Marquis, what is that to you?'

'A Marquis! He is no more a Marquis than I am a King! Someone ought to do something,' Woodstock says and is reproached by a glance from Gaunt, but still he continues: 'All I say is that accidents happen. It is hardly the first time that a King has chosen his advisors poorly.'

'The people rose up against what they thought were the King's bad advisors. They broke into the Tower and put heads on spikes.' Gaunt tries to hold back a sneer. 'I lost my home in London to the rebel mob. If it is all the same to you, Thomas, I should prefer for the people to stay in their rightful place where they belong. Let the enemy take de Vere, if they can, but we ought to concern ourselves with other matters. I do not want another rebellion on my hands, not with all the King's might mustered here in the north.'

'I would take rebellion any day, if it would put his head on a spike.' Woodstock returns to perusing the map before him, avoiding Gaunt's furious glare. He traces the outline of the Scottish border with a ringed finger and looks at Edmund. 'Have you been to Scotland before, Sire?'

'No, my Lord.' Edmund despises being servile to Woodstock, but since he has all but sanctioned the removal of de Vere, Edmund decides to keep his peace with the youngest royal uncle for now. De Vere is clearly a thorn in Woodstock's paw, perhaps Edmund can use that to his advantage. He looks at the map. 'Though I have been in the north before, I have yet to cross the border.'

'Nor I. But my brother has much experience in looking over the border, do you not, John?'

Edmund can tell that Gaunt struggles to ignore Woodstock's jibe. 'Now, we will cross it together, Thomas, and make war on Scotland.'

'But will we win?'

'The Scots are clever. They know they cannot take on the English army.' Gaunt steps close to the table, inviting Edmund to join them. 'They will attempt to break our lines; they may even succeed. We will have to stretch thin to manage the terrain.'

Woodstock flicks imaginary dust from his impeccable, dark-green cape, which is lined with fox fur. 'Why not just carve a road through the woods, as our great-grandfather did?'

'This is not Wales,' Gaunt says and points. 'These are not flat lands and marches; these are rocky hillsides. If we attempt to carve a road, we will be there for years, decades.'

Edmund can tell Gaunt is already exasperated and decides to weigh in, pointing to the map. 'The Scots are famous for their warfare. They are ruthless and know these mountains as we can never hope to. The thinner the line, the greater the risk, my Lord. I should avoid going too far north, best to stay in the lowlands. Even so, the woods are dense.'

'We must try to keep as close as we can.' Gaunt sighs. 'But we will lose men, of that I have no doubt. I have seen what the raiding parties that ride south of the border can do and they are but a few men. Once we are in the lowlands, our numbers matter little enough.'

'Is there no news of where the main host is?' Woodstock feigns an interest, but Edmund can tell he is done with war council for now. 'They can be made to do battle, surely?'

'My scouts have seen a few groups of men scattered about, none of them big enough to be the main host. For my part,' Gaunt says and scours the map, 'I would say that they are not amassing. They will not give battle.'

This sparks Edmund's interest. 'What will they do, my Lord?'

Gaunt's face hardens. 'They will go around us and sack the cities we pass.'

'Surely not! That is unchivalrous!' Woodstock looks appalled, but Edmund knows this kind of warfare, was forged in similar circumstances. He understands Gaunt's concern.

'This is war.' Gaunt looks at his brother. 'There is no chivalry in war. Is there, Sir Edmund?'

'The burnt land tactic. Which I have practiced often enough myself.' Edmund studies the map. 'No, my Lord, chivalry and war do not mix. In war, there are only winners and losers.' And I mean to win, Edmund thinks, I mean to make the most of this war, as I have of all the wars and all the battles I have ever fought for your family. Some way, somehow, I will come out victorious.

'Losing is not an option,' Gaunt says and rolls up the map. 'We must advise the King wisely, prevail upon him that there is no room for rash decisions. I look to you, Sir Edmund, to be a voice of reason on the council later today – and every other council that we will undoubtedly attend while we are in this wretched land.'

Woodstock laughs out his contempt. 'The King has his uncles at hand, what difference does a lowly knight make?'

The look Gaunt gives his frilly brother almost makes Edmund cringe. Clearly, Gaunt has had enough. 'Sometimes it is he who tips the scales. But if it consoles you, brother, let us pray it does not come to that.'

## 8 August 1385 – Edinburgh

Edmund looks at the city. Burn them. The King's words ring in his ears, the high-pitched voice of an angry adolescent frustrated that all of his efforts to lure the Scots to fight have failed. So here we are, Edmund thinks, and it falls to me to tip the scales.

Next to him, Argyle surveys the road and surrounding area. In some ways, he is slow to learn and, in others, such as understanding the landscape and judging what is the right way to proceed seems second nature to him. He will be a warrior, just as I am, Edmund thinks, but the idea does little to soothe him.

Behind them, the English camp rumbles through the thin stretch of woods that lies between the English army and Edinburgh, which is silent as a tomb. There will be no one there but women and children, Edmund thinks, that is what I would have done, surely that is what the Scots have done too. And our fool of a King wants to set an example.

'Would that the King should change his orders. Sacking a city is one thing, it will give the men something to fight for and lift morale, which God knows we need … But burning it is folly!' Edmund cannot contain his rage; there is no honour or glory in burning innocents, he will gain nothing by fulfilling the King's command.

Argyle's eyes flash with defiance. 'You should not speak thus!'

'I will speak as I find, and I have already laid my concerns before the King.' Edmund slaps his gloves against his palm and turns from the view of Edinburgh. 'You mark my words; this will end badly. I understand why the King does not want to go from here without a clear statement. But burning the city when there is but women and children left is the wrong kind of statement!'

Woodstock should never have told the King about the burnt land tactic. But then, Woodstock would be the man to make such a mistake, if indeed it was a mistake. Edmund is far from certain.

'And what would you do?' Edmund recognises the rash anger of youth in Argyle's voice. 'It is the King's command, and surely …'

'Surely, he must have the right of it?' Edmund cuts off Argyle; he has to be disciplined, to be brought to understand the difference between necessity and recklessness. Edmund is done losing men to the King's cause. 'That is what you are meant to believe, and yet none of his advisors – not even your brother – thinks it is the right course of action. The whole council was in uproar, Lord Gaunt arguing from a position of great knowledge. One that I back! If this had but been in the time of the Prince, we would have gone about it quite differently. The King must see reason.'

Edmund steps off the path and a strand of brambles grips his hose. He can tell that Argyle is struggling to harness his anger. When next he speaks, it is through gritted teeth. 'And what reason might that be?'

'That it is better to sack a city, plundering its residents but leaving them alive, than it is to burn every last soul in there.' Forcing a calm demeanour, he does not feel, Edmund leans on a tree. 'Poor bastards.'

Something in Argyle snaps and his stance changes. 'The Scots are our enemy! And the people in that city too! I believe the King is in the right! And even if I did not, it is his command that we burn the city!'

Edmund grips the handle of his sword, his gloves creaking. Fool of a boy, why did I bring you when you are of no use at all? he thinks and allows himself a moment to calm down before he replies. 'If the King had any true knowledge of chivalry, he would know that a knight does not burn innocents. Women and children are innocents; even you cannot argue differently. They did not choose this war. All they see are strangers forcing themselves on their lands.'

Cries and screams rise as a mighty flood in Edmund's mind, they ring in his ears, dead eyes staring at him, a girl covered in sick bleeding out in his arms. Is this going to be another Limoges? Even after all these years, his failure to change the mind of a Prince haunts him, it was his greatest loss and he will not abide another. Edmund hisses. 'They would gladly let their possessions go to live another day.'

'I cannot believe you!' Argyle takes a step forward, his eyes glittering in the twilight. 'What kind of a solider are you to doubt your King's command? What kind of a friend?'

Edmund grabs Argyle by the wrist and squeezes until the boy squirms. 'I have been too lenient with you! You are overstepping your mark. I fear what will happen when we return to England with nothing to show for it but a city of burned women and children. I am the kind of friend who understands what is truly at stake for our King!' He lets go of Argyle, anger surging through his veins. 'Never doubt my loyalty to the King! Or my love for him!'

Argyle looks at the ground, no doubt to hide his tears. 'Then how can you disagree with your orders, Sire?'

Something in Argyle's voice prods Edmund's pride. If he cannot even get his squire to obey, to blindly follow his master, how can he hope to check the King? How can he win the day if he cannot sway a simple boy?

Mastering his temper with great effort, Edmund lowers his voice, adds fervour to his words. 'I am not alone in my concerns, squire. It may surprise you to know that your brother feels as I do; it is not right to burn the city. Even now, I assume the King's uncles are trying to dissuade him. We risk the lives of fourteen thousand English soldiers if we linger here.' Edmund turns from Argyle's appalling, tear-stained face and points to Edinburgh. 'This may be the only way in – but it is also the only way out. We have no ships, and I will wager that the Scots did not leave a fleet for us to commandeer. I would not want to be here when the fire licks up the walls.'

'But Sire, surely the Scots are days away if they have just burned Carlisle?' Argyle's voice reveals that he is coming around, and Edmund allows himself to relax for a moment.

'Days? We are on their land; they know it like the back of their hand, and I am certain they did not march all their men to Carlisle. We would have come upon their main host if they did. Have you not felt eyes on the back of your neck as we marched here?' Edmund watches Argyle crumble before him. Every time he thinks the boy has learned his lesson there is another one waiting to be taught. It is disquieting.

'No. The King has had scouts out roaming the hills and woods this whole time. He would know.' But now, Argyle's words waver. 'You are an old and frightened man!'

'You are too like the King – rash and unchecked!' When Edmund sees pride in Argyle's face, he sours, he will not raise a fool, he will not abide such open insubordination. It must be crushed at once. 'There are larger forces afoot in our realm than can be controlled, Master Argyle – even by the King. If he chooses unwisely, I am not certain any of us will return unscathed!'

Fat drops of cold rain are not enough to cool Edmund's fury. He turns away, leaving Argyle in the thicket, Edmund feels the bite of the brambles that cling to his hose, but he does not stop. Tonight's heated words have made one thing brilliantly clear; the boy must be checked, brought to heel, and there he must stay for the rest of his life. He is even more useless than Edmund had thought. But there are others in camp who can be worked on, and for that he is grateful.

He looks over his shoulder and when he cannot see Argyle, Edmund turns from the path and trudges through the mud to get to a higher part of camp. It is not long before he is soaked to the skin, but at least the rain has forced most of the soldiers into their tents. The lonely sentry outside the big tent stands aside as soon as he sees Edmund and he pushes through the flaps and into a damp heat. 'My Lord.'

Gaunt rubs his eyes and looks up, his face tired and drawn. 'Sir Edmund.'

Pale steam rises from Edmund's clothes, increasing the damp, cloying feeling in the tent. 'I have inspected the road leading into the city, my Lord. If we carry out his order and march into Edinburgh, we will be walking into a trap. I will not send my men in there and what is more, I cannot burn innocent women and children. There must be another way.'

'Then you must make the King see reason. I have tried and failed more times than I care to admit; if he wants the city burned, who is left to change his mind if, between us, we cannot?' Gaunt reaches for a pitcher and pours a cup. 'He is becoming what we always wanted, Sir Edmund, the spitting image of his father.'

'His father in his later years,' Edmund grumbles and wipes his eyes. 'Wilful and self-important. It is beginning to rub off on others in the most unfortunate way.'

Gaunt leans back and looks to be contemplating Edmund. 'You are all that stands between youthful pride and massacre. How appropriate that you are given a second chance; now, you might put right past failure.'

The sneering undertone is not lost on Edmund, but he has · to acknowledge that Gaunt has the right of it. 'I see that the tides are changing, my Lord, and I do not care for it. The King listens to the wrong sort of people.'

'He has you.' Gaunt rises and pulls off his hardened leather jerkin. 'Does he not?'

Slowly, warmth replaces the bone-chilling, damp cold of the Scottish rain and Edmund squeezes water from his cloak. 'You heard him today, he does not listen to reason. If we are to change his mind, we must go about it with more craftiness than wringing his arm until he submits. We must make new allies if we are to avoid disaster.'

'New allies?' Plunging his hands into the washbasin, Gaunt looks up before splashing his face. and rubbing at his ink-stained fingers. 'I am glad you see reason at last, for we are about to repeat the sins of the father, and I will not assent to it. If the King wishes to burn the city to the ground, be it on his head. My men will not partake. I will not partake. If I cannot stop him, he will breach the walls of Edinburgh without the support of Lancaster.'

'Daring, my Lord.' Edmund is encouraged by Gaunt's words; as long as he plays this right, he will be able to get Gaunt on board. 'I feel the same. Although the loss of my men will be but a drop in the ocean, if many enough of us can agree …'

'You are suggesting treason?'

'Call it what you will, but you think as I do on this account, my Lord.' Edmund turns in front of the brazier. 'We must impress upon the King the repercussions of his decision. You and I can remind him of what happened to his father …'

'Ah, but will he listen, Sire?' Gaunt wipes his face and wrings his pointed beard. 'Will he take the advice of old men when a horde of young hotheads cheer him on?'

'Can you swear to me that the screams of hundreds of women and children set alight, burned while you watch, will not drive you mad, my Lord?' Edmund can tell he has struck a nerve. 'I still have a trick or two up my sleeve, and you wear longer sleeves than I do. Certainly, with your powers of persuasion, you can rally enough of those young hotheads to your cause?'

'Do my ears deceive me, Sire, or are you offering to put your services – dubious though they may be – at my disposal.'

Taking a cup from the tray, Edmund grabs the pitcher and pours wine for himself. 'This one time, my Lord, let us join forces and not allow past events to overshadow what we might accomplish if only we trust one another.'

Gaunt hesitates for just a moment before he throws away the towel. 'Whom can you rally?'

'Mowbray for one.' For all his talk of trust, Edmund does not trust Gaunt and yet, he has to make an offer of information to achieve what he wants. 'You?'

'Besides my wayward brother Thomas?' Gaunt strokes his beard to get the last drops of water out. They fall into the sputtering candle sitting next to the washbasin. 'I see you are surprised, Sire, but I will have you know that, whatever else Thomas is, he is loyal to his family. With your namesake Edmund at his side to ensure he will not cause trouble; he will join me, they both will. Now, you have three Dukes in support of your cause. I also count Arundel loyal to me.'

'I can bring de la Pole to the table,' Edmund offers and smiles as surprise changes hands. 'Yes, my Lord, I make friends quite easily.'

'De Vere will never back us.' Stepping close, Gaunt's eyes roam across Edmund's face. 'And I wonder how you will manage to persuade Mowbray to side with me.'

'I employ his youngest brother.' Edmund enjoys the last of the wine, soon he will have to brave the Scottish rain again. 'Moreover, he is an ambitious bastard who will stop at nothing to assert his own authority. I am quite confident that I can win him over.'

'The King and he were best friends,' Gaunt says.

'They were, my Lord, but that is in the past. I believe that Thomas Mowbray has little love to spare for de Vere, a man who not only replaced

Mowbray as the King's favourite, but also a man thoroughly unworthy of such interest. At least the Baron Mowbray thinks so, and who are we to argue?' The death of John Mowbray transferred the title of Baron to Thomas, a matter that Edmund has found great satisfaction in of late.

Silently, Gaunt dresses anew, summoning his squire and two servants to help him. Edmund watches from the shadows as a mighty golden chain is laid carefully around Gaunt's shoulders and clasped at the back. When the squire offers up Gaunt's cloak, he points to the luxurious cot, and the squire lays the cloak out flat, bows low and ushers the two servants from the tent, dripping a trail of rain in their wake.

In the pause, Gaunt seems to have made up his mind. 'Let us proceed at once. This is not a matter that can be kept waiting, we must strike now, and strike true.'

Edmund shakes out his wet cloak and throws it over his shoulders, it falls heavy around his legs and clings to his shoulders. 'When this is done, I suspect we will both be out of favour for a while.'

'I always envied your optimism, Sire.' Gaunt's eyes glitter. 'I think that we will be out of favour for a long time. I have other pursuits to entertain, but what will you do? For you cannot expect me to offer you a place in my service.'

This time, Edmund does smile. 'What I do is for the good of the Crown to protect England. No King can ask for any more than that.'

Gaunt picks up his cloak and strokes the ermine trim. 'You mean to let someone else take the fall for you.'

'Let some young hothead stumble, what is that to me? Or to you, my Lord?'

'Sometimes, I forget how well that I like the way you think, Sir Edmund, even if you are a devil.' Gaunt turns the gold and garnet ring on his finger. 'This, perhaps, is why men look up to you, because you are never tainted by deceit, even when you are the one deceiving everyone else.'

'I learned to play the game from the greatest of them all,' Edmund says eager to be away. If they are to succeed at the council tomorrow morning, they must move fast; the time for idle conversation is over. 'What will you do once the deed is done?'

'Castile needs a King; I need a crown.' A languid smile plays at the corners of Gaunt's mouth. 'But first, we must do our deed.'

'Bring your brothers and Lord Arundel to the table, and I shall provide the rest,' Edmund promises. 'I am certain that Lord Warwick can be prevailed upon. As can Montagu, he and I have often seen eye to eye. The only thing I ask is that you do not look to me to speak up tomorrow.'

'Someone must,' Gaunt says; threat and warning lace his words.

'Leave that to me. After all, there is someone here in camp who thinks himself far above all of us – even above you. Someone who thinks himself untouchable.' Edmund pushes the flaps open. 'He will do the job, and well too, I expect, for he is a man even the King cannot deny.'

# CHAPTER 27

## 3 September 1385 – Westminster Palace

'I blame you, uncle, for this fiasco!' The young King glares at Gaunt. 'I had such expectations, but you failed me utterly.'

Gaunt struggles to keep his temper contained. 'I did warn you, nephew …'

'Warn me that the Scots would not fight? Warn me that I would look a fool in front of all my subjects? Oh no, uncle, I do believe you never once said any such words.' The King looks about and his young followers snigger. 'You never were worth your salt as an advisor. You did a poor job by my father; you did a poor job by my grandfather and all of London hates you!'

Westminster Palace is a bright beacon of riches and power, but today, the King's chambers seem dark and oppressing. The weather is as downcast as the English army that returned from Scotland, no one is satisfied, no one feels safe anymore. Just the way Edmund likes it best. These days, it does not do to trust in anyone, only in yourself, but Edmund counts new followers and friends among the men who went to Scotland, and for that he is pleased.

'I always supported your father in his endeavours, your Grace, and my father too,' Gaunt says, his grey eyes flashing. 'Even in their foolish war to aid King Peter, which ultimately resulted in what sits before me today. A child King with no idea how to govern a country; who will not listen to reason.'

'Mind yourself, my Lord,' Warwick says with a smirk. 'Beware you do not find yourself speaking treason.'

Gaunt looks equally insulted and incensed. 'Do not presume yourself above me, my Lord! I have given as good council as any of you. I supported you when you asked the King to spare Edinburgh, you are as much to blame for this fiasco as I am, if not more!'

This is going rather well, Edmund thinks, let them bicker amongst themselves. He lingers in the shadows, certain that neither Gaunt nor Warwick will ever deign to draw Edmund into the discussion. After all, they cannot be seen to take advice from a lowly knight and, besides, old animosity is the best fuel for a fight. Edmund is still pleased that he convinced Warwick to back Mowbray when he went before the King, knelt and pleaded for Edinburgh to be spared. The moment Mowbray won the argument was when he insisted that to burn innocent women and children was unholy and unchivalrous, words Edmund had put into his mouth.

'My dear friend Warwick saved me from a cruel fate, uncle,' the King sneers and glares at Gaunt. 'But it does not diminish the shame that I feel of what came to pass. I do blame you for my misfortunes in Scotland, for without your vague council, I would never have suffered as I did. My army would never have suffered as it did! You are bad luck; everyone knows it. I should never have trusted you with any responsibility; I should have left you at home. It is your fault that I had to go to Scotland in the first place!'

'How so, nephew?' Gaunt no longer attempts to be civil. 'How am I responsible for your rash and immature decisions?'

Unsettled, the King looks about for friendly support and finds it easily in his young followers. Edmund tries to gauge the mood in the room; if Gaunt is sent packing, there is a sudden opening at the King's side, and this time, Edmund will not let some child snatch it up. He means take what is his by right; a seat at the King's table and Edmund's words in the King's ear. There is no doubt in Edmund's mind that the King is far from ready to govern England on his own, but given the right kind of advice and guidance – by the right kind of people – he may in time be shaped and forged into the King his father never got to be.

'I remember how you wanted to rush home when the peasants entered London!' The King's words come out a little weak, but acknowledging grunts from the assembled men encourage the King. 'You should have trusted me, uncle, to be able to control my own people. As I well proved. Did not I brave the archers and disperse the rebels? Did I not pay them back in kind? I am full well capable of making my own decisions. While you – you are bad luck! You should have stayed at the border and struck a deal with the tiresome Scots, as I instructed; you should have made them acknowledge me as their sovereign and we would have had done with them!'

Gaunt grips the hilt of his sword. From behind, Edmund sees how his fingernails dig into his palms, spilling blood. Naturally, Gaunt is enraged, for it was the King himself who called Gaunt back from the border when the rebellion was stamped out. Edmund slides his hand to his own sword.

'Is that so, your Grace?' Gaunt's words freeze the room.

'Yes, uncle, that is so.' The King rises. 'I would never have had to leave my cherished wife. I could have concerned myself with governing my lands, not playing at war with a people who will not give it! You FAILED!'

'You failed.' Gaunt's words splinter like glass on tiles.

Stepping close, the King stares into Gaunt's face. They are now of a height, but the King is still a growing youth whereas Gaunt has reached his prime. It is a battle of wills and neither will bend to the other. Edmund notices that Langley and Woodstock are eyeing the power play with disinterest, why are they not more concerned about what might happen if Gaunt and the King fall out?

'I failed?' Incredulous the King shakes his head. 'No, uncle, I believe you will find that if you had followed my orders rather than lecture me at Edinburgh, we would have had our battle with the Scots. We would have triumphed, and history would remember me as the King who finally had the savages of the north bend their knee to the King of England. Instead, you have let me return a fool.'

'The truth is never what we wish it to be, nephew.' Gaunt glances at Edmund, but finds no help from him, just as he promised. Aggravated, Gaunt tugs at his beard. 'In time, you will discover that your decision to spare the Scots will serve you well. When we enter into new negotiations …'

'If you think that I shall ever trust such a task to you again, my Lord,' the King flares, 'you are sadly mistaken! While I might grow weary of some of my advisors, I find I have no use of you at all!'

Finally, Woodstock steps forward, as Edmund expected he would, with a slick smile on his face. 'Your Grace, dear nephew, we none of us can imagine the pressure you endure as King. We understand, do we not, Sir Edmund, that the decisions you face are never simple. We understand that to govern is not easy. I do believe that perhaps my brother simply forgets himself.'

Irritated that Woodstock draws him into an otherwise entertaining argument, Edmund decides to make the most of it. 'My Lord Woodstock speaks true, your Grace; I should never presume to understand the burden placed upon your shoulders.'

'Lick his boots all you like, brother,' Gaunt says eying Woodstock and ignoring Edmund. 'I for one am done.'

'I hear Henry misses his father,' de Vere titters, and the King laughs out loud.

'Well said, dear friend. Yes, uncle why do you not go and find your son, who was so strangely absent from this endeavour. Tell him that I sent you, so that he might not feel alone anymore.' The King has his arm around de Vere's shoulder the two of them smirking. 'Is he still afraid of the dark?'

Edmund looks at Gaunt whose face has turned to stone. In the end, it is Thomas Mowbray who interferes, as Edmund suspected he might do; he never can keep out of a good argument. With his silver tongue, he never should, Edmund thinks, as long as he works for me.

'Your Grace is in the right. Lord Gaunt might prefer to have some time with his wife, some chance of winning his own fame on the field and even a crown for his head.' Thomas glances at Gaunt. 'You have plenty of advisors.'

The King sobers and looks intently at Mowbray. 'You think that you can do a better job, my Lord?'

'I presume no such thing,' Mowbray says with a callous gesture. 'You are free to choose your advisors as you see fit.'

Mention my name, you little twat, for once in your life think of someone other than yourself, Edmund thinks, and name me as principal advisor. You hate de Vere as much as I do, what can you possibly hope to achieve by putting such notions as these into the King's head? You know full well that he will turn to his pet, a man wholly without spine, and you would let him? For the first time, Edmund thinks that Thomas is as skilled in duplicity as he is himself – perhaps even a little better.

'Yes, so I am, my Lord, so I am.' The King looks up and catches Edmund's eye. Something runs across his face, but before Edmund can tell what it is, it is gone. 'Very well, uncle, if you wish to pursue your own fortune, so be it. It will get you far away from me, and that is what I want! The very last thing I need is a Judas at my court, whispering in my ear. You will see that I can do better by myself with my own appointed advisors than I ever have with you!'

'Is that so, your Grace?'

'Oh yes uncle, I see it quite clearly now!' The King does a round in the room, ending up next to Edmund. He looks up and smiles. 'I have Sir Edmund – he will be the seasoned voice of reason. After all, he fought beside my father and caught a French prince for him when you did nothing. He rode across enemy lands to send word to my grandfather that my father lay sick and ruined in Aquitaine. He has served me faithfully since I was a small boy, and he gives sound advice. He will do fine!'

Edmund lets a smile play on his lips and looks at Gaunt, who is realising that he has been pushed into a corner, been played for a fool and that he has done so to himself. Would that Gaunt could see the look upon his own face, for it is as amusing as it is liberating.

Gaunt's angry gaze comes to rest not on the King but on Edmund. 'Then I wish you good luck.'

Across from Edmund, de Vere wears a sneer and a rattled expression all at once. It must be dawning on him that I have won, Edmund thinks, he must be realising that he is cast aside for once. I have struck two birds with one arrow.

'He needs no well-wishes from you,' the King says. 'He is honest and a great friend. Unlike you, uncle, who only ever coveted my crown and my throne. Truly, everyone sees it!'

'Your Grace,' Woodstock says in his melted butter voice. 'Perhaps …'

'Perhaps you need to consider whom to back, uncle Thomas.' Danger surges in the King's voice. 'Perhaps now is a good time to keep quiet.

Perhaps you should consider yourself lucky that you are not asked to leave too!'

Flustered, Woodstock steps back, Langley patting his back. The two brothers exchange an inscrutable glance and then turn their attention to their oldest brother. Gaunt has released his grip on the hilt, markings of the intricate pattern embossing his palm.

'You may go, my Lord Gaunt.' New sniggers and woops spur on the King. 'I release you from your duties. I remove you from my council. Your services are no longer required.'

Turning without bowing to his nephew, Gaunt brushes past Edmund, Woodstock and Langley half-running to catch up. 'Brother!'

Waves of laughter wash over the shamed Gaunt and push him and his brothers through the doors. De Vere is clasping the King's hand congratulating him on a job well done and no doubt hoping he can save his position and outwit Edmund. Others are quick to mimic the King's friend hoping a little of de Vere's prestige will rub off on them, and the King is too preoccupied with his young cohort to notice that Edmund slips from the room. In the badly lit hall, Woodstock is grabbing Gaunt by the shoulder, whispering something in urging tones while sad-eyed, Langley shakes his head.

'Brother, I implore you not to leave,' Langley says as Edmund comes close. 'The King cannot spare you.'

'You heard the little cockerel. It is time to let him drown in his own misconceptions. I am done! My brother never listened to me until it was too late and, even then, it was only to tell me that I should have spoken up sooner, insisted harder. Now, I try to do just that, speak up at once and insist harder.' Gaunt is tense with anger. 'But it falls on deaf ears! No more!'

'He will never like being gainsaid!' Woodstock snorts. 'It does not matter if it is you or someone else. He will only ever listen to those foolish enough to support him.' Catching sight of Edmund, Woodstock points. 'Fools such as him. The glorious Sir Edmund!'

Edmund knows better than to defend himself. If the King's ears are closed to advisors speaking against him, Woodstock's are closed to all those daring to speak at all. When Edmund looks at Gaunt, he gives the smallest of nods, before he shakes off Woodstock's hand and slams open the massive doors leading into the courtyard. A crown awaits in Castile, and

Gaunt's head is bare. 'NO! I have suffered enough insults. You make your own choices, but I shall not stay in a country where my advice is not wanted!'

From the shadows, Edmund watches Gaunt snatch the reins from his squire's hand and jump into the saddle as if the Devil is biting at his heels. Gaunt careers out of the courtyard, his retinue scrambling to follow suit.

A moment later, Edmund walks into the sunlight, turning a smile to the sunny sky. First to meet him is Argyle, his blue eyes wide at the commotion. Carelessly, Edmund brushes off Argyle's questions, he knows that the King's mistake is his luck. The path is cleared for Edmund to become the voice of reason, as the King himself claims that he is. With Gaunt out of the way, the King can roam free and will no doubt make the most of his newfound freedom – and Edmund means to make equally much of his. Woodstock and Langley are poor substitutes for Gaunt's hard-earned knowledge and ability to teach life-lessons, but Edmund can teach some life-lessons of his own, and gain favour to boot.

'Are my men ready?'

'Yes, Sire. But what …' Argyle's baffled face makes him look simple. Edmund hates that he has fathered a simple boy.

'None of our concern. Perhaps a few egos were bruised, but that is naught to us.' Edmund takes the reins from Argyle and swings himself into the saddle, rejoicing in the subtle leather padding and the shining pommel. His saddle has always brought equanimity. 'Make sure everything is packed before you ride out.'

He leaves Argyle with a stunned look on his face. The dust from Gaunt's retinue dances on the horizon, and Edmund is happy to meet the first cross-roads and see nothing but the bright blue horizon when he turns south.

My time has finally come, he thinks as he spurs his horse into a canter, his four men-at-arms a few feet behind him, and I mean to make the most of it.

# CHAPTER 28

## 27 July 1392 – Westminster Palace

'I always wondered how you got de Vere to cross blades with the King.'

I knew much and more about him than he cared for the King to know, Edmund thought, and that is what I used. 'It was a game of high stakes, my Lord and, in such a game, someone is bound to lose his head and act out of turn and character. In this case, I called in a favour; I never spoke to de Vere at all.'

Gaunt tapped his finger on the armrest. 'Not many could goad him, but I suppose that you found someone who could.'

'Whatever the case,' Edmund said evasively and listened as the bells tolled announcing the coming of a new day. Midnight already, Edmund thought, I must not dawdle. He looked at Gaunt, 'it changed the King's mind. It saved the lives of thousands of Scots, and it took us back to England. Well, almost all of us. But then, you had already decided to leave at that point, I believe.'

'If I had known what trouble you would land my nephew in once I was gone, perhaps I would have acted differently.' Gaunt let his finger trace the edge of the worn document. 'Perhaps, I would not have gone so willingly to Castile.'

Edmund looked up into the ceiling. 'I did what no one else could have done, my Lord. And I did it at your bidding. If you had stayed in England, perhaps everything had been different, but who is to say it would have turned out for the better? Will you have me believe you would have accused your own son of treason?'

'My duty to England comes before all else.'

'We both swore an oath to assist the King in every way, to protect the Crown,' Edmund smiled at Gaunt's displeasure. 'Only you saw fit to leave me to do your dirty work when your son could not. I saved the King as I have always promised I would, and now, I am about to do so again.'

'If you were indeed the mountain among men that everyone speaks off, you would be the most splendid knight that ever lived.' Gaunt gave Edmund a dark look. 'But we both know better.'

'What we both know, my Lord,' Edmund said, 'is that if I had not been present to intervene, someone very different and much less deserving would still govern England. I would remind you that I was here when you were not, I saw what you did not see. If you think for a moment, I believe your son's fanciful tales above my own recollection of events, you are sorely mistaken.'

Gaunt rose and worked his arms, no doubt trying to wake himself up, to stay sharp. 'The mind is a curious thing.'

'Mine has never led me astray as your boy's did him.' Edmund shook his head. 'For all that I am, in your eyes, unworthy scum, remember this: if I had not befriended a certain person, had not swayed him and in turn had him sway the others, England would be at war with itself. And you would be to blame.'

## 25 January 1388 – Beauworth

'This is what you get for poking at snakes,' Edmund says to Warden who is holding the reins of the grey horse. 'Keep the peace of my house until I return, Master Warden. I look to you to ensure that trouble does not flare up in my absence. No matter the news from court, stamp it out at once.'

'Off you get, Reggie, back to bed.' Warden waves at a scrawny stable boy standing nearby. 'He's as nosy as they come, M'lord, but good with the horses. Best to be weary of what you say around him though.'

They watch Reggie scuttle off into the warm darkness of the stables. Edmund realises that he hardly knows any of the stable boys and decides that, when he returns, he will make it his business to be re-acquainted with every single soul under his roof. He needs to know that he can trust his household, all of it. After two years of relative peace and prosperity in England, and a steady flow of riches from the King's grateful hand into Edmund's coffers, something ugly has reared its head. He has to cut it off before it turns its spiteful eyes at him.

'I have received a royal summons,' Edmund lowers his voice. Though he knows what must be done, he finds that, for once, he wants someone with whom to share the disturbing news. Warden is a man with a knack for keeping things to himself, and for that reason alone, Edmund would keep him employed for the rest of his life.

'The King is taken prisoner in the Tower, confined to a single room and constantly surrounded by his enemies. It seems his uncle, Woodstock,' Edmund spits the name, 'has decided it is time that the English should have a new King, a fully grown man.'

'Not his older brother?' Warden's tone betrays his calm expression.

'From what I can gather, Lord Gaunt has naught to do with this uprising.' Edmund strokes the horse trying to soak up the animal's calm. He knows that Gaunt is in Aquitaine, enjoying the company of his constant companion Lady Catherine and their children. He also knows that Gaunt would never give orders for such a clumsy attempt to seize the English throne. However, it seems that someone would.

Edmund draws Warden close. 'Unfortunately, his son is one of the King's so-called companions. As is Lord Mowbray. And his Grace intimates that those two blowhards are involved. It seems that the King is pressed into a corner and harried day and night. All of his friends have been sent from court; they are outlawed and hunted throughout the land. Our King is alone and heavily guarded.'

That Mowbray is involved is what goads Edmund more than anything else. Since their return from Scotland, Mowbray has risen in the King's estimation because Edmund has kept drawing attention to him. For the Baron to turn his back on Edmund and conjure up such a foolish plot as this is disturbing and leaves Edmund seething inside.

'How did the King manage to smuggle out a letter for you?' Unlike others who might have been breathless from scandalous excitement, Warden's whispered question holds true concern.

'Even now, luckily, he has some still loyal to his service,' Edmund says, but does not tell Warden that those loyal servants are in Edmund's pay and consist mainly of young girls working in the King's kitchens.

Not long ago, Edmund sent word that the King should take care to have his shirts washed, and the King had understood the message for what it was intended, for surely none of the Lords currently holed up with the King would have allowed him to send a message to his most faithful knight.

'What news of de Vere?'

Edmund takes hold of the pummel and pauses with his foot in the stirrup, the cold of the smooth metal seeps through the sole of his well-worn boot. This is the only topic which has his back up. It is poorly executed and he berates himself for choices made in the past.

'Escaped, but only just. He is in France. If I am right, and part of me prays it will be so, he will live out his days there.' He would have had de Vere killed, not just on the run. As long as he is alive, he poses a threat.

Warden pats the horse on the neck. 'In safety?'

'In exile,' Edmund says and swings into the saddle. 'While I believe that the nobles are out of their league to present any kind of demands before the King, I cannot pretend that I shall miss de Vere much. He has a knack for getting the King into trouble, and with rumours running wild at court, it is better that the young buck be removed. However, they are wrong about some of the King's friends. So very wrong.'

Warden lets go of the reins. 'Maybe it's difficult to tell one kind of friend from another these days.'

'Let us hope the nobles are able to.' Edmund wields the horse around. One nobleman in particular will feel his wrath when he gets to London. 'I shall not return until I know more. Keep the peace here, Master Warden. I trust my household to you.'

Edmund raises a hand, 'Out!' he calls and his men fall in behind him. 'Keep vigilant, men! We ride against the tide!'

As soon as they have cleared out of the courtyard, Edmund hears the rattle of the portcullis. Beauworth is as safe in the hands of Warden as it would be if he were in charge himself, but if the King's desperate message is to be believed everything hangs in the balance.

Edmund growls under his breath. He has grown lazy and content, and this is how the world repays him. Once, he was the first to be asked advice and the only one who had any hold over the King. He has befriended men, he dreams of killing, and for what? So that they might rise, the moment he turns his back? How dare they imprison the King in his own castle without even consulting Edmund first? And more importantly, whose heads will roll for the King to keep his seat?

Indignation tortures Edmund as he weaves his way through the woods. The world turns from black to grey, but the sun keeps away, and the mood of his men is surly and subdued. Edmund cannot resent them, for they know only that danger roams the land, not how much is at stake nor if they will ever see Beauworth again. If the King is imprisoned then so too must his friends prepare to be, and Edmund still counts himself as one of the King's friends.

The frozen snow creaks and cracks under the horses' hooves, the sounds oddly muffled in the moist air, no wind to stir the barren branches or give flight to heavy thoughts.

'We turn here, Sire,' Ellis Archer says. As the other men, Archer is wrapped in a thick woollen cloak which hides his armour from sight. He carries a sword at his hip and, no doubt, at least one dagger concealed somewhere on his body. Behind his saddle, a bundle containing a tent and some provisions is bound tight to the horse. 'Do we know …?'

One glance at Edmund and Archer's question trails away. 'There is no telling what we might incur, so I want vigilance from all of you. The ground is hard for now, but if the weather turns, this will prove a long and arduous journey. I prefer the frost and cold to soft and slippery ground. We will break only to water the horses and to sleep. With any luck we will have roofs over our heads the whole way.'

His men nod grimly and push ahead, the horses trotting two abreast on the narrow road. As the only one, Edmund rides alone in the middle, though it is no consolation. While his men are pressed against each other, he is squashed under the weight of his own concerns, tormented by being blindsided by men he thought he had outsmarted and, most of all, he is angry that he has been kept in the dark. Fortunately, his solitude also provides the answers he needs.

Before they reach London, Edmund sends two of his men north; he needs leverage, and he knows where to get it.

## 30 January 1388 – The Tower, London

'You are brave to come here, Sire!'

Edmund bows his head in what may appear to the others as submission, but is really to hide his extreme displeasure. 'I was summoned.'

'By whom?' The hint of mockery makes Edmund concentrate hard to stay indifferent.

'Perhaps you will be kind enough to tell me, soldier, where I might find the King?'

The small slit in the door slams shut, and Edmund hears shouts and a commotion behind the barred gate. He is surprised that the Tower has been locked down in this fashion; it is worse than he had envisioned on his long journey to London. It seems no one had thought that anyone would come demanding to see the King, and the sounds behind the massive wood slabs confirm his suspicion.

Edmund stands his ground as the bell tolls for the second time. He will wait here through the night if need be even though the freezing cold has pierced to his bones already, and he cannot feel his feet. He has experienced much worse in the past, and he knows that the city is watching. The citizens and guard will see a knight come to protect his King, and they will cheer for Edmund, in the end.

Finally, the door in the gate opens and a guard waves him through. Edmund nods and sends away his men rather than demand they enter with him. Clearly, he is to be admitted alone or not at all, but to have the upper hand and appear in control is a matter of pride and power. Edmund will be seen to have both, even as he enters on foot. As soon as he is through, the door is slammed shut and barred, two guards crossing their halberds.

'This way, Sire,' a youth says and hurries towards the big, white tower looming amidst the sprawling courtyard.

Edmund peers this way and that while he follows the servant, who has set a quick pace to get him to wherever he is going. He knows better than to ask, for this boy is not in the King's employ.

A quick knock on the door is all that the servant performs before he whisks away to a no doubt much warmer and friendlier place than this deserted hallway. Edmund waits impatiently as the door slowly opens, a golden flicker crawling around the frame and beckoning him inside.

'Sir Edmund. I am surprised to see you!'

Edmund bows before Woodstock. 'I had not expected to be here, my Lord.' And that is the truth of it, Edmund thinks on, for I was asking for the King, not his tiresome uncle. I might have known that you were behind this mindless plot. Although this just proves who is in charge; such matters might change at the flick of a wrist, and Edmund is not too concerned.

'I, on the other hand, had expected the King to send word to someone. Now that he has so few friends left in England, I might have guessed he would look to you.' The words are spoken without emotion, but Edmund knows better than to relax before the mighty courtier. For all his well-bred manners, Woodstock is of Plantagenet stock, and the worst kind there is, for he has neither the dignity of the late Prince, nor the cunning of his older brother Gaunt. All he has is raw, unbridled ambition, he reeks of it.

'I did indeed receive word of a most peculiar nature from the King, my Lord.' Edmund wants to refuse the cup of mulled wine offered to him by a servant, but he is frozen to the bone and lets the warm fluid wash through his body with extreme satisfaction, 'Thank you.'

Woodstock sweeps a gesture towards a chair near the fire and Edmund accepts. Once their cups are replenished, Woodstock sends the servant away with a whisper and turns to Edmund. 'To business then.'

'I am here to see the King as you well know, my Lord,' Edmund says and thinks, and if I could, I would snap your neck and trample over your body to get to him.

'I regret that it is impossible for me to allow that you visit him.' Woodstock folds his hands and pyramids his index fingers, briefly resting them against his lips. 'The King is in council.'

'And yet, you are here?' Edmund does not care if his question is impertinent, he has brought his battleaxe of words and if blood is to be spilled, he will do it. 'Not to mention that I have received no summons for council and, as far as I can tell, neither has any of the other knights who usually sit at the table. Surely, whatever is keeping the King in council is something that might be deferred, now that I have arrived at his own command.'

'There are other able men in the realm,' Woodstock says obliquely. 'Some who may believe they know more about the ruling of a country than you – or even I.'

'You must forgive me, my Lord, if I choose not to believe you. I am tired, I am cold and I will have the truth.' Edmund can feel the warmth of the cup of mulled wine seep into his fingers. 'Why have you put the King behind bars?'

'You make it sound as if he is a prisoner.' Woodstock sips from his elaborate cup, which glistens in the firelight, gemstones bouncing bolts of colour into the room's dark corners. 'He is in council with men who can be trusted to act in England's best interest. There is nothing to concern yourself with, Sir Edmund.'

Here it is, Edmund thinks, the truth of it all. His council consists of those who feel slighted, of small-minded men with pathetic visions and little imagination. Nothing good will come from acting rash or hot-headed and so Edmund smiles to stifle his anger. 'Is Lord Bolingbroke with him?'

'Yes, my nephew is with the King.' Woodstock seems to weigh how much to elaborate on, and Edmund feels his patience stretch thin, but he does not show it. After another sip, Woodstock sighs, 'There is unrest in the country, Sir Edmund. You know as well as I do that our young King, for all he tries and is determined to rule, is no match for the King we were so cruelly denied.'

Are you hinting at the late Prince Edward, or are you lamenting your own perceived slight? Edmund thinks but keeps quiet. It is best to let Woodstock decide where the conversation goes and what is to be said. He can always probe and prod if needs be, but for now, let Woodstock think that he is in charge.

'You are clever not to press me, but then my brother always says that about you. That if you had not been such an excellent soldier, such a magnificent fighter and a fiercely loyal subject, you would have made one hell of a courtier!' Woodstock's laugh is unsettling.

'I should not presume to reach beyond my station,' Edmund says through gritted teeth. He can smell the ambition oozing from Woodstock, who is, in every way, no match for the Prince who Edmund loved as a brother. At the best of times, Woodstock is a pale replica, an empty vessel, and at worst, he is a cruel enemy.

'No, others did that for you.' Woodstock taps the armrest. 'Very well. My somewhat wayward nephew, Henry, has got it into his head that the King's friends were trying to depose all of the English noble families, to seize power and control over the King and make demands well beyond their scope. Unlike his father, Henry is never slow to react, and it seems that, to some extent, he has the right of it. Otherwise, why would the King have called upon de Vere to muster an army and march on London? Had it not been for Lord Mowbray, he might even have succeeded, and then where would we be?'

Thank you for telling me, Edmund thinks and lets time expand before asking, 'What says Lord Gaunt about his son's involvement, my Lord?'

'I could not say if he knows what goes on or not. He has enough on his plate in Castile. We need not bother him with this trifling. Though I might imagine that Henry would do nothing if his father had not sanctioned it. And while I am here, I can stand his father's role and advise him on the best course of action.' Woodstock smiles. 'I suppose if John was here, he would accuse me of being hot-headed. He might call it the curse of the young.'

'This curse is about to unleash mayhem,' Edmund reflects, he is curious. 'What happens if you succeed? What would that make you, my Lord?'

'The brother of a King,' Woodstock says icily. 'I have spent many years advising my nephew, I know as much about governing a country as anyone. I am invested in England, and in my nephew's future. I would never let Henry, or any other man, overstep the mark.'

There is something cruel and dangerous in Woodstock's words; with Gaunt far away, who is to steady the eager hand that reaches for a crown? Edmund represses a growing concern. For all that Woodstock tries to present himself as a mere servant, ready to pass the crown to his older brother, Edmund does not believe a word he says. If Woodstock takes the throne, Gaunt stands to lose much and more, for he has long since staked his success on the young King, and Edmund does not doubt that

Woodstock will never allow for Gaunt to continue in his many offices. If there is one thing Gaunt truly loves, it is his wealth. Only a threat upon his lands might induce him to return promptly to England. Edmund wonders if he can set a plan in motion that might just prove to be such a threat.

'I am certain my brother is comforted in knowing that Henry is part of this. If he has informed his father, which I assume he has,' Woodstock finishes. 'I might say that you are foolish and rash to come here, Sir Edmund, but then we all know what you are.'

Rather than take the bait, Edmund adds innocence to his reply, 'Or you might say that I am loyal to a fault, which is no more than I am expected to be.'

'You understand that no matter what transpires, Sire, your position in England is fragile at best?' Woodstock runs his finger around the rim of the cup, the slow movement is most hypnotising. 'The King loves you dearly and that is a dangerous feeling to be the recipient of.'

'Yes, my Lord,' Edmund says and puts aside his empty cup. 'And to ignore a royal summons, no matter what peril I might find myself in, is even more dangerous. Or am I mistaken? I would look to you for advice, for you seem to be so willing to dole it out, even when it is not wanted or called upon.'

'You have in your household a young man, is that not so? Someone who might prove dangerous to you.' Woodstock eyes Edmund for a moment before continuing. 'Lord Mowbray's brother.'

'Argyle, yes.' An unfamiliar tingling makes Edmund's hair stand on end. 'Though I am not aware that he is dangerous?'

'When his brother is part of the show …,' Woodstock begins and looks around in irritation, 'Where is my servant, that wretched … Ah, there you are! More wine!'

The youth who had left Edmund by the door appears from the shadows with a steaming pitcher and carefully pours first into Woodstock's cup and then Edmund's.

'Did you get my message through?'

'Yes, my Lord,' the boy whispers, 'he is coming forthwith.'

Woodstock nods condescendingly, and the boy slips back into the shadows. 'Then we shall soon have the truth of it.'

They drink in silence, the gnawing, crackling noise from the fire the only sound to fill the large apartment. Unlike his brother, who always received Edmund in his study, Woodstock entertains his company in a generously decorated and lavish parlour, the walls hung with heavy tapestries as well as large paintings and the colourful shutters barred against thick windowpanes. Edmund is looking about when a hidden door opens.

'Henry!' There is forced affection in Woodstock voice. 'Come stand by the fire, my dear nephew. I have a visitor.'

'Sir Edmund.' Henry of Bolingbroke has inherited some of his father's booming voice, but there is an elegance to it, which his father lacks. Some say that he has also inherited some of his mother's pale beauty, but Edmund knows better. Tonight, Bolingbroke looks tired and harried. 'I would have a word in private, uncle.'

'Sir Edmund must hear what you have to say,' Woodstock says and briefly pats Bolingbroke's arm. 'He will not relay our conversation. Will you?'

'No, my Lord.' A word easily given can be taken away again, Edmund thinks, let them think I can be cowed if it helps me.

'Go on.' Woodstock gestures for the servant to bring another cup of wine, which Bolingbroke takes without even acknowledging the boy's presence. Edmund notices the petulant glance as the boy slinks back into the shadows. Here is another soul who wants to wrench free from the shackles of submission.

'I am afraid things are getting out of hand.' Bolingbroke does nothing to conceal his dismay. 'Truly, uncle, I believe we must beg the assistance of my father! Warwick is running wild. If not I and Lord Mowbray – what an unlikely ally to depend on – were there, I think he would have pulled the King's garments off his back without a second thought!'

Bolingbroke is clearly shaken, but Edmund knows only too well who orders about Warwick. Woodstock will not lift a finger to change the situation, as long as it is going his way. For once, Edmund almost admires Woodstock's cold calculation, but he is also a fool who can be easily overrun when the time is right.

Woodstock offers his seat by the fire to Bolingbroke who sinks into the chair with a sigh. 'It will not be long before we must make our move.' Bolingbroke glances at Edmund. 'You are sure?'

'Yes, nephew, whatever else Sir Edmund is, he is first and foremost a champion of England,' Woodstock says in that strange soothing manner, 'I have heard him swear so before my father on bended knee.'

Edmund swallows a smile and nods.

'If you say he is to be trusted … I will not depose my cousin!' Bolingbroke's voice breaks. 'I cannot! Not even if the others were to suggest that I … NO! I never would! You have sworn allegiance to the King and so have I. We may not see eye to eye on many a matter, but to depose a King? God would strike me down! Not even for my father!'

'What do you suggest?' Woodstock asks, and Edmund spies in his face a mixture of grim satisfaction and unbridled pride.

'An allegiance with Mowbray, God help me,' Bolingbroke exhales. 'If the three of us can hammer out an accord in which we satisfy most of the noblemen's desires, we can sway Arundel. Warwick may be ambitious, but he is not stupid. He will come around, even if it is only to bide his time. It allows for my father to return. Which I believe he must.'

'How do you propose to achieve this accord, my Lord?' Edmund knows full well that a choice word or two whispered in Thomas Mowbray's ear is enough to change his mind. He is a wily man only interested in lining his own pockets. That makes him easy to work with, easy to flip.

'My cousin must agree to call Parliament. He must be made to see that, in order for him to remain King of England, needs must that he turns his back on his friends and takes advice from those more naturally inclined to be good counsellors. I will debate with him night and day until he is made to see reason.' Bolingbroke rubs his eyes. 'It will come to pass, Sir Edmund, never fear. If nothing else, my father has taught me every aspect of diplomacy, and I shall strain to do him proud. England will not fall into depravity as long as I am here. I will not allow it.'

'And Lord Mowbray agrees with you?'

Woodstock turns away from Edmund's question. Perhaps he has wondered why the King's most faithful childhood friend has decided to turn against him. Edmund knows why, or at least he believes that he does. The pieces are slowly coming together, forming a picture that is most pleasing.

'Thomas is a greedy man – and we have much wealth to bestow upon him,' Bolingbroke grumbles. 'I worry not about him nor about Arundel. I believe that once they saw what Warwick wishes to achieve, they were as appalled as I. Beyond anything, I do not think Thomas will like to see anyone else on the throne, for it would serve him ill. If Thomas helps me, we can persuade the King to agree to our terms.'

'But we must be certain that he will do as we say.' Woodstock bends over his desk, drawing paper and quill close. 'Terms must be made that will satisfy the needs of our fellow noblemen. I care not if it shocks my nephew, for if I were to go before the Lords of this land and profess that the King's friends be spared, I might as well condemn myself to Hell. Heads will roll.'

He makes a fine speech, Edmund thinks, but I see that he does not mean it. Woodstock has his eye fixed on a golden prize, and no one will be able to deter him, unless Bolingbroke manages to change Mowbray's mind. Satisfied that Edmund has, at last, understood the game, he leans back in his chair and lets the two men talk. It is better to be silent than show your hand too soon.

Bolingbroke stares into the hearth, the flames cast strange and unsettling shadows over his young face. When he speaks, his voice seems to come from far away. 'Fear not, Sir Edmund. We may not agree on much, in the great scheme of things, but neither of us wants to see a new King rise.'

'There will be trials then?' Edmund curses the many who fled England as soon as the King was in trouble. He will have to retire to Beauworth for a time and work through others. It might be done, but he does not like to put his faith in those who can be bought.

'I will make the King call Parliament, and yes, there will be trials. I suspect none of the nobles will rest before de Vere is condemned to death. They loathe him the most, and I do not resent them for he was too close to the King, too much a distraction and a danger to the government of England. Which means that he can never be allowed to return to England. The same is true for Neville and Suffolk. If only we had caught them before they made their escape.' Bolingbroke drinks the last of his wine and winces. 'They will be stripped of their lands and offices, which will be handed over to more deserving men.'

'And what of me?' Edmund does nothing to veil his curiosity.

The scratch of Woodstock's quill stops. 'You must leave at once.' Ending his writing with a flourish, Woodstock melts some wax and seals the message. 'This will see you safely back to Beauworth where you must stay. You cannot harbour any of the King's friends, no matter how well you know them. If you stay completely neutral and come only to London when I or Henry bid you, you will have nothing to fear.'

'Why me, my Lord?' Edmund asks and wonders, and for how long?

'You once fought alongside my brother, you captured a Prince of France, you survived wounds that lesser men would have succumbed to. And though you may not believe me, I think that you have only ever offered the King sound advice. For those reasons, I cannot make myself get rid of you. For now.' Woodstock claps his hands once, the sound absorbed by the thick tapestries, and the young servant appears. 'Take Sir Edmund to the back gate. Tell no one that he was here – or I will have your head off, regardless of who your mother is!'

The youth bows low and casts an angry glance at Bolingbroke who once more stares into the flames, seemingly lost in thought.

'Go now, and keep to your own house. Bring back word that the King is safe and that I – for the time being – have been appointed to aid the King.' Woodstock rises from his seat, an amused glint in his eyes. 'And rule alongside him.'

With the door in the Tower gate locked behind him, Edmund sniffs the cold midnight air. They think they are rid of me; they think I can be cowed and why would they not. It is better to be underestimated by fools than to be watched over by those who are wise to my ways.

For the first time, Edmund is pleased that Gaunt is thousands of miles away fighting for his own crown. Not that it is going well. Edmund has regular news from Gaunt's household and finds amusement in seeing this mighty Lord slighted not only by the noblemen in his new kingdom, but also by the commoners who will not accept him as their king. At times, Edmund has even wondered if perhaps Gaunt will relent and call upon Edmund's services, but Gaunt never has.

Knowledge and information are what makes a man truly powerful, Edmund muses and turns for the nearest tavern where his men are waiting for him. Woodstock told him to be on his way, but Edmund has one more thing to do before he leaves London. All he needs is to be certain that his men have reached their destination. He decides it is best to wait somewhere outside London as Woodstock has no doubt put men on the task of ensuring that Edmund leaves as agreed.

Besides making war, playing this game is what Edmund likes best and, for now, he will take pleasure in knowing that there are at least three fools locked up with the King. All he needs is one willing accomplice to guarantee that everything will turn out for the best.

At the tavern, Edmund settles the bill and gestures for his men to mount up.

'We're leaving, Sir Edmund?' Archer asks, wiping droplets of ale from his beard.

'It is no weather for either man or beast, Archer, I know,' Edmund says and clasps a hand on the soldier's shoulder. 'But we must be away, for I fear that lingering here will cause trouble for the King, and he needs no more trouble.'

Edmund is careful to say the last loud enough for the barmaid to hear him. Gossip never travels as fast as on the lips of young women eager to impress young men, and this one will no doubt be telling everyone she serves, for the next many days, that one of the King's closest friends fears for his wellbeing. Edmund smiles at her and then turns for the door. 'We ride for Beauworth to wait out the result of this most impossible situation.'

Outside and mounted, Edmund leans towards Archer. 'I hope you trust me?'

Archer lowers his voice. 'I would give my life for you.'

'That will not be necessary,' Edmund says with a carefully measured smile. 'I need you to ride north too, at the halfway mark, contract a messenger and have him go the rest of the way. To Framlingham. I have need of fast information, and I trust you to ensure I get it.'

Two by two, the men ride into the night. As soon as they are outside the city gates and into the sliver of trees that line the road south, Archer swerves and disappears. Edmund is confident that he will not have to wait long for his visitor. But it never hurts to be prepared.

## 4 February 1388 – Camberwell, outside London

'What do you want?' As usual, disdain drips off Mowbray's tongue, but his face betrays his words.

'I am given to understand that you have been approached by Lord Bolingbroke.' When Mowbray winces, Edmund pushes his thumb in further. 'Perhaps you have already forged a prosperous alliance, my Lord?'

'You no more think of me as *my Lord* than I think of you as an honest man,' Mowbray spits and hisses when Edmund smiles, 'you are too easy in your ways and too free with your smiles. As is my useless brother, who dwells under your roof and never answers any of my letters. Tell me, Sir Edmund, is he deliberately disobedient to me because you have told him to be, or is he just a dolt?'

The small inn chamber is clean and tidy, the linen white with blue stripes and the mattress new. The small table by the window and the chair Edmund is currently occupying are well-made and spotless. To be indoors in a place with plenty of food and drink and a soft bed to sleep on when the weather is foul is not a bad way to spend time waiting. Even for a reluctant visitor. Still, the inn grows more cramped every day he has to stay in his room, and Edmund is ready to leave. He just has to ensure that Mowbray knows his place.

'I knew not that you were in contact so regularly,' Edmund says careful to keep his smile on. 'Perhaps he is simply young and forgetful? It happens to us all, is that not so? Just as you have forgotten whom you serve.'

Mowbray grabs the nearest cup and throws back the wine. He wipes his chin and scowls. 'I have forgotten nothing, and do not think for a single moment that I serve you!'

'I should imagine you serve the King.' Edmund takes a sip of his own drink. 'Though you serve him badly at the moment.'

'His friends had to go.'

Edmund puts his cup down. The motion is slow and careful, measured to underline that he has the upper hand. 'On whose orders?'

This time, it is Mowbray who smiles, but it just makes him look sick. 'I should think yours, Sire, for I distinctly remember you saying that de Vere had to be got rid of. That he had outlived his purpose and was a bad influence on the King. Well, you got what you wanted, I did your dirty deed. The King's worrisome friend is exiled and cannot return.'

'What would you have done if you had captured him?' Edmund is honestly curious. 'For you understand, do you not, that if you had brought de Vere back to London in chains, your accomplices would have had him beheaded. Regardless of what the King had said or done.'

Mowbray pours another drink, his hand trembling. 'Lucky then, is it not, that de Vere escaped? You see, you are not the only one who knows how to play the game anymore. There are many and more pieces on the board than you take into consideration, and many more who move them. The simple times of old are gone, Sire, and so should you be. You are no use anymore, and I should not have come.'

When Mowbray reaches for the door, Edmund says indifferently, 'I almost forgot – your wife sends her regards. And your eldest son too.'

The hand floats, shudders and then balls into a fist. Though he does not turn, Edmund knows that Thomas Mowbray is caught, and he is furious.

'I want you to accept the deal that Bolingbroke proposes.' Edmund takes another sip. 'Make what you can for yourself from it, I care not. Make sure some heads do roll, I grant you that it is necessary – and needless to say, my head will not be among them. Perhaps it will soothe some of the bristling Lords if de Vere is condemned to death.'

'You hate him that much?' Mowbray's voice is barely a whisper.

'He has certainly outlived his purpose, and he is a poor defender of the King, as he proved when you attacked him,' Edmund says and waits for Mowbray to turn around. 'If he were to return, all hell would break loose and you know it. If he returns, he will pave the way for Woodstock to do what he truly desires, though he was quick to dismiss the notion when I met with him. He will not stand aside to let anyone else close.'

'He desires the crown for his own.' Finally, the young Baron turns, his cheeks flush red. 'If I do what you ask, what do you want in return?'

'I have already secured my position and without any effort at all. Naturally, I will play the part of thwarted friend to the King, I will rumble in my halls and lash out at those who took the King captive.' Edmund gestures. 'It is to be expected of his most ardent friend.'

Mowbray looks around the simple, well-equipped room, his face laced with enmity. 'You want to keep Beauworth and all your pensions. Is that it?'

'A suitable compensation for sitting idle, do you not think so, my Lord?'

Again, Mowbray hisses and slams his hand against the limewashed wall. 'You are not my master! You do not tell me what to do, whom to speak to or what deals to make!'

'I would never presume to tell you anything.' Edmund rises and, in two easy strides, blocks the door. 'I only offer council, as I have done so many times before. What you make of it is entirely your business.'

Although it is evident that Mowbray knows he is beaten, he puts up a fight. 'I never sought your council; what use would a Baron have of a lowly knight? You live on the grace of the Crown, and right now, the Crown is not held by a boy whom you can have dance after your pipe! It is in the hands of a devious man with plans of his own that would curdle your blood.'

Edmund leans against the door, the wood worn smooth in patches, but rough under his shoulder blades. 'Woodstock means to have the crown to himself, even if he has to topple a King and kill him.'

Mowbray sits on the bed; his whole being trembling. It is one thing to think of malice, Edmund contemplates, it is another thing entirely to have it thrown in your face. It is a good that I can still scare him with words alone.

'You know it is the truth as well as I do,' Edmund says, never breaking eye contact. 'Woodstock is a heartless brute, but fortunately, he is also a fool. One that will play into our hands – into your hands – if you let him.'

The Baron hides his face in his hands. Edmund is almost certain he has won, but to be careless at a time like this would be unwise. Instead, he drives home the point, 'A few days ago, he was indiscreet enough to tell me that he will accept a deal, if it is brokered between you and Bolingbroke, and you get Arundel on your side. I assume that the latter is easily achieved as he is your father-in-law.'

'And you have Elizabeth?'

Edmund cannot help but laugh. 'I am no gaoler, my Lord. I do not "have" her as you say. I merely have a few men ensuring that I know where she is. As a precaution. We would not want anything to befall your family. God only knows who lurks in the shadows.'

'I should not be surprised if it was you,' Mowbray says weakly. 'What is this deal you keep speaking of?'

'You bring Arundel to the table, and he in turn convinces Warwick that to overthrow a King is a terrible idea. Another thing upon which we can agree without problem, I should wager. Let Bolingbroke lead the way, he knows what the English Lords want, and what they will accept as a fair deal.' Edmund enjoys Mowbray's meek nods. 'We cannot prevent Woodstock from assuming some power, but only for a while. If anything, this provides an opportunity for you to learn to bide your time, as I have done often enough, and wait for the winds to change. Clean up the King's entourage and make sure you stay close to him and all will be well.'

Mowbray snorts dispirited. 'And if I fail?'

'I am sure you will not.' Edmund steps away from the door. 'You have too much to gain by succeeding. Among others, you will be close to the King once more, the only young man at his side who is not family. He will turn to you for comfort, and you will provide it.'

When Mowbray rises and walks to the door, he looks up at Edmund. 'My brother thinks you a saint, do you know that, Sire? A more noble and chivalrous man he has ever met. For the longest time, I thought him a simple fool, but the more I hear about you the more I think that you have charmed and deceived a whole kingdom, and I would sorely like to know how you did it.'

Edmund opens the door. 'More can be won with smiles than sneers, my Lord. That is all I know.'

'Call back your men,' Mowbray whispers, his face still strained. 'Now.'

'As soon as word reaches me that you have gone into Parliament, arm in arm with your fellow applicants and bent the knee to our King, I shall.' Edmund looks down at his guest. 'And not a moment sooner.'

# Part 5

# Legacy

# CHAPTER 29

## 27 July 1392 – Westminster Palace

Gaunt laughed, low and genuine. 'I should have known that you had a hand in that travesty. It is one thing that my son bent the knee, I would have advised the same, and he is no fool. But to walk into the hall, arms locked with his accomplices, it was well much for me to stomach.'

'A little theatre never hurt anyone,' Edmund said. 'Though I confess, I was surprised that Mowbray managed to persuade them, especially Woodstock, to make such a blatant display.'

For a while, Gaunt sat with his eyes closed, a thoughtful look on his worn face. Then he asked: 'You truly never intended to harm Mowbray's wife or child?'

'He is a weak man in many ways, though I believe that if I had acted out, he would have hounded me to the ends of the earth.' Edmund rubbed his arm. 'But no, I had no such intent. You see, I know things about Mowbray that would bring him down without my ever having to visit Nottingham. Fortunately for all, he is a clever fellow and understood that I was to be disregarded no more.'

'They underestimated you.'

Edmund grunted a laugh. 'They forgot about me. Which is a much worse crime, my Lord.'

Gaunt tipped his cup at Edmund and sent a solitary, nasty smile. 'And what about your bastard boy?'

'He was as loyal then as he is now.' The thought of Argyle, a grown man, tall, broad-chested and strong, makes Edmund smile in earnest. 'His brother has earned the family an unfortunate reputation for switching alliances faster than a snake can strike, but I caution you, my Lord, do not mistake Argyle for Thomas.'

'I have worked too long with Thomas Mowbray to put anything past him,' Gaunt concedes, 'and I know too little about Argyle to make my mind up. Perhaps I will get to know him better in future.'

'I certainly got to know your son very well.' Another smile dawned on Edmund's face when Gaunt looked stunned. 'How did you think I kept informed during my voluntary exile?'

## 6 March 1388 – Beauworth

Edmund waits for the servant to close the door before he opens the sealed letter. There is no crest stamped into the wax to reveal whom it is from, but Edmund knows. It is from the same man who has been keeping a steady flow of information coming to Beauworth for the past month or so. Bolingbroke; written in his own, immaculate hand.

How fortunate that I chose to send word to him that I had returned here, Edmund thinks, that he might trust me to be an honest man. In the weak light from his candle, Edmund has to rub his eyes to focus on the compressed words.

*Now that the King has decided to let us return England to peace, we are all hard at work. Woodstock is at the head, always attempting to root out new conspiracies and more of the King's friends. How de Vere and Surrey must congratulate themselves that they are safely away from our shores. They may have a death warrant hanging over their heads, but if rumours are to be believed, at least de Vere is living comfortably enough with his destiny and has, since the divorce from my cousin Philippa, taken a new wife, a former chamber maid to the Queen no less. She now lives in exile with him, and so, I am forced to acknowledge that perhaps he has some love in his heart to call her to his side. They say the couple has been welcomed at the French court and lacks for nothing in the way of companions or pleasures. But then I suppose that such flatterers as he most certainly is can thank his easy manners that he will never want for companionship. You must know that Brembre has been condemned to death and now awaits the executioner. He suffered it quite well. It is not he, nor the others I worry about. My chief concern is my cousin the King. His desire to fight has quite gone out of him. He seems most dejected and downcast.*

Edmund looks up just in time to see an early messenger of spring swooping down outside his window. Following the swallow with his eyes, Edmund thinks that to everyone at court, he must be congratulating himself that he has not fallen prey to the vindictive Lords, but he loathes being cooped up at Beauworth while others have the King in their hands. Not even the fair prospect over the grounds and forests soothes him anymore.

Turning to the letter, Edmund is surprised as he reads on.

*Sir Simon was next to be tried for his alleged crimes, though we both know that all he ever did was be a friend and mentor. Woodstock was keen to make sure this one too would face the executioner. No matter how much the King pleaded to spare Sir Simon's life, Woodstock would display his supreme power. I tried to intervene and so too did Mowbray, for all the good it did us. In the end, the Queen went down upon her knees, crying and begging for Sir Simon's life. If the scene had not been so horrendous, I might have smiled a little at her theatrics, but Woodstock would not be moved. We did all that we could, even my uncle York attempted to sway his younger brother behind closed doors and later in the courtroom, but to no avail. Sir Simon was taken directly to the block and now his head adorns the gates to the Tower. I know that he is wholly without blame. It is appalling. It is unnecessary. I try to applaud myself that we saved the King, but I cannot. He may look dispirited now, but if he is anything like his father and grandfather, the repercussions of what has transpired thus far will beggar belief. He will not stand for this; I know he will not! If only he remembers that I tried to save his tutor's life. But I doubt it. I have sent word to my father too that he might know what has happened here, and I confess that I have urged him to come as soon as possible to check his brother. All we can do now is pray.*

When any man assumes such power as Woodstock has claimed for himself in such a short span of time, it seems terror must flow in its wake.

Edmund wonders how differently he would have managed the situation had he only been present at court. But since he is not, all he can do is let his imagination roam free and plan a future that seems far away. At least it seems that Bolingbroke is every bit as loyal to the King as his father is. That is something to hold on to, because it ensures that Woodstock will be checked, especially if and when Gaunt decides to return from his frugal attempts to put the Castilian crown upon his head.

But Edmund also agrees with Bolingbroke that the King will never forgive the men whose actions set in motion the fall and death of his favourite tutor, Sir Simon. Or the lifelong exile of de Vere. If only de Vere would have the decency to fall ill and die, some of the King's vengeance might be stifled.

If Woodstock believes, even for a moment, that taking all the King's closest friends to the chopping block is enough to ensure the King will never stray again, Edmund knows that Woodstock reckons without his host. It is a matter of time before something happens that rekindles the King's fighting spirit and sets new wheels in motion. Until such a time, Edmund must find something else to occupy his thoughts.

Since Thomas Mowbray has proven to be an ally, although reluctant, Edmund decides it is time to test the loyalty of another Mowbray. Argyle has received no letters from court, Edmund knows, because he has men and women in his pay at court, and Argyle suffers the injustice of being suspected of treasonous acts by all of Edmund's servants. They keep a sharp eye out, and Edmund pays them well to do so.

Still, he must know that the boy is loyal. Thomas let slip that sometimes he sent word to Argyle, and that will not do. For though Edmund knows that, this time, Mowbray did as he was bid, he might not do so again in the future. And if this is to be the last time, Edmund can use the Baron, he must secure the only remaining brother onto himself, swear him to his house and his service. Mould Argyle in Edmund's image and make him realise that he cannot serve two masters.

He opens the door to the hallway and stops a passing page. 'Fetch me Master Argyle.'

When Argyle steps through the door, Edmund feels a surge of unexpected pride. The young man is tall, broad of frame and has the most striking golden hair, which sets off his shocking blue eyes. If he is not

Edmund's son then what is he? Anyone can tell that there is not a drop of Mowbray blood in him.

Then and there, Edmund decides to tell Argyle most of what he knows and even voice a few of his concerns. If he is to be of any use to Edmund, Argyle must know what is at stake. Time to prove once and for all, if Thomas Mowbray was right about his brother, or if there is more to Argyle than meets the eye. Edmund hopes for the latter.

'I should think you would be interested in the latest news from court, Master Argyle. Or have you already heard?'

## 18 August 1388 – Westminster Palace

Edmund is waiting in the grand reception room outside the King's private chambers. The shifty mood of the room seeps into Edmund's skin and mingles with his sweat. Everyone seems out of sorts; do they know what is happening?

'Sir Edmund.'

With all the courtesy he can muster, Edmund bows. 'My Lord Mowbray.'

'How long since we have seen the King's great friend here in London. Should we be honoured?'

Thomas Mowbray may look like his father, Edmund thinks, but he is a pale reflection in opaque glass, his ambition so strong it hangs about him as a stink. Edmund knows that etiquette dictates he is to respond, but he does not. Although his hold on Thomas has weakened, there is still vague disconcert in the young man's eyes, and that is enough to tell Edmund that all is not yet lost.

In the end, it is the Baron who speaks again, 'Ah well, all will be revealed soon enough, would you not say?'

'If the King would only see me.'

'Which one?' Mowbray whispers and winks as if to convince Edmund that they are still allies. 'The one on the throne or the one with the seal? I have access to both these days.'

'The King is lucky to have such great friends as you, and such great council as his uncle.' His words are sticky as summer honey, and Mowbray shrinks a little. 'I hear that you never stray far from the King's side in these troubled times, and you must allow me to express my gratitude for your constancy.'

Something in Mowbray's demeanour changes and Edmund thinks; good, you can still be caught by surprise. This will prove to be of great value to me later on, because I mean to make the most of this first olive branch someone has been foolish enough to extend to me.

The young Baron puts a hand on Edmund's shoulder. 'Once the audience is over, seek me out. There is something we must discuss.'

'Sir Edmund!' Woodstock's voice snakes around Edmund's ankles like silken shackles. 'I wonder what has teased you from your lair?!'

'My Lord Woodstock.' Edmund bows low and arranges his face. 'A royal command.'

The whisper of concern on Woodstock's face is quickly replaced by a smile. 'I see, how curious. How very curious indeed. Well, I am sure you are most welcome at court and have been long missed by our King. Though as you know, kingship requires much from any man who sits the throne and our beloved ruler has been busy of late.'

Busy dangling from your strings, Edmund thinks and nods along. 'Will the King be able to see me today, my Lord?'

'Let me determine if it is worth the King's while to grant you an audience, or if we may between us lay to rest whatever is troubling you.' By his words, Woodstock acknowledges what rumours have long whispered about; that he is regent and the King a puppet. Woodstock ignores Mowbray who in turn stares idly into the distance. 'This way.'

Edmund matches Woodstock's rapid pace with ease, but the prying eyes in the reception room follow him to the door and beyond. Behind closed doors, Woodstock's smile turns into a sneer and he grabs Edmund's arm. 'Why are you really here?'

'A letter with the royal seal.' Edmund resists the urge to shake off Woodstock's touch. Let him think he has the upper hand. Glancing around, Edmund lowers his voice. 'I am surprised you did not know, but as it is I had to come, my Lord. Is it true?'

Woodstock pushes Edmund into an alcove and draws the thick curtains behind him, burying them both in the stifling August heat. 'Is what true?'

'That the King is amassing his own army? Soldiers loyal only to him?' Though Woodstock's expression remains immovable, Edmund can taste fresh fear oozing from the opulently dressed royal uncle. 'Or is it perhaps your doing, my Lord?'

'Why would I encourage the King to build his own army? When all he has to do is call upon the Lords of England to muster their men.' Woodstock puts a hand on Edmund's shoulder and turns him to the narrow, soaring window. 'Have you announced your arrival?'

'To enter the palace these days, it seems you must,' Edmund says and feels Woodstock's hand tighten. 'I did not leave Beauworth with an easy conscience, for I know you do not want me here.'

'No. A letter would have sufficed. Directed to me. The King should not be alerted to such lies and deceit as has raced across the land to you. Might this be another attempt from the south to rise against their rightful Lords?' Woodstock's voice never reaches above a whisper, but his fury burns bright. 'If you are here to stir up trouble with tales of how the King must raise his own army, let me be the first to warn you, Sire, you will not succeed!'

Edmund looks at Woodstock, though he is certainly handsome, there is something uniquely distasteful about him. 'We have an agreement, my Lord, and one that I intend to honour, but what would it look like if I disregarded a royal command? How would you explain away that I did not come directly? How would I? If you want to keep the King in the dark, you must play your part. More fool you, if you think I would hatch such a half-witted plan. For that is what this is. He has no need of an army, you say, but I understand perfectly if he disagrees with you. And you would do well to acknowledge that fact too.'

'Perhaps.' Woodstock removes his hand as understanding finally dawns. 'You are refusing to join his cause?'

'Is this your way of telling me that what was treasonous a moment ago is indeed the King's true intent, hatched by him and not someone else?'

Footsteps approach and Woodstock holds up a hand. In the silent wait for whomever is on the other side of the curtain to pass and move on, Edmund enjoys the sight of Woodstock squirming next to him. Though a tall man, Edmund towers over him and in such close quarters, even Woodstock's vanity cannot protect him from feeling inferior.

'There have been whispered rumours,' Woodstock says when he is satisfied that they are once more alone. 'And my nephew has been much in Chester of late, but I thought he was there to rest and grow strong and to show the Queen a change of scenery. Even court can grow tedious for a young couple.'

You have never cared two straws for the Queen, Edmund thinks, but I see that with the King in Chester, much of your work here is easier to carry out. How dreadful you must feel to know that the man you tried so hard to rid yourself of earlier this year has played you. For though the King is little loved in England, Woodstock cannot even claim love in his own dukedom.

Edmund leans against the cool stone wall and looks down at the small walled garden below. He lets Woodstock flounder a little longer before he speaks, 'I have no reason to think that the King would lie about building an army. Though I confess that I did, briefly, suspect this to be a plot to remove him from power, and I am glad to be proven wrong. If he has indeed been much in Chester, no doubt it is not the countryside that has called out to him, but more likely the fact that in Chester they excel in the use of bow and arrow.'

'If the King …'

'He will have to look elsewhere for a seasoned knight to head his army,' Edmund says dismissively and sees relief in Woodstock's eyes. The trap is set. 'I am here to renew my pledge to defend the Crown of England with my life. And to remind the King that to call into question the allegiance of a man knighted by his own father and sworn in by his own grandfather is a grave mistake. I have little doubt he will see reason, once I am granted an audience.'

'Then you agree with me that the King has no need of an army.' Comforted by Edmund's words, Woodstock returns to his natural state of superiority. 'I had imagined you would jump at the opportunity to return to royal favour.'

'I fell out of it because of you, my Lord.' Below the window the King walks with his Queen, smiling at something she says. Edmund is pleased that they are together. Many at court underestimate the Queen, but Edmund has a fair notion that she is a power to be reckoned with.

Woodstock too looks at the young couple. 'She needs to provide an heir.'

'I am certain the Queen knows her duties. At least they look at peace.' The air in the little alcove is stifling, and Edmund turns away from the view. 'I wish to speak to him. Alone.'

'You were banned from court by all the Lords.' A smug undertone sneaks into Woodstock's voice. 'I cannot be seen to suddenly favour you.'

'My Lord, I have kept word with you until today, and I only come here because I fear that the King's idea of a personal army will drive a further wedge between the Crown and the nobility. England cannot survive more strife; in that we must agree?'

The ring on Woodstock's hand glitters in the dull light as he smooths his lavish silk gown. 'I am here to ensure that the rift does not grow larger. Leave it to me, Sire.'

If you are so certain of your power, Edmund thinks, then why do you hide my presence? He looks again at the royal couple, the King offering his Queen a yellow rose. 'For how long?'

'Until he is brought to heel.' Woodstock scowls at Edmund. 'However, too many have already seen you prancing about and so, I shall arrange for the King to see you later today. I trust that you will repeat your refusal to join his army.' He pushes back the curtains and a burst of fresh air cools Edmund's neck. 'I shall grant you this boon and then you will be gone from court until such a time as I see fit for you to return. If I were you, I would not expect to come here again until you are an old man.'

At least I know now that you are still afraid of me, Edmund smiles to himself and watches Woodstock saunter back into the reception room, courtiers parting as waves before a ship's bow. How fortunate for me that he is ignorant enough to think that five minutes with the King will make no difference.

Mowbray turns his back when Woodstock approaches, and Edmund has to temper a laugh at the look of affront on Woodstock's face. Here is another Lord who is not deceived by the King's uncle and that is a good thing. Entering the great hall himself, Edmund makes sure he is seen by everyone. He smiles brightly at the many ladies, exchanges polite remarks with the courtiers and accepts refreshment when it is offered. At the opposite side of the hall, Woodstock holds court, his eyes constantly moving, taking in everything that goes on.

'All he lacks is a pretty crown to place upon his fair hair.' Mowbray sidles up next to Edmund and looks at him askance. 'I hear that he tried the King's, but it did not fit his big, pompous head.'

Repressing a laugh, Edmund follows Mowbray towards the garden doors, which are kept open to let in the soft summer sun. 'The King asks that you join him and the Queen for a breath of fresh air.' Mowbray leans in. 'I am certain that Woodstock has spun you a tale that you can meet the King later, but do not believe him. And remember me for the favour I offer you now; there may come a time when we need each other once more.'

'It will do.' Edmund allows himself to be a little surprised that Mowbray will openly defy Woodstock's supremacy. He also wonders what the Baron wants in return. For with Mowbray there is always a hidden agenda. Something Edmund takes credit for teaching him.

'Come find me afterwards,' Mowbray says in an undertone. 'I insist.'

Edmund looks about and catches Woodstock's eye. He smiles and inclines his head. 'Perhaps it is better that you find me, my Lord. You know only too well that the court has eyes and ears.'

'So does every house in England, and many of those eyes are in your pay.' Mowbray opens the doors with a great flourish. 'I will send word.'

The King looks up, a flicker of disbelief in his eyes before it is replaced with a wide smile. 'Sir Edmund! Is it really you?'

'I come to beg a moment of your time, your Grace.'

The King releases the Queen's hand and gestures to a bench. 'Then you must have it.'

ଓ ଓ ଓ ଓ

Edmund looks out into the narrow street and relishes in the stirring breeze that wafts through the window-hole. One of the shutters hangs askew, the boards are rimmed with dirt and cobwebs. He watches the life of London wind down, men pushing carts towards the river, little children trailing in their wake hoping something might fall off for them to pinch. A couple of women hustle by, their faces worn beyond their years; no doubt they work at night.

At the serving hatch, the madam and her husband quarrel with an old drunkard, his voice slurred from drink and his missing teeth. The madam slaps the man's hand away from her bulky skirt and her husband shouts over his shoulder for a platter of food to be prepared. The old man tries to fight off the madam, but she is a sturdy woman and quick to turn out his pockets and snatch what little coin he has. Then she grabs his arm and as she elbows open the door to push the boozer out, a cloaked figure slides in.

Edmund nurses his cup with no real intent to drink. When he fetched it, a quick look through the hatch was enough to quench his thirst. A candle stub melted into a mountain of old greying wax provides the only light besides the torches of passing watchmen, their flickering flames make shadows dance on the dreary low-built houses across the street.

'A fine establishment.' Mowbray pushes back his hood, careful to wrap his light brown cloak around him before sitting down. 'How is the wine?'

'Non-existent I should imagine,' Edmund says and snaps his fingers.

The madam ambles towards their table, her wide hips swaying. Mowbray gives her a brief glance. 'Now that would make lesser men seasick.'

She bends over, her breasts resting on her stomach and gives Edmund her best smile. 'Yes, M'lord knight?'

'Another cup.' Edmund returns her smile and watches red roses bloom on her blotchy cheeks. 'If you would be so kind. My friend is just come in from the docks.'

'He's thirsty then, poor bean,' she says in what is meant to be a flirtatious tone, locks of her greasy hair dangling before Edmund's nose. 'You're not, sweetheart?'

'I am enjoying your fine drink.' Another smile to seduce her into leaving. 'He will too, once he gets it.'

She squeezes Edmund's thigh before she straightens with some effort and sails away to the serving hatch from where her husband sends Edmund an irritated glance.

'Always ready to charm.' Mowbray straightens his dark hair. 'How was the King?'

'Upset and suspicious; he is a ship lost in a sea of animosity. Though he was pleased to see me, at least until I told him why I had come.' Edmund looks about. 'You are alone?'

The corner of Mowbray's mouth curls. 'Of course. You think that I would let anyone see me enter this mean hovel?'

'I once picked up your father not far from here.' Edmund leans back. 'Enjoying an establishment not unlike this one.'

'Cleaner, I hope,' Mowbray says with an edge. 'You will find that I am nothing like my father.'

'Courtier, Lord, politician. You share many traits. And yet, I agree with you, you are nothing like your father; perhaps we should both take comfort in that.'

A nod from Mowbray turns Edmund's attention to the madam, swaying her way to their table. 'Your cog returns.'

Laughing, Edmund takes the mug from her and presses a couple of coins in her palm. 'Thank you, Madam.'

She is wise enough to understand and takes herself away with a last curious glance at Mowbray, who looks at the mug with discomfort. 'You drink this?'

'No, I caught a glimpse of the kitchens beyond. But to sit in a tavern with nothing to drink will rouse suspicion. I prefer to come and go here today with no one knowing. To that end, I must be inconspicuous, as must you.'

'You think you can go unnoticed anywhere?' A watchman passes the window and Mowbray looks down, his dark hair obscuring his distinct features. 'The King?'

'As the Queen was present, he managed his temper though with some difficulty. I told him that I am as loyal to the Crown as the day I swore my oath, but to join his army while the Lords send their young men to my household to learn the art of warfare is a bad idea. I doubt he believes me, but he had to accept my explanation, what else can he do? He needs what little friends he has left.' Edmund turns his cup; it sticks to his palm. 'Now, tell me why we are here, my Lord.'

'Together we thwarted a great injustice, you and I. I swore then never to deal with you again, but it seems I have to endure you once more.' The urgency in Mowbray's voice catches Edmund off guard. 'I cannot go to Bolingbroke; he is the most distrustful man in England. Anything you say to him is sure to get to Gaunt before long, and as I am no longer certain that he has the King's best interest at heart, I have to turn elsewhere.'

How this pains you, Edmund muses and looks at Mowbray, how you hate to be here, begging me for a favour. And you should, for I will use you as a shield to gain access to the innermost workings of the court, and I will not seize until I am at my rightful place beside the King once more.

Mowbray glances out into the dark street, his long, delicate fingers tapping on the table. 'It seems Gaunt is well-informed of all that goes on in England and that he wishes for matters to unfold for the time being. At least, that is what Bolingbroke says. It appears that Gaunt is not very concerned with the King's safety.'

'And you are?' Edmund works hard to suppress a laugh; this is as outrageous as it is hilarious. 'As a spy-master yourself, you will acknowledge that Gaunt is only playing the same game as you. As all of us. Without men in our pay, how can we learn anything of importance? Rich men have but one flaw – one that we all use – that they believe themselves alone behind their own walls.'

'I did as you asked,' Mowbray sulks, his voice childish. 'Now, you will do me a favour in return.'

Edmund snorts. 'I took you in and taught you all that you know about courtly games, my Lord. I should say that my benevolence has long since returned your little favour tenfold. Tell me the real reason we are here or begone. I have long suspected that our dealings were almost at an end, perhaps it is time you stand alone. Truly alone.'

Mowbray shakes his head. 'Are you as reckless as Lord Woodstock? I would not have thought so but, now, I wonder if that is the case or if you are simply annoyed that you are not in the centre ring anymore. Even if you do not wish to serve the King in his personal army, for reasons I will never presume to understand, I still think the notion that he is to have an army brings a bitter taste to your mouth. Tell me that you are as clever as I have always thought you to be.'

Rather than voice his resentment, Edmund gestures for Mowbray to continue, which he seems more than happy to do. 'Woodstock does not understand what the King means to do once he has his own legions of archers and soldiers. He thinks it a mere past-time for the King to keep him from the council and ensure he signs whatever papers Woodstock places in front of him.'

'I have always thought Woodstock to be an idiot, although he hides it well enough.' Edmund lets a smile snake its way onto his face. 'Tell me what you plan to do.'

'I am one of a few young men still allowed to sit with the King at night, to entertain him in his private chambers,' Mowbray says. 'Do you think all we do is play cards and drink?' He pauses when another watchman walks past, shining his torch through the open window hole. When the shadows on the opposite wall flitter away, Mowbray continues. 'We discuss how he goes about reclaiming what is his by right. The army is the first step. It is just outrageous enough for Woodstock to dismiss it as a passing fancy.'

Mowbray returns Edmund's savage smile. 'I see you think as I did that it would be too great a test, but it turns out that Woodstock still views the King as a tiresome child. He does not understand that the King is a man grown, eager to assert himself. Thus, Woodstock believes that if it takes a small personal army to keep the King occupied …'

'… it is a fair price to pay to keep his place as regent,' Edmund finishes. 'I see how it is.'

'I hope you do, for there will come a time when you are once more asked to prove your loyalty, Sire, and I believe it may come sooner than you think. Consider this my final favour to you, and then we are done.' Mowbray nods and Edmund sees the madam whispering with two young men, pointing to Edmund's table. 'I think, we are about to be shown the door.'

Edmund rises and smiles at the madam whose demeanour seems to change. 'Best we leave at our own accord. But I have one final question.'

'Argyle did not know.' Mowbray pulls up his hood. 'He cannot know. I charge you with the task of keeping my brother out of trouble. I am in the thick of it as you have made sure to make me, but I have finally learned my lesson – John would have been proud of me. He always said that I was too cocky to care about learning, but I have proved him wrong. I know who to back. I am loyal.'

'Why do you not want Argyle to know?' If Edmund is to make this most curious assent, he wants something useful in return.

'Because he never did know how to keep his mouth shut.' Mowbray gives a curt nod to the madam and walks out. 'He believes the truth should always be spoken, whereas you and I know that most dealings are best left in the shadows.'

On impulse, Edmund grabs the madam's hand and presses a kiss on her rough skin and a couple of coins into her palm. He leaves her blushing in the doorway, her hand at her heart.

Mowbray is right, Edmund thinks as he turns towards the river, there are many kinds of loyalty, and the best of them are bought and paid for. But with Argyle, he will have to choose a different approach, for no matter what Edmund thinks of his son, it seems Argyle is impossible to bribe.

# CHAPTER 30

## 27 July 1392 – Westminster Palace

'I have always wondered why you passed on the opportunity to command the King's private army.'

'If nothing else, I hate to be predictable.' Edmund sighed. 'If I had said yes, I would have missed many opportunities to make an impact where it might make the biggest difference. As the King's personal general, I would have been confined to always take his side.'

'I should have known that you were never truly out of the power struggle,' Gaunt said and a smidge of admiration snuck its way into his voice. 'Even when you were confined all those years to Beauworth. I confess, I am disappointed that my own son would include you in his dealings, but then Henry is a trusting soul. You always knew all that went on.'

'And more,' Edmund agreed. 'Fortunately, it seems the King is pleased still to have a personal army of just a few hundred archers and a regiment of soldiers. I only hope it continues so. No matter what, my actions allowed me to return to my place on the King's council when he finally spoke up and claimed the crown for his own again. And there, I worked to keep the peace, for I knew then that my allegiance with the King could not suffer another prolonged absence.'

Gaunt cracked his knuckles and blinked. 'Which brings us to the present.'

'I admit, I was surprised when the Queen cornered me a week ago outside the King's chambers. But then, I have always said that she holds more power than we might imagine.' Edmund's mind wandered to six days ago.

ଔ ஐ ଔ ஐ

## 20 July 1392 – Westminster Palace

'You are certain, your Grace?' Edmund can easily believe what the King has just told him, but it does not do to let him know that this is old news.

In the corner, Queen Anne leans lightly against the back of a chair, her face is as white as the veil on her headdress. She is as slender and willowy as the day the King married her, her bosom small and her waist narrow. At the moment, she looks more like an ornament than a real person, but then she would know how to stay in the background as all Queens must.

'Quite certain.' The King's voice is cold and stilted. 'It is no secret that several among my closest relatives have never come to terms with me as their King. My uncles are far too ambitious to sit quietly in the countryside and tend to the tedious business of being proprietors. They want more. They have always wanted more.'

'I can well believe it of Lord Woodstock, but my Lord Gaunt …' Edmund pauses; he wonders why the King has suddenly decided that his chief advisor cannot be trusted. 'He made an oath to your father on his deathbed, and I know that what he promised he has honoured, your Grace. He is loyal.'

The King gives a false smile. 'Yes, my uncle John has certainly put on a show to rival the best performers in the world. Still, his own son tried to dethrone me only a few years ago. How can either think that I will not keep a keen eye on all their dealings?'

'He did not succeed.' Edmund is tiring of this worn topic and means to stamp it out. 'You decided to believe me then, and I trust you have not changed your mind about my allegiance?'

A little crestfallen, the King fiddles with his sleeve. 'Of course not, La Fontaine, I trust you with my life. But lately, rumours have flooded my court that someone is plotting against me.'

'You are a King; someone will always plot against you.' Edmund struggles not to sigh, has the King learned nothing from his years of being governed by others? He catches a glance from Queen Anne and shakes his head. 'Tell me about these rumours, your Grace, and I shall help you decide if there is any truth to them.'

As usual, the King's mood is quick to switch, now he is revived and his foot taps restlessly. 'It was Mowbray who first told me …'

Edmund grasps his hands behind his back to keep still. 'Is that so?'

'I know that you care little for Lord Mowbray,' Queen Anne finally speaks, her voice still thick with accent despite her many years in England. 'Nevertheless, I believe in him, I find him a true friend. As I find you. You promised to hear my husband's complaint, and so you must let him speak.'

A royal port for a royal storm, Edmund thinks when the Queen crosses the room to touch the King's shoulder. He acknowledges her caress by kissing the back of her hand. 'Yes, my beloved. You have never found fault with Mowbray, and so neither shall I.'

I wonder how Mowbray has succeeded in charming the Queen, Edmund considers while the royal couple is afforded a brief moment of intimacy without the entire court staring at them, judging whether the Queen is with child and whether the King is finally ready for a mistress. Edmund knows that while the Queen lives, and long may that be, the King will never have eyes for anyone else. It has frustrated many a courtier and nobleman, who has a few too many daughters, that all this time the King has shown no interest in any other woman. They even speculate that he has not the natural appetites of a man, dangerous whispers that Edmund has kept from reaching the King's ear. To Edmund the royal couple's sincere infatuation with one another is a blessing, it means he only has to contend with guiding the hands of two people and not a score of mistresses and their impossible fathers.

'Mowbray says that my uncles plot to have me overthrown.' The King's cold words defy the burning fire in his eyes. 'He has heard whispers for some time, but nothing to prove when and who might do it.'

Edmund listens in silence. He wills the King to continue, but it is Queen Anne who picks up the thread. 'I have told you, my love, that I do not believe your uncle John has anything to do with it. I agree with Sir Edmund that he has never failed you and therefore must be without fault. But I can well believe that your uncle Thomas has plans of his own.'

'I know you always speak truth, dear wife.' The King weaves his fingers with the Queen's and turns to face Edmund. 'What to do, La Fontaine? Whom can I trust but you?'

Edmund shakes his head slowly. 'I cannot say, your Grace. If indeed you are in the right and Lord Woodstock plots against you, you can do but little until the plot is revealed. If someone else is at play, how can we know who and why?'

'Why is easy! Mine is a seat anyone in the kingdom – in the world! – dreams of seizing!' The King is working his way into another tantrum, red flames spring to life on his cheeks. 'Ever since my grandfather died and left the crown to me, hardly a day has gone by that someone has not vied for it, lusted for it and clawed for favour! Am I to let them?'

'No, my love,' the Queen says. 'But how can you expect Sir Edmund to offer up answers to questions even you cannot answer?'

Shrewd, Edmund thinks, as always, she is so very shrewd and knows just how to handle her temperamental husband. Edmund admires her for it and knows that he is lucky she has taken to his charms and sings his praises even when he is not at court. Without her as an ally, he would have a harder job of keeping close to the King. As it is, Edmund finds it an easy feat to always see the King when he needs to. But if she changes her mind, Edmund will have to work very hard not to fall out of favour with the King. That is why it always pays to agree with her, especially when there is nothing very much at stake.

'Thank you, my Queen,' Edmund says and inclines his head. 'I would have to know more about these whispers before I can be of use to you, your Grace. But if you would permit, I shall seek out Lord Mowbray for a quiet word. If there is anything I can do, I will do it.'

The King gives a low growl and gestures at Edmund to leave the room. He is not best pleased that he has to see Mowbray, but if that is what it takes to put the King's mind at ease, then so be it.

Something rustles vaguely behind him. 'A word, Sir Edmund.'

'My Queen.' Edmund turns and sweeps a bow. 'What might I do for you?'

'My husband is greatly troubled. Wearing the crown is a lonely position, and he has experienced much – perhaps too much – inconsistency from people he once trusted blindly. If you truly meant what you said …' The Queen turns her face away and brushes her cheek. 'Beware that he may ask something of you that you would otherwise refuse.'

Edmund lets her regain her composure and looks out the window at London's distant rooftops bathing in the sinking sun. He wonders if the fields of wheat and barley are ripening as they ought; he needs to stock Beauworth for the winter. Inside, Edmund laughs at himself, he has grown soft to worry about something as tedious as crops and winter-stores.

'He is afraid.' The Queen too is looking out of the window. 'I have no reason to discredit Lord Gaunt, between the two of us, I believe as you do that he is loyal. But why then would Lord Mowbray speak as he does? At the moment though, I am more concerned with Lord Bolingbroke; he …'

'… is another matter entirely,' Edmund completes the Queen's insinuation. 'I cannot believe that Lord Bolingbroke will disobey his father.'

'You make it sound as if Henry has no opinion of his own.' The Queen tries to hide a smile. 'Truly, I believe we all underestimate my husband's cousin. Much more so than may be good for us. I think, one day, we will wake to realise what a mistake we have all made in assuming that he does nothing on his own.'

Edmund shakes his head. 'While Lord Bolingbroke is certainly his own man in many ways, he is still under the influence of his father. And …'

'… so is my husband.' The Queen rests a hand briefly on Edmund's sleeve, the touch ever so light and gone in an instant. 'We will never disagree on this matter for I believe that Lord Gaunt's influence benefits my husband. You have never treated me as a mere woman, Sir Edmund, as someone without opinion or wits. I am ever grateful for your good favour. It may surprise you that Lord Gaunt is the only other man here at court who has shown me the same kindness.'

Acknowledging Gaunt's astute decision to favour the Queen, Edmund draws breath. 'Then he is a wise man and rises high in my opinion, your Grace.'

'Good.' The Queen pauses and fiddles with her pearl and diamond necklace. 'For I have a personal favour to ask of you.'

☙ ❧ ☙ ❧

I should have known that I would end up here. Edmund stares at the massive oak door, its many rivets glitter in the flickering flames from the torches anchored in the wall at either side of the frame. Above the door the royal crest impaled by the royal arms of Castile and Leòn looms. Edmund picks his teeth with his meat knife and then pushes it back in his belt, best get on with it.

The door swings open to let out a cool breeze and faint laughter from the courtyard below. 'Sir Edmund!'

Edmund enters and glances about the room. No matter how many times he is in the presence of Gaunt, it never seizes to amaze him how many stacks of books and papers always sit atop his table. Time has taken away some of the neat and tidy impression, but Edmund knows that everything is in its proper place. As always.

A silhouette is carved amidst the open window, stark black against the rich opulent gold and red that shimmer outside. 'Sir Edmund.' The voice is deep, rich and at once both unsettling and soothing.

'My Lord Gaunt,' Edmund says and waits for Gaunt to turn from the view. 'The Queen sent me.'

'I thought she might' Gaunt snaps his fingers for a servant to pour two glasses of wine. 'She is a great patron of mine. Much more so than I deserve.'

'Surely not, my Lord.' Edmund has played the game of courtiers for so long that even such tired phrases as these sound sincere and earnest, a show put on for the servants. 'The Queen is concerned. I am convinced it is a trifling matter, but I promised that I would visit.'

Gaunt's servant slips from the room and Gaunt points at a pair of ill-matched chairs beside the window. One has a high, elaborately carved back and thick, sturdy legs, in its seat lays a comfortable crimson and gold cushion. The other is a low stool with an equally low back, it looks worn and tired, but robust nonetheless. Edmund takes his seat. Low to the ground it still brings him at eye-level with Gaunt when he sits down.

'If only the King would listen to me, trust me as the Queen does, we would not be here. If only he were not so hellbent on stating his own affairs as more important than that of the country, we might indeed have more peace in the land.'

'If only your own brother would come to terms with his place in the scheme of things,' Edmund replies. 'Rumour has it that Woodstock is clawing for the crown once more. Do not tell me you are ignorant to the whispers of a plot.'

'Thomas is always up to no good; I should pay little heed to whispers and rumours.'

'I do, but the Queen does not. And neither does the King, who called me for a private audience this morning, berating me for having done nothing to chasten your brother.' Edmund leans his arm on the windowsill, the angle is awkward. 'Just tell me that you have him under control.'

Edmund and Gaunt both attend the King's council meetings, and they exchange curtsies whenever anyone is listening. They often enough agree on matters of state, sometimes argue about taxes and how to manage the royal mint, and never deign to disagree in public about insignificant matters. The only times they are at each other's throats is when talk of war and campaigns arise. Edmund wants to see battle, Gaunt is adamant that they must preserve peace at all costs. But they do agree on one thing; Woodstock must never again be allowed within reach of the throne of England.

Gaunt folds his hands under his pointed chin, his beard has grown grey over the years. 'Many years ago, you swore eternal fealty to my brother. Not long after, you repeated your oath to my father. When Richard was made King, you bent the knee and offered up your sword.'

'All knights must.' Edmund only half-listens, he is busy deciding which of the Queen's new ladies-in-waiting to court and bed tonight. If there is one good thing about being at court it is the fair prospect of a little private entertainment. This matter of Woodstock plotting against the King is old news that has circled around court for half a year already with nothing to show for it. Edmund knows, he has spies everywhere, even in Woodstock's bedchamber.

'Later, you told me that you would do anything to ensure the King's seat upon the throne is never again unsettled. Do you remember?'

'I am sworn to serve the Crown and defend England. What of it, my Lord?'

'Mowbray is right. My brother is plotting against the King,' Gaunt says bluntly, not moving. 'He is a dog with a bone, he will not let it go. Day and night, he tries to rally men to his cause. He fabricates lies, diminishes the King's decisions.'

Gaunt's words settle between Edmund's shoulder blades and bites into his skin. He fights to keep calm. 'And you let him?'

'I have my eye on him.'

Edmund tries to sound out what Gaunt is planning. 'But you do nothing?'

'Believe me, if I thought it would make a difference, I would barge into the King's private chambers, my brother wrapped in chains, and proclaim him a traitor myself. But I have no evidence. Nothing to tie him with any plot but gossip. No letters, no coded messages. Nothing. It seems that my brother has finally grown a little wiser in his dealings.' Gaunt leans back and taps a finger on the carved armrest. 'Unlike others here at court, who also have the King's ear, I do not lay merit upon gossip alone.'

Thomas Mowbray, Edmund thinks, and looks out at the evening sky. 'You are certain, my Lord?'

'I know my brother. I know that he is biding his time and making trouble for the King, waiting for an opening, waiting to topple him.' Gaunt leans in, resting his elbows on his thighs. 'The question is: what will you do about it?'

I could have him beg, Edmund thinks, I truly think that I could make him beg, but then he would hold it against me forever. He glides a hand through his hair. 'You want something from me. You want me to intercede on the King's behalf that much is clear. Now why would I do that, my Lord, when you have no proof of any misdeeds?'

'You owe me. You owe him.'

This close, Gaunt looks old and Edmund wonders if he too looks this old, after all they are the same age. Living at court and being a part of the royal family has a price it seems. Being one of the King's close friends has a price too, but Edmund has never let it take its toll on him as it has on Gaunt. If he is not careful, he will wind up with a crooked back and a furrowed brow, Edmund thinks.

'You think that he is going to stage a coup.' Edmund stretches his leg. 'But you do not want to stick out your neck, in case there is no truth to it. So now, you are looking for someone else to seize your brother and cast him in a cell. You think me a fool, my Lord?'

'No more than you think me a scoundrel.' A smile twitches on Gaunt's lips. 'Come now, Sir Edmund, we do not need to tread this pointless dance. Let us get to business. You are wondering why the Queen sent you to my door today.'

There is no backrest on the low chair, and the seat bites into Edmund's thighs, but he stays seated and pretends to be comfortable. 'She too knows what your brother is capable of, and unlike you and I, she is not quick to dismiss him. If I did not know any better, I should say that it is you who put her up to this.'

Gaunt gives a harsh laugh. 'And if I did not know you better, I would say that you have grown cynical, Sir Edmund. Perhaps you have finally tired of courtly competition? The game of princes is not for the fainthearted.'

'I have been trapped in it too long. If it were a game of chess, I should sit on the throne myself by now, a mere peasant raised to king.' Edmund rubs his shoulder; the old war wound gives off a quiet cry of agony. 'We both know that the King must be kept safe. I will honour my pledge to your brother and father. What else is there to do?'

Relief is plain on Gaunt's face, but in his eyes is a haunting shadow of sadness, a strange emotion that Edmund has rarely seen in him. In the distance, a sliver of light tears the sky apart, the roll of thunder slow to present itself, a storm is gathering both outside and within the palace walls it seems.

'What is said here tonight must never be repeated. I will have your word, Sire,' Gaunt says and seems satisfied when Edmund nods. 'The Queen and I have spoken often of late. She is ever careful to keep it from the King as his temper is, well, erratic at best. But she knows how to soothe him. A quality required by any woman who takes a place in our family, and it is a quality that, sadly, my brother's wife does not possess.'

A lesser man might quiver in fear to hear you speak this way, Edmund thinks, but if the King hears of your secret meetings with his wife he will explode in a fit of rage. Perhaps I might use this information to my own advantage. Edmund accepts a glass of wine. 'What have you and the Queen been discussing?'

'When she heard that my son had left court to pursue other affairs abroad, she approached me to thank me.' Gaunt sits straight-backed in his chair. 'Obviously, I conceded that I had nothing to do with it. Henry decided to leave on his own accord, as there is very little for him to do here. Except being a constant suspect in the King's eyes. I am sad that my own good fortune where my nephew is concerned has not rubbed off on Henry.'

'Your son can hardly blame the King for keeping an eye on him, my Lord.' Edmund raises the glass to his lips; the wine is sweet and cool. 'For all that Lord Bolingbroke saved the King's position, he also earned enmity from his actions. He decided to back your brother.'

'He did not know what Thomas was plotting!' Gaunt drinks too, it seems to calm his temper. 'As soon as Henry realised what had happened, he forged an alliance and brokered peace.'

On my prompt and Mowbray's actions, Edmund thinks and puts the glass on the windowsill. 'Still, he cannot hope to earn the King's trust any time soon.'

'They should have been close. Edward wanted it so and my father likewise. Even I wanted it,' Gaunt says in wry tones. 'But they are too different. Henry is a man forged for war. And Richard? He detests battle. His little army will never raise a bow to anyone.'

War, Edmund thinks, conquest? That is what you desire, even after all this time, even after seeing your brother brought to his knees by his thirst for battle? After all these years of Gaunt cautioning the King against war-making, it seems Gaunt and Edmund are finally on the same side. 'You should call upon me if you want bows to be raised, my Lord. Between us we might take the crown your father never managed to snatch up for himself and place it on the head of our own King.'

'As tempting as the idea of you far away from court is, Sir Edmund,' Gaunt says with an irritated air, 'I cannot accept your proposition. Your duty is first and foremost to my family, and my family needs you here.'

'My duty is to the Crown and England,' Edmund corrects him. 'But let us not waste time mincing words and pining for what is not to be. Tell me about your brother's scheming – and what you and the Queen plan to do about it.'

Gaunt looks from his wine to Edmund. 'She feels, as I do, that something must be done to ward off Thomas once and for all. You see, we need someone who is willing to do anything to save his King. Even if it means …'

The unspoken words hang between Edmund and Gaunt, stuck as flies in a spider's web. Is he really asking what I think he is? Edmund's brain is struggling to absorb the enormity of the favour about to be asked. Could this be his crowning moment?

'I would do it, if I thought it would make a difference,' Gaunt continues without feeling. 'I have spent my life serving my nephew and I will do anything to keep him on his throne. But what will he do once I am gone? How will he govern? England will suffer and break apart. And my son will return home to avenge me. No, I cannot do it, the risk is too great. And yet we must root out the evil that dwells at court.'

Not too long ago, you had me marked as that evil, Edmund contemplates and nods, Gaunt is right of course, England will fall apart without his steady hand, his advice in the King's ear. Clearly, he does not think the same to be true if Edmund is gone. How little they know about his power. Still, this is a golden opportunity and Edmund pretends to be shocked to allow himself a moment feign recovery before he asks: 'What do you mean to use as your ruse to draw out the plot?'

'You do not wish to know what the consequence will be for you?' Gaunt cannot hide a note of surprise in his question.

'I will not blindly accept anything, nor give my word without explanation. You and I have known each other for too long to mince words as I already said.' Edmund looks into Gaunt's cold, grey eyes. 'I know what you are asking. All that is left is to decide whether I believe that it is worth doing. After all, I have my own position to concern myself with.'

Something in Gaunt's demeanour changes, satisfaction steals across the proud face and a small, almost warm smile plays at the corner of his mouth. 'Perchance I have been wrong about you. Maybe you truly are the glorious knight everyone else thinks you are.'

Or maybe I see an opportunity to make my mark on history, to be remembered forever, Edmund thinks and feigns distaste. 'If you want me to fall on my sword, you might want to flatter me rather than degrade me.'

'And if I thought you truly cared about my opinion, Sire, I would. But that will remain a hypothetical discussion, do you not think? When there are much more pressing matters for us to deliberate.' Gaunt rises and gestures for Edmund to follow him.

Acknowledging that he will not best Gaunt this evening, Edmund follows him to his desk. Outside the windows, more white gashes mar the darkening skies. How apt that a storm is coming outside, when inside another storm is brewing. 'What is your plan?'

Gaunt draws a piece of paper from a small chest and places it before Edmund. 'To use this, of which it seems, my brother has squirreled away many copies.'

The royal crest sits prominently at the bottom of an almost empty page. Edmund traces the outline of the bulky wax while understanding dawns. He looks at Gaunt. 'Do tell.'

## 25 July 1392 – Westminster Palace

No sooner has the door closed behind Edmund than Gaunt pounds his fist into the table. It is a good thing that it is sturdy oak, otherwise it would have crumbled. Last time Edmund was here, he had left to be caught up in a hailstorm. Now, it seems that he is to weather another storm, only this time it blows with the gale of a royal tantrum.

Gaunt's eyes are wild with fury, but his voice is measured when he speaks. 'We have unearthed another will in my father's hand. It states clearly the line of succession.' Gaunt licks his lips and pushes the document towards Edmund. 'How long have you known?'

Edmund does not have to look at the paper to know what has Gaunt in a fit. Instead, he nods with an overbearing smile. 'What does it matter? I have never acted upon it.'

'You lied to me.' Gaunt snorts and thrusts the will into Edmund's hand. 'How long?'

Turning the paper, Edmund smooths it against his thigh and tries to hand it back. 'For certain? About ten years.'

Paling, Gaunt takes his seat, a hand on his chest. The gold and ruby signet ring gives a flash of blood before it vanishes beneath his beard. 'Ten years?'

'What does it matter, my Lord?' Edmund has fight not to beam another smile at Gaunt. Instead, he places the will on Gaunt's desk which is uncommonly empty. 'If you are worried that I will now barge into the line of succession and proclaim myself a possible heir, you are mistaken. I want no crown, strange as it may sound to you, for I have seen what crowns do to people. I am a warrior, a knight, a hero. Not some landlord chained to his desk and his duties to his people. A drop of royal blood in my veins changes nothing.'

'You are my rival,' Gaunt says in a puzzled tone, he grabs the will but does not look at it.

'I was never your rival.' Looking out of the window, Edmund breathes deep. 'Oh, I might have made something of it. No doubt, your brother would have been pleased; he often said that he wished I had been his brother by blood and not just by deed. How easy it would have been to tell him on his deathbed that he could have me for a brother. But to what end?'

Gaunt opens his mouth but no words come out, and Edmund crushes another smile. 'You wonder why someone, as greedy for fame and fortune as I am, did not use his knowledge?' When Gaunt nods, Edmund continues: 'I have seen what happens to the men in your – or should I say our – family. How they vie for crowns and fight among each other. I have seen them fall out and clamour, and I have seen the King dreaming of the day when he can punish them all. I would never overthrow my good hold on the King for such a fate. I am not Plantagenet; I am La Fontaine.'

Finally Gaunt regains his speech. 'Am I to believe that never once during these past years of having the King's ear did you whisper that you were more than a knight? That you were an uncle? That unlike his other uncles you had proven yourself to him, you could be trusted above all others, that he must acknowledge you and any offspring as part of the succession?'

He speaks of the girls, Edmund thinks, not of Argyle. He cannot know for everyone who did know is dead, apart from me. 'It did occur to me that I might use this to my own ends, but then the King seems to have grown weary of uncles, would you not say?'

'If he knew,' Gaunt says and points at the will, 'do you think that he would favour you?'

Edmund puts a hand on the parchment; one corner is singed; it leaves a smudge on the desk. 'No, I would be another contender. Imagine what he might do if he found out. I wield my power from the shadows, not from the centre aisle. I leave that to you.'

'But you are a contender, and a force to be reckoned with as you have often enough boasted.' Gaunt sighs, 'A fourth brother still alive.'

'If Woodstock found out it would cast a shadow over his efforts, would you not say, my Lord?' Edmund teases. 'After all, I push him down the line and into obscurity.'

Outside the window three seagulls swoop and play, one of them has a fish in its beak. It tosses its head and catches the fish in the air, swallowing it up in one big gulp. The other two birds scream.

Gaunt seems lost in thought and Edmund takes a seat by the empty hearth. Ever since Lady Blanche told him the truth about his heritage, Edmund has tried to drown it out. Why would the old fool make a will and name him in it? When he gets nothing but a massive headache. No gold, no lands, nothing but a place in a family that hates him. Except the King, he does not hate Edmund – not yet.

'The will matters not,' Edmund says to break the silence. 'I have bigger fish to fry, and I would have you help me fry them.'

Gaunt lifts his head. 'What?'

'I have already accepted your ploy, my Lord. I have agreed to do what must be done to ensure Woodstock gets his black mark, which he so rightly deserves.' Edmund looks across the room at Gaunt. 'If only he were as clever as you or I and had played the hand fate dealt him, we would not be in this mess.'

'You would still proceed?'

'Is the document drawn up and delivered?' Edmund inquires. It is best to know all rather than act rash.

Gaunt looks down at the will, new determination on his face. 'Yes. It went out yesterday.'

'And it was accepted?'

'I have no cause to think differently.' Gaunt rolls up the will. 'I could have thrown this in the fire.'

This time, Edmund does smile. 'Then you would have had to light one first, and who would care to do so on a sunny day like this? Besides, I think someone else tried to burn it and failed. Perhaps you should keep it, in case Woodstock lashes out again. You can rub his nose in it and tell him that, even if I am gone, there is another in the line of succession before him.'

Something approaching curiosity sneaks into Gaunt's eyes. 'You have a son? Such secrets you have been keeping, Sir Edmund. I find that I would have your story before the day arrives.'

Edmund rises; his grey and blue silk gown sticks to his back. 'I am invited to dine with the King tonight. You will have to wait until he dismisses me.'

'I take it that you will want wine to wet your tongue,' Gaunt says and gestures for Edmund to leave.

'I think we will both need something to drink before the night is over.'

# CHAPTER 31

## 27 July 1392 – Westminster Palace

'I wish I had never asked for you to tell me all,' Gaunt admitted and rubbed hands together. 'Then I might simply have been content to send an unwanted bastard to his death.'

'But then we would not have had the pleasure of each other's company one last time, my Lord. We have seen some strange things these past many years. We have fought together on the battlefield and at opposite sides in council.' Edmund leaned forward to stretch his back. 'I would not have been without it.'

'Your true home has always been the battlefield. You are forged by blood and steel. But you have transformed into a mighty courtier, just as Edward once predicted.' Fingering the will laid out between them, folding and unfolding one corner, Gaunt nodded slowly, clearly deliberating something. Edmund leaned back; his tale was at an end. All he wanted now was to go to bed. Later today, he would make his last performance and he wanted everyone remember him as a man in his prime, not some haggard old washout. He would give the King what he had commanded and make a mighty show to taint Edmund's wicked half-brother Woodstock.

'I never thought I would say it, but England – no I, owe you a debt of gratitude. Not just for the counsel you have given over the years while the

King was young, but for never revealing who you are. I do not like all that I have heard here tonight, but then, who is truly innocent anymore?'

Satisfied that Edmund had Gaunt where he wanted him, confused by his many admissions, tired from the long night of tales and weary of his own family, Edmund nodded. 'You call the battlefield my home, but I have long called Beauworth home. I have trained the King's men, better than any other knight. I have educated more noblemen's sons and bastards than anyone else. Without complaint.' Edmund scratched his cheek. 'It has made me rich, but only because I have served the Crown. Even you cannot complain of my loyalty on that score, my Lord.'

'My father made a mistake when he gave you Beauworth. It belongs in our family, and my father had vowed never to let it out of our bloodline again. It should never have been yours.' Gaunt glanced at the will and his look soured.

Edmund pulled a scroll of paper form inside his shirt. 'Sanction this and it never will.'

'How long have you been preparing to die, Sire?' Gaunt stroked his pointed beard but made no move to take the scroll. 'How long have you known that, one day, someone would call upon you to do what you swore to do?'

Holding the scroll out, Edmund smiled. 'Since the day Prince Edward lay his sword on my shoulder and slapped my cheek with his gauntlet hand. He marked me and I always knew that, sooner or later, I would be called upon. I have lived my life as I saw fit, I am ashamed of nothing I have done, I am rich because of my loyalty. I am here because of it too. Everything I have ever done I did on my honour and my oath.'

Gaunt's loud laugh rolled along the richly decorated walls. 'You are the cleverest man that I have ever met, but honourable, I would not call you! Certainly not after what you have told me tonight. Once your final part is played out what is to stop me from picking apart your reputation, as the crows would pick your eyes from your scull if you had fallen on the battlefield?'

'You need the death of a hero,' Edmund said, his smile tight on his face. 'Otherwise, it will all be in vain. You will have gained nothing by my death if you taint my name when I am gone. Fortunately, I know you to be a man capable of rising above your own petty desire for revenge to save the kingdom you claim to love.'

Finally, Gaunt took the scroll from Edmund's outstretched hand. Gaunt tapped it slowly against his palm. 'You are the most tainted hero the world has ever seen.'

'But the world will never know.' Edmund's smile rested comfortably on his lips once more. 'I am the piece you need to win the board. Without getting your hands dirty, though naturally you would never admit it.'

Gaunt pulled the leather cord from the paper and began reading, nodding here and there, frowning once. When he was done, he laid it down on top of the will. 'This is your wish?'

'Not long ago, I was reminded of something Lady Blanche said to me on the night before I left Framlingham for the very last time,' Edmund said and looked into the night beyond the glass panes. 'She was angry at me for something I said, I remember not what, but I remember her words: "Children are more than a nuisance! They are your only way of securing a legacy. Their existence in the world is all that stands between being forgotten and being remembered when you are gone. They are what can keep you alive forever. My nephew was wise enough to understand that this is the only truth in the world. I expect you to be equally wise." It stuck in my mind.'

'You are willing to do anything to be remembered?'

Edmund turned his gaze back to Gaunt. 'Argyle will not know I was his father, there is no point in it. He is not the only legacy I leave behind. I trust to the common folk to remember me as the golden knight who died on the jousting field, plucked from life by a monster. And I trust you to instil in the King the urge to find out who did it. Everything will go according to your plan. In the end, all evidence of foul play will point to the only man who should never be allowed near the King again. I will have my name whispered in awe throughout the centuries. I will be remembered as the knight who laid down his life to save his King. You will aid in that endeavour any way you can.'

'How will you know that I will keep my word?' Gaunt sounded faintly amused, but Edmund was past caring.

'If I think that you might waver, even for a moment, I shall go onto that field tomorrow and lay waste to every opponent you send at me. When I am done, I shall tell the King who I truly am.' Edmund grinned. 'And then you will have one more brother to contend with, only this one is no fool. He knows how to play the game, and he has the love of the King. Fear not, my Lord, before I am done, the King will love me above all others, even if he is upset at first.'

Gaunt's hands trembled with anger as he signed the document, melted the crimson wax and pushed his signet ring into the sticky fluid. He thrust the paper at Edmund who took it with pleasure. 'I knew that I could count on you, my Lord.' He looked at the emblem embedded in red. 'In return, allow me to part with a word of warning. You should never have forced the King to grant Lancashire to you for life. It was perhaps your greatest mistake. He sees you not as a loyal uncle but as a contender, and he will never trust you or your son, no matter what you do. The greatest threat always comes from within your own family.' Edmund paused for effect, 'Just as you suspect your brother of a plot, so too will the King constantly suspect you. One day, you will have to choose between your own blood and your oath to the King, I hope you choose wisely.'

'Carry out your deed and I shall honour my pledge to you.' Though Gaunt's expression was calm, his voice betrayed him. 'Make it to the final round and then die. That is all I ask.'

'As long as you give me your word that the evidence of Woodstock's hand in the plot is unearthed, I will honour our agreement. After all, I swore to give my life for the safety of England, and I shall honour that vow.' Edmund turned for the door, tucking the document back inside his shirt. 'You see, my Lord, I learned to die long ago.'

# CHAPTER 32

## 27 July 1392 – London

The house was dark save for a single window, in which Edmund could just make out the uneven flicker of a candle. Never let it be said that his reluctant host was lavish in his extravagances. But then it was to be expected that a man who loved gold above all else would hoard and not squander. Whether he ever actually enjoyed his riches, Edmund did not know. Surely, his own spending had led to fun and pleasure, and now that he was about to leave this world, Edmund was quite pleased with himself.

The future of Beauworth secured, enough money to last at least two generations and a sealed deal with the richest man in the realm that if anything turned sour for Edmund's heir, Gaunt would recompense him. Edmund let the stable boy lead his horse away and looked once more at the single, grey window with its sad little golden fleck.

Lady Blanche was right, he knew it, children were all any man could hope to leave behind, other than his earthly possessions, and most of those should certainly be entailed upon his children. But it never hurt to be vigilant, and it definitely never hurt to take precautions.

A servant ushered Edmund through the dark hall and into a gloomy study, where the grey ghosts of furniture seemed all that was up to greet him. From the chair by the empty hearth, Edmund heard faint breathing.

He pushed back his cloak and grabbed a bundle of documents from inside a hidden pocket. 'My Lord.'

'In the dead of night, I think we can forego our civilities.' The voice was raw, a testament that, not long ago, its owner had been sound asleep, no doubt convinced that all was well in the world. 'Sit down, La Fontaine.'

'Thomas.' Edmund took the chair opposite Mowbray and stretched his legs. He longed for the comfort of his own bed but this could not wait. 'I come straight from court.'

'What is that to me?' There was danger as well as dejection in Mowbray's eyes. 'I was asleep and now, here I sit as an obedient child waiting for a tutor to arrive. We agreed that we were done.'

'You agreed,' Edmund said. 'I have only ever let you think, I was of similar understanding. But let us put past animosities aside, for there were times where we worked together and did it well. I would have you remember those times now.'

'What do you want?' Thomas' hands curled around his armrests.

Edmund held out his parcel of secrets. The Baron squinted in the pale light of the sole candle, sighed and took a twig, dipped it in the flickering flame and lit three more candles. Then he leaned back and looked at Edmund. 'What are those?'

'Collateral. In case a certain person proves to be indisposed to honour the agreement I struck with him not half an hour ago.'

'Striking bargains in the dark will only gain you ill-tempered associates, as you well know,' Mowbray said, but his voice betrayed his interest. 'And who was it who was foolish enough to deal with you?'

'Gaunt.' Edmund let the name sink in before he continued. 'Tomorrow on the field, I will meet my destiny.'

'Ever the poet … when you choose to be.'

Shaking his head, Edmund half-smiled. 'I neither claimed to be one, nor to understand it when other men spent hours on end labouring with pen and paper to produce a few lines that rarely stirred the woman they desired.'

'No, you always chose a more aggressive approach.' It was Mowbray's turn to smile. 'As half the court will profess to. Is there a noblewoman in England you have not bedded?'

'I believe, I have yet to have the pleasure of entertaining your wife,' Edmund nodded at the ceiling and Mowbray's face darkened. 'Nor the

Queen, of course. Perhaps a handful of others. But you will find that those who did enjoy my company came willingly, and most of them sought me out, not the other way around.'

'Women flock to you as moths to a flame, much as they do to my unfortunate brother. But with you, they all burn their wings.' Thomas drew a hand through his thinning dark hair. 'What do you want from me with that pile of paper?'

'You are a cunning man,' Edmund said with true acknowledgement. 'I have always congratulated myself that I had some small hand in your creation. You will forgive me when I also call you a fool.'

Rather than growl and agonise, Mowbray looked observantly at Edmund, the trace of understanding creeping into his eyes. 'You are offering me something of value. Something you would never part with unless …' Edmund nodded and, with dawning interest, Mowbray turned his unsettling, grey eyes to the documents. Edmund held one out, and Thomas took it to study the seal. 'Gaunt's own crest. The wax still warm.'

'Signed this night. It testaments that Gaunt will let Argyle take possession of Beauworth should anything befall me.' Edmund gestured to the rest of the papers. 'These are further insurance that he keeps his word to me. And that his son will continue to do so when Gaunt is dead.'

'You did not seal the rest?' Thomas' ill-hidden surprise was strangely comforting.

'I will, once you have read them.' Edmund rested his hand on the parcel and looked at Thomas. 'Before you do, I will have you know that what is in there is more than your brother knows.' Every fibre in Thomas' being seemed to vibrate at the prospect, and Edmund cut him off with a gesture. 'I would have you swear to me that you will never breathe a word of it to anyone before you read the contents. I will have your oath now, or I shall leave you wondering forever what you were denied access to.'

Edmund could tell that Mowbray was pretending to struggle with his conscience. Fortunately, he would come around and knowing Thomas – though he made a great show of being indifferent to Argyle – he would immediately know why none of this was to be mentioned ever again. 'I accept your terms.'

'Your oath, my Lord,' Edmund said to Thomas' disgruntled face. 'Now.'

'I swear upon my honour,' Thomas began and when Edmund snorted, Thomas continued,' upon my life and upon the Mowbray name that I shall never repeat my knowledge to anyone. Whatever these papers contain, I shall take my knowledge with me to the grave.'

'Except if anything should happen that puts the King or the Crown in jeopardy and you can find no other way but to expose those mentioned within. Only then, as a last resort, you may use your knowledge for the greater good of this country and its people,' Edmund added and nodded for Mowbray to repeat his words. After a brief pause, Thomas did and held out his hand, palm up.

'This may be one of the greatest secrets you have ever been sworn to keep,' Edmund said and handed over the neat stack of documents. 'No, it is the greatest secret. Fortunately, I know you to be a man of many – and varied – secrets, and I know you will keep this one to yourself.'

Thomas slid the leather tie from the first scroll and sat down at his desk, drawing a candle closer to the paper. As he read, his expression kept fluctuating between outright disbelief and shrewd understanding.

Meanwhile, Edmund enjoyed picking out trinkets and artefacts that he had previously seen in the care of the late Baron Mowbray, Edmund's old friend. Clearly, Thomas was a family-man first, and that only served to prevent him speaking out of hand or acting rash. A family-man was the best weapon against a flood of unpleasant secrets being revealed.

'Tell me again why you are giving me these?' If Mowbray was surprised by what he read and now knew about Gaunt and Bolingbroke, he hid it exceedingly well. Thomas' efforts made Edmund feel strangely proud.

'In your hands, they are safe while, in other hands, they would be weapons. You will know what to do with them if anything should happen. I trust you to keep your word.' Sleep clawed at Edmund's eyes, but he pushed it away with an effort. This needed saying. 'Beware you keep them safe, tell no one, not even that conniving wife of yours.'

Thomas heated the stiff plate of wax in the melting spoon, the brass black on the outside from its continued, and no doubt, frequent use. 'I cannot help but wonder if you are right not to tell Argyle.'

Edmund took off his great signet ring and twirled it between his fingers. 'You once said he is too honest and too stupid to keep secrets. Well, I know that we were both mistaken in that belief. He is not the wide-eyed boy that he once was. The world has hardened him, has made him a man. His loyalty outweighs even his extreme desire for honesty. Still, this he would not be able to keep secret and it would cost him his life.'

'You speak about loyalty, but Argyle is not bound to Gaunt,' Thomas huffed and dipped the spoon further into the flame. 'I grant you that he is loyal to the King, but will not these secrets merely serve to make the King safe in his position?'

'Argyle is loyal to the Crown,' Edmund said and added in thought, I was very careful he swore his allegiance to the Crown and not the man wearing it. He looked at his ring and continued, 'He knows that it is paramount to keep Gaunt by the King's side to ensure that England remains safe from her enemies. And I would have the King safe in his position, as Argyle well knows. For that reason, he will take what little he knows to the grave, as will you, Thomas.'

Edmund dismissed the idea of putting his own crest on the documents, it would not serve. Instead, he took the garnet and gold ring the King had given him years ago after a tournament and pressed it into the glob of wax, Mowbray had deftly poured onto the first piece of folded up paper. When all documents were sealed, Edmund sat down opposite Thomas, the bulky desk a vast expanse between them. The smell of warm wax stung in Edmund's nose. 'How far we have gone together, Thomas. How much we have seen, and done, to protect the King.'

'And serve ourselves,' Thomas offered in return. 'Do not tell me, La Fontaine, that you did all of this just to save my brother's inheritance?'

'I did it to thwart Gaunt and his family, of course,' Edmund admitted. 'But I also did a great deal of it to ensure my legacy lives on. Once I am gone, you can tell Argyle that I was the father he never had if you wish, and you will ensure I am spoken of often and in reverent tones at court.'

Thomas' face turned sneaky. 'And if I do not?'

'Your brother has his own orders. And he will not disobey me. Beware you never reveal who Argyle's true grandfather was though, that I will have your oath on.' Edmund was tired and wanted to be in bed. Better get it done quickly, before he blurted out the truth that he had not told Argyle everything. This was his final gamble, and he wanted it kept between as few men as possible. 'As I said, if anything threatens the Crown of England, I want you to go directly to Paris and put this in the hands of one of my girls.

You have their family name from the document, and I am certain, you have already memorised it?' When Thomas nodded, Edmund continued. 'They have orders too and will know what to do.'

Thomas rose and rummaged in a dark corner; a lock clicked once, then twice. He returned to the dead fireplace; his hands empty. He pulled at his lower lip and then asked, 'How long have you suspected that I knew about Argyle?'

The chair was hard and uncomfortable, Edmund knew he had to leave soon, but he would grant Thomas a few more moments of his time before he crossed London to return to his home and his bed. 'I think, on some level, you have always wondered. But I was certain that you knew you had the right of it when I petitioned the King to leave my estate to Argyle.'

'If half the court was not so busy looking up their own arses, they would know too. No one who sees the two of you together can doubt that your relation goes well beyond that of a knight and his soldier. Which I have been meaning to speak to you about,' Mowbray said and leaned forward. 'Why did you hesitate to elevate him from squire? Why make him a soldier and not knight him on your own?'

'You earn a knighthood on the field, or doing the King's bidding.' Edmund yawned. 'He has yet to prove himself.'

'It is as I suspected, he was telling the truth all along.' Thomas rubbed his forehead. 'He is too honest for his own good.'

'Perhaps he needs to be, to counteract his father and his brother.' Edmund's shoulder ached and the notion of putting on his armour tomorrow had never seemed less attractive, but he had a part to play, and he intended to play it well. 'Not to worry, you will soon enough be rid of me. When I am gone, I look to you to keep your brother safe from the hatefulness of the world. While I would have liked him to take after me, I have realised tonight that perhaps it is a good thing that he does not. Honest and loyal men have their place in the world and, with any luck, what I am about to do will rid you of a few enemies and serve to keep everyone safe for a long time to come, my Lord.'

Mowbray gave a sickening smile that Edmund not only recognised but also enjoyed. He would agree. He might ask a few more questions, but in the end, Thomas loved his brother more than he would ever confess to, and that was all Edmund needed to know.

'I will not ask what you infer to, Sire, for it will not change your mind, I see that plain upon your face. I also agree with you that, in some cases, honesty is all any of us can strive for, and my brother has it without even knowing what a gift he possesses.' Mowbray shook his head. 'He is my brother, and the world will never learn differently. Who knows, perhaps it is time that the King is introduced to an honest man.'

'Make whatever you can of him,' Edmund said and they both knew who he referred to. 'But know this; when I am gone, the world will be a very different place. You once said that you were done changing allegiance and yet perhaps you have to do so once or twice more before all is set straight. Do your King's bidding in good faith, Thomas, and steer him clear when he is about to sail too close to the wind. Your brother is a warrior, he will not thrive at court, but he will have to come and more often than he likes, I will wager. You are the greatest courtier that I have ever met, greater still than any royal uncle and, between you and Argyle, you can rein in the King and make England prosper.'

Thomas had laughed but now his laughter stilled. 'You would have me believe that you care about England?'

'Not as others do,' Edmund agreed and earned a nod. 'But I will have you believe that I care about my legacy. In that we may see eye to eye.'

'Legacy is everything.' Thomas' eyes strayed from Edmund to the empty hearth. 'You have my word, Sire.'

Edmund rose, his legs stiff, his eyes stinging from lack of sleep and his mouth almost empty of words. He looked out at the dawning city; a new day beckoned. His last day. Edmund turned to Thomas. 'I am not concerned about Gaunt; for all his faults, he holds England in his heart,' Edmund professed. 'Bolingbroke is another matter, for at his core lies a secret that makes him dangerous. I do not know if Gaunt ever told him the truth, but they are too close for us to trust that Bolingbroke is ignorant of his true heritage. I charge you with this task; whatever the King believes, always counsel him against falling out with his cousin. Remind him of the past if you must, but only to caution him of repetition.'

Thomas rose too, walked past Edmund and rested his hand on the door. 'I fear sleep-deprivation has made you unhinged, Sire.'

When Edmund walked past him into the dark hall, he saw understanding on Thomas' face and nodded. 'Perhaps you are right. But I learned long ago that the real danger is not in the enemy we know,' Edmund said as way of parting, 'but in the enemy, we overlook.'

'Good luck on the field tomorrow, Sir Edmund,' Mowbray said to Edmund's back. 'God's grace goes with you.'

And all of Hell's devils, Edmund thought and could not suppress a laugh. Perhaps he was unhinged, but he had done it to himself, and he was pleased with what he had accomplished.

All that was left to do was to die a clean death.

# CHAPTER 33

## 27 July 1392 – London

'Shield!'

The world was encapsulated in two small slits. Edmund stretched out an arm and felt Argyle tie the shield into place. The last joust. When Coxcombe fell two rounds back, Edmund was more pleased that he wanted to admit. He did not desire to lose to Coxcombe, he would have gone back on his word to Gaunt if he had ended up opposite him. Coxcombe would never have given him a clean death, there was too much bad blood between them.

Instead, it was another relic from Limoges who turned his steed towards Edmund; Lockley, the strange boy who had grown to be a man. Edmund had watched his progress in the tournament and was surprised at what raw strength could do for a man who had little skill with a lance. It was not what he had hoped for, but Lockley would do.

Edmund settled the lance on his hip and rode to the end of range. A glance at the tribune revealed the King leaning forward, his gaze intent while the Queen struggled to smile and chat with one of her ladies. Edmund felt the wind kick up; fine-grained water prickled through his visor and into his eyes. He turned Noble and adjusted his seat.

In the distance, Lockley finally took the field, pausing only for a moment to salute the King on his dais. The Queen rose and Edmund let his mind go blank. The armour muffled the sound from the crowd; the only thing he heard was the rush of his own blood, rising as the Queen raised her handkerchief. It fluttered. His breath slowed.

Lockley turned his horse about and gave a perfunctory nod. Through the slits, Edmund watched Lockley tighten his grip and then he bore down on his horse.

Edmund kicked Noble and felt the familiar lurch as it jumped forward. The horse became part of Edmund, its ears pricked up and it gnawed the bit. When Lockley lowered his lance, Edmund adjusted his seat to take true aim.

When his lance struck Lockley's shield, the impact bit into Edmund's arm, numbing his muscles. He turned Noble about and saw the King settle in his seat. In the minute world of the helmet, Edmund could not see Gaunt or Woodstock anywhere. He could hardly make out Argyle in the increasing rain.

'His seat is bad!' Argyle shouted and handed Edmund the next lance. 'You will win!'

Edmund pretended not to hear and brought Noble about.

The herald dropped his hand. Noble lurched. Edmund lowered his lance. So did Lockely. For a second, Edmund saw the white in his opponent's eyes. Then both lances hit their marks, and Edmund's arm burned again. He looped Noble around for the final turn and the world rotated on its axis.

He landed on his back, orange pain tearing at his side, sand spraying through the slits and into his eyes. He felt the thud of Noble's hooves through the ground. He wanted to shout. He wanted to scream.

Blue eyes swam into view. His head was released.

'Remove it and he dies,' Lockley whispered from far away.

Edmund could not breathe. He could not move. Strange white sparks shot across the skies. Green tendrils burrowed their way through his flesh, rushing to his heart. Where was the glory he desired? Where was the clean death he was promised?

Liars, they were all liars. Anger and humiliation clashed and joined; their struggle plunged Edmund into darkness.

*Is this death?*

## 28 July 1392 – London

'Boy …' Edmund cloyed on acrid spit.

Argyle was at his side, pouring water on his lips. He could not drink. The cold spray never entered his mouth, it rolled from his lips onto his burning cheek, evaporating.

Argyle set the cup aside and saw something; with a look of great distress, he reached over.

'No … no need to look.' Edmund did not recognise his own voice. 'It will not … heal.'

'Sire, do not speak!' Argyle's shout split Edmund's world in half and he closed his eyes. He could feel Argyle's hand on his arm. 'I shall get a physician.'

I must stop him, Edmund thought idly, he cannot undo what has been done. We have to flush out the enemy. It is all as we agreed. All except my valiant death, how dare they take that from me? Dots of red fury danced before his eyes. Twirled and entwined with the amber haze of pain. Edmund shook his head with great force. It hardly moved. Instead, he put a leaden hand on Argyle's and locked eyes with him. 'No. It won't be long now. I feel … You must be watchful.'

Argyle squirmed and Edmund put what force he had left into his grasp. It felt weak, as if his fingers were detached from his body. How could his mind be so alert when his body was defective? With an effort, he drew Argyle close. 'Listen to me! You must be watchful. The court is full of dangers … I had not …'

His voice drowned in blood and spittle; he lost control of his fingers. A strange thought took hold of him; was this how the Prince suffered for years? How was it that he clung to life for so long while I cannot but put voice to my words? Am I that much a lesser man than the broken Prince?

'Sire … What do you mean?' Argyle's breath was cold on Edmund's burning skin.

'The King …' Edmund coughed. Now, he felt life trickling from his body in drops of blood that seeped down his side. It was velvety raw and oddly comfortable.

'The King?' Argyle's voice took on an urgent tone that dribbled into Edmund's conscious and sparked it.

'The King knows …' Edmund tried to get up, but his body was not his to command anymore. It belonged to death. 'He will ask your help. You … do not …'

Helplessly, his head fell back on the pillow and, for a moment, he loathed himself, loathed his weak vessel and hated, above all else, those who had fooled him. Was this all a ruse from the get go? Had he grown so used to being the one laying traps that he did not recognise one when it was laid for him? Inward, Edmund cursed his own arrogance, his inability to believe anyone to be as clever as himself. But what use would his death be if that was all they hoped to achieve? No, there was truth in Gaunt's eyes last night, Edmund told himself, there was honesty and fear too. My death is not in vain.

There was a ruckus far away; someone shouted an order and footsteps faded into grey.

'Sire?'

Edmund willed his eyes to focus, his voice to return. Life ebbed away. 'Do not trust … anyone.' Through the veil drawn over his eyes, Edmund could not see Argyle clearly any more. He could only hope that he was there. 'No one.'

Let them sing about me. Let their voices soar to the sky. I will have my chivalrous end. I have come too far to die for nothing. Edmund's head rolled to the left and he smiled at an old friend.

*So – you are death.*

# EPILOGUE

## 1401 – Château Gaillard, Rouen

Argyle rubbed his forehead. He recognised La Fontaine's writing, but most of the words were of another, and the contents even more disturbing than the disclosure of Bolingbroke's true heritage. It opened a chasm under Argyle, threatening to plunge his family into chaos.

Instead of having a droplet of royal blood, his children had a river. What he hated Isobel for bringing to the marriage bed, he had brought too. He was as responsible for endangering his sons as she, more perhaps because he had not known or rather, had not acknowledged the affinity he had felt for La Fontaine since the first time he set eyes on the knight.

La Fontaine might have failed in bringing about Woodstock's downfall, but Argyle would strive to ensure his legacy be remembered forever as was his true aim. If only there was a way to achieve his goal without feeding his children to the fierce English lions that held the seat of royal power. What luck that La Fontaine's parting gift had provided the escape Argyle so desperately needed.

Through the windowpanes, the sun begged for Argyle to take comfort in its rays. He brought the letter and settled in the window bay, one foot on the sill, the other on the floor. For the first time in more than a year, the ground sighed and rolled beneath him, reminding him of all the troubles he had faced to discover the truth, and how all he wished for now was to forget it. He wanted to erase all that he had read. He wanted to be washed clean.

Instead, Argyle re-read the pages, his mind bringing the words to life in La Fontaine's voice:

*Madam,*

*I break my promise of silence to you only to relay news of my daughter's recent passing. What I feared has come to pass, her love for a King brought down the wrath of God upon her head, her punishment was to fall victim to the great mortality, but the Devil has protected her bastard son, who survived his mother and buried her. I suppose that is his atonement for his part in tearing a family apart and denying his mother a chance of happiness, which she would have been awarded, had we never crossed paths.*

*Do not think, Madam, that I now regret saving you that night, nor that I would have turned your party from my door, for I believe it was meant to be. You have never aged nor diminished in my estimation, though what you brought with you, I can never forgive. You called it then the folly of two young people. I called it adultery. Perhaps the years have wizened you, and we may now agree that what was done behind closed doors, in secret, was a sinful act against God himself, a smear on a good marriage.*

*My other reason for writing is that the boy now dwells with me, and here he cannot stay. He is a constant reminder of what was done to my family. I know that I should love the boy, but I find that I cannot, and I fear that if he is not soon gone from my sight, he will drive me mad, and I might turn to sin to cleanse my halls of old misdeeds.*

*Therefore, I besiege you to relay my news to your brother and ask that he come to fetch what does not belong to me. In time, the boy may prove himself an apt soldier. At night, I dream that he might die in battle and bring some comfort to what remains of a broken family.*

*I know that our King plans once more to take the crown that is his by right. Perhaps in some small way what he placed at my hearth can be returned to him; can aid his efforts in reclaiming France for himself.*

*All I ask is that the boy never returns to my house. I will not suffer the taunt that is in his every word and breath. He must be gone. You must make your brother come for him; it is what was promised and now must be fulfilled. Know this; until your brother comes, I shall teach the boy all he needs to know and learn to be of value to the King's cause. He has the face of a warrior and the mind of a strategist. Your brother will not be disappointed in his new charge.*

*Madam, if you grant me this kindness, I shall never again make any requests, I shall respond to no letters. I will be as dead to him as he is already to me. I want no news.*

*Your obedient servant and saviour*

*Aymard La Fontaine*

Crumbling the paper, Argyle's chest tightened and his breath grew shallow anew. This letter, along with the rest of the pouch of documents, was a living testament that he had never truly known Edmund La Fontaine. That such secrets lived between them that they might as well have been strangers to one another. It also burned to know that Thomas had known the truth and deceived him. Had called him brother to his face and placated with him to preserve the Mowbray honour.

The pain in his chest intensified, and Argyle closed his eyes on the setting sun and sat for a moment, a golden sheen travelling through his eyelids drowning his memories in an otherworldly gleam. Then he looked at the last piece of paper again. He squinted. In the top corner was a faint trace of a scrawl. Something was written on the other side in ink so faded that it was almost gone. Argyle held it up against last rays of sunlight and the words came to life.

*Ma chere Madame Blanche*

*I write to you because I have nowhere else to turn. Those who know my secret shun me and I cannot live in this wretched place a moment longer. When I turn up at your doorstep, please do not turn me away; please show me the kindness that has been so long denied from my own kin.*

*I bring with me a beautiful boy, made from love. In him, you will see a man who holds a special place in both our hearts, you will see that he is a mirror image of his father, a golden boy, blessed by God and all his angels. I am resolved to leave my home and make my way to England. I fear what my father might do once my precious boy comes of age. More than anything, I must keep him safe and out of harm's way. He must remain forever a secret.*

*Sylvie La Fontaine*

Out of the window, Argyle watched Madame walking from the stables, her copper hair caught in a net, her hands pale half-circles around her dark riding gloves. His half-sister. Argyle wondered how she could walk so lightly through life with such a heavy burden on her shoulders. How Madame could serve a man who should be her sworn enemy, who should bow before her if the past had been different. One with whom she was equal if not superior.

Watching her gave Argyle the courage and conviction to do what had to be done. He went to the small desk and drew out a piece of paper. It was time to send a warning of what was coming. Time to bind a past pledge of protection to an oath of silence. Time to show his hand and play his trump card. His only card.

He wet the tip and dipped it in ink. The sins of the fathers are the fate of the sons, Argyle thought. While he was prepared to accept his fate and do what La Fontaine had done for him, he would not pass on his sins to his sons, he would fall on his sword to save them and put an end to this madness.

His quill scratched a slow dance over the paper, carving out the future.

*My Lord,*

*An embassy approaches your shores seeking to wrench power from you. Though my freedom is no longer mine to command, I have a few still loyal to me, and in them I entrust this message to be delivered sealed and safe in your hands. The enemy comes. Beware, for they know all of your secrets and they will not rest until you return to them what is more dear to their hearts than their thirst for your blood and their desire for your crown. Once we arrive, I entreat you; trust no one …*

Not even me, Argyle thought as he sealed the letter hastily. It seems, I am my father's son after all.

☙ ❧ ☙ ❧

# HISTORICAL NOTE

The Hundred Year War was one of the most tumultuous times in English history. The Plantagenet kings strove to take back the French throne, originally claimed by King Edward III as his ancestral legacy. Naturally, the French royal family resisted and this plunged the two countries into a war that extended for almost a century on and off.

During the reign of Edward III, his eldest son and heir Prince Edward, known to posterity as the Black Prince, spent much of his time harrying the French countryside, aided by many of Edward III's best commanders and closest friends, among which you find the Duke of Lancaster, Henry of Grosmont.

It is also during this time that some of the most epic battles took place, including the battles of Crecy and Poitiers, the latter being one occasion where Edward III's sons gathered to aid each other in defeating the French forces. It was also the first time the King of France openly came onto the battlefield and his capture was seen by many, at the time, as the end of the war. But prolonged negotiations for his release, the immense ransom the English demanded for King John and the general unrest in France led to new troubles.

The decision to aid the hated King Peter of Castile to reconquer his crown after he was thrown out of his own realm by his half-brother Henry of Trastamara is cited by several historians as one of the worst decisions made by the Plantagenets. Not only was Edward III deep in debt over his constant war with France, which ultimately resulted in Parliament refusing to send money to the campaign, it was also undertaken at the worst possible time. Whatever happened to render prince Edward sick after his victory near Najera, he never again resumed the strength he had been known for. Some historians argue that these factors made Edward III lose sight of what he wanted; the French crown.

The strife within Edward III's household, the constant rivalry between most of his sons, is also historically accurate. When prince Edward fell sick, John of Gaunt was already waiting in the wings, vying for the English crown. In the end, he gained another crown by way of marriage, the crown of Castile. Though he never managed to get a firm hold of Castile, his daughter by the Castilian princess Constance did in the end take the throne with her husband. John of Gaunt went on to be a stout supporter of king Richard II, who came to the throne when first his father and then his grandfather died. Richard was a child when he was anointed and lived to see the Peasants' Revolt, in which he valiantly rode towards the peasant rebels to have them cease their uprising. The aftermath of the revolt and Richard II's years as king were known to be turbulent and he to be a fickle king, surrounded by many poor advisors, such as Robert de Vere, who is featured prominently in this story.

Something that struck me while researching for this book was how many girls John of Gaunt had by his first wife, Blanche of Lancaster. The sons they had together all died in infancy, except Henry of Bolingbroke. However, John of Gaunt had three sons by his mistress and final wife, Katherine Swynford, all of whom survived to adulthood. The idea that perhaps Henry of Bolingbroke was not a legitimate son of Blanche and Gaunt was too good to pass up and it makes for some of the entanglement in this book.

Finally, Edmund la Fontaine is a figment of my imagination, and the insinuation that he might be a bastard child of king Edward III is likewise pure fiction. By all accounts, Edward III was devoted to his wife, Philippa of Hainault, by whom he had 13 children in all. Nonetheless, the idea that someone could rise from obscurity to fame at this time is well-founded. Several of the Plantagenet kings and princes are known to have struck up what some might call ill-advised friendships with young men from lesser families or worse, from doubtful backgrounds. It is easy to speculate that one such man could catch the eye of prince Edward and even become a confidant when he did not trust his own brothers. Some knights were bequeathed great estates, lands etc. for their services to England and the king, and in return, they were expected to go readily into war.

A man forged at the field of Poitiers might well have thought that to live and die by the sword was the only way. Such a man would most certainly take his knighthood pledge very seriously. Perhaps enough so that he would allow for an inferior adversary to take him out on the jousting field, if it would save England.

# ABOUT THE AUTHOR

Mette Holm is a writer of historical fiction focusing on last of the Plantagenet rulers beginning with Richard II. The Mowbray family caught her eye when she was first researching the age and especially Thomas Mowbray was so fascinating, she simply had to write about him and the Mowbray family. The decision led to her first book: At the King's Command. In this sequel, she once more delves into the vipers' nest that was the English court.

Mette Holm has been telling stories all her life, be it in school, at university or even in her day-job as an independent business owner and copywriter. While historical fiction holds a special place in her heart, a yet unfinished fantasy manuscript occupies her top drawer and rumour has it that it will in time be dug out and finished. As a quirk despite her Danish heritage, she knows more about medieval England than she does about Danish medieval history.

For more information please visit: metteholmbooks.com and follow Mette Holm on Facebook @MetteHolmBooks or on Instagram @authormetteholm

If you want to make absolutely certain, you don't miss a beat – sign up for her newsletter at this address: www.metteholmbooks.com

# The Mowbray Chronicles will return …

## October 1415 – Agincourt

'Cousin John', Edmund half-shouted as he barged through the tent flap. His question froze on his lips. 'My Lord Holland, Sir John ...'

Edmund's cousin frowned and stepped in front of the low table. 'Yes?'

John Holland still looked a mess from the fight in the tunnel yesterday, but he was in a fine mood. 'Let him come in, Mowbray. Perhaps he can shed new light on our situation.'

# ALSO BY METTE HOLM

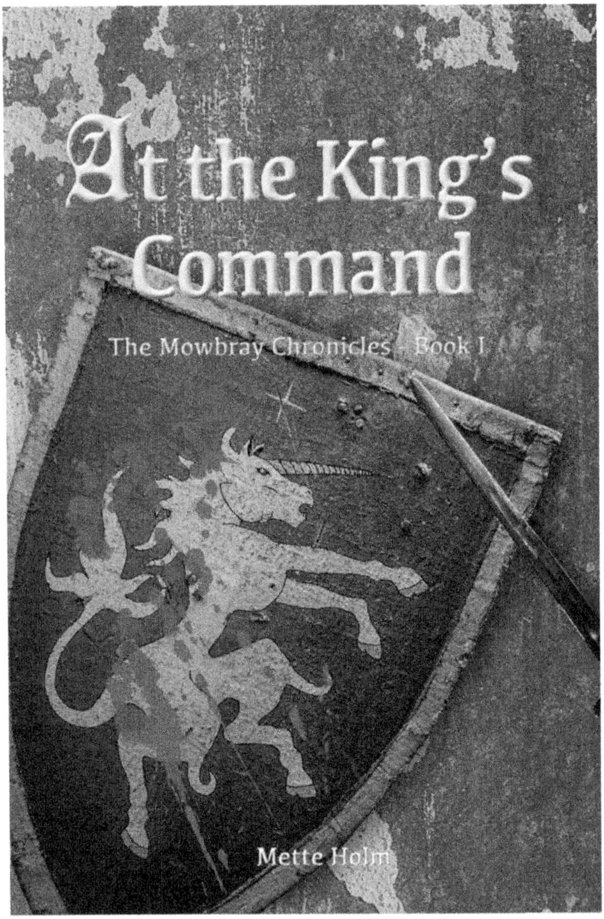


At the King's Command

Court of Deadly Whispers

Web of Lies

Shield of Blood

Printed in Great Britain
by Amazon

40798413R00249